The Driftwood Fire

Close to the brink, he stopped. 'Told you the view was magnificent, didn't I? Look, Anna, look down there.' He grasped the back of her dress and urged her forward.

Anna screamed. He was holding her just a foot from the edge. The cliffs dropped almost vertically to the stone and shingle cove at the bottom. Below her, seabirds cruised back and forth to nests built on narrow shelves in the rock. Heady scents of salt and seaweed floated up to her, and the cries of the gulls echoed shrilly in the abyss.

'What was I saying just now?' Guy went on. 'Oh yes, we were talking about your old flame, your penniless artist. Did you marry me on the rebound, Anna? And did you think to flaunt my money in front of Peggy? I'm not flattered.'

'It wasn't like that, Guy!'

'No?'

'Well – not exactly.'

Elizabeth Ann Hill was born in London in 1952 but grew up in South Wales and Cornwall where she now lives. She is the author of six previous novels.

The Driftwood Fire

ELIZABETH ANN HILL

Mandarin

A Mandarin Paperback
THE DRIFTWOOD FIRE

First published in Great Britain 1996
by Mandarin Paperbacks
and William Heinemann Ltd
imprints of Reed International Books Ltd
Michelin House, 81 Fulham Road, London SW3 6RB
and Auckland, Melbourne, Singapore and Toronto

A CIP catalogue record for this title
is available from the British Library
ISBN 0 7493 1875 9

Printed and bound in Great Britain by
Cox & Wyman Ltd, Reading
Phototypeset by Intype London Ltd

One

The card beneath the painting read: 'Portrait of the Artist's Wife'. The girl in the picture was dark and curly-haired, brown-skinned and brown-eyed. She was wearing a mauve cotton dress and a radiant smile. The work was beautifully done in oils, the shading delicate and fine. Set in a light oak frame, the portrait took pride of place among the others on display. It was not for sale.

Anna stared intently at the painting, with eyes that were green and flecked like polished serpentine. The artist's wife – Peggy – she of the broad local accent and bawdy laugh. Anna's hands clenched and unclenched at her sides. Any moment now, she was going to cry.

She cast a quick glance round her, finding with relief that she was alone. The gallery was silent, and bare of everything except the score of oils and watercolours hung around the walls. All the work of Hallam Pentreath.

Her Hal.

This was his first exhibition. Anna had long imagined how she would share with him in the pride and excitement of it. But no, she had been ousted, robbed. She couldn't bear it, seeing that portrait up there, mocking her. The triumphant face of someone else in the place where her own should be. And not just anyone else, but her oldest enemy.

Why had she come here to torture herself? Well – why did people pick at cuts and make them bleed? She had planned to ignore the exhibition, but in the end the temptation to look had been too great. She had known it would hurt, but not this much. The portrait of Peggy was unexpected.

Overcome by rage and pain, Anna turned to leave. But as she went out, she passed the workroom where materials were prepared. The door was ajar and a table stood just inside. On it lay a wooden frame, together with a piece of artist's linen, primed and ready to be tacked across it. Beside it was a large, sharp pair of scissors.

Anna stopped dead in her tracks, eyeing them, seized by an awful temptation. It was lunchtime and Hal was out. Downstairs, the gallery's owner was minding the shop. She licked her lips and struggled briefly with herself, fury battling with her better nature.

Fury won. A moment later, she had the scissors and was back in the gallery, using them to gouge the smiling face of the artist's wife, puncturing the canvas, dragging the metal through the fabric – downward strokes, diagonals, and many punching stabs. Hot tears ran down Anna's face. In half a minute, the painting had no face at all.

Breathless, she stopped, blinking through a salty blur at what she had done. She was glad and appalled, exultant and terrified, all at once. Such an explosion from Anna Trevena, gentle, dignified Anna. For the first time in her life, she knew the thrill of doing something wicked.

After a moment, however, the glee was replaced by panic. She had better slip away quickly before anyone came in. She had better wipe her face and make herself scarce. Dropping the scissors, she fumbled for her handkerchief.

But then:

'Oh, Anna . . .' The voice came from the doorway, just behind her. 'Anna, what good did that do?'

She froze. Oh God. Oh no.

'It's been nearly a year. Are you still so grieved?'

Turning, speechless with humiliation, Anna stared helplessly at Hal Pentreath. The young man gazed back at her with pitying reproach. He was gracefully built, with wavy, sandy-coloured hair and grey eyes. Over an old pair of trousers, he wore a faded canvas smock. Were it not for the paint stains on his clothes, he would have been taken for a fisherman.

She hadn't heard him come up the stairs. How long had he been standing there? Had he watched her do it? What did it matter? Even if she had escaped unseen, he would have guessed the culprit.

'Anna,' he said steadily, 'there's no sense in this. Peggy and I are married, we have a child, and you have to accept that. For pity's sake . . .'

Anna scarcely heard what else he said. She only knew she had shamed herself, made a fool of herself. Mortified, she pushed past him, rushed for the door and clattered down the stairs as fast as her legs would carry her.

Old Mr Jackman, who owned the art shop and the gallery above it, looked up in surprise as a girl in a cream summer frock dashed by his counter, pulled the door wide and went out. Peering over the top of his glasses, he saw her go running past the window, to disappear amid the bustle of Temperance Street. As the tinkle of the door bell died away, Mr Jackman turned to Hal, who had come to the foot of the stairs.

3

'What was all that about, Mr Pentreath? Some sort of trouble?'

'It's nothing,' the artist said quietly.

'The young lady appeared upset. Wasn't she a friend of yours at one time?'

'Yes.'

'I seem to recall that she once came in here and bought you a fine set of brushes – birthday present, wasn't it?'

'Mm,' nodded Hal, loath to be reminded of that. 'Look, I, um, think I'll change one of the paintings, if you don't mind. I have a still life I'd like to show. I'll take home the one of my wife.'

'All right, as you please.' Then: 'Perhaps the young woman wasn't well?' persisted Mr Jackman.

'Not her normal self, that's for sure,' sighed Hal, retreating upstairs.

To get home, go up to her bedroom and hide, was all Anna wanted. She ran the whole way, all uphill.

Trezawne was a steep little town on Cornwall's north coast. A few miles inland, the rising ground met the edge of Bodmin Moor. Once a mere fishing village, Trezawne had started to grow during late Victorian times, spreading up and back over the hills behind the harbour. Now it was 1930 and the town had reached four times its original size, with a population of almost thirteen thousand. People spoke of 'higher' and 'lower' Trezawne. The terms were informal, used to describe two very different areas and, by implication, sum up the people who lived in them. The farther up the hill, the smarter the dwellings. At the top there were tree-lined residential roads – villas with gardens, detached houses with little balconies to the bedroom windows,

4

homes with names instead of numbers. A leafy, peaceful part of town, where doctors, solicitors and other professionals lived, and where the tennis and bowling clubs were found, as well as the grammar schools.

As she reached the turning to her home, Anna slowed to a walk, trying to compose herself and get her breath back. She dried her eyes and blew her nose, praying that she might creep in without being seen by her mother.

Mrs Trevena ran a guest house. It was one of a terrace of ten, halfway down the hill, and was called *Lamorva*. Anna's mother would always say that the Trevenas lived in higher Trezawne. Certainly, their house was not part of the original fishing village, and by that definition perhaps she was right. Those at the top of the town, however, would not agree that she was one of them.

Just like all its neighbours, *Lamorva* was painted white. It had a small front garden and three steps up to the door. Outside each house was a board, announcing 'Bed and Breakfast. Dinner Optional'. Mrs Trevena charged rather more than her neighbours, in order to ensure a better class of guest.

Anna went indoors, hoping to slip quietly upstairs. She guessed her eyes must be red, and the tears were ready to come again at any time. Her mother, she knew, would not be sympathetic.

The house was silent; the guests were expected to go out straight after breakfast and not to show their faces again until evening. Anna was greeted by the usual smell of polish. The hallway had flowered wallpaper, and a little table on which stood a vase of dried grasses, together with the telephone, a message book and pen.

An immaculate housekeeper, Mrs Trevena. Very keen of hearing, too. Anna shut the front door softly, but as she turned around, her mother came out of the kitchen.

'I expected you in for lunch, Anna. Where have you been? You'll have to make do now with something cold . . .'

She paused and her eyes flickered over Anna's face. They were pale, prominent eyes. There was no concern in them, only puzzlement.

'Have you been crying? Why?'

Then the puzzlement changed to irritation and she answered the question herself.

'Oh, don't tell me – that wretched exhibition. You went to see it. Anna, how could you be so silly?'

The girl was silent. No use hoping for comfort or understanding. Delia Trevena was not a motherly woman. Everything about her was stiff and controlled; she was tidiness incarnate, with her crimped hair and starched frilly apron. She always smelt of talcum powder. Mother and daughter were nothing alike, for Anna's looks had come from her late father. At nineteen, she was tall and slender, pale-skinned and fine-featured, with light brown hair which was smoothly bobbed. Mrs Trevena, by contrast, was short and plain.

'Come into the kitchen,' she ordered. 'Have something to eat.'

'I'm not hungry.'

'Some tea, then. I want to talk to you.'

Anna followed her, resigned. Now, on top of everything else, she would have to endure one of her Mother's lectures.

The kitchen was flawlessly clean, not a speck or a spillage anywhere. Mrs Trevena was very proud of

6

its modern gadgetry. *Lamorva* had 'gone electric' the previous year, the first house in the terrace to do so, and Mrs Trevena was the owner of an electric kettle, toaster and coffee percolator, all made by the Magnet company.

Anna sat down at the table.

'Now listen to me,' her mother said, setting her tea in front of her and taking the chair opposite, 'it's high time for this to stop. Hal Pentreath was never the sort of man I wanted for you. You can do better by far than the likes of him. Fancy a girl like you, brought up in a nice home like this, moping over a scruffy lad who'll never amount to anything. What were his family? China clay workers! My dear life!'

'That's not what Hal is, Mother.'

'Oh!' Mrs Trevena rolled her eyes, then she drew in her chin and knowingly pursed her mouth. 'Yes, of course, he's an artist. A neat way of avoiding real work, if you ask me. A lot of idlers call themselves artists. They don't even have to be good at it nowadays, they only have to pretend and give themselves airs. Some of the stuff you see on show – well, a two year old could do it.'

'Hal isn't that sort of artist. You've seen his work.'

'I don't care what sort he is. Believe me, even the best of them face a struggle in the early years, and many still die poor in the end, even after making a name for themselves. They can't handle money when they get it. They're certainly not reliable providers. Marry an artist, Anna, and hear the wolf at the door.'

Anna had to bite her tongue. Her mother was wont to dismiss any number of types as shiftless, sinister or in various other ways undesirable. Methodists, miners, liberals, publicans, anyone whose speech was rough, anyone who had too many children – her list of the disdained was lengthy, and artists had always featured on it.

'Of course,' continued Mrs Trevena, 'it's a very nice hobby for gentlemen. It can even be a harmless full-time pursuit for people who have other means of support. But Hal? At best, he's a dreamer, at worst, he's work-shy.'

'He has a gift and he's right to use it,' protested Anna. 'He can do anything – landscapes, portraits, still lifes, caricatures . . .'

'Monkeys can do tricks, but they're still monkeys and ought to remember it,' sniffed her mother. 'That Peggy Angilley – she'll be sorry, don't you worry. The joke's on her, my dear. I know you feel she stole him from you, Anna. Well, what she stole was a packet of trouble. He'll be a burden to her, wait and see. She'll get what she deserves for being loose.' Mrs Trevena's nose and mouth gave a twitch, as if she could smell rotten eggs. 'Letting him take advantage of her, falling pregnant – well enough for one of those Angilleys. I brought you up a lady, thank the Lord, taught you to keep your virtue and your self-respect.'

Brought me up untouchable, reflected Anna. Perhaps if I'd been a bit less proper, it would have been *my* portrait up there on the wall.

Mrs Trevena pulled a face. 'I never liked him coming round here, looking so down-at-heel.'

'You needn't tell me,' muttered Anna mournfully. 'You used to keep him waiting on the doorstep like a tradesman.'

'And I make no apologies for it. I knew he was no good for you. I'm very thankful that it's over and he's married.'

8

Anna forlornly sipped her tea and made no reply.

'You must think about the future now,' her mother went on. 'Make good use of your schooling, Anna. Just having been to the grammar school gives you a certain distinction, you know. You could marry a professional man and not feel at all out of place among his friends and colleagues.' A faraway smile touched her face. 'Of course,' she added complacently, 'you were always good material. It's inborn.'

Mrs Trevena thought herself a cut above. Her father had done something clerical at the post office, while her mother had kept the appointments and records at a doctor's surgery. The young Delia had consolidated her grandeur by marrying Mark Trevena, who was on the local council. His early death from kidney failure had provided her with a useful sum of life insurance. She had never felt the urge to marry again. It was nicer to be in complete control of everything.

Sometimes her mother's pathetic snobbery simply made Anna smile. She would humour her and nod in tolerant agreement. More often, though, it grated, made her wince and stoked a desperate longing to escape – to go somewhere dust and clutter wouldn't matter, live with someone who didn't care what the neighbours thought. Somebody messy and happy and unconcerned with money or social position.

Hal Pentreath was such a person, and that was half his attraction. An artist, in Anna's scheme of things, was a breed apart, with no fixed place on the ladder. An artist was a romantic figure, a creator. No matter how poor, he was made acceptable by 'culture'. Never mind his accent or his origins, all was excused by talent. What Anna felt she had lost, and what she grieved for as much as the man, was what she deemed to be a glamorous and picturesque style of life. 'Bohemian' was her favourite term.

'Money,' Delia was saying, 'that's what matters, Anna. It's the great sustainer, my dear. Love and idealism are all very well, but you have to look at a man's financial prospects. Always marry money, Anna, if you have the chance. There's nothing idyllic in poverty, I promise you . . .'

On she went, and on, until Anna finished her tea and escaped upstairs. She hardly dared imagine what her mother would say if she knew what had happened at the gallery. She wondered if Hal would tell Peggy, and if Peggy would spread it around. The fear brought on a throbbing headache and Anna decided to take a few hours' sleep.

Lamorva had three storeys and her room was at the top, with a view of the sea and lower Trezawne. Sunlight slanted brightly in upon the red carpet and pink candlewick bedspread. Like the rest of the house, the room was very neat and smelt of lavender wax.

Anna went to draw her curtains, and lingered a while at the window, gazing out. From here, she was looking down on the rooftops of the fishing quarter. Squares and rectangles of grey slate, joined and jumbled together at awkward angles. Beneath each one was a poky granite cottage. Much of lower Trezawne had been built in the seventeenth century, and some of its streets were so narrow that a man could almost span them with outstretched arms. The shabby part of town, and yet the one which drew the visitors and, of course, the artists. Hal's world, and Peggy's, lively and eccentric. A far cry from the propriety of the terrace and *Lamorva*.

Money or no, it was Hal she had wanted. Hal and

the artistic life, or what she imagined it to be. And she would have caught him, she felt sure, if not for the Angilley girl. Peggy, the scheming little cat, had trapped him in the age-old way, guessing that Hal would be soft enough to do the decent thing and marry her. If only he had been a bit less honourable.

Taking off her shoes and dress, Anna lay down on the bed in her slip. But as soon as she closed her eyes, there came the image of Hal's incredulous, pitying face, and an echo of his voice with its soft burr:

'Oh, Anna . . .'

How could she have done such a thing? She'd been raised to be well-mannered, self-possessed. Ah, but that was Mother's influence, only a veneer. Underneath was a dreamy, susceptible girl who had fallen very hard for the warm and easy-going Hal.

Had her father been alive, he would have comforted Anna, stroking and patting her, allowing her to cry and talk about her loss. As it was, she was unconsoled in her misery. All Mrs Trevena had ever done was tell her to pull herself together, sniffing that Hal was quite unsuitable anyway. She was irritated by Anna's pain, had no patience with it.

Today, in the gallery, it had found explosive release – and made everything worse. Anna rolled on to her side, curling up into a ball, and silently wept again.

Two

It was twenty-five past five, and the shop and gallery were about to close for the day. Hal had wrapped the ruined portrait in brown paper and tied it round with string. A still life of fruit and flowers now hung in its place.

He paused before he left, looking round him. His first exhibition. It made him feel like a real professional. For someone completely self-taught, he felt he was doing pretty well. No art school for him, the youngest of a family of ten. On his eighteenth birthday, Hal had walked out of a job in the kaolin quarries at St Austell and come up here to Trezawne with just three pounds in his pocket. Casual jobs on the ferries and as a pub cellarman had paid for cheap lodgings, and in his spare time he had started to paint, hawking his work round shops and restaurants. Nowadays, Hal did nothing but paint. It was an uncertain living, but he wanted no other.

He had made that clear to Peggy, and she had accepted it. He was bent on a precarious career. All right, she said, she didn't mind, she would take her chances with him. Anyway, her mother would help them out.

He frowned to himself as he thought again about Anna. In a young man's careless way, Hal had been seeing both girls the previous summer; Peggy because she was always good fun, Anna because she believed in him and would listen for hours while he talked about art. He hadn't realised he was doing any great harm, had thought it a bit of a joke, in fact, that Peggy and Anna squabbled over him – just as they vied over everything else. He wasn't sure, even now, what had caused the grudge between them.

Would he ever have married Anna? To be practical, realistic, Hal doubted it. He liked her company, of course. She was beautiful, and how could he not be flattered by the interest she took in him? But her mother had hated him, and Anna came from such a tidy, comfortable home. Hal was used to a rough and ready life, and he doubted that such an existence would really suit Anna. She only imagined that it would. Hal suspected that she had read too many romantic biographies of painters and poets.

No, if the truth were told, Peggy was more his sort. Tough, hot-tempered Peggy. Generous Peggy, who allowed him liberties, and shared his enjoyment. Anna was always far too ladylike for that. But he hadn't meant to injure her, hadn't bargained for the way she took on. Of course, it might not have been so bad if her rival had been anyone else but Peggy. Hal didn't find their feud the least bit funny any more.

Going downstairs with the painting under his arm, he found Mr Jackman ready to lock up. This was the smartest shop in town, double-fronted, with large windows and white paintwork. It sold artists' materials, and work by local painters and craftsmen, the latter evidenced by stands displaying hand-made pottery and carvings. There was always classical music playing, usually Handel or Bach.

Mr Jackman was a gentle, well-bred man, past sixty and going grey. Sympathetic towards a young artist who was gifted but lacking the benefits of education and private means, he had always given Hal a good deal on his paintings. For this exhibition he was accepting just thirty per cent commission and allowing some of the work to be hung unframed – a very decent concession indeed, Hal thought.

He bid the old man good evening and went on his way. Outside, he paused to look at his poster and savour a thrill of pride.

EXHIBITION HERE OF WORK BY LOCAL ARTIST

HALLAM PENTREATH

15–25 MAY, 1930

10 a.m. – 5.30 p.m. Daily

No Admission Charge

MANY WORKS AVAILABLE FOR SALE

Yes, his first exhibition, and at a quality gallery, too. Hal felt things were going well for him.

Temperance Street was on the eastern side of Trezawne. Here were the banks, the larger shops and the post office. It ended at the town square, where the library and council offices were found, and where the buses parked. Once across the square, Hal's route home took him down a short side-street. At the end of it, he stepped from shadow into brilliant sunshine and before him lay the harbour and cottages of lower Trezawne.

When, as now, the tide was low, it revealed a stretch of fine, pale sand. Late May had brought a heatwave, and even at this hour the beach was still scattered with people. Children frolicked at the water's edge, while old people dozed in deckchairs. Mothers were setting out picnic teas, waving flies away and picking sand out of the food.

Hal walked on across the quayside. Underfoot were cobblestones. A row of granite cottages fronted the beach and harbour. One of the occupants, a widow named Mrs Opie, always turned her parlour into a tea-room during the summer months. A notice hung in the window:

CREAM TEAS 1/-
Scones, Jam and Clotted Cream, all home-made

So tiny was Mrs Opie's parlour that she could only serve six people at a time. Almost everything here was like that; small-scale, with tightly clustered, crooked little dwellings, divided only by narrow streets and alleys, tiny courtyards. No gardens – no room for them in such a hive – only occasional window-boxes full of geraniums or nasturtiums.

High and dry on the sand beside the west quay, Trezawne's fishing boats awaited the incoming tide and another night's work. The mackerel season was nearing its end. Soon the men would go drifting for pilchards instead, or put on board baskets of long line and set out in search of skate and ling, brill and conger eel. However, the old way of life now existed cheek by jowl with something new. Enticed by the Great Western Railway posters of Cornwall, and conveyed to Trezawne by the branch line from Bodmin, a growing number of visitors came every summer to sit on its beaches. They were mostly middle-class and comfortable. Up-country, grim depression was taking hold, but Trezawne, like the rest of Cornwall, only saw the sort of 'foreigners' who could afford a holiday, and the

15

nation's economic troubles were felt less keenly by working people here. Hardship in a place like lower Trezawne had other, more natural causes, none of them new – things like sickness, death of a father at sea, scarcity of fish, or loss of gear in a storm. For the fishing families, the chief concerns remained tides and catches, local gossip and chapel, and most of the old villagers merely regarded the holiday people with mild curiosity. There were, however, some who seized the chance to profit from them. Hence, a few seaside amenities had appeared.

As Hal passed by, the deckchair man was folding up his sign and stacking chairs away. On the beach, the last Punch and Judy show was drawing to a close. The donkeys were still plodding back and forth across the sand, bearing tiny riders in bathing costumes. Dandy and Syrup, penny a ride. The donkeys wore Venetian straw hats with red ribbons and always looked dejected, but were quite plump and well cared for. Jack Tresize, the donkey man, collected up their droppings with a shovel and sold them by the sackload for manure.

Hal was living with Peggy's family. Her mother was one of the enterprising kind and owned a business, with living quarters overhead. Standing right on the harbourside, just opposite the slipway to the beach, the shop occupied the whole ground floor of what had once been a boat chandler's store. Cheap and topsy-turvy, it was known as Angilley's Bazaar. In summer it had a fairground look about it, because of the wealth of colourful items hanging round the door and stacked outside on the cobbles; big rubber beach balls striped yellow and green, tin buckets and spades, children's fishing nets and floppy white linen sun hats, box kites and racks of penny postcards.

To go inside was to find oneself all at once within a toyshop, an ironmonger's and a haberdashery, which also sold newspapers, old books and musical instruments, sweets and bottles of ginger beer.

A Jew's-harp, a penny whistle, an accordion? Maisie Angilley probably had one in stock. Pots and pans, boot polish, blacking brushes? Of course. Mousetraps, paraffin? Naturally. Ribbons and braids and buttons? Whatever you needed was here. A twopenny yo-yo, a hoop and stick, a box of lead soldiers, a spinning top? Just come and choose.

The side window of the bazaar faced on to Pawlyn's Hill, which led right up to the parish church at the top of the town. So steep was Pawlyn's Hill that the pavement on one side was cut into steps and an iron handrail was provided for the breathless. Before he went inside, Hal paused to look in this window, where a large array of his paintings hung on show. Two gone since this morning. They were only little views, of course, fetching ten shillings each, but income was income. It was very convenient, living here and having the shop to sell the bread-and-butter stuff. Better still, he had the loft for a studio.

Going into the bazaar, Hal was greeted by the usual ping and clatter of slot machines. In a side room, Maisie kept a collection of bagatelle games, a weighing machine, one that told fortunes, and sundry other amusements, many of them rather ancient. A ha'penny to peep at fading sepia photographs of plump women in underwear, to flick the marbles into the holes, making eyes and nose for the clown, to spin a numbered wheel and win a silly novelty, to make the Jack

17

Tar roar with laughter or the model tin mine work its engine beam. No matter how gimcrack the prizes, the machines were always popular. Children were constantly scampering in and out, and back and forth to the old brass till, requesting change.

Behind the counter sat Maisie Angilley. She was forty-two, with a slightly knobbly nose and small, twinkling eyes, her wiry hair chopped off at ear length. She always wore gingham pinnies, which usually clashed with the print of her dress. Maisie was humorous and shrewd, plain and durable as coconut matting. Wherever Peggy's good looks had come from, it was certainly not from her mother. In character, however, they were very much alike.

Maisie was fond of her son-in-law. Yes, he had got her daughter into trouble, but it always took two and she knew Peggy well. Anyway, Hal had done the right thing by her. What more could anyone ask? Everybody knew, of course, that it had been an 'urgent' wedding, but Maisie Angilley was never one to care what the neighbours thought.

'Had a good day?' she asked him.

'Yes, I made a sale – six guineas.'

'Ooh,' said Maisie, impressed. Then she noticed the parcel under his arm. 'What's that?'

'Oh – I changed one of the paintings.'

'Did you? Why? Which one?'

Hal hesitated a moment, then he told her what Anna had done.

'She must be cracked,' said Maisie, indignant. 'I hope you'll make her pay for it?'

He shook his head. 'I wasn't going to sell the portrait anyway.'

'That's not the point. It was your property and she

18

destroyed it. Think of the time and work you put into it.'

'Maisie, she was in an awful state, and I felt it was partly my fault. Anna's not normally spiteful or reckless. She's a lovely girl when you get to know her.'

'Better not let Peggy hear you say that. And I still don't think there's any excuse. We all have disappointments in our love lives, one time or another. Miss Trevena must learn to live with the fact she can't have everything she wants. Snooty little madam,' bridled Maisie. 'Just like her mother.'

Hal could have argued on that point, but knew it was futile. Maisie and Peggy were solidly united in dislike of the Trevenas.

'Just the same, I felt sorry for her,' he said, as he started upstairs.

'You're too soft, Hal,' Maisie sighed. 'Don't know what Peggy will say, I'm sure.'

After the initial shock, Peggy burst out laughing. She held the portrait at arm's length, surveying the damage with disbelieving eyes.

'Anna Trevena? Starchy old Anna did this? You saw her?'

A rueful nod.

Peggy's eyes danced and she laughed again. One of the very dark Cornish, she could easily have passed for a southern Italian.

It was seven o'clock and they were upstairs in the loft, which was reached by a short staircase off the first floor landing. The massive ceiling beams were rough and studded with nails, from which, a generation past, drift nets had hung to be mended. These days, the nails held a few of Hal's paintings. He had made himself at home in the big sunny room, where three sizeable windows gave excellent light. He had moved in a few pieces of furniture, including a sagging old couch. The tables and shelves were littered with crusted palettes, tubes and cakes of paint, brushes and stubs of charcoal, and rags with multi-hued stains. The place smelt pungently of oils and turpentine. Peggy and Hal liked to come and sit up here of an evening, away from the rest of the family.

'Lord,' she murmured, 'how she must be chafing, and after all this time.'

'Peggy,' said Hal, 'don't gloat. I don't like you when you're like this.'

'I can't help it, she's so stiff and haughty. She's always looked down her nose at me.'

'No, it's just that you take her that way. And she isn't starchy. Anna has feelings like anyone else.'

'So it appears,' admitted Peggy. 'Fierce ones, too. But aren't you angry about this?' She flipped her fingers against the painting.

'I can always do another.'

Putting the portrait down, she flopped beside him on the couch. She was wearing a green cotton frock and flat sandals. Peggy was partial to pastel colours, and she went about in sandals almost all year round. By the window, in a basket, the baby crooned and mewed. They had named her Joy and she was nearly three months old.

'Well,' said Peggy, grinning again, 'you know, that portrait wasn't really very much like me.'

Bending his head, he peered down at her.

'How can you say that?'

'It was far too angelic.'

He had to admit, she had a point. He nuzzled her neck and Peggy giggled.

'I'm quite sure that Anna felt you'd been too kind to me. Your work always shows the way you feel about the subject.'

Yes, he thought, it was painted with love, and Anna had seen the affection in it. Poor Anna.

Peggy could never think of her as 'poor Anna'. Peggy could only think of her as 'Miss high-and-mighty who reckons she's better than me'.

How had it begun, this enmity? Peggy lay beside her sleeping husband that night, remembering – or trying to. There seemed to be no firm starting point to the feud, just jumbled memories of slights and counterattacks and petty rivalries.

They had first met at junior school, and something about the Trevena girl had simply antagonised Peggy from the start. Perhaps it was Anna's oh-so-upright bearing, or the neatness of her dress and the fact that she studied hard. Without a doubt, Anna's quiet reserve had been construed by Peggy as 'stuck-up'. But what had turned this judgement into real animosity?

A certain defensiveness, perhaps. Just by being the way she was, Anna had somehow made Peggy feel 'rough'. She recalled with special humiliation and wrath the day when Anna informed her that the midday meal was lunch, not dinner. Even at the age of nine, Peggy had sensed the import of that correction. It carried such a wealth of superiority.

Still, Peggy had always been popular, one of the gang, while Anna was a child who remained on the sidelines. That had been Peggy's consolation and her weapon. She was always the centre of everything and usually 'boss of the game'. A powerful position, being boss of the game – rather like that of a hiring foreman. If you wanted to join in the rounders or tag or whatever it was, you had to ask permission from the boss. Anna could always be sure of refusal from Peggy.

Thus, a distance had been maintained between them, and with it, misunderstanding. All sorts of incidents had served to create more ill-will as time went on. Many were trivial, some were more painful, but over the years the drips of resentment had pooled into a reservoir of mutual dislike. It had led, on one occasion, to a playground fight. As a consequence, the mothers had quarrelled too, when Mrs Trevena called at the shop to complain about Peggy. Like mother, like daughter, Maisie had assumed, thereby labelling Anna with Mrs Trevena's snobbery.

It had always appeared to Peggy that Anna was favoured by the 'better class'. Gazing up at the moon-light on the ceiling, she remembered competing with her for the rôle of Meg when the school put on a play of *Little Women* – and losing, being given a very minor part. Just a silly school production, yet Peggy could still relive the bitter pain of being deemed less worthy.

'You're not the right type, dear,' the teacher had said. The same up-country teacher who had no trouble with Anna's surname, but carelessly listed Peggy in the programme as Peggy Anne Gilley.

Peggy was always conscious, too, of the difference between *Lamorva* and her own family's quarters above the bazaar. She knew that Anna's home was on the telephone and enjoyed the luxuries of indoor plumbing – no squatting in a tin bath for her. No sticky lino on the floors; the Trevenas had carpets – their advertisement in the local paper said so. The Angilleys had mains water but no electricity, still relying on paraffin lamps. The kitchen boasted a gas stove and water heater, and that was all. Maisie was old-fashioned that way. The latest thing might save some work, but she preferred to save the money. Bathrooms and indoor lavatories were extravagances, in her view, and the little brick outhouse in the yard was quite good enough. It was what Peggy had always been used to, and she only minded it when she thought about the comforts and refinements of Anna's home. It disturbed her somehow, undermined her sense of being all right just as she was.

A parting of the ways had come when the girls reached the age of eleven, because Anna Trevena went to the grammar school. Anna had a special chance in life; she was a rare gold nugget, sifted from amongst the gravel. Again, it seemed to Peggy, the world had made a distinction between the best and the dross, and she felt belittled.

Fifteen, that was Peggy's age when she left school. What did it matter? Maisie had said. She'd be married with babies before very long. Schooling didn't really matter all that much for a woman. Nature had its plans for her, and some man always came along to put them into effect.

Yes. Men, marriage, the next stage in life. And a new field of combat for Peggy and Anna, when both of them fell for Hal Pentreath.

Lying here now in the dark, listening to Hal's quiet breathing, Peggy smiled to herself, recalling a night the previous summer. She remembered the cool, soft sand in the dunes of Tolgarth beach, the tufts of marram grass in spiky silhouette against the moonlit sky. Full moon, a cloudless night. The sea looking just like silver foil. And down on the beach, a stack of blazing driftwood with people sitting round it, sharing baked potatoes and sausages and cider. A bit of a party for Midsummer Eve; swimming before the sun set, singing afterwards. And for Peggy and Hal, the chance to slip away into the dunes together.

Peggy had won the contest that night. Her ace, her trump, had been to conceive the child. Looking back, she had worked out that it must have been that night. Not that she had made a deliberate bid to get herself pregnant; she had simply taken a chance and it had happened.

Anna doubtless believed it was calculated. Well, let her think so.

Three

Hal was woken at dawn next morning by the sharp cries of gulls and the skittering scratch of their claws on the roof. Coming as he did from the moors outside St Austell, he had never grown used to the sound.

He left Peggy sleeping, rose and dressed, and went up to the loft to put in some work before breakfast. He enjoyed the misty, milky light and the almost unearthly stillness at break of day. Down at the quay, the boats were coming in from their night's fishing, and he took up his sketch pad and charcoal to make a drawing or two.

Most of the craft were Victorian luggers, with rust-brown sails, and hulls tarred black, their numbers and names picked out in white. As yet, there were only two vessels with engines fishing out of Trezawne. The tide was high and by seven o'clock two big mackerel drivers were tied up alongside the jetty. From his windows, Hal could watch the figures moving around on board. Sturdy men in caps and thigh boots and heavy woollen jerseys, men in oilskins or smocks like his own, all of them burnt by sun and wind, made muscular by years of hauling heavy nets by hand. His charcoal skimmed over the paper as baskets of fish were lined up on the quay. Soon the wharf was littered with heaps of net and corks and canvas floats, as the crews unloaded gear for barking or mending, and washed down the boats.

By the time they trudged off home to sleep, the scent of bacon was summoning Hal to breakfast. Going down the steps to the first floor, he went into the kitchen.

The Angilleys were people who lived in their kitchen. When they were all together, they sat, ate and fought around a big square table covered with oil-cloth. Breakfast, in fact, was normally a peaceful meal, since Peggy's father and brother rarely rose in time for it. This morning, however, Hal found them both at the table.

When there was trouble in the family, it was nearly always caused by Walter and Jasper Angilley. As far as Hal was concerned, they were the only disadvantage to life at Angilley's Bazaar. Maisie was pleased to have him there; to the menfolk, he was thoroughly unwelcome.

Jasper Angilley jeered as his brother-in-law came in. 'Here's Rembrandt,' he said. Tall and gangly, Jasper had a receding chin and was rarely without a grin on his face.

Ignoring him, Hal sat down beside Peggy. Maisie put a plate of bacon and eggs in front of him.

Walter Angilley eyed the lean rashers of bacon and curled his lip. 'I see you saved the best for Michelangelo.'

Maisie, passing behind his chair, poked him between the shoulder-blades. 'That's enough of that.'

'My bacon's fatty,' Walter complained in his usual guttural tones.

'Don't pretend you're hard done by, you like it that way.'

Walter lapsed into surly silence. Flabby and short, he was always in need of a shave and went about without a shirt collar. Even when at table, he wore a grey tweed cap. Beneath it was a face full of broken veins. His presence at breakfast this morning was thanks to the fact that a job had come his way – by no means a regular occurrence.

Eyeing him cynically, Maisie sat down to her meal. 'What's this work you've found, then?'

'Bit of plastering,' mumbled Walter.

'Where?'

'Up the hill. New people moved in near the church. I said I'd do it for two pound ten and they were delighted.'

'Poor trusting souls,' grunted Peggy.

Her father scowled at her. Walter was an odd-job man, and not a very good one, either. When he worked at all, he worked cheap. The result was always shoddy: a clumsy roof repair, a new window pane which would soon fall out, a rough coat of paint which would start to flake within a month. Thus, he had earned a reputation which ensured he wasn't offered too much work, and then only by the unsuspecting, never those who knew him. Between jobs, Walter spent most of his time in the pub. Maisie gave him pocket money just to get him out of her way.

Jasper Angilley was taking after his father, every bit as shiftless and fond of beer. He was twenty and showed not the slightest sign of ever amounting to anything. When Walter had a job to do, he took Jasper along to help, charging for two men's labour and making twice the hash of the work.

'Nice house, is it?' Maisie asked.

'Smart,' confirmed Walter. 'All fancy mouldings and friezes.'

'Well, try not to do too much damage,' his wife said drily.

'Or leave the job half finished,' added Peggy.

'Nothing wrong with our workmanship,' snapped Walter. 'It's fair enough for what we charge.'

'If people don't pay a lot, they can't expect a lot, can they?' Jasper agreed through a mouthful of food.

'They could pay three times the going rate and you'd still botch it,' Peggy sniffed.

Her brother's grin faded, his sloping chin quivered.

'At least it's man's work,' he retorted, intending a sideswipe at Hal.

'Mmph,' mumbled Walter, nodding. He was gobbling fried bread, and grease was running down his chin.

Peggy opened her mouth to reply, but her husband nudged her, winked and shook his head. Walter and Jasper were constantly trying to goad him, but Hal was peaceable by nature and seldom rose to the bait.

Jasper slashed at his bacon and stuffed a forkful into his mouth. He champed a bit of rind, then spat it out. It missed the edge of his plate and plopped onto the oil-cloth. He was mightily peeved that his mother thought so highly of Hal Pentreath. Maisie wished Jasper were more like him, and was always saying so. It was 'Hal this' and 'Hal that'. Walter scoffingly called him 'the golden boy', while Jasper whined that a mother ought to favour her own flesh and blood. He was endlessly indignant that Maisie had turned him out of his bedroom so that the married couple and their baby could have it. He slept in Peggy's old room now, and found it cramped. He kept banging his head on the slanting ceiling.

But it was no good arguing with Mother. It was her money which had purchased the bazaar, and her efforts, too, which kept it going. Therefore, Maisie wore the trousers. She supported her husband and son, and never tired of reminding them of it. In return for a lazy life, they sulkily accepted her authority. Now and again, Walter would thump his chest and shout, but everyone knew it was all bravado.

Maisie would often ask herself why she'd married Walter Angilley. The answer always came back the same: 'Well, being so plain, I wasn't spoiled for choice and I wanted children.' She had also made the classic mistake of thinking marriage would reform him. She knew better now.

Peggy was her consolation, the one she loved and the only good thing to come out of her marriage. Peggy, who helped in the shop and around the house. Peggy, who had given her a beautiful granddaughter. Jasper often referred to Joy as 'the accident', to which his mother would retort that *he* was a calamity.

Later, when Hal had returned to the loft, and her husband and son had slouched off to their plastering, Maisie handed Peggy some money, a shopping list and a note with the name of a horse in the four o'clock at Newton Abbot. Maisie liked a little flutter on the races every week.

Peggy went out by way of the back gate in the yard, en route for the grocer's and the betting shop. Lower Trezawne had nothing resembling a main street. Most of its shops, like Mrs Opie's tea-room, were converted front rooms and were therefore located wherever the owners happened to live – which meant a tour round a warren of lanes and alleys whenever there was much to get.

The age of lower Trezawne made itself strongly felt in these back streets. There were cottages with sunken, wavy roofs, little bedroom windows squeezed up close beneath the eaves, and ill-shaped doorways with low lintels. A few of them were whitewashed, but most were plain dark granite. More than half had flights of outside steps from the street to the upper floor, which meant a fish cellar underneath. Nothing here ever changed, except that railings grew a little more rusty year by year, cobbles a little smoother, and patches of lichen on walls and roofs imperceptibly larger.

Peggy went up Salter's Op, along The Ropewalk and down Tabernacle Row, the pat-pat-patting of her sandals the only sound to disturb the quiet, her lilac frock a flash of brilliance in the sunlight. In Spargo Lane, she passed the workshop belonging to Jimmy Polsue, who made barrels, together with blocks and spars for rigging. Polsue was elderly and a fervent chapel-goer. A stooping figure in dungarees, he was scraping old paint off his gate as she passed, and bade her a grave 'Good morning'. She answered him brightly and his sombre gaze followed her with concern as she walked on, because she was a sinner and hadn't been saved. Mr Polsue was sorely afraid that all the Angilleys were candidates for hell. They didn't even go to church, let alone chapel.

Peggy's first stop was the betting shop, a seedy little place tucked away beside an empty lock-up store. The windows were whitened over, as if for shame at the business conducted inside. Peggy breezed in, put a shilling each way on Fire-in-the-hole and then carried on to the grocer's.

Along the way was Curnow's remnant shop with its heaps of gaudy fabrics, and round the next corner, Daisy Martin's second-hand (in truth, a pawn shop), and Freddie Williams's junk yard, full of bits and pieces off old boats. Freddie owned a motorbike and side-car, the only motor vehicle ever seen in these narrow back streets.

Pascoe the butcher was boiling down dripping as Peggy went by and the smell was awful. She quickened her steps, turned up yet another sidestreet and reached the grocer's shop. Screwed on to the wall above the door was an old enamel sign, rusty at the edges, advertising Hudson's Dry Soap, and a newer one for Cooper's Powder Dip. The windows were crowded with packets of Rinso, Glee and Ipso, drums of salt, and dog biscuits called Melox Marvels.

The shop was run by Mrs Rowe, who wore her hair in a bun and viewed the world through wire-rimmed spectacles. A new Home and Colonial had just opened in Temperance Street, but Peggy preferred to come here. She liked Mrs Rowe and the shabby old shop. It smelt of tea, cheese and dried fruit. Joints of bacon encased in muslin were hung from the rafters, and against the counter were propped sacks of flour and tapioca, split peas and Demerara sugar. Mrs Rowe measured everything with a big brass scoop and scales. It all went into stout paper bags which were coloured dark blue.

Peggy bought eggs, a tin of treacle and a pound of butter beans. As she weighed out the beans, Mrs Rowe remarked:

'I see your husband's having a bit of a show at the gallery.'

'And people are buying his pictures,' said Peggy. 'It's been a real success.'

'Has it?' The beans rattled into the bag from the lip of the bowl on the scales. 'Well, that's wonderful, isn't it? I'm very pleased for you, dear.'

She was, too. There was no jealousy in Mrs Rowe, nothing two-faced about her.

Sadly, the same could not be said for everyone. Lower Trezawne, like anywhere else, had its more spiteful inhabitants. As Peggy paid for her goods, another customer came in: Ruby Tabb, a spinster of fifty, whose skinny body was topped by a large head, on which grew a shock of grey hair.

'Morning, Peggy. How's the baby?' Her smile was too taut to be friendly.

'Flourishing, Ruby, thank you.' Peggy took her change and turned to leave.

'I went in and looked at your husband's paintings. Asking a lot for them, isn't he?'

'And getting it,' said Peggy cheerfully.

Ruby's eyes darted over her, noting the length of her dress. Too short, she decided – only just below the knee. No wonder Peggy had got herself in trouble. 'Mm, well, that's nice, of course. But when's he going to find a proper job?'

Behind the counter, Mrs Rowe sucked in her cheeks and gave a small shake of her head.

'After all,' continued Ruby, 'it isn't real employment for somebody like Hal.'

A glint appeared in Peggy's eyes. 'Now, what do you mean by that?'

Ruby bridled. 'It's not as if he's an educated man.' She shrugged. 'He's just ordinary, like the rest of us. Very nice lad, of course – but don't you think he ought to come down to earth?'

'What should he be doing instead?'

'Fishing or something, I suppose.'

'Oh, he'd make a fortune that way, wouldn't he?'

'It's always been good enough for the other men round here,' Ruby sniffed.

'Hal is different,' said Peggy sweetly. 'And he's doing well.'

'Oh, all right, if it doesn't worry you. Just seems to me a very chancy way of making a living. Still, I suppose you can always count on your mother if things start going badly. Maisie's used to carrying everyone.'

'Did you want to buy something, Ruby?' Mrs Rowe interrupted sharply.

'Lard,' came the answer. 'Half a pound.'

Peggy was stony-faced. 'We pay our way. Mam will never have to carry us.'

'Well, I hope you're right, dear, for your own sakes and for hers. A man must grow up and face his responsibilities once he's married – even if it was carelessness that got him into it.'

Disdaining to answer that, Peggy bid good-day to Mrs Rowe and went on her way. For a minute or two she stalked down the street feeling ruffled. Ruby Tabb was a bitter old bitch, by no means typical of local people, but Peggy was aware that some did regard Hal's occupation as a substitute for work. They looked upon artists as oddities belonging to a different species – educated people, as Ruby had said. Many thought it a bit of a joke that the rough and ready Angilleys now had one in the family, and a few would say that Hal was foolishly aping his betters.

Quickly, however, Peggy shrugged it off. Ruby's nastiness was merely proof that Hal's success had stuck in her throat, and the time would soon come when all the doubters would have to admit they were wrong. Peggy gave a couple of skips and the spring returned to her step. She walked on down to the waterfront, swinging her basket, and turned towards home.

It was late morning now. Over on the west quay, the old men were out on their bench by the harbour wall. Four retired fishermen in peaked caps and bowlers, black boots and navy blue jerseys. Every fine day they'd be there, smoking their Gold Flakes and pipes of Digger. Hal said he was going to paint them before the summer was out.

Briefly, Peggy thought again about Ruby's jibe:

'He's just ordinary, like the rest of us.'

No, Peggy told herself fondly, he's not. My Hal is someone special.

Four

The following morning at *Lamorva*, Anna was serving breakfast, as usual. She moved among the tables in the guests' dining-room, collecting up empty fruit juice glasses and putting down plates of bacon and eggs. There was murmured conversation and a delicate clink of knives and forks. Mrs Trevena presently had a full house – eight boarders, mostly elderly couples.

The dining-room was sunny, with a large bay window full of aspidistras. The table linen was white and stiff, the crockery and cutlery carefully chosen to be nice but not worth stealing. One never knew, one couldn't be too careful, Mother said.

Anna went round with the coffee and tea pots, offering the second cup to which everyone was entitled. Then she returned to the kitchen and sat down to a frugal slice of toast.

Mrs Trevena eyed her primly. 'What are you going to do today?'

Anna shrugged, nibbling the crust of toast without much appetite.

'You're not to mope about. Make yourself useful and run a few errands for me. You can pay some money into the bank, and then go to the *West Briton* office, ask them to run our advertisement again. Oh, and I need a prescription filled at the chemist's. When you come back, you can help me to pull out the beds and sweep underneath.'

It was Thursday morning. The day was very hot as Anna dawdled down the hill to Temperance Street. Her head still ached from another night of weeping. She had to wait at the bank and again at the newspaper office. From there, she crossed the street to Lindow's Pharmacy.

Lindow's always smelt of lavender water and embrocation, and was very old-fashioned. The walls were lined with dark oak cupboards, each having many little drawers. Ornamental flasks of coloured water, red and purple, were ranged along the top of them, in company with scores of fluted green glass bottles. It always made Anna think of Victorian poisoners. A sign on the counter demanded to know: 'Are you constipated?', concluded that you probably were and recommended a ferocious laxative. Another sternly warned that no girl was likely to marry unless she took Bile Beans.

Anna had brought a prescription for a liniment. She handed it to Mr Lindow.

'It'll take ten minutes,' he said.

'I'll wait.'

He disappeared into the back room. An advertisement card for 'Star' cosmetics caught Anna's attention as she wandered round. Words like 'allure' and 'bewitching' were used. She paused to ponder over the trays of eyebrow pencils and nail varnish. There were boxes of face powder, too, and cakes of rouge and lipsticks with sultry names.

Perhaps if I'd worn some of this, she thought wistfully, Hal might never have looked at Peggy Angilley.

As she browsed, the doorbell tinkled and someone else came in; a youngish man in casual clothes. Anna had seen him around the town, but didn't know him. He looked at her, smiled and wished her good morning.

'Good morning,' she said shyly, and turned away.

The bell brought Mr Lindow once more to the counter. He took a prescription from the man and disappeared again.

Anna picked up a perfume sampler and dabbed a spot on her wrist. It was light and sweet; she liked it, and toyed with the notion of buying some just to cheer herself up.

The man was watching her, looking her up and down. After a moment, he remarked:

'Nice and cool in here.'

She looked round. 'I beg your pardon?'

'I said it's cool in here.'

'Oh – yes.'

A pause and then: 'Left school now, have you?'

She blinked a question at him.

'I used to see you about in the uniform,' he explained.

'Oh. Yes, I left last summer, Mr . . .?'

'Buckman.' He smiled again. 'I'm Guy. And you are . . .?'

'Anna Trevena,' she said, with some reluctance. She was in no mood to make his acquaintance.

'Do you have a job or anything?'

'I help out at home. My mother runs a guesthouse.'

'Indeed? We're in much the same line of business, then. I own Elestren Manor.'

'Really?' Her eyebrows lifted. Despite herself, she was interested. Elestren Manor was a small but very smart and expensive hotel. It stood in grounds of seven acres at the western edge of the town. 'I've heard wonderful things about it,' she said, 'especially the food.'

'Thank you. And where's your mother's guesthouse?'

Anna told him.

'Ah, yes, very nice up there.'

She regarded him curiously, wondering how old he was. Early thirties, at a guess. His face possessed the odd quality of being both handsome and ugly all at once. The ugliness lay around the mouth. It was full and well-shaped and yet it had an unkind downward turn when in repose. A smile or a grin brought it back into harmony with the rest of his features, which were pleasant. His eyes were hazel, rather large. His hair was brown and straight, combed back and smoothly dressed. Anna was tall, but he stood a head above her, and his leanness emphasised his height.

'Buckman, that's not a Cornish name,' she observed.

'My family came here from the Midlands.'

'Oh, I see.'

Mr Lindow emerged again, bearing both prescriptions. Guy Buckman opened the door for Anna as they left.

'Which way are you going?' he asked, as they stepped outside.

'Straight home, I've things to do.'

He cocked an eyebrow. 'I don't suppose you're looking for extra work, by any chance? I need a girl for the office, just part-time.'

Apologetically, Anna smiled. 'I'm sorry, no.'

'I'd pay you well.'

'I'm sure you would, but I've never done anything like that before.'

'There's nothing to it. You'd pick it up in a couple of days, bright girl like you.'

'You're very kind, but no.'

'Oh, go on, think it over this weekend.' His smile was boyish, very engaging. 'Call in on Monday morning if you want the job.'

'All right,' she said, just to get away. 'I'll consider it, Mr Buckman.'

'Call me Guy.'

'When you've asked me to work for you? Surely your staff don't do that?' queried Anna, surprised.

'Um, well, not normally.' Again the big, disarming grin.

She nodded knowingly. 'I thought not. Well, goodbye.'

By the time she reached home she'd forgotten about him. It wasn't until nearly bedtime that he crossed her mind again. She was sitting with her mother in their private parlour and Mrs Trevena had the wireless on. The news programmes were full of reports about Amy Johnson, whose plane was on the last leg of its flight to Australia.

'Do you know, I was offered a job today,' Anna said, glancing up from her book.

Mrs Trevena stared at her over her spectacles. 'Oh? By whom? What sort of job?'

'Mr Buckman who owns Elestren Manor. He wanted a receptionist.'

Her mother dropped her knitting. 'Who?' she asked, her green eyes bulging.

'Guy Buckman. He owns . . .'

'I know, I know. Elestren Manor.' Mrs Trevena switched the wireless off. 'Well, what did you say?'

'I said thank you, but no.'

'Oh, Anna! Why didn't you accept, you silly girl?'

'I didn't want the job. Anyway . . .' Anna suppressed a smile. '. . . I was a bit suspicious of his motives. He wanted me to call him by his Christian name. Probably a married man with a roving eye. You know the type.'

'That's just where you're wrong, my dear. He's single, he's eligible.'

'How do you know?'

'I heard it from Mrs Kellow at the florist's shop. She was telling me not long ago that she supplies Elestren Manor – said he was a charming man and she couldn't understand why he wasn't married.'

'Really? Well, don't get carried away. He offered me a job, not a diamond ring.'

'One thing can lead to another, Anna dear.'

'Doesn't seem likely to me. In any case, he's not my sort.'

'He's precisely your sort, unlike that Pentreath boy.'

'Mr Buckman's much older than me.'

'What's wrong with maturity?' Mrs Trevena sniffed. 'Anyway, you're exaggerating. It might be a matter of ten years, and that's nothing. I've seen him, I can tell.'

'Even so, I didn't feel I wanted to know him better – or take the job.'

Her mother pondered for a while and then said craftily: 'You know, Anna, you made rather a fool of yourself over that wretched Hal.'

Flushing, Anna hid behind her book. Mother had no idea how big a fool.

'You've never concealed your feelings well. Everyone knows how hurt you were when he married that Peggy.'

'Who's everyone?' queried Anna, peering at her over the book.

'Our neighbours, dear. Your schoolfriends.'

The blush went from red to maroon.

'If you want to restore your dignity, Anna – better still, come out on top – I can't think of a better way than being seen with a man like Mr Buckman. Show that Hal Pentreath you're not pining for him. Then, at least, you can hold your head up and know they're no longer laughing at you.'

'That seems a very bad reason for taking up with a man.'

'Oh, don't be such a prig.' Mrs Trevena's tone became wheedling. 'Wouldn't it be galling for Peggy Angilley? Imagine it.'

Anna did. The book sank to her lap. A thoughtful look came over her face.

'Why don't you telephone Mr Buckman in the morning?' her mother pressed. 'Tell him you've changed your mind and you'll take up his offer. You never know where it might lead. Anyway, it would do you good to have a little job, help to take your mind off all that other nonsense. It's a glamorous place, you know, Elestren Manor. Lots of excitement, always something going on.'

For a moment, Anna was almost tempted, but then she shook herself and went back to her book.

'Don't ask me why,' she said, 'but I just don't like the idea.'

Breathing heavily down her nose, Mrs Trevena took up her knitting and carried on. There was irritation in the rapid click of the needles. 'You're your own worst enemy, my girl,' she said.

Five

Hal's exhibition ended the following day. He had sold eleven paintings. Favourable things had been said of his work in the local press, and the Town Council had offered him facilities for another show at a future date. On Saturday morning, he took Peggy out and bought her a frock in celebration – yellow cotton trimmed with broderie anglaise – and a necklace of big amber beads to go with it.

'I'll wear it,' she said to the assistant in the shop, and the woman obligingly put her old dress in a carrier bag.

'Pleased?' asked Hal, as they walked down the street, arm-in-arm. 'You look lovely, Peggy.'

And she did. The fabric, crisp and pretty, set off her brown skin, and the beads at her throat seemed to glow in the sun like drops of honey.

'Let's have a day out,' she suggested, kissing him. 'Let's go to Newquay, just the two of us. Mam will look after Joy.'

They caught the bus at the old town square, and rode down the coast to reach Newquay in time for a lunch of crab at a café. Afterwards, they wandered down to the beach under Narrowcliff.

The day was the kind of misty blue which promised more fine weather. Barefoot, carrying their shoes, Hal and Peggy threaded their way through the Saturday crowds, the dry sand hot and silky between their toes.

42

Walking out to the tideline, they followed its trail of shiny pebbles, heading towards Lusty Glaze. The sea-smell was heady, the water shockingly cold whenever an incoming wave touched their feet.

Leaving the crowds behind, they reached a lonely stretch of the beach, where Peggy tucked her skirt up into her drawers and waded into the tide up to her shins. Rolling up his trousers, Hal followed her and they ran along for half a mile, kicking water at each other like a pair of ten year olds. Before very long, their clothes were soaked and Hal took off his shirt. There was very fine down on his broad brown back, and it shone in the sun like powdered gold.

As the tide fell lower, it left a great expanse of flat, wet sand.

'Draw me something,' Peggy demanded. 'Go on, artist, use your toe.'

He thought for a moment, then started to hop around, outlining the contours of a face. A few skips here and there, a few deft strokes and touches, and upon the sand lay a pretty good caricature of Walter Angilley.

Peggy hooted and clapped her hands. 'Exactly! That's Father exactly! Now do one of me.'

A minute or two and there she was, looking pugnacious.

'Oh, you beast!' shrieked Peggy, laughing.

'What about this one, then? You'll like this better.' He drew two hugging matchstick figures, ten feet high. Bending, he scrawled with his finger: 'Hal loves Peggy', and added a heart.

'Best thing you've ever done, I think.' She giggled as he scooped her up and swung her round and round. 'Perhaps you ought to take up painting with your feet.'

By mid-afternoon they reached the headland at the limit of the beach. The cliffs were high and rugged here, with many lofty ledges occupied by nesting gulls. Flopping down in the shade of an overhang, they sat to rest for half an hour. Peggy leaned back against the rock and folded an arm behind her head, contemplating the plumes of horsetail clouds sketched on the sky. A gull was gliding so high up there, it looked no bigger than a moth. Far out from where she sat, Atlantic breakers swelled and rolled, curling, booming, diminishing to leisurely golden ripples flowing in gently over the sand.

She closed her eyes and smiled, inhaling scents of brine and seaweed. This was perfect happiness. She adored her husband and life was filled with promise. These were good, good times, and this an especially wonderful day. Her skin felt full of the heat of the sun, and quivering breezes patted her like cool, ethereal hands.

A sandfly tickled her face and she blinked as she brushed it away. 'Look at those,' she murmured to Hal, pointing out a tuft of flowers growing high on a buttress of rock nearby. 'Beautiful, aren't they? I've always loved pinks.'

He shaded his eyes, scanned the rockface a moment, then bobbed to his feet.

'I'll get them for you.'

'What?' Suddenly frightened, Peggy sat up. 'Hal, no!'

But he was already running across the sand to the foot of the cliff. Peggy set off after him, but in no time he was scrambling upwards, twenty feet from the ground. 'Hal!' she shouted. 'You come down! Hal, don't be so stupid!'

His voice came back. 'It's all right, I can see a way up.'

'Never mind. I don't want the flowers.'

'Of course you do.'

He swung himself up a few more feet.

'Hal, please!'

'Don't worry so.'

Peggy watched him helplessly, cursing herself for the careless remark which had given him such a rash idea. She'd forgotten that Hal could be just like a child, acting on impulse, not stopping to think. It was one of his lovable traits, yet also the one thing about him which sometimes worried her. Peggy was never exactly cautious, but Hal seemed to live by a cheerful faith that the worst would never befall, no matter what he did.

Pressing a hand to her mouth, she watched him climbing. The wind was tugging at his hair, and mobs of gulls, disturbed from their nests, kept swooping past him, screaming.

He reached a ledge and shuffled along it a fraction at a time. Below him was a drop of sixty feet. One slip now and all his promise, all their future, would go in an instant. Peggy saw his hands moving gingerly over the rockface and fancied she could almost feel the rough brown stone herself, as if her own fingers were inching across it, their fleshy pads pressing hard into little grooves and gripping at ridges.

If he fell, she thought she would die herself. What an end to a golden day.

But finally he cleared the ledge. Beyond it were generous footholds, easy handholds. He hopped across to a safer perch atop a jutting shelf of rock, raised a waving hand above his head and shouted something

Peggy couldn't catch. Then, turning, he clambered over to the little outcrop where the flowers grew, picked them and tucked the stems in his belt.

With anxious eyes, she watched him make his descent. At last, he reached bottom safely and came towards her, full of bounce, with the posy of pinks now clutched in his hand.

'Thought I couldn't do it, eh?'

'Oh, you idiot!'

'Here you are.' He held out the flowers.

'You might have broken your neck, or been crippled!'

'Go on with you, it was easy.'

At first she wouldn't take the pinks. 'You irresponsible . . .! I was so afraid! You could have made a widow of me, and for what?'

'Peggy . . .' He looked reproachful. 'Here.'

He held out the flowers once more, and this time, slowly, she took them, running her fingers over their petals. What a gesture it had been. No matter how angry, she had to recognise that.

'Don't you ever scare me like that again,' she warned quietly. 'I mean it, Hal.'

'I'm sorry.'

Peggy looked down at the pinks and couldn't repress a smile. 'They're lovely,' she admitted. 'If only they could last forever.'

'Tell you what, I'll paint you with them, seeing you need a new portrait.' Squeezing her, he whispered: 'I wouldn't have made such a climb for Anna, you know.'

'So you say.'

'It's true.'

'I'm not so sure. You're a great silly fool and a showoff,' she sniffed – then screamed as he pinched her behind.

They started the long walk back to town and she kept a tight arm round his waist. Peggy could hardly imagine life without him. Except for Joy, Hal was everything in the world to her.

That evening, they went for a drink in the pub next door to Angilley's Bazaar. Billy Nancarrow's place, known as *The Old Solace*.

Billy's pub presented a shabby façade – grubby whitewash crossed with black timbering. The lintel of the door was lopsided, giving a foretaste of what lay within. The ground had never been properly levelled before the place was built and consequently all the walls and floors were out of true. If ever Walter Angilley had put up a building, it would probably have looked very much like *The Old Solace*.

The regular customers were all of a kind, and they congregated at Billy's because few of them were tolerated anywhere else. Most had been banned from every other licensed house in town, whether for brawling, foul language, breakages or threatening the landlord. They comprised a selection of salty riff-raff, along with sundry misfits like Walter and Jasper. Billy Nancarrow enjoyed a certain esteem among them as 'their' publican. He was bald and very large, and heavily tattooed. No one ever threatened Billy Nancarrow.

Saturday evening attracted additional custom because it was sing-song night. Maisie Angilley always said that God never made anyone totally useless, citing the fact that her husband and son had a measure of musical talent. It was they who provided the tunes every Saturday night, playing in company with two other local men. Walter was handy with an accordion, and Jasper skilled with a fiddle. No amount of drink seemed to impair their abilities. The other members of the makeshift band were a grubby old man with a piccolo, and a fat youth expert on the ukelele. Billy paid them fifteen shillings each, with a free meal thrown in. It was the nearest thing to regular employment Walter and Jasper had ever known.

The Old Solace was packed that night. Even though Peggy and Hal arrived early, it wasn't easy to find a seat. At last they squeezed in at a rough oak table alongside Jack Tresize, the donkey man, and the Penpraze brothers, two burly types who ran a couple of pleasure ferries from Victoria pier. Skinny Jack was known as 'Soon-be-dead' because he professed to be gravely ill. He had been insisting for thirty years that he had 'something terminal'. Hal was well acquainted with Saul and Noah Penpraze, because they had given him a job when first he came to Trezawne. They still took a certain proud interest in all that he did.

'Got your name up in lights, boy?' Noah nudged him as he sat down. 'Saw the piece in the paper. You're doing some well.'

'Might be a rich man one of these days,' agreed Saul. 'You could have bidders fighting at auction to own a genuine Pentreath.'

'Get on with you,' scoffed Hal, but he was pleased by the compliment.

Peggy flashed him a look which said: It may not be so very far-fetched. Who knows?

'We'll be able to say we knew you before you were famous,' added Jack.

'Don't go giving Peggy ideas,' sighed Hal.

'Let us buy you a drink, boy,' Noah said. 'Bitter? And barley wine for Peggy?'

He fetched the round and everyone toasted Hal's success.

Fondly, Hal watched his wife clapping and singing along to the bouncing tunes. The air was fragrant with pipe-smoke, and the smells of cork, beer and pies. Some of the songs were ribald or just plain silly, but Peggy enjoyed them. He could never have asked Anna here for an evening like this, he thought. She would have been uncomfortable, and so would he.

Anna's neat home, her education, had always bothered Hal, reminding him of his humbler origins. There had been times when she used words he didn't understand, though pride had never allowed him to point that out. Evidence of schooling always intimidated Hal. That was why he never mixed with the other local painters. There was a small society for artists in Trezawne, but he wouldn't join. All the painters he had met were better educated than himself. Most had received formal training in art and all came from gentler backgrounds. Deliberately or not, they made him feel at a disadvantage.

'I'm not much for clubs or meetings or discussions,' he had told Peggy. 'I think it's a waste of time, and I don't want to be influenced by other people and their ideas. I might lose what's my own, if you know what I mean.'

She had never questioned that, whereas Anna had argued about it.

Peggy caught him looking at her and reached out for his hand. She seemed to see a golden glow around her husband's head. It was just the lamplight, the twinkle of brasses and copperware hung round the walls, but to her it looked like the aura of genius.

Late that night, they sat on their bed together with

49

notes and coins strewn all around them, counting out the proceeds of the exhibition. It had earned Hal something over seventy pounds, net of Jackman's commission. Peggy's face was radiant as she handled the cash.

'Seventy-two pounds fifteen and six,' she said with satisfaction. 'That's not bad, is it? Not bad at all.' She was sitting cross-legged, in her nightdress, with the money in her lap. Ecstatically, she clutched a bunch of pound notes in either hand. 'Oh, Hal . . .' She wrapped her arms about his neck and kissed him.

Propping the pillows up against the brass bedstead, he lay back, pulling her into the crook of his arm. He was half undressed, wearing only his trousers, and Peggy toyed thoughtfully with the line of hair running down his stomach.

'When will the next one be?' she asked.

'The council have offered me the use of a room next spring.'

Her eyes shone. 'What shall we buy with the money?'

He tucked an arm behind his head. 'We'll save most of it. I'll open an account at the post office. And one day, Peggy, not too far ahead, we'll buy a house of our own.'

'Will we? Really?' The question was breathless.

'I promise you. One of these days.'

A house of their own, one of these days. Privately, Maisie Angilley was in no hurry to see that day.

She was out in the yard on Monday morning when one of her neighbours looked over the back wall and enquired:

'Your Peggy be moving out, will she, now her husband's doing well?'

Maisie looked up from her mangling, and there was Lily Craze, a couple of clothes pegs in her mouth, throwing a sheet across her washing line. Today the courtyards all over Trezawne were strung with flapping laundry, and the smell of boiling linen was in the wind. A ten-foot obstacle course lay between the back door and the lavatory, for Maisie's yard was congested with tin baths and buckets.

'They'll be wanting more room sometime, I dare say.' Maisie cranked the mangle, panting. 'But it's early yet to talk of that.'

Lily jammed the pegs down over the sheet and took up another. She was sixty, still wore black taffeta to the ankles, and was locally known as Lily Greasypockets, though no one could quite remember why. Nicknaming was always a favourite Cornish habit. Her husband had an allotment up the hill and was keen on compost; therefore he was known as Steaming Heaps.

'You ought to throw Walter and Jasper out. Keep Peggy and her family home with you,' said Lily, cackling.

'Perhaps I will.'

'If my old man behaved like those two, he'd soon have his marching orders.'

Maisie grunted as a lump of twisted fabric squeezed through the rollers. 'They're the cross I have to bear. I made the vows and I knew Walter was no bargain.' She straightened up, flexing her back, and swiped the hair back from her eyes. The front of her pinafore was soaking wet.

'Could be worse, I suppose,' allowed Lily. 'At least he doesn't knock you around.'

'Walter?' shrilled Maisie. 'Couldn't knock the top off a boiled egg. Too tired to get out of his own way.' She

51

shook out a pillowcase flattened by the the mangle and pinned it to the line above her head. 'Peggy's learned from my mistake. She's married a better man.'

'An artist,' Lily mused, picking up her empty clothes basket. 'Never heard of young men going in for such things in my day. They went to sea or down the mines and that was that.'

'Everything's changing,' Maisie agreed.

'That's a fact. I often feel like something left behind from yesterday, as if I shouldn't still be here.' Lily's eyes grew absent, thoughtful. 'These are funny days, Maisie, the tail-end of what always belonged to be. It's all just slipping quietly away. I ask you, what'll it be like in years to come?'

Maisie knew, but she said nothing. She had known from the time the railway reached Trezawne how the future would be.

Lily shook herself. 'Ah, well, better go on in and starch the old man's collars.'

Hauling a tablecloth out of the rinsing bath, Maisie fed the corner between the wooden rollers and started forcing the handle round again. As she laboured, Lily's question came back to her:

'Your Peggy be moving out, will she . . .?'

Maisie devoutly hoped not. What would be left for her if her daughter and family were gone? The dismal company of Walter and Jasper, that was what. No one to help in the house, no one with whom to laugh, no baby to cosset.

If the truth were told, Maisie would agree with Ruby Tabb and Mrs Trevena on one thing: painting was a chancy way of making a living. She was pleased that Hal's exhibition had been a success, but knew it was no guarantee at all of future prosperity. Maisie felt a great affection for her son-in-law; he was good-tempered, optimistic, and zealous about his work. He had made Peggy happy. But – Hal wasn't practical, not the most sensible of men, and probably never would be. He was too impulsive, too blithe for that. Maisie had diagnosed this from the day she first met him. Still, Peggy had wanted him and her mother had thought:

Oh, well, I don't mind very much if he's not the best of providers. Peggy knows she can always turn to me. I wouldn't want her to marry a man who'd take her over, take her away. If they need a bit of help, it'll serve to keep them close, and that's fine by me.

Six

May turned into June. On another cloudless day, Anna was leaning on the railings near Victoria pier, watching the ferry boats come and go. This was where she had first seen Hal Pentreath three years ago. She was then only sixteen, standing here in this same spot, killing time on a summer's day. The memory came back clearly of a queue of people filing down the steps to the Padstow ferry, and a young man standing at the bottom, helping them aboard. Something about him had seized her interest even then – the bright fair hair, and a kind of happy aura all about him. A pleasing manner, both relaxed and civil. Once or twice, his laughter had reached her, making her smile too, because it was such a joyful sound. Some months later, at a party, a friend of hers had introduced him.

'Anna, this is Hal Pentreath. He's an artist, you know . . .'

Anna stared dolefully down at the bottle-green water which lapped at the wall of the quay. A crust of barnacles coated the great granite blocks, and fringes of pale green weed, wet and silky, hung from the ropes of small boats moored below. There was no escape from memories in a small town like Trezawne. Everywhere she went, she was reminded of the time when Hal did this or said that, or . . .

All of a sudden, a voice at her shoulder broke in on her thoughts.

'Decided against the job, then, did you?'

Anna started, looked around. Guy Buckman was the last person on her mind, but there he stood, smiling at her.

'Oh,' she said, collecting herself, 'hello. Yes. Still, I expect you've found someone by now?'

He nodded.

'I'm glad.'

He rested his forearms on the railings. 'Well,' he said, 'it was only a ploy anyway.'

'I beg your pardon?'

He grinned. 'I wanted to get to know you.'

'Mm, I guessed as much.'

'Transparent, was I?'

She smiled and said nothing.

Still he lingered, looking at her. Anna was wearing a white cotton blouse with pin-tucks and glass buttons. Her straight linen skirt was calf-length. She was never bold enough to go about in gaudy colours and candy-stripes, as Peggy often did.

'Well then, I may as well be direct. Have lunch with me?'

She stared at him, half shook her head. 'Oh – no, I don't think I could.'

'Why not? Wouldn't you like that? Come on.'

Anna was about to refuse him, but snippets of her mother's words echoed in her head and made her hesitate.

'. . . you made rather a fool of yourself . . . Everyone knows how hurt you were . . . Wouldn't it be galling for Peggy Angilley?'

'Umm . . .' She struggled with indecision.

'Scallops, perhaps, at *The Buttery*?'

'Oh,' she said again. She was tempted. What harm

55

could it do? A splendid little restaurant, *The Buttery*, with its oak panelling and bow windows. Perhaps it would help to take her mind off Hal for just a while.

'Strawberries to follow?' he coaxed.

'I don't know, it does sound lovely . . .'

'Are you expected home?'

'It isn't that.'

'You're quite presentable, if that's what you're worried about.'

Still she dithered. But why hold back? Because he was ten or twelve years older? So slight an acquaintance? Anna could pinpoint no other reason. But then, how did any relationship start? And what did she have to lose, except an hour or two of painful brooding? Taking a deep breath, she laughed and gave in.

'Well, all right. You're very kind. How can I say no?'

When Anna returned home in mid-afternoon, Mrs Trevena wanted to know where she had been. The answer set her twittering with excitement.

'Now tell me all about it. What a feather in your cap! You say he took you to *The Buttery*?'

'Hmm. The bill was nearly four pounds,' added Anna with awe. 'That was what he gave the waiter, and he told him to forget the change.'

'Oh, that's nothing to Mr Buckman. Has he asked to see you again?'

'He wants to take me for a drive on Saturday.'

'Ooh!' Her mother was in raptures. 'You said yes, of course?'

'I did, but . . .'

'But what?' demanded Mrs Trevena. 'Don't tell me you're having second thoughts?'

'I don't know. While I was with him it was all so

novel and exciting. I was feeling – buoyant – and really keen for more of his company. But after I left him, as I was on my way up the hill, something . . .' Anna's forehead furrowed. 'I can't explain. I just wished I hadn't been so hasty.'

'Oh, Anna, what a goose you are! For heaven's sake, don't go thinking up a lot of ifs and buts. Just go out with him, give the man a chance.'

Covertly, Anna threw her a look of annoyance. Mrs Trevena's advice had been just the opposite concerning Hal. Stop, consider, have a care. But then, Hal Pentreath had no money and that was Mother's yardstick. Delia Trevena had never met Guy Buckman, knew little about him, except that he owned that very prestigious hotel. That, however, was enough; she was ready and eager to call the banns. Anna suspected it wouldn't matter to her mother if Guy had two club feet, crossed eyes and a dangerous psychosis. She would still look upon him with favour.

Still, Anna had to admit he was attractive. Some women would be positively thrilled by the cruel set to his mouth. It was almost a cliché of steamy films and novels.

'Well,' she said, 'I've promised to go, so I will. I suppose it's just that he's a stranger and I met him in such a casual way.'

'Was a stranger,' corrected Mrs Trevena. 'And it doesn't matter how it happened, I'm just grateful it did. Will he collect you from here?'

'Yes. About eleven o'clock.'

'I can't wait to meet him. You must bring him back for dinner.'

'As a matter of fact, he suggested an evening meal at the hotel.'

Mrs Trevena's mouth formed a big, approving 'Oh', and then closed into a prim little smile.

'He isn't wasting any time, is he? I think you've really made a conquest, Anna.'

She had, too. Anna knew she had. The signs were easy to read. The way he had looked at her over lunch – so admiring. His reluctance to part with her. Walking away, she had looked back twice – and found that he was standing, watching her.

Anna was flattered by it, immensely flattered, and wondered why she also felt vaguely disturbed. Perhaps because things were threatening to move too quickly. She felt she had blundered into something without quite knowing what she was doing. Mother, of course, would say that fate had taken over and was acting for the best. Anna supposed she could be right.

'I think I'll buy you a few new clothes,' Mrs Trevena said. 'You've nothing really smart enough for dinner at Elestren Manor. You must have a nice frock, something simple and good that will do for afternoon and evening. Silk would be very suitable. You've never had a silk dress, have you?'

Anna stared at her. 'Do you mean it?'

'I'm not given to joking, dear. You shall have a nice new pair of court shoes too, and a bag to match. We'll take the train to Truro tomorrow, just as soon as the guests go out.'

A silk dress, new shoes. Anna began to feel a genuine sense of occasion.

'I wonder what kind of a car he has,' mused Mrs Trevena. 'I expect it's something smart and sporty. I can just imagine all the neighbours peeping from behind their curtains. This will give them something to think about.'

Anna pulled a wry face, but said nothing. She had always been one more thing for Mother to brag about. Dad's important job at the town hall had been Mrs Trevena's favourite talking point when Anna was a child. Then, when he died, it had been Anna's place at the grammar school, proud reports of all her little achievements. To impress, outshine, was ever Mrs Trevena's priority.

All the same, thought Anna, perhaps in this case Mother was right. Being courted by Guy Buckman might be something of a coup – especially if she were seen with him by Peggy Pentreath.

Guy arrived punctually on Saturday morning, driving an MG Midget and dressed in white flannel trousers and shirt, plus a cricketer's V-neck jersey.

Mrs Trevena insisted on giving him coffee before they left. She ushered him into the parlour and fluttered off to get out the best china in his honour. He sat there patiently with Anna, his presence seeming to fill the little room.

'I'm sorry,' she said. 'Mother always likes to inspect my friends.'

Guy smiled and shrugged it off, lounging expansively in one of the chairs. His long legs took up a lot of room. He was used to surroundings much more spacious, and it showed. Anna remembered how her father used to sit, neat and upright in his chair. A very unobtrusive man, not like Guy at all.

Mrs Trevena quickly returned with a tray. Coffee and biscuits and slices of Bakewell tart. Placing it on a low table, she seated herself and began to pour.

'Well, isn't this nice?' she said, handing Guy his cup.

Her manner was coy, and a bit subservient, Anna thought.

Leaning forward, he took it with a murmur of thanks. His sleeves were rolled to the elbows and his forearms were sinewy, tanned. For the first time, Anna noticed how bony his hands were, the knuckles especially prominent.

As they all drank their coffee, Mrs Trevena did most of the talking. It was largely in praise of Anna – which caused the girl to squirm. Guy listened politely, but as soon as courtesy allowed, he glanced at his watch and stood up.

'Time's flying, we'd best be off.'

Relieved, Anna bounced to her feet, picking up her bag. It was black leather, to go with the patent shoes and the blue silk dress her mother had bought for her in Truro the day before. Guy looked her over and winked. 'You look gorgeous,' he whispered.

'Well then,' cooed Mrs Trevena, beaming from one to the other, 'where are you thinking of going this lovely day?'

Guy glanced at Anna. 'Fancy a spin across Bodmin Moor?'

She was rarely fussy, always amenable. 'That would be lovely,' she said.

Turning to Mrs Trevena, Guy told her: 'Anna's coming to dinner with me this evening.'

'Yes, I know.' She was all smiles.

'I'll bring her home around ten, if that's all right?'

'Of course, of course. You just be sure to enjoy yourselves.' Mrs Trevena clasped her hands together, ecstatic. As Guy escorted Anna down to the car, she stood on the front step, self-consciously glancing around in hopes that a neighbour or two might be looking. She gave a little wave as the car pulled away.

Anna enjoyed the drive. A car-ride was a novelty for her. Laying her head against the back of the seat, she watched the road unfold, a grey asphalt ribbon, and felt the hot wind flowing towards her under a sky of unbroken blue. After weeks without rain, the moorland was shrivelled and crisp, patterned with brownish-purple heather and bristly swathes of yellow gorse. A landscape dry enough to burn, with only dabs of green to relieve it.

Once again, Guy Buckman's genial company lifted her spirits, just as it had in the restaurant a few days before. He had a way of making her feel very special, glamorous. Anna had always thought herself uninterested in money, but in the silk dress she was sharply conscious how nice it was to wear expensive things. She felt at home in the soft brown leather passenger seat of the Midget, and couldn't help thinking how good it would be to dress this way and be driven around and fêted all the time.

Guy took her up to Gunnislake for lunch at a celebrated country restaurant. The prices horrified and thrilled her, but he didn't turn a hair. Anna found herself torn between fright and wanting more of this. She felt overawed and out of her depth, but privileged too, and excited. Part of her, however, also entertained suspicions. It all seemed too good to be true. Why had he taken an interest in her, young and inexperienced as she was? Perhaps he was one of those men who had different girlfriends all the time and quickly tired of them. That would certainly explain why he wasn't yet married.

That evening, when they arrived back in Trezawne, Guy drove her straight to Elestren Manor. The hotel, with its twenty bedrooms, lay in a vale about half a mile beyond the edge of the town. A pair of high granite gateposts marked the entrance. They were spanned by an arch with the name 'Elestren Manor' in wrought-iron. A left turn off the road led up a shady lane through a tunnel of beeches which ran for fifty yards. The drive then emerged into bright sunshine, with lawns and beds of blue and yellow irises on either side, and ended before an extensive granite house – once the private home of a rich gentleman. One side of the house was swathed in ivy, luxuriant dark green against the light grey stone. There were big sash windows in eighteenth-century style, eighteen panes to every window, the frames picked out in clean white. A large conservatory ran along the western side.

On a square of gravel near the front entrance stood eight or nine smart cars. Guy parked the Midget beside them. He pointed to a big saloon as they got out.

'That green one's mine as well. I've a fondness for Rileys. I buy a new one every year.'

Anna nodded, unsurprised. He wouldn't make do with one car, would he? Not a man like Guy. Again, she felt a thrill of nervousness. It was all so – overwhelming.

They went inside. The front hall had a red and gold carpet, which ran down a corridor towards the lounge and dining-room, and up a flight of stairs to the bedrooms. Part of this lobby had been partitioned off by a counter, to make an office. Behind the counter sat a girl of roughly Anna's age. She looked up when they entered and seemed, as if by reflex, to straighten up in her seat.

'Good evening, Mr Buckman.'

'Good evening, Sarah.' He paused at the desk and held out his hand. 'How many have we tonight?'

She passed him a small ledger and a handwritten list. 'Twenty-eight residents, and a chance booking for five at half-past eight.'

'Anyone still to arrive?'

'Mr and Mrs Anstey. They'll be in room nine.'

The receptionist was in evening dress, and had curly blonde hair. As Guy scanned the list, the girl watched him with a certain tension. But then he handed it back and said:

'Good. Everything's under control, then?'

'Yes, Mr Buckman.'

He turned to Anna. 'I have to go up and change. Shan't be very long. Sarah will show you where the ladies' cloakroom is. Come along to the bar when you're ready.' He indicated double glass doors near the foot of the stairs.

Anna spent fifteen minutes washing her face and hands and combing the tangles out of her hair. She dawdled a while at the mirror, wishing she had worn some pearls or something to make her appear less young and ingenuous.

Finally, she made her way down the corridor to the bar. Guy was already waiting for her, perched on a high stool and sipping whisky. He had put on a suit and tie. About a dozen other people sat around at tables.

'What would you like?' he asked, as she took the seat beside him.

'Just orange juice.'

As soon as she said it, she thought how juvenile it sounded. Orange juice, when she was faced with such a display of wines and spirits and liqueurs. Crème de menthe and kirsch, curaçao, grenadine, and a score of other brightly coloured liqueurs of which she had never even heard, all glowing like jewels under the spot-lights. And ten different kinds of everything else, it seemed. Guy, however, offered no argument. The barman, hovering nearby, made a few swift movements and a glass of orange juice appeared smartly before her. Again, Guy held out his hand in that casual manner. Silently, the barman passed him two menus, and he gave one to Anna.

'You seem to be forever feeding me,' she said.

'It's my trade. Can't break the habit.'

She spent a while poring over the menu. The French presented no difficulty, but the choice was bewildering. Nowhere else for miles around could one buy food like this. In the end she opted for trout, while Guy decided on steak for himself.

The barman slipped out to the kitchen with the order and returned a moment later to carry on polishing glasses. He was young, with sleekly oiled hair and a dickie-bow. Hardly a chatty soul, observed Anna. This was a servant, who spoke if and when he was spoken to. He would probably make careful small talk with a guest, but always remember his place. His impassive face revealed nothing of how he felt about it.

They went in to dinner at eight o'clock. Here in the dining-room, the same efficiency, the same unobtrusive movements by staff, the same anticipation of the diners' wants and needs. Everything was pristine, a gleaming vision of white napery, silver, and blue-flamed flambé lamps. There was dark blue carpet and gold flock wallpaper. Wall lights with amber glass shades were set between six-foot mirrors in wavy mahogany frames. At one end of the room, some steps led down to a polished dance floor.

'No music tonight?' asked Anna.

'No, but there's a dinner and dance next week. We have one every fortnight.'

'Who comes to the dances, the higher Trezawne crowd?'

'Mostly, yes. Same faces all the time. Trezawne is such a backwater, they'd have to go a long way to find a better night out. The residents join in, of course. I hire a band from Plymouth. They're excellent, very versatile. You'll see for yourself next week.'

She looked at him. Brightly, he lifted an eyebrow. 'You do like dancing, Anna?'

'Well, yes . . .'

'It'll be enormous fun.'

'I'm sure,' she said uneasily.

His expression sobered somewhat. 'Sorry – was I jumping the gun?'

She supposed that was it. Something had made her draw back for a moment – a sense of being taken over. Who was in charge of Anna's life? Herself? Or fate? Or Guy and her mother?

'I'm being presumptuous,' said Guy. 'I apologise. I should be asking if you want to see me again at all?' This with his most winning smile. 'It's just that I've enjoyed today so much. Perhaps you haven't?'

She had, and how could she deny it, sitting here, eating his delectable food? How could she offend him, generous man that he was?

'No, truly, I've had a lovely time.'

'What's the matter, then?'

What indeed? Perhaps it was a female suspicion that he might want some sort of repayment from her. She coloured up at the thought, more because of its baseness than anything else.

'Nothing. Nothing at all. I'd love to come.'

'Good. I'll introduce you to all my friends.'

I'll need another dress, Anna thought. She doubted her mother would mind. The sweet trolley arrived, but Guy sent it away, suggesting instead that they should have crêpes Suzette. The head waiter would cook the dish at the table.

It was all so beautiful, Anna thought, as she watched the man flipping the little pancakes, adding liqueur and burning it off in rushes of flame. Her face was lit by a flush of excitement. Glancing at Guy, she saw him watching her intently, almost amused.

'Quite a show, isn't it?' he said. 'Next time you come, you must have one of Chef's flaming sword kebabs.'

Later that evening, he drove Anna home and parked beneath the street lamp outside *Lamorva*.

'Shall I ring you in a day or two? he asked.

'All right.'

'Perhaps you can think of something you'd like to do next Saturday – your turn to choose.'

Pleased, she agreed. 'I'll give it some thought.'

Guy peered up at the house and whispered: 'Your mother's got us under surveillance.'

Sure enough, a bulky shadow loomed behind the sitting-room curtains. Through a gap came a slit of light, and one popping eye could be discerned.

Anna sighed. 'I'd better go in. Thank you for everything. It was wonderful.'

'Thank you for your lovely company, Anna.'

She thought just then that he might try to kiss her, but he made no move. Did she want him to? Not really.

Nice as he was, it was still too soon. Perhaps he knew and respected that, was anxious not to frighten her off.

'See you next week, then,' he called, as Anna got out of the car. Roaring away, he sounded a farewell toot on his horn.

Seven

Next day was Sunday. Everything stopped in lower Trezawne on Sundays. Methodism still had a powerful grip and the chapels were full. No Cornish fisherman worked on the Sabbath, no café opened its doors for trade. A stillness descended upon the old village, and there were no donkey rides, no deck chairs for hire at the beach.

There wasn't a family in all the town less religious than the Angilleys. Sunday, however, was the one day when Maisie put her feet up and declined to do a thing. She read the papers and played her gramophone records all the morning, while Peggy cooked the joint for lunch. Maisie's gramophone was an elderly Monarch Senior with a big green horn. She always used Songster needles, and her taste ran to jaunty popular tunes. Chapel folk passing along the back lane were offended each week by the sounds floating out through the Angilleys' kitchen window. After a good sermon full of damnation, 'Yes, we have no bananas' struck a jarring note. 'Let a smile be your umbrella', advised the gramophone. 'Tiptoe through the tulips', it suggested. 'You're the cream in my coffee', it told them merrily. It wasn't decent, not on a Sunday, declared the more intolerant.

To Hal Pentreath, every day was the same, and a Sunday afternoon as good a time as any other to go out and sketch something. He found an old courtyard that fine, warm day, and a couple of elderly women sitting outside on their fish cellar steps in the sun. Could he draw them? he asked. They didn't object, and carried right on with their scandalmongering as he set to work.

There was many a yard like this in lower Trezawne, littered with barrels and baskets and pressing stones, hung about with ropes and a few broken crab pots. All the surrounding cottages had an air of cheerful neglect; a bit of flaking whitewash here and rotten woodwork there, a slipping slate or two, a window with a crack. Tufts of weed grew out of little gaps between the flagstones, and a buddleia bush was sprouting from a crevice in a wall. Attracted by the scent of fish, yowling cats prowled everywhere.

In careful detail, he copied everything, each eccentric little dwelling, all the clutter, the crumpled faces and plain, faded clothes of the women, catching the feel of a place closed in and people long unchanged.

Hal was never aware of the passing hours when he was working, only of differences in the light, and the length and angles of shadows. He had all but finished when he heard a brisk, familiar step approaching down the alley.

'I've been looking everywhere for you,' said Peggy. 'It's gone six. Don't you want any tea?'

'I suppose so. I forgot the time. Look, what do you think?'

He showed her the drawing, then passed it across for the two old women to see. They studied it with nods and cackles, quietly flattered, even if it was just a bit of 'that old art nonsense'.

'It's good. Going to make an oil of it?' asked Peggy.

'Don't know, I might.'

He tucked the sketch pad under one arm and draped the other round her shoulders as they headed homewards. A shortcut through the maze of streets took them past the Methodist chapel, whence came the strains of the closing hymn of the early-evening service.

'O God, our help in ages past, our hope for years to come . . .'

They were good bass voices, strong and controlled. Trezawne was known for its male voice choir, as well as a fine brass band. Worldly as she was, Peggy found the singing pleasant and hummed a few bars of the tune as she went by.

A few yards further down the street, however, was the rear entrance to *The Old Solace*, where Peggy heard sounds of a less uplifting kind. A rattle and clink of bottles was followed by curses in response to the crash of breaking glass. Drawing near, the couple came upon a sordid sight. Outside the back door of the pub, Walter and Jasper were going through the empties and drinking the dregs. Billy Nancarrow had neatly stacked a score of crates, ready for the brewer's man next morning. Now they were strewn all over his yard, and brown bottles rolled everywhere.

Jasper had found half a pint of pale ale which had gone flat, and was sitting on the back step, guzzling it. His father was pouring trickles of this and that into a beer glass, thrown out because it had no handle – indiscriminately mixing bitter, barley wine and stout, anything to make up a quantity, a few good gulps.

Peggy and Hal stopped dead in their tracks.

'My God,' she said, revolted, 'if you could see yourselves!'

'Uh?' Walter swung around. 'Aw, 'tis you.' He scowled at her, then carried on.

'For pity's sake, Father, stop it! Have some self-respect.'

'Bugger off,' snapped Walter.

Jasper chortled, swigged from his bottle and leered at Hal. 'Been busy, Rembrandt? Done another masterpiece?'

Pentreath looked him up and down. 'You're pitiful,' he said.

'Don't you say that about my boy,' growled Walter. 'Soppy article like you.'

'Like to clout me for it? Like to try?'

Angilley glowered at him, but took a step back. Neither he nor his son was a fighter. Hal was a much bigger man and came from tough stock. Despite his gentle occupation, he was able to handle himself and the Angilleys sensed it.

'What's the matter?' taunted Peggy. 'Couldn't you wait for opening time? Must be some hard for you on Sundays, with the shorter drinking hours.'

'Ah, go to hell!'

'You shame us, you do,' Peggy told her father fiercely. 'Mam and me, we may not be genteel, but you're a disgrace.'

'Prissy, prissy, prissy,' Jasper mocked in mincing tones. He drained his bottle and tossed it away, and there was another smash.

'You'll have Billy out here in a minute,' Peggy warned.

'Don't care,' grunted Walter. 'Take your scolding face and clear off home.'

'Come on, maid,' said Hal, 'don't bother, leave them to it.'

71

'Do you want to be seen like this when the people come out from chapel?' demanded Peggy.

'None of their business,' snorted Jasper.

'Lovely way to behave on a Sunday.'

'What do you care about Sunday?' Walter sneered. 'You didn't even get married in church. Rush job at the town hall was what you had. Nothing very holy about you.' Then, looking past her up the street, he raised his voice. 'Well, here they come!'

Peggy glanced over her shoulder and saw the congregation filing out through the chapel doors.

'Been God-bothering again?' bawled out Walter.

People on the steps turned round to look.

'Shut up, Father!' Peggy hissed.

'Been sucking up to the Almighty?' bellowed Angilley. 'Sanctimonious buggers, always begging for this or apologising for that . . .'

'Stop it!' Peggy yelled. She raised her hand to him, but Hal quickly pulled her away.

'Don't upset yourself, maid, that's what he wants.'

'Damn you, Father, they're our neighbours and they're mostly nice people, they're not all prigs. A lot of them come in the shop all year round to buy from us, and we're glad of the trade. Trying to lose us money, are you? Trying to ruin Mother?'

Walter grew sullenly silent. He hadn't thought of that. To damage his means of support was the last thing he wanted.

The chapel people walked away up the street, muttering between themselves and shaking their heads.

'I shouldn't worry,' said Hal to Peggy. 'They all know what he is, they won't blame Maisie.'

And that was true. Walter Angilley was widely disliked. He had no friends whatever, save his son. Sometimes when she looked at Jasper, Peggy felt a certain pity for him. He'd never been exactly bright and was easily led.

'It's us against the women, boy,' Walter had told him from the time Jasper was knee-high. 'They'll nag you and drive you and find fault every minute if you let them. You take my tip, stick by your old dad, please yourself and enjoy your life.'

And Jasper had, because, after all, effort and discipline weren't much fun. Indolence came much more naturally.

He wouldn't have turned out a bad lad, Peggy thought, given a decent father, a better example. He wasn't ill-natured, merely dopey, whereas Walter could be malevolent.

Especially where his daughter was concerned. Peggy's sharp tongue had always nettled Walter. Since she was no more than six years old, he'd been seeing those dark eyes fixed upon him, full of scorn. Once, when she was eight, she had told him that he smelt. Because he was her father, he had the gall to think that Peggy owed him some respect, no matter how appalling his behaviour. The day she confessed she was pregnant, Walter had hoped to see her sent packing – but Maisie hadn't said a single angry word to her. Instead, she had welcomed Hal and the baby into the house.

Now Walter rounded on his son-in-law. 'They all know what I am, do they? And what are you? You don't mind living cheap with us. Why don't you move out and rent your own place? You're making a bit of money, but you like holding on to it.' His eyes were turning red, as they always did when his bile was rising. He thrust his face at Peggy, a bead of spittle glistening at the corner of his mouth. 'If you had to get yourself in trouble, you could at least have picked a man who'd give you a home of your own. Jasper and me, we'd be thankful to see the back of you.'

'We'll have a house, don't worry, and what's more, we'll own it,' retorted Peggy. 'We'll have a bit of property, something you could never hope for, not in a million years. And don't you tell us we live cheap, when you don't pay for anything. You're a couple of spongers, you and that great fool there. A pair of clowns, boorish and proud of it.'

Jasper belched and giggled. He lolled against the pub's back door, his long legs stuck out straight in front of him.

'Peggy,' said Hal, 'come on, let's go. This won't do any good.' He took her arm and she turned away with a parting glare at her father.

Walter shouted after her as they walked off: 'I'll see my day with you, you carping little article. Sooner or later. A time always comes, don't think it won't.'

Peggy and Hal went in through the back gate of the house and she slammed it behind her. The skirmish had left her down-in-the-mouth. Ruffling her hair, Hal said:

'That was only bluster, maid. What could he do to hurt you?'

She snorted. 'Oh, his threats don't worry me. But when I remember all the times those two wasters have made me feel small . . .' She shook her head. 'He may be my father, Hal, but I loathe him and I know he hates me. He'll take hard words from Mother because she keeps him, he needs her. But he gets nothing out of me, so I'm the worst in the world. As for Jasper, he's not much cop, but that's the old man's doing. He's

74

turned my brother into rubbish, just so he'll have company.'

'Yes, well, that's Jasper's lookout. Don't you let it get you down. I don't let them upset me.'

Wanly, Peggy smiled, but the memory of the chapel people staring made her wince. No matter how good she was feeling, Walter could always embarrass her, spoil her day. That was another reason she had envied Anna when they were children – for having a quiet, pleasant father who obviously loved her and never let her down.

Eight

Tolgarth beach had always been one of Anna's favourite haunts, and that was where she went with Guy the next time he took her out. The beach lay two miles west of Trezawne. Beyond the town the road began to wind uphill through a belt of trees. At the top, it came out into the open, with heathery moorland on one side and cliffs on the other. Some people called this a dangerous road. In places it ran within yards of the cliff edge and there was no barrier. Below, a slope fell steeply away to the brink of an eighty-foot drop. A mile further on, the road made a zig-zag to skirt around the deep chasm which split the cliffs just outside the town. This was the zawn, the steep-sided inlet cut like a giant wedge from the rock, as if by a Titan's axe. At high tide the sea rolled in there with an eerie moan, which on stormy days became a bellow. The town had taken its name from this cleft, which appeared on the map as Zawn Fell – Cruel Zawn. Some way past it, the road began to go downhill again, as cliffs gradually gave way to sand dunes – the gentle approach to Tolgarth beach, a three-mile sweep of soft beige sand which was usually deserted.

Anna had suggested Tolgarth for reasons she wouldn't dream of mentioning to Guy. At the back of her mind was the thought that it might help soothe the painful memories and restore a little of her pride, to come here with another man and walk where she had often walked with Hal.

They left the car and made their way down through the tussocks of marram grass and along the sands. The tideline was marked by a scattering of débris – razorfish shells and cuttlebones, even the odd mermaid's purse. Bits of feathery green and red weed had been left by the ebbing water. There was driftwood everywhere, bleached and smoothed by the sea.

Driftwood. Before she could stop it, an image leapt into Anna's mind of darkness and crackling flames. They had gathered up driftwood that night the previous summer, piled it into a heap and lit it as the sun went down. A score of girls and young men from Trezawne, celebrating Midsummer Eve with fire in the old Celtic way. Anna and a few of her friends, Hal, some other chaps and their girls, Peggy Angilley . . .

Anna remembered Hal in the firelight, laughing and pouring cider for others in the party. She remembered, too, seeing Peggy Angilley watching her across the blaze. A current of challenge had passed between them, unspoken but clearly understood.

He's mine.

He's mine.

Hands off.

You just leave him alone.

Sometime later, when everyone was singing, she had seen Hal get up and go off into the dark – to answer a call of nature, Anna had thought at first. But then she had realised that Peggy had disappeared too.

'You're quiet,' Guy observed. 'What are you thinking about?'

'Nothing important,' said Anna quickly. 'Nothing much at all.'

'*Don't you tell him about that Hal Pentreath,*' her mother had warned her. '*Don't you let Guy Buckman know you made such an ass of yourself.*'

Anna hardly needed such advice. Turning to Guy, she clasped his arm, smiled up at him.

'Going to stay for dinner again this evening?' he asked.

'I'd love to. Can you really afford to spend so much time entertaining me?'

'People always make time for things they truly want to do.'

'Your staff seem very dependable. I suppose that gives you a certain freedom?'

He laughed. 'Oh, don't delude yourself. I have to crack the whip. The business would go downhill very fast if I didn't. I do have some employees who take a pride in their work, but most will get away with what they can, that's human nature. It's the same everywhere, of course – people dawdle, get sloppy – but down here there's something else as well, an attitude that there's never any hurry. What's that word they use? Directly. Or "dreckly", as it comes out. I'll do it directly, they say. Directly means "*mañana*", only more so. Drives me mad.'

Anna chuckled softly. 'Dreckly' – this week, next week, sometime, never. It was a Cornish trait, there was no denying that. Nevertheless, she said: 'I hope you're not one of those foreigners who like our county but don't like us?'

'Sorry, I didn't mean to malign your whole tribe.'

'I know how irritating it is. Still, we're not all alike. Mother's very brisk and fussy, always chivvying the tradesmen.'

He regarded her from under his lashes, eyes half closed against the sun.

'Do you get on with her? Are you close?'

She shook her head.

'I thought not.'

Anna murmured: 'She's very impressed with you, may I say. Calls you a perfect gentleman.'

A smile touched his mouth. Then: 'I lost my mother in 1923. I was more attached to my father. He died two years ago. I'll show you a photograph of him when we go back. In fact, you must let me show you my flat. I'm sure you'll like it.'

Anna glanced at him, briefly wary.

'It's all right.' Eyes wide, he held up his hands. 'I'm a perfect gentleman, remember?'

Guy's rooms were situated at the rear western corner of Elestren Manor. The suite comprised a sitting-room, dressing-room, bedroom and bathroom. Below the windows, the lawn stretched away into shrubbery, thick and dark – mostly towering rhododendrons, the red-flowered variety known as 'Cornish Giant'.

'It's lovely,' Anna said. 'So quiet up here.'

She wandered round the sitting-room, looking at everything. Mahogany furniture, an open fireplace, lots of china ornaments and family photographs.

From the writing table by the window, she picked up one in a tortoiseshell frame.

'Is this your mother?'

Guy was lounging in an armchair, hands behind his head.

'Yes, that was taken when I was quite small.'

'She looks very sweet. What was she called?'

'Helen.'

79

Anna studied the picture a moment longer. A woman of roughly twenty-five smiled out at her. Mrs Buckman was cutting blooms from a rambler. Over her left arm hung a basket, half-filled with flowers, and in her right hand was a pair of pruning shears. She looked so nice, Anna thought. Such a pretty, kindly face.

'She couldn't have been very old when she died. How did it happen?'

'Cancer.'

'Oh. I'm so sorry.' Anna put the picture back, took up another. 'And this is your father?'

'Yes, that's the old man. Wonderful person. His name was Matthew.'

Anna considered the photograph. Taken on the terrace outside the residents' lounge, it showed a man in a wheelchair. His hair and brows and beard were very thick and greying. Anna noticed he had rather podgy hands. They rested on the cover of a book, the plump fingers barely spanning the width of it. Matthew Buckman's general build was stocky, in which respect he was not at all like Guy. The breadth of his beard suggested a brutal jaw.

'Why was he in a wheelchair, Guy?'

'Rheumatoid arthritis. Had it the last seven years of his life. It was heart trouble, though, that killed him.'

'Did he suffer a lot of pain?'

'With the arthritis? Some days.'

'Oh dear,' murmured Anna. She scanned the other photographs. There was quite an array, including many of Guy in childhood and youth. As a toddler, he was usually posing with both parents. As he grew bigger, he was more often alone or with Matthew. Matthew before the arthritis began – short, thickset and powerful. Only in two small pictures did someone else appear

80

– a solemn little girl, aged about seven and then about ten.

'Who's this?'

'My sister, Elaine.'

'Rather serious-looking.'

'Mm. No sense of humour.'

'You don't get on?'

'We didn't. I never see her now. I get a card at Christmas and that's all. She works in London, does something in a laboratory. Medical research – tropical diseases, if you ever did. Eventually she wants to go abroad to fly-blown countries and be an angel of mercy.'

It seemed a worthy ambition to Anna, but he spoke of it with something close to contempt.

'It sounds interesting.'

He shook his head. 'Can't understand any woman wanting to do that. What's worse, she's neglecting her natural rôle in life. She's twenty-six and ought to be married with children by now. She'll end up a lonely old spinster, you wait and see.'

'I take it you don't approve of women with careers?'

He admitted: 'No. I suppose I'm the old-fashioned sort. Anyway, for all her high-flown talk about helping the suffering, she did damn-all here at home. Buzzed off as soon as Mother died – and just when the arthritis was getting a real grip on Father. He'd just lost his wife, was becoming disabled, and his daughter chose to clear off. Charming, eh?'

'Sounds a bit selfish, I must agree.'

'Mind you, it wasn't that Father needed her to look after him. We had plenty of money, plenty of staff. We hired a nurse towards the end. But it's the principle of the thing. Elaine never came back to visit him. She attended the funeral, that was all. I haven't seen her since. Father never forgave her for taking off the way she did. Didn't leave her a thing in his will.'

Anna looked at him.

'No, not a bean. Elestren Manor's mine, all mine. So are the stocks and shares and a few other worthwhile assets Dad accumulated.'

Anna sat down in an armchair. 'It must feel good to be so secure.'

'It just feels normal. I've always had everything I wanted.'

'I daresay your sister's found out what it's like to be hard up?'

'Oh, I think she earns a decent salary. Anyway, she made her choice, didn't she?'

Briefly, something troubled Anna. Yes, his sister had made her choice – and apparently been punished for it. Had it instead been Guy who left to pursue a career of that sort, would he have been penalised the same way?

Well, perhaps he would. Anna supposed she had no right to pass judgement, knowing so little of Elaine or Matthew Buckman.

'Did she realise what it would cost her?'

'I believe the old man warned her.'

'She must be very dedicated,' Anna said.

'Noble old Elaine,' smiled Guy, and she sensed he was teasing her. More seriously, he conceded: 'To give her due credit, she isn't mercenary. Me, I'd hate to live more modestly.' He glanced through the window and then at his watch. 'Lovely sunny evening,' he said. 'We've a tennis court, you know. It's a couple of hours until dinner. Care for a game to work up an appetite?'

'Oh . . .' She was suddenly on the defensive. 'I haven't any kit.'

'I can find you some, I'm sure.'

'And I really can't play at all well,' she said anxiously. 'In fact, I'm hopeless at sports. Hockey, tennis, netball – they despaired of me in school.'

'I don't mind how bad you are. It's only for fun. Who knows – perhaps you can learn better from me than from some hectoring old teacher? Come on, let's try. I promise not to bully you. We'll just have a knockabout.'

Anna sighed. 'All right, but I warn you, it won't be much of a game.'

She was right about that, and yet, for the first time ever, she enjoyed herself out on a court. It was pleasantly private, surrounded by tall rhododendrons and therefore out of sight of the hotel. There was no one but Guy to witness her awkwardness, and he dismissed her blunders with amusement. Anna lost two balls by lobbing them clear over the chain fence and into the shrubbery. She scurried hither and thither, missing three shots out of four and seldom clearing the net when she managed to hit one. Her serve was a wild and desperate gesture. Guy said she looked for all the world like someone trying to shoo off a wasp. Every so often he hopped over the net and showed her once more the proper stance and grip and swinging motion. Anna was pink with exertion and full of apologies, while he was perfectly cool, not even slightly out of breath, and happy to demonstrate over and over again.

So much patience, Anna thought. And how elegant he looked, walking back to the other end of the court, swinging his racket, his left hand in the pocket of his flannels. A willowy, white-clad figure against the green of the rhododendrons. Ease and grace were the words he called to mind. Ease and grace in his speech and dress and manner and all his movements. Fumbling and stumbling, she felt like a clot, but he made light of it all. That was the essence of good manners, her father had once said – making people feel comfortable, smoothing over little embarrassments. Guy had a talent for that – a joke, an adroit and timely change of subject, and the difficulty was past. So relaxed and good-humoured was he, that after a while her play began to improve a little.

As the sun set behind the rhododendrons, the court grew shadowy and cool.

'Time to go in, I think,' said Guy. 'Half an hour to freshen up and change for dinner, eh?'

'Yes, lovely.' Anna was chirpy. 'You know, I really enjoyed that, Guy. I honestly think I learned a thing or two.'

'I'm sure of it. We'll do it again. You'll soon get your confidence.'

Before much longer, Guy had Anna's confidence entirely. What had begun for her with unaccountable misgivings, became an easy habit and a consolation for what she had lost. She had less and less time to think about Hal, for Guy was always on the telephone, or knocking at the door to collect her for another delightful outing. At her mother's behest and expense, Anna was always out buying new clothes, always getting ready for something. She went to all the dinner dances, becoming casually friendly with Guy's acquaintances from the top end of town. And he was always at hand, attentive, making her feel so central, so important – powerful salve indeed for her grief and wounded pride.

An acceptance steadily grew in Anna that this, after all, might be the sort of life for which she was meant – one of drinks and parties, of being waited on and chauffeured about. The thought of life with Hal even began to seem slightly ludicrous. It had been, as Mother said, a misguided youthful fancy, a wrong-headed infatuation from which Anna had now been saved.

By summer's end, she was spending half her time at Elestren Manor. It didn't matter if Guy was busy, she was always welcome. She could sit in the garden and read or sunbathe, amuse herself as she wanted to, and then they would have a meal or go out for a while. She was recognised by the staff as having a special status, someone free to come and go where and whenever she pleased, someone to whom everything was available and nothing was to be charged. In a rare moment of familiarity, Sarah the receptionist confided:

'Mr Buckman's had several other girlfriends in the past, or so I'm told, but none of them lasted very long or were treated the way he treats you. He must have decided you're The One.'

Indeed he had. Anna had known him a little less than four months when he proposed. She would always remember the date: 28 September.

They were out in the garden behind the hotel. Slung between two trees was a hammock and Guy was lazing in it – sleeping, Anna thought. She had a garden chair for herself and was writing a letter to a friend. A sun still very warm for the time of year was high in the sky, and the light was greenish-gold beneath the trees. Anna was halfway through a sentence when a voice from the hammock enquired:

'When are you going to marry me, then? How about next spring?'

Her pen stopped moving. She had always expected some sort of preamble, so the abruptness of it left her briefly speechless. But after all, everything was taken for granted, wasn't it? Elestren Manor was her second home already.

He opened one eye, peered at her. 'Why the shocked silence?'

Anna stared at him a few seconds longer. 'I don't know, really.'

'You must have been expecting it?'

'Perhaps not quite so soon.'

'Oh dear, am I rushing you again? We'll be engaged for a good six months. Plenty of time to back out, if you suddenly find you can't stand me.'

'Engaged,' she repeated, savouring the word, the idea.

'Yes, you know – betrothed, affianced, spoken for. I give you this bauble and your mother puts a notice in the paper. That's the usual drill, isn't it?' Fumbling in his trouser pocket, he drew out a little box. His lean hand dangled over the side of the hammock, offering it to Anna.

She took it and opened it, gasped. An emerald, sur-rounded by diamonds.

'Large, but not big enough to be vulgar,' Guy said. 'Like it?'

'Oh!' She was breathless. 'How could I not?'

Rolling over on his side, he grinned at her. 'Try it on, then, let's see if it fits.'

Anna slipped the ring on. Perfect.

'Hmm,' said Guy approvingly. 'Yes, it suits your hand.'

'It must have cost a fortune,' she whispered, admiring it.

'Nothing's too good for my future wife. I take it you do accept me?'

'Oh, of course!'

Nine

Hal and Peggy had enjoyed a very successful summer. Their savings account at the post office had grown to £123.18.4d. Every so often, Peggy would take the passbook out of her dressing table drawer and do sums in her head, working out the interest at sixpence in the pound, estimating how much they might add next year and the year after that. It amused her and conjured golden visions for the future. Hal had promised they would have a house. Peggy imagined one just as nice as *Lamorva*. Maybe even a street or two higher up the hill.

But her hopes of going one better than Anna were very soon squashed. One morning in early October, she was minding the bazaar. It was nearly midday and a few local children were in the side room, feeding ha'pennies into the slot machines. Peggy was just serving a little boy with a huge pink and green striped lollipop, when a dumpy shape darkened the doorway. Peggy gave it a quick glance, then a second, astonished look which followed it around as it entered and started sauntering among the displays of goods.

Delia Trevena, attired in a smart tweed coat and a hat with a turned-down brim. Anna's mother, walking between the shelves, picking things up and putting them down with just a hint of disdain.

Now what can she want? Peggy thought suspiciously.

'Miss . . .? Miss?'

The little boy was staring worriedly up at her, clutching his lolly. It was round and as big as a tea-plate, half hiding his face. He stretched up a sticky palm for his change.

She had frozen with the coins in her hand. Shaking herself, she passed him his two pennies and he scampered off.

Mrs Trevena came to the counter. 'Good morning, Peggy.'

'Morning, Mrs Trevena.'

'I've come to buy a stereoscope and some cards. A present for an old friend.'

Peggy nodded towards a shelf by the window. 'They're over there.'

'I tried everywhere else in town first,' Mrs Trevena went on, 'but no one had precisely what I wanted. You're my last resort. I hope you can help, it's really not worth a trip to Wadebridge.'

Peggy looked at her, expressionless.

'Any local views?' asked Mrs Trevena.

'Plenty. Just choose what you want.'

'Thank you.'

A small frown came to Peggy's brow as she watched the woman select her purchases. Whatever her reason for calling here, it was not the stereoscope and cards. Peggy could think of at least two other shops where she could have bought the same.

Mrs Trevena returned to the till. 'I'll take these, I think.' Delving in her handbag, she drew out her purse.

'Eighteen and six,' said Peggy, flapping open a paper bag.

Mrs Trevena paused. 'I don't suppose you wrap things as gifts? No, of course not. Silly me. Now, let me see.' She started counting out small coins. 'I expect you're always glad of change, aren't you?'

'Money's money,' Peggy said.

'It certainly is.' Mrs Trevena dumped a handful of sixpences, pennies and threepenny bits in front of her. As Peggy checked the amount, Mrs Trevena remarked:

'I should think it's very cramped for you and Hal, living up above here with the baby?'

'We've plenty of room.' Peggy continued, whisking the coins off the glass top, counting under her breath.

'Have you?' queried Mrs Trevena, her tone full of doubt. 'Well, possibly for now, but when more children come along . . . You will be having more, won't you? Planning on a big family, I expect?'

A cold: 'No.'

'Indeed? You surprise me.'

'Anything else we can sell you, Mrs Trevena?'

'No, Peggy, I don't think so.' The woman glanced around her. 'Had a good season, I trust?'

'Exceptional.'

'Yes, so have we. Some lovely people as guests this year. Both Anna and I have made wonderful new friends.' This with a peep from the corner of her eye.

Something was coming, Peggy thought. She was getting to it now, whatever had brought her here.

But then Mrs Trevena changed the subject. 'I see you have some of your husband's paintings on show. I must say, they fit in very well here with the other merchandise.'

Meaning the other rubbish. Peggy cocked her head and wryly smiled. Whatever tiny claims to superiority Anna's mother might have, a knowledge of art was not among them.

'Does he sell any?'

'Quite a few.'

'Of course, you get just the right sort of customer here. Know your level, aim at a certain clientele, that's the whole secret of good trade, isn't it?'

Peggy wanted very badly to hit her. Instead she said: 'Hal's exhibition at Jackman's was a great success. None of the paintings he sold there was cheap. They all went to very good homes.' A glint appeared in her eyes. 'Sadly, one also went into the dustbin, thanks to your daughter.'

Mrs Trevena's smirk was replaced by puzzlement.

'Don't pretend you've forgotten. Or didn't you know?'

'Know what? Don't talk in riddles, girl.'

'What Anna did to my portrait,' said Peggy softly, smiling.

Mrs Trevena looked blank.

'Ah, I can see she didn't tell you. Well, I'm not surprised. Come to think of it, I doubt you'd have had the gall to show your face here if you'd known. We could have prosecuted her, you know. Vandalism, wilful damage. Hal didn't even make her pay. You owe him thanks for that.'

'I don't know what you're talking about.'

'Anna destroyed a portrait of me. It was part of the exhibition. Ripped it to shreds,' said Peggy. 'My husband saw her do it. He's much more forgiving and much more discreet than I am, Mrs Trevena. I would have spread it all over town, if Hal hadn't made me promise to keep quiet.'

Crimson washed over Mrs Trevena's face. She remembered now – Anna coming in so upset that day. So very upset. Peggy wasn't lying, that was clear. Mrs Trevena would have a few things to say to her daughter when she got home.

In her embarrassment, she almost fled the shop. But then she remembered her purpose in coming.

'Oh, well . . .' She grimaced and shrugged. 'I can't deny that Anna was foolishly infatuated with young Hal at one time. And all young women have silly moments, little outbursts of passion. I'm sure you've had yours. But Anna's completely over that now. She's outgrown that ridiculous crush and found her proper element. She hasn't given Hal a second thought since she met Guy Buckman.'

Peggy's eyes widened, her grin slipped.

'Yes,' purred Mrs Trevena, 'you know who he is, don't you?'

Peggy struggled to hide her dismay. This was it. Now she knew why the old cat had come.

Mrs Trevena moved in with the painful details.

'They've been courting four months, you know. Guy simply adores my daughter. He takes her out driving and – oh, to all sorts of places. She's always dining with him at the hotel.' Mrs Trevena clasped her hands together, full of playful malice. 'They look simply perfect together. The engagement party's on Saturday. I couldn't be more pleased.'

'How nice,' said Peggy carelessly. She felt sick with shock, but was desperate not to show it. To make matters worse, two figures had just appeared in the doorway. Walter and Jasper, home for their lunch, were standing there with hands in pockets, listening.

'Things have a way of turning out for the best, don't they?' continued Mrs Trevena. 'Truly, Peggy, I'm grateful to you, you know. Hal was never any good for Anna and you've saved her from wasting any more time on him. Now she has Guy, who's entirely suitable for her.' She picked up the bag with the stereoscope. 'I thought you'd be interested to know that, dear. Imagine what Anna's life will be like in years to come, compared with yours.'

Peggy, so rarely bereft of a retort, was speechless for once.

'Yes,' said Mrs Trevena softly, 'you chew on that, my girl.'

Turning to leave, she was confronted by Walter and Jasper.

'Going to be a society wedding is there, dear?' Angilley said.

Jasper's dopey grin became a gurgling chuckle.

'King'll be lending you the gold coach, will he?'

'Excuse me.' Mrs Trevena tried to sidestep them, but they moved this way and that, pretending confusion, and all three seemed to do a little shuffling dance.

'Oh, get out of the way!' she snapped.

'Well, go on, Jasper, shift!' commanded Walter. 'Stand aside for Lady Muck.'

A loud guffaw from Jasper. He jumped back, clicked his heels, saluted.

Mrs Trevena hustled past them. 'Louts,' she muttered.

'Where's it going to be, then? Truro Cathedral?' Walter shouted as she hurried off. 'Or have you booked Westminster Abbey?' Knowingly, he eyed his daughter. 'Came here bragging, did she? Came here to upset you?'

'I reckon she managed that, all right,' sniggered Jasper.

Peggy flushed. 'It'd take more than her, or anything she can boast,' she muttered.

'Oh, yes?' Walter mocked. 'Is that why there's a face on you as long as a fiddle?'

They both slouched past her and up the stairs, Jasper still chortling and Walter still sneering. Peggy sat down heavily on the stool behind the counter. Elestren Manor? Anna was going to marry Guy Buckman, live there? Peggy was crushed. Suddenly, everything she had seemed worthless, all her hopes and plans a joke. Everything good which had happened was now of little consequence. Hal's exhibition – insignificant. The savings account – pathetic. Their bedroom here above the shop – cramped and without privacy.

Comparison. Everything was relative. Until Anna's mother came in, Peggy had been fairly content with her lot. Now, suddenly, it seemed beggarly. Guy Buckman took Anna out driving and eating in fine restaurants. With Hal, a bus ride to Bodmin and a plate of fish and chips was a big day out. Hal could earn a modest living and put a few pounds away, but Anna Trevena had snared a man who could buy her the best of everything. Beside Elestren Manor, even the houses in higher Trezawne were unimpressive, so the day would never dawn when Peggy could boast a better address than that of her old rival.

The tables were turned once more. Anna had achieved a coup. No longer alone and humiliated, she was going to be the privileged wife of a well-to-do man.

Peggy was briefly conscious of her own spite. What had she wanted – to see Anna spend her whole life grieving for Hal, to see her die an old maid? Well – no. Peggy had vaguely thought that Anna would settle for someone else eventually. Someone second-best. Dull and respectable, probably. Nothing to envy.

Instead, she had caught the biggest fish in the small pool of Trezawne, and before her stretched a life of ease and pleasure. Peggy had never been one to mind housework – even Delia Trevena had to do that. Yet now, when she realised that Anna was set to escape domestic toil, she was gripped by a brand new resentment.

Later, when Maisie came in from shopping, Peggy went upstairs to clear up in the kitchen. Walter and Jasper had left their usual mess. Peggy ran some hot water into the sink – a deep porcelain sink, the surface yellowed and crazed. Collecting up the dishes, she dropped them in and they made a noise like rattling bones as they sank to the bottom. Flinging in some soft soap, she gave a huge, wretched sigh, then reached listlessly into the water and started mopping.

Pork fat and cabbage stuck stubbornly round the edge of Jasper's plate, and she dug savagely at it with her thumbnail. Anna would never have to do jobs like this once she married Guy Buckman. Anna would have staff to do everything for her. Peggy banged the plate down on the draining board, seized another dish and swirled the mop around it. Anna would never have to cook or make a bed or sweep a floor. Anna was going to have the last laugh, wasn't she?

Peggy's hand sank into the greasy water, convulsively squeezing at the dishmop. A faint smell of gas made her queasy. Raising her eyes, she stared at the blue pilot light of the water heater. It swayed from side to side like an eastern dancer.

Such a smart place, Elestren Manor, and Anna would fit in there, just as she had at the grammar school.

As I never could, Peggy thought. Except as a chambermaid or a dishwasher.

A hideous sense of inferiority seized her, examples of Angilley vulgarity flashing through her mind. Walter and Jasper belching at meals, or lifting a leg and loudly passing wind. Maisie, standing by the stove and gobbling out of a saucepan. Good as she was, she had some awful habits. Walter, piddling in this very sink because he was too idle to go outside to the lavatory. Jasper always scratching his genitals – unaware half the time that he was doing it, just absent-mindedly squeezing at his fly. Walter shambling about the house in a sweaty vest, his braces hanging down over his trousers and beergut oozing over his waist-band. Maisie, going out shopping in a torn, filthy apron, with her hair still in curlers. Jasper's idiotic guffaw . . .

Exploding with fury, Peggy dashed the dishmop into the sink, raising a splosh of water that spattered the floor. Much as she loved her husband and child, she felt she was the loser after all.

Hal received the news with his evening meal. Peggy hadn't said a word, but Jasper was eager to tell him.

'Hear about your old girlfriend?' he asked through a mouthful of cold beef and pickles.

Hal declined to look up from his plate.

'Don't know what you mean.'

'Peggy hasn't told you, then?' Jasper, chomping food, was grinning at him.

'Obviously not,' said Hal with weary patience.

'Found herself another man. A rich one,' Jasper informed him. 'Got tired of carrying a torch for you.'

Hal glanced at Peggy, who sat at the end of the table, dolefully turning a spoon round and round in her tea.

'Delia Trevena was here today,' she told him quietly. 'Anna's engaged.'

'Oh? Really? Well, good, I'm very pleased for her.'

Then, thoughtfully, he added: 'That was quick, though, wasn't it?'

'Yes, reeled him in fast. Should think she would. Lost a sprat and caught herself a turbot,' taunted Jasper, spluttering with mirth.

He received a long, unsmiling look from his brother-in-law. Drunk or sober, the same imbecile humour, thought Hal. Walter was at least quiet when he had no drink in him – morose and idle, but quiet – whereas Jasper would clatter and thump about, banging doors or singing and whistling to himself. He seemed unable to tolerate silence.

Jasper's grin faltered and his gaze dropped. He thrust a pickled onion into his mouth and crunched it loudly. A hard stare from another man would always subdue him.

'Who's she marrying?' Hal asked Peggy.

'That man Buckman, who owns Elestren Manor.'

'Ah.' Hal emitted a grunt of amusement. 'That'll make her old woman preen and swagger.'

'That was what she came here for, to rub my nose in it.'

'Jealous, she is,' crowed Jasper, jerking his head at his sister. 'Pea-green and sick with envy. How do you feel about that?'

'Shut up!' Peggy hissed.

'Well, you are.' Jasper's fists thumped on the table, holding his knife and fork on end. 'Can't stand it, can you? Been sore as a boil all day.'

'That's enough,' growled Hal.

'I'm just telling the truth.' There came a rattle of slack-jawed laughter. 'Peggy's old enemy's hit the jackpot. Last laugh's always the best.'

Angrily, Peggy bounced to her feet and left the table.

Hal heard her running down the stairs and then the shop door slammed.

'You miserable toad,' he said to Jasper.

The other man snorted, then smirked. 'This won't be so good for you, Pentreath. She'll always be comparing now, you wait and see. You won't be able to give her much and she'll always have an eye on how that other one's doing. I know Peggy. She won't be so content with you after this, you and your ten-bob paintings.'

Hal didn't bother to argue with him, but left him chuckling over his food and went out in search of Peggy.

He found her sitting on the quayside in the fading light. The streets were all but deserted, though the waterfront pubs were already busy. The sky was pink and grey, and the fishing boats were just setting out for their night's work at sea, the sails black angular shapes against the sinking sun. Peggy was watching their dark silhouettes heading south and west. She sat beside a mooring bollard, her legs dangling over the side of the quay.

Hal seated himself beside her. 'What's the matter, Peggy?'

She shook her head and wouldn't answer.

'You're thinking we'll never be rich?'

She was silent.

He clasped her hand. 'Well, you're right, we probably won't. I'm not the type to be famous and make a fortune, despite all that silly talk in the pub from Saul and Jack. Very few painters see much money – especially while they're alive to enjoy it. I don't kid myself that I'm one of the élite. I just love the work. I'm good at it. I can make a living, and one day I'm going to buy you a house, but I've never pretended to you that we'd be wealthy, Peggy.'

'I know.'

'And it didn't bother you before.'

She looked away.

'Not until this morning, eh? Not until you heard about Anna?'

Peggy sucked her bottom lip.

He turned her face to him. 'Maid, for God's sake, give it up. Give up competing with her. Even a boxer knows when to throw in the towel. What's the point of it all? And where does it stop?'

'I don't suppose you've ever had an enemy. You don't understand.'

'Enemy!' he muttered. 'God, the drama! You're still a couple of bickering schoolgirls, scoring off each other. Well, there's nothing you can do this time, so you'd better accept that you can't beat her. Not when it comes to money. I can't be another Buckman for you.'

'I haven't asked you to.'

'But will you be discontented now?' he asked uneasily. 'Are you going to be angry, Peggy, because I can't buy you the best and keep you in style?'

'Of course not,' she said quickly. Then: 'Not with you.'

'Or with the way the wheel turns, if you're wise.'

'She always . . .' Peggy faltered, stopped. 'How is it, she always . . .?' Again, she was at a loss.

'Goes one better?'

'No, I didn't mean that.'

'Yes, you did. As Jasper said, she lost a sprat and caught a turbot. That's what you're thinking.'

She put her arms around him. 'It's only the money, it isn't you. I didn't mean I'd rather have Guy Buckman. It's just seeing her being – swanky – that nettles me so.'

'Nothing personal, eh? Well, that's a relief.'

For a while they sat cuddled together there on the quay in the gathering dusk. The moon was rising and broken trails of golden light from *The Old Solace* windows lay on the quiet waters of the harbour.

'We have a nice life, don't we?' Hal said. 'We're lucky, Peggy.'

'Yes.' Her voice was small.

'It's crazy to let envy and old grudges spoil it.'

'Hmm.'

He knew that tone. Peggy trying to convince herself of something.

Musing, he added: 'Hope Anna knows what she's doing.'

Peggy looked up at him.

'She can't have known the man long,' Hal said. 'All seems a bit hasty to me.'

'If you strike gold, you stake a claim fast,' came the cynical reply.

'Perhaps she's in trouble?' Hal suggested, eyebrows lifting at the idea.

They looked at each other and Peggy laughed despite herself. 'Not in a million years.'

Briefly, there was silence. Then: 'Anyway, I wish her well,' Hal said. He nudged her. 'Go on, Peggy, be generous, do the same.'

The answering voice was wry. 'She doesn't need my good wishes. Anna's one of fortune's favourites.'

Ten

Guy and Anna were married on the last Saturday in April of 1931. Emerging from the parish church, which was very near the top of the hill and overlooked almost all of Trezawne, the new Mr and Mrs Buckman paused on the steps for photographs. Everyone was cheering and throwing rice, while the church bells peeled with frantic merriment. Anna was in a full white satin frock and orange blossom headdress, her husband in grey top hat and tails.

Mrs Trevena had spent half a season's profits on the flowers and cars and the dresses for her daughter and the bridesmaids. Clothed from head to foot in salmon pink, she contrived to appear in nearly all the photographs. Later, she cornered the reporter sent by the local paper and talked at him so long that he ended up with ten pages of shorthand notes.

The reception – a four-course meal – was naturally to be held at Elestren Manor at Guy's expense. The procession of cars set off down Pawlyn's Hill en route for the hotel, and that was where Peggy chanced to see them as she was making her way to the cobbler's shop with a pair of Hal's shoes.

Her footsteps slowed as the big black car containing the bride and groom drew near. As it passed, she caught a shadowy glimpse of Anna, whose frothing white gown seemed to fill the back seat. Guy Buckman was on the side closest to Peggy. As they went by, he looked out and she saw him clearly. He smiled at her and then he was gone and another car was approaching. One of its passengers wore a big pink hat.

Peggy quickly switched her gaze away and went on up the hill. She had no desire to meet Mrs Trevena's eye. She stopped again, however, when the last of the cars had passed, and watched them turn left beside the bazaar at the bottom of the hill.

All just a silly, expensive show, she tried to tell herself, but envy had its way with her, just the same. Her own quick visit to the registrar's office seemed so drab and furtive by comparison, although she'd felt elated on the day.

That frock . . . Peggy thought, when the last of the cars had disappeared. How would it have felt to be married in something like that, with bridesmaids and hymns and a church full of flowers? Peggy would never know, and she felt she had missed one of life's great thrills.

Grasping the handrail, she plodded on. What a turnabout, what a fairytale for Anna. Then she recalled something Maisie had said – that every fairy story had its wicked witch or ogre. And Hal's words, too:

'All seems a bit hasty to me. Hope Anna knows what she's doing.'

Peggy pulled a wry face. Her mother and husband could say what they liked, it was hard to imagine anything but happiness for Anna now.

The reception was lavish, as might be expected, with food and drink of the very best. At half-past two, the newlyweds left their revelling guests and set off on the long drive to the channel port. They were catching the overnight ferry to Ostend. The honeymoon was going to be in Switzerland, where Guy had rented a chalet in the Alps. Dressed in a beige shantung suit and a white picture hat, Anna twisted around in her seat as the car sped down towards the gate, and waved a happy farewell to the crowd assembled on the lawn to see the couple off. As they rounded the bend in the drive and the hotel was lost from view, she turned and looked at her husband with shining eyes.

'Oh, Guy, it all went so well, didn't it? I really enjoyed it, every minute.'

He grinned. 'Why so surprised? You know I never allow things to be less than perfect.'

'No,' she said, 'that's right, you don't. But even the weather's been kind today, you must admit. I'm only sorry your sister couldn't come. I'd have liked so much to meet her.'

Elaine Buckman had sent her regrets – along with what Guy dismissed as excuses. Unbreakable commitments, Elaine called them. Her brother claimed indifference.

'To hell with her, she can please herself,' he had said.

He made no comment now. Instead, he asked: 'Got your passport all ready, I trust?'

'Yes.' She sighed happily. 'Switzerland. Oh, I'm so looking forward to it.'

'Ever been abroad before?'

'No, it's very exciting. I'm sure I'm going to love it. This really is the most wonderful day of my life.'

Twelve hours later, Anna was feeling far less certain of that.

The moon was up and the sea was very calm. She leaned on the guardrail, looking down at the wash of the cross-channel ferry.

She felt frightened and soiled.

A change had come over Guy the moment their clothes were off. A change abrupt and total, as if a switch had been thrown. Such a gentleman all the time they were courting – but tonight, in bed, he was anything but that. One moment quite impersonal, as if she were some object he had hired to service him. The next, deliberately doing things she didn't like. Any protest brought a set look to his face, a stubborn persistence, as if to show her who was boss. He hadn't been exactly violent, and yet he had shown a determination to impose on Anna anything she didn't want. No allowances were made for her virginity. It shook her that a man so outwardly polished could be so goatish. Worse, she had gained the strongest impression that he enjoyed her distress, was excited by it.

He hadn't spoken to her once from start to finish.

Anna stared down into the blackness of the water with its ghostly trail of foam. It was nearly two in the morning and almost every cabin was in darkness. Wrapping her dressing gown more tightly around her, she shivered. No one had told her it could be like that. Mother hadn't warned her – but then, what did Mother know, who had never had any man but Anna's mild-mannered father? Books and films made no mention of anything like this. What they portrayed was coy, or sugary, or tempestuous. There had never been a hint of anything quite so unnerving as that which she had just experienced from Guy. A mask had dropped away. He had her now, and in bed he abandoned all consideration for her feelings.

They were spending this night in a first-class cabin. She felt she would always remember the soft hum of the ship's engines whenever she recalled this initiation. No loving words from her husband, no whispers or laughter, just his rhythmic grunts and the low, pumping murmur of machines from down below.

All right, she was inexperienced and bound to be somewhat bashful, but there was something human missing from his treatment of her. Anna had once seen a tom cat holding down a she by the scruff of her neck. She had felt a bit like that – held still and skewered. She supposed it was impossible for anyone to preserve much dignity in lovemaking. The very nature of the act precluded it. But she hadn't expected to feel so soullessly used.

Suddenly, from the darkness behind her, came Guy's voice. She hadn't heard him padding up to her, barefoot. She gave a start.

'What are you doing out here, Anna?'

She turned and he was very close, almost pressing up against her. Wearing – nothing at all.

'Oh my God!' She glanced to right and left along the decks. 'Guy, go inside!'

Casually, he turned his head, looking this way, that way. Wooden planking stretched away on either side, lit spectrally at intervals by small lamps. Towards the bow and stern the walkway disappeared into darkness.

'It's all right, everyone's asleep.' He started opening her wrap, pulling up her nightdress.

'Not everyone. The crew . . .'

'Don't worry, there's no one about.'

She felt the guardrail, hard and cold against the small of her back.

'Not here!'

'Yes, Anna, here and now. Don't you love the night air and the smell of the sea?'

'Please . . .'

'Can't wait now.'

He pinned and took her with a jolt, bending her backwards over the rail. Wordless again, but faster this time, and slamming so hard she fancied with horror the rail might give way. Then down they would go together in the black night sea, and be left behind as the lights of the ship grew ever more dim and tiny and far away . . .

It was terrifying, but mercifully quick.

Afterwards, back in the cabin, he sat chuckling on the bed.

'Imagine if someone had caught us, Anna.'

She was silent, still shaking. She didn't like the way he looked naked. He lacked the good covering of flesh that made bodies lovable.

'Oh, for God's sake, you're not upset? Where's your sense of fun?'

She muttered: 'I thought my wedding night would be a lot more – romantic.' Climbing into bed, she rolled on her side, away from him.

His tone when he answered was full of amusement. 'I had to have you there and then, out in the moonlight, under the stars. What could be more romantic than that?'

Anna made no reply. She had felt like some whore, doing it for sixpence in a shop doorway.

'Come on.' He leaned over her, whispering. He smelt of aftershave and his skin was cool. 'When was I ever slushy with you, Anna? It's not my way, you know that. When did I ever spout a lot of silly mush?'

When, indeed, had he ever said he loved her? Thinking on it now, she couldn't remember a single time. There had been charm and generosity and a subtle taking of control which said he considered her his, and

106

finally the offer of marriage – and didn't that mean love? She had assumed so, taken it for granted.

Was that a mistake? Had she been wrong?

'Wasn't that out there just now more thrilling than hearts and flowers?' persisted Guy.

'No. I hated it. You frightened me.'

He wasn't at all disconcerted. 'Fathead,' he laughed. 'We were perfectly safe.' Then, silkily: 'Don't worry, Anna, you'll learn to like everything I like. That's a promise.'

She closed her eyes and refused to answer.

Late the following day, they arrived in Interlaken. It was wet and the streets of the town were all but deserted. The mountains were hidden by hanging clouds, so low that Anna fancied she could almost see the raindrops crystallising out of them. The world seemed grey and white and stony, the vegetation a washed-out green. It hadn't looked like this in the pictures Anna had seen. They had been emerald and blue, full of celestial peaks and alpine flowers – the land of Heidi and cuckoo clocks and chocolate. Her first reaction was to wish they had gone to Vienna instead, or better still, Florence.

The chalet was just outside the town, perched on a slope near a small, white-painted church with a belltower. Both buildings seemed stuck on to the grassy hillside like ornaments. Behind them, clusters of pine trees pierced the mist with their spiky tops. The chalet was typical – rich brown wood, window-boxes, painted flowers on the shutters and the door, a log pile at the side.

That evening they had supper at a cellar restaurant. There was candlelight, accordion music and singing.

Anna drank a great deal of schnapps, which went straight to her head and fortified her somewhat for the night to come.

Later, in bed, she was only half aware of what Guy did, but in the morning she was very sore, and had a hangover.

The weather, however, had undergone a miraculous change which lifted her mood. She walked out on to the upstairs balcony, and there before her were lush green foothills with swathes of dark forest. The lakes and sky were purest blue. Beyond, dreaming over the valley, serrated ridges and peaks, all clothed with snow; the bosomy Jungfrau, the Eiger and Mönch.

They went out to a small hotel for a breakfast of coffee and croissants.

'Shall we go for a cable car ride?' Guy suggested, as they paid the bill and left. 'I'll show you a breath-taking view. It'll clear your head for you.'

He was at his most cheerful this morning, his laughing, boyish best. She tried to recall exactly what had happened last night, what he had done to her, but could only summon fragments of memory. At any rate, Guy seemed pleased with her. He was full of jokes, affectionate.

Perhaps I'm a prude, she thought. I don't know what other people do. Guy likes things I never read about in biology books. I thought there was no more to it than that. It appears biology books only give you the elementary stuff. Perhaps I should try and get hold of something more – advanced.

They took their ride in the cable car, warmly dressed against the cold, Anna in a red woollen jacket, tam and slacks, Guy in corduroy trousers and a heavy jersey which made him look almost sturdy. The light was brilliant, and all the contours of the mountains sharp. In places the snows were beginning to melt, revealing a hard grey landscape of rubble and naked rock.

Guy was right about her headache. In the mountain air the grogginess fled, as if the flapping wind pulled it out of her skull and bore it away. Standing by the railings at an observation point, she looked out over mile upon mile of snowfields and jagged summits, exhilarated and grateful to have seen this.

'Magnificent, isn't it?' said Guy.

'Oh, it's wonderful.'

'How's your head?'

'Completely better,' she said happily. 'I feel so wide awake.'

'Told you, didn't I?' Looking around, he spotted a couple of skiers, went across with his camera and asked the man to take a snap. The stranger obligingly photographed them, hugging and windblown and smiling, against the glorious tableau of mountains.

Trusting again, Anna clasped Guy's arm.

'You'll learn to like everything I like,' he had said.

She resolved to try. My husband, she thought. He knows more of the world, more of life, than I do. There isn't anything wrong. I just have to get used to it.

On the way back down the mountain, they had the cable car to themselves. Anna watched the crags go by and gazed down, fascinated, at the towering trees which looked so tiny from above.

Suddenly, however, she became aware of her husband's stare as he studied her profile. She looked at him and he reached out a hand, toying thoughtfully with a lock of her hair.

'Must stop in London on the way home and get this done properly,' he murmured.

'What?' A slight frown touched her brow.

'Your hair. You must have it decently styled. You need a touch of make-up, too, and some really good clothes.'

'Mother bought me a trousseau, Guy.'

'I know, but it simply won't do.'

She blinked uneasily. 'Don't you like me as I am?'

'I adore you . . .' He kissed the tip of her nose. '. . . But there's room for improvement.'

Anna didn't know what to say. So – she had short-comings, wasn't quite up to his standards, it appeared. She looked down at herself, then, worriedly, back at him.

'What's wrong with me?'

'You just don't make the best of yourself. I knew from the day I first saw you what a beauty you could be if you were dressed and groomed the right way.'

'Did you?' she said uncertainly. It was a compliment, and yet it made her feel like something suitable for renovation.

'Don't look so apprehensive,' he chaffed. His smile was dazzling, his manner playful. 'I promise you'll love the result. I'm going to transform you, Anna.'

Eleven

It was while the Buckmans were away that Hal had his exhibition at Trezawne town hall. He was given the big wood-panelled meeting chamber on the first floor – room enough to show the full spectrum of his talents – and there he displayed watercolour landscapes, oils of the town and harbour, charcoal animal portraits and, in a lighter vein, some caricatures. The latter were faces everyone in lower Trezawne would recognise: Billy Nancarrow, the craggy Penpraze brothers and Jack Tresize, Lily Greasypockets and her husband Steaming Heaps, the old men on their bench by the harbour wall, and a handful of others goodnatured enough to sit for Hal and give the town a chuckle at their expense.

Again he was widely praised and made a lot of sales. Elated by his success, Peggy forgot all about her old rival for a while. One Saturday, by way of celebration, she went across to Temperance Street and Mr Jackman's shop, to buy her husband some fresh materials.

Faint amusement crossed the old man's face when he saw her come in. She was wearing a red and green striped dress. Atop the black curls rested a straw hat with a poppy on the brim. Always so vivid, Mrs Pentreath. No wonder Hal, with his love of colour, had married her. She was carrying Joy, who had recently passed her first birthday and was just as dark and rosy and brightly dressed.

111

'Well, Mrs Pentreath . . .' Mr Jackman beamed at her over his glasses '. . . I hear all's going nicely once again?'

'Oh, yes, Hal's delighted, so am I.' Peggy glanced around her at the shelves. 'He's running out of everything, so I thought I'd come and fetch him some supplies. You'd better tell me what he buys, I haven't much idea.'

Mr Jackman turned to the racks and stands behind his counter, and started picking items from the display.

The baby pointed, goggling, at the rainbow array of coloured inks, jars of tempera and sticks of pastel. Peggy always thought brand new artists' materials had a pristine beauty all their own. Fat, glossy tubes and smooth cakes of colour, virgin – unmixed, unsmeared, unclotted. Perfectly pointed pencils, factory sharp and still smelling of shaved wood. White and toned papers and silky brushes, all so immaculate.

'He uses a lot of rose madder,' mused Mr Jackman, assembling some tubes on the counter. 'And raw Sienna and Prussian blue. What else? He'll want terre verte, I should think. Titanium white, certainly. That'll do for oils. Watercolours – he normally buys this brand – ten good basic shades in this box. Paper – he favours fine ones, medium weight, so this should suit. Then he'll want some charcoal, linseed oil and flake white powder. I expect that's enough to be going on with, don't you?'

He put it all in a bag and gave her a discount of half a crown on the total.

'You're kind, Mr Jackman,' she said.

'Your husband's a good customer, my dear.'

'He's had a lot of help from you over the years. We both appreciate it very much.'

The old man smiled. 'He deserves encouragement. From the day he first showed me his work and told me he'd taught himself, I knew he had the vocation. Few young men with similar backgrounds would even think of pursuing such a career, let alone risk trying it. And I dare say he takes a bit of ribbing from some quarters?'

'Mm,' Peggy confirmed with a nod.

'Indeed, but that sort of thing will never stop him, because he isn't a dabbler, a pastime artist, it's a necessity to him.'

'I know,' Peggy said. 'He's lucky that he can make a living doing the thing he loves so much.'

'Very few are so fortunate,' Jackman agreed. Then, thoughtfully, he added: 'He's young, of course. What he's turning out at present is good but not unusual. As he grows older, as life changes him, so his painting will change. One day he could start producing work that's excellent, unique. But that'll come in its own good time, and he might have to suffer some ups and downs before he achieves his very best and receives real recognition. Always support him, Mrs Pentreath, even if the road is rocky, always cheer him on.'

Peggy wasn't quite sure what he meant, but she said: 'Yes, of course.'

'Send him in to see me. We must talk . . .'

Mr Jackman suddenly faltered and seemed for a moment to forget that Peggy was there. He pressed a hand to the side of his cheek and braced the other against the counter to stop himself swaying.

'Mr Jackman?' She put down the bag and reached out to him. 'What's the matter? Are you ill?'

He blinked behind his spectacles; he plainly couldn't focus properly. Then, just as quickly as it had come, the spasm passed and he laughed awkwardly.

113

'Oh – I'm sorry, Mrs Pentreath. What was I saying?'

'Mr Jackman, is there something wrong? I thought for a minute that you were about to black out.'

'It's just old age, my dear. Now – oh, yes – I was about to suggest another little show upstairs for your husband later this year. As I said before, ask him to come in and see me, we'll talk it over.'

'All right,' said Peggy, eyeing him uneasily. 'But are you certain you wouldn't like me to call a doctor for you?'

'Oh, no, no, no!' He was quite himself again. 'Just felt a bit light-headed. Didn't have much breakfast, that'll be the cause.'

'If you're sure,' said Peggy doubtfully.

'Yes, yes. Now mind what I say and ask Mr Pentreath to call by. I have one or two contacts in London who may be of help to him. I'd like to invite them down to see his work.'

Bidding him goodbye, Peggy set off down the street to the square and the town hall. The town clock was striking one as she went upstairs to the exhibition room. It wasn't as nice as Jackman's gallery, more like a school assembly hall, with a parquet floor and a musty smell. There were several people looking around at the works on show. In the corner, at a table, Hal was just completing a pencil drawing. He took the baby from his wife and kissed Peggy fondly when she showed him what she'd bought.

'Are you coming home for something to eat?' she asked.

'All right, I'd be glad to get out for a breath of air. May as well take these home, too.' He picked up a couple of watercolours he'd done during the week to pass the time.

As soon as the people had gone, he hung a notice on the door: *Back at 2.15.*

Out in the square, Trezawne brass band was giving a Saturday concert, as it often did in spring and summer. Strains of favourite hymns and classics alternated with popular tunes, flowing skilfully from 'Hills of the North, Rejoice!' into the 'Radetzsky March' and on to such trifles as 'Bye-bye, Blackbird'. The band all wore maroon livery. With their highly polished brass, they made a brilliant splash of colour underneath the lime trees by the Great War memorial.

On passing the greengrocer's shop, Peggy caught sight of some big mixed baskets of strawberries and cherries on show outside. 'Imported, 3lbs Weight per basket' said a scrawl on a bit of old cardboard propped behind them.

'Oh, Hal.' She stopped. 'Have you got any money?'

'Not just now.'

'Nor have I, I'm spent out. Oh damn!' She lingered, eyeing them. 'They do look beautiful.'

'Handsome price, too,' Hal observed.

'I know, but . . . Perhaps I'll come over again later and get some, if they're not all gone.'

There was the briefest hesitation, then he said, 'Wait here,' and went into the shop.

Moments later, he emerged minus one of his paintings, selected a basket of fruit and handed it to her.

She stared at him. 'Hal, you didn't . . .?'

'Yes, why not?'

'You're mad! That picture was worth a guinea, easily.'

'It's only money, and look, the man threw in a pound of yellow pears. Tell you what, let's not go home. Let's go over by the library and wolf the lot.' He was laughing now in that sunny way which always touched her

115

heart. 'What's life if we can't be a bit extravagant sometimes?'

Alongside the library was a small public garden, with laurels and red and white May trees and wooden seats. No one was there to see, so they shamelessly gorged on the fruit, feeding each other and spitting the stones on the grass all around.

'Mr Jackman wants you to go in and see him,' Peggy said through a mouthful of strawberry. 'He'll arrange another show for you. He said something about asking some people he knows to come and look. From London, Hal, people with influence, I expect.'

He looked at her, half scared and half excited. 'That's a fact?'

'Mm.' She pulled a handkerchief out of her pocket and wiped Joy's face and hands clean. 'It could mean a step up for you.' Her forehead furrowed. 'One thing, though – I didn't think Mr Jackman seemed too well.'

'How do you mean?'

'He – went funny – for a moment while I was there. Dizzy. I don't think he could see properly. Then all of a sudden he was all right again.'

Hal shrugged. 'Doesn't sound like much to worry about.'

'I hope not. Anyway, mind you go and see him.' Taking the very last cherry, she extracted the stone and slipped the sweet black flesh into the baby's mouth. There was nothing left in the basket now but a pile of strawberry husks and pear cores. 'Oh, aren't we awful gluttons?' She clutched her stomach and started to laugh.

'Wanton,' Hal agreed. 'Let's do it again tomorrow.'

He started pulling faces for Joy and tumbling about

on the grass to amuse her. The baby's rolling chuckles echoed round the little park.

No matter how wealthy Guy Buckman is, I'll bet he's not half so much fun as my Hal, reflected Peggy.

Twelve

Guy and Anna returned home in mid-May. Sarah was on duty in the office when they arrived. Her eyes grew wide with surprise at the sight of Anna, for Guy had been as good as his word; his wife had been transformed.

'Welcome back, Mrs Buckman,' Sarah said. 'Did you have a nice time?'

'Yes, it was splendid.'

'I do like your hair,' the girl ventured. 'It looks elegant.'

'Thank you. I'm not quite used to it yet.' Anna's hand moved nervously to touch it. An expensive London hairdresser had rendered the crown of her head sleek and shiny, and rippled the sides with Marcel waves. She was wearing make-up too, eyebrow pencil and lipstick and rouge. Her suit was tight-waisted and rather tight-skirted, her heels higher than any she had worn before. The outfit was strikingly smart, but Anna felt strange in it, half hobbled. She hadn't chosen it herself.

'Big improvement, isn't it, Sarah?' Guy said, smiling.

'Yes, Mr Buckman.'

He took Anna's arm and they started up the stairs. 'I've a surprise for you,' he said, as they went along to the flat. 'I telephoned Sarah yesterday and she says it's all ready.'

'Surprise? Something more, after all you've given me?'

118

He pushed the key in the lock of their door and turned it. 'I never do anything by halves.'

The door swung back and Anna stepped inside, exclaiming: 'Oh!' and looking round her with delight. The rooms had been redecorated. They still smelt faintly of paint, and the scent of new carpet hung in the air.

Anna was thrilled with the bedroom. The décor was simple but pretty, with white walls and a sandy-coloured carpet, lacy curtains and furnishings in walnut. There were chairs upholstered in deep turquoise, and a satin quilt on the bed in the exact same shade. The most ornate touch was the bedstead, a swirling design in gilded wrought-iron at both head and foot.

'Like it?' asked Guy.

'Oh, yes, it's so airy and light.'

He showed her the bathroom. Same colour scheme, brand new fittings. Lots of graceful bottles and jars full of lotions and oils for milady.

The sitting-room was painted in peachy shades, with a chocolate brown carpet. The armchairs had been re-covered in a beige and green tapestry fabric. Upon the sideboard sat an enormous crystal rose bowl filled with blood-red blooms.

'It's wonderful, Guy!' she said, hugging him.

'Only the best will do for my wife.'

Just inside the sitting-room door stood a small trunk – Anna's things from home, delivered while the couple were away. After tea and sandwiches, she began to unpack them.

Guy had gone downstairs to hear what had happened while he was away. Anna hummed to herself, arranging her little possessions about the flat. She had brought a few books and some favourite gramophone records. On the dressing-table, she placed her brush and comb set, and a jewellery box which played 'Für Elise' when the lid was opened. There was a photograph in a silver frame of her mother and father – her favourite one of Dad – and another of her class at grammar school, taken in their upper sixth form year.

Turning to the other cases, Anna started putting away her clothes. Everything was new, the trousseau her mother had bought her, and a set of far more stylish, costly garments purchased in London on the way home. Anna's forehead creased as she recalled the shopping spree. Thoughtfully, she stroked the fabrics, hanging up the formal day dresses, the floaty frocks and blouses, tailored costumes and elegant evening wear. They were lovely, of course, but the taste was not her own. Guy's suggestions, his preferences, had prevailed. Tutting and shaking his head, or smiling his approval, he had steered her away from so many things she had wanted, directed her to other choices. Better ones, he firmly said. Well, she did indeed look very smart in everything he had bought. A lovely new wardrobe, no doubt about that. She had been mindful all the time that he was paying and therefore entitled to a powerful say. The clothes were in tune with the hair and the make-up, creating a style which was complete, with nothing out of place. Nothing wrong with that, in principle.

Only – a whisper of unease kept telling Anna that something had been taken away from her. Catching sight of herself in the wardrobe mirror, she fingered her powdered skin and felt, for a moment, troubled. At a plush London salon, they had varnished her nails and plucked her eyebrows, painted her face as if she were a doll. It was all very expertly done and not at all clownish, but in the mirror she saw, not Anna Trevena, so lately a schoolgirl, but the garnished wife of an affluent man. Not quite herself – or perhaps a version of herself which should have waited another ten years to appear.

Anna fought down her misgivings. She was Mrs Guy Buckman now and had to look the part. She had to be as fashionable as the women who stayed in her husband's hotel. Undeniably, she now looked more suitable for Guy, closer to his age. A gulf which could never truly be closed was at least concealed by illusion.

When everything had been put away, Anna went to the bedroom window, opened it and stepped out on the little balcony. All the first-floor rooms on this side of the house had balconies. They made her think of Shakespeare's Juliet. A parapet ran from each one to the next, but only the most determined Romeo would risk trying to cross.

Anna leaned on the railing, looking out over the lawn. There was sunshine and birdsong, the smell of freshly cut grass. Beyond the rhododendrons were several acres of pretty woods – all hers to roam. Her home, this beautiful place. What a privilege, what great good fortune.

She was still standing there when Guy returned. He came up behind her, grasped her round the waist and pulled her back hard against him.

'Come on, Anna, let's christen the bed,' said his voice at her ear.

'What? Guy, it's only four o'clock!'

'So?' He spun her round to face him, gently tweaking the end of her nose. His grin grew broad and he drew her back into the bedroom, started to undress her with a brisk determination. Anna felt a bit like a parcel in the hands of some impatient child. Her husband softly swore as a button declined to slip out of its hole. He pulled and a darkness crossed his face. The threads gave way and the button flew across the room.

'Let me . . .' she began.

But he seemed not to hear, bearing her down on the bed, tugging at her clothes and at his own. What ensued was a sprawling rut among a tangle of half-unfastened garments. Afterwards, pinned beneath his snoozing weight, Anna looked around her with a feeling of unreality. Such a gross display in this pretty room by her elegant husband. Some would say she should be flattered that he lost his head for her, showed such passion. A man like Guy, well-educated, smooth.

Instead, it made her feel ugly, sordid, being half-dressed. Her with her pants still around her right ankle, him with his buttocks rising above his shoved-down trousers. The fact he had his socks and shoes on, and she had her brassière pushed up under her armpits. Awful. So undignified, calling up images of louts and tarts groping in alleys or under railway bridges. And there was no need for it. The louts and tarts had nowhere else to go, but Guy and Anna were married, they had this beautiful bedroom and plenty of time. It could have been quiet, loving. That was what she would have liked.

Panic rose and then subsided, rose and fell again. He had given her so much, she was going to lead a pampered life, but something still seemed ominous, wrong. Whether the fault lay with him or with her, she wasn't sure.

Anna lay and stared at the ceiling, full of confusion.

A glamorous place, Elestren Manor. So Mrs Trevena

had said and so it was. A constant stream of well-dressed, well-heeled people came and went, staying a weekend, a fortnight, a month. Couples of all ages – but rarely children, Anna had noticed. It was not a family hotel, but a place for cocktail drinkers and cigar smokers, people who ordered dinner late, sitting down to eat around nine and still talking over the liqueurs at eleven. A place where twosomes and foursomes wandered in and out in tennis whites, where guests would come to the desk enquiring for the nearest riding stables.

Often, there were furtive goings-on among the residents. Assignations, midnight creepings from room to room. Elestren Manor was a favourite venue for romantic interludes. Guy, more baldly, called it 'the dirty weekend trade'.

'A lot of the couples who come here aren't married, you know,' he told Anna. 'Now and then we have a terrific drama when a wife tracks down her husband here and catches him with his fancy bit.'

'You don't mind that sort of thing?'

'Why should I care about people's morals, so long as they pay their bills? You must learn to be broad-minded, Anna.'

Broad-minded, yes, but not too democratic. So far as Anna's relationship with the staff was concerned, Guy had very definite views.

'Don't be too friendly,' he told her, 'not even with the office girls. It diminishes your authority and they'll only take advantage. Anyway, there isn't much point in getting to know the employees, because they come and go all the time. That's how it is in this business, here today and gone tomorrow. You must have noticed a good many changes of personnel since you started coming here?'

She admitted she had.

'They're mostly young, you see, and restless. Careless, too – I often have to fire someone. I have a high regard for the chef because of his excellent work, but he's about the only fixture. Oh – and Mrs Roseveare, the housekeeper. She's been with us since Mother died. Completely trustworthy. The rest of them are ships in the night. It isn't like a big family, don't think that.'

In truth, the warning was superfluous. Anna sensed that she was liked by the hotel staff, but most of them kept a respectful distance, as if afraid of exchanging amiable words with the boss's wife.

During her first week, Anna explored the hotel from top to bottom. Guy gave her a set of keys and she went round looking at all the bedrooms, the cellars and the stores and utility rooms. There were four little attic bedrooms for live-in staff like Sarah and Mrs Roseveare, but most lived out.

The noisy, busy hub of everything was, of course, the kitchen – nothing short of hell on earth when meals were being served. A sweltering place where figures scurried to and fro amid the clatter and crash of dishes, the rising steam from the bain-marie and the great boiling pots atop the stoves. Heat, heat and more heat. Three large gas ovens, two hotplates, a salamander roaring. Crockery and serving platters, all too hot to touch without a thickly folded cloth. Delicious aromas of food intermingled with a fainter scent suggestive of scorched metal. Over all this presided a chef named Lionel. He was fat and excitable. For much of the time he went about bellowing and throwing things, and sometimes threatened to kill people, brandishing a ladle or a carving knife.

'Of course, he's all talk,' Guy said. 'Tempers get frayed in the rush when they're serving. You needn't take any notice of him.'

He might be right, but Anna elected to stay out of the kitchen as much as she could. The only time she ventured there was during the afternoon break or late at night when the work was finished and everyone had gone.

Her own little part in the business was the dainty job of doing the flower arrangements for the front hall and lounge. That, and a couple of shifts in the office each week when the girls had their days off. Sarah explained to her all the routines. They were simple enough, but they needed care.

'Do double-check when you're taking a reservation over the telephone,' she said. 'Make very sure you've drawn in the correct arrival and departure dates and allocated the right sort of room, especially at times when the hotel is busy. An error can cause the most terrible trouble. All the bookings must dovetail perfectly when the house is full. Make a mistake and it's often very hard, if not impossible, to rectify.'

Anna nodded, looking at the grid of dates and rooms. A simple cross-reference. Easy enough, she thought.

Sarah pulled down some folders from a shelf. 'Now, this is the filing system – at least, the only part of it you'll need to use, Mrs Buckman. As you see, room confirmations in this file, function details in this one, general correspondence in this one. Everything is in alphabetical and date order with the most recent letters on top. So long as Mr Buckman finds everything in its proper place when he wants it, all's well. If not . . .' She rolled her eyes and affected a shiver. 'Once, when I was filing, I accidentally clipped two letters together and put them both under "J", when one should have gone under "T". It took us twenty minutes to find it and he was awfully angry. You have to watch things like that.'

As she went on, Anna became aware of a scrupulous and fearful attention to detail. The ledgers, the cash – well, yes, of course accuracy was essential. Yet Sarah seemed excessively worried about the odd penny adrift, or crossings-out, or use of black ink where blue was the norm. And she spoke of certain errors as if they were heinous crimes: forgetting to order a newspaper, or ordering the wrong one, putting a guest down for morning tea when he'd asked for coffee, running out of anything the residents might want, such as postcards and stamps. Any of a host of little human slip-ups, easily made when one was busy. Sarah stressed a score or more of these vital points to watch and Anna noticed again and again her use of such words as 'precisely', 'thoroughly', 'neatly', and phrases like 'be very certain', 'must not', 'dare not'.

Perhaps Sarah was meticulous by nature, but Anna felt driven to ask: 'Do you enjoy working here?'

'Mr Buckman pays me generously,' said Sarah. 'And I like to do my job well,' she added quickly.

'All right,' Anna said, 'I'll do my best to be as conscientious as you are. My husband won't be able to say you haven't taught me properly.'

It was only in part a joke. Sarah's smile was hugely grateful.

Well, thought Anna afterwards, it was probably as Guy had said. Employees would grow sloppy if they weren't kept on their toes, and Elestren Manor had such a reputation to maintain.

'How did you get on with Sarah?' he asked her. 'Think you'll be able to cope?'

'I don't see why not.'

'That's my girl.'

'And this is all I'll have to do? It doesn't seem very much.'

'Oh, of course you'll mingle and be charming, make all the men envy me for my wife, and all the women envy you for the way you look. You'll grace the place and be a lovely hostess.' He tidied a lock of her hair, smiling down at her. 'Shouldn't be difficult for you.'

'I'll have to practise,' she said seriously.

'You'll be fine. I won't let you go wrong.'

That same evening, just before dinner, he took her out for another tennis lesson. It was the first time they had played since the previous summer.

'We'll just have an hour on the court,' said Guy. 'I hope you haven't forgotten all I taught you.'

But she had. Most of the good had been undone by lack of practice during the winter months. He sighed and started to coach her all over again. He demonstrated swings and serves and she strove to copy him.

After about twenty minutes, he began to show signs of impatience.

'Again,' he said heavily, as she hit the net for the sixth time, attempting to serve.

'Again.' The word became rather clipped as she missed an easy forehand.

'Again!' A ball came whistling over with the force of annoyance behind it.

'No! No, no, no! You're not even properly placed!'

'I'm sorry, Guy . . .'

'How many times have I shown you the way to take one like that?'

'I know, I'm sorry . . .'

'Try again.' Another ball speeding towards her.

She fluffed it – largely because she kept glancing at his face. It wore a tight expression of irritation.

'Once more!' It was almost a bark.

She dithered this way, that way, and again the ball flashed past her.

'Oh, I give up!' He threw his racket at the fence.

'Guy, I'm doing my best!'

'You just can't be bothered.'

'I want to play, truly I do!' She ran for a stray ball, picked it up. 'Let me try serving again.'

She tossed up the ball, swiped at it, missed. It plopped at her feet with a couple of listless bounces and rolled away.

From the other end of the court came a groan. She didn't know whether he meant her to hear it, but she clearly caught the words.

'Oh, you dumb bitch! That's enough. Let's go in.'

Anna stood rooted, staring at him.

Hands on hips, he bent his head for a moment as if he were pondering something. Then he was coming towards her, looking contrite.

'Sorry. You know I didn't mean that.' He forced a smile.

She hesitated just a second, then turned and walked back to the hotel without waiting for him.

Thirteen

Of all the staff at Elestren Manor, Anna found Mrs Roseveare to be the most congenial. She was one of those hefty, talkative Cornish women with what Anna always thought of as a 'plump' voice – warm, sweet, reassuring bubbles of sound. Mrs Roseveare liked to gossip and seemed the only female employee prepared to chat with Anna woman-to-woman.

Passing along an upstairs corridor the following morning, Anna saw the door to the best room wide open and heard the gurgle of running water from the bathroom. The housekeeper's mop and bucket were propped just inside the bedroom door.

Anna went in to say good morning. She found Mrs Roseveare down on her knees, cleaning out the tub.

'Nearly finished here, Mrs Buckman,' she said, panting. 'I'll be along shortly to do the flat for you.'

'All right, no hurry.'

Anna sat down on the corner of the bath. She had been disturbed all night, upset by Guy's little outburst on the tennis court. He'd been as sweet as honey ever since, but Anna was left with a sense of unease. For some reason, too, she kept thinking about his sister, the estranged and somewhat maligned Elaine. She wondered how well Mrs Roseveare remembered her. She said:

'You've been here eight years, haven't you?'

'That's right, my dear. Why do you ask?'

'Oh, I was just thinking about Guy's sister. I've never met her, you know. Can you recall her?'

Mrs Roseveare went on scouring at the enamel. 'Never saw much of her myself. She went away soon after I started here. Quiet sort of girl, as I recall. Clever, I think. Always civil. That's all I can tell you.' A hesitation, then: 'I don't think her father liked her. Don't know why.'

'Was it mutual?'

'I fancy it was, or she wouldn't have left home so eagerly, especially with him becoming an invalid.'

Anna was thoughtfully silent a moment.

'Was he very severely disabled?'

'Oh, yes, towards the end. Could hardly do a thing for himself. He grew to be very cantankerous.'

'Due to the pain, I dare say?'

'I don't think it was that, so much. He hated being helpless. He'd always been an active man, I believe, in charge of everything and everybody. It used to enrage him, being stuck in his chair and dependent on others.'

'I gather he had a nurse?'

'He had three, to tell you the truth. Couldn't stand any of them. The first one only stayed two months, the second was here for just under a year. The third one lasted eighteen months and saw him out.'

'Of course, he would have preferred his wife to look after him, wouldn't he? Shame that she died when she did.'

The housekeeper didn't answer that. Her back was jerking now as she rubbed energetically at the tidemark.

'Did you know Mrs Buckman at all, or did she die before you came?' asked Anna.

130

The woman knelt back, sitting on her heels. She looked up at Anna, her chubby face sober.

'I'd been here just a fortnight when it happened. Oh, it was pitiful. Poor, poor thing.'

'What was she like?'

Absent-mindedly, Mrs Roseveare squeezed at the dripping cloth in her hand.

'Not much resemblance to that picture he keeps, that one where she's cutting the roses. Thin, she was, haggard. And preoccupied, silent. Hardly said a word to me, although what she did say was kind. I think she was a nice soul, a very well-bred woman, but by the time I met her she was – well, a wreck, to put no fine point on it. A funny thing, the mind. Amazing what it can do.'

Anna frowned. 'The mind?' she queried. 'What do you mean?'

'Well, she worried herself into that condition, didn't she? Poor soul. It wasn't as if she was really ill.'

Staring at her, Anna said: 'But she had cancer, didn't she?'

'Why no, my dear, I think you're a bit mixed up. She thought she had it, certainly, and that was why she took the tablets.'

'Tablets?'

'All those sleeping tablets. I was the one who found her. It was . . .' Mrs Roseveare hesitated. 'I – I thought you knew.'

There was a silence. Then: 'She killed herself? Is that what you're saying?'

Troubled now, the housekeeper lumbered to her feet. 'Oh, now I wonder if I've said something I shouldn't? I assumed that Mr Buckman had told you all about it.

Anyway, you'd be bound to hear sooner or later, it's no great secret. It was in the papers at the time.'

'I was only a child then,' said Anna. Indignantly, she stated: 'My husband told me she had cancer!'

Mrs Roseveare moistened her lips. 'I expect you misheard him or misunderstood, my dear.'

'It was a deliberate overdose? You're sure?'

'I don't think I should say any more, Mrs Buckman. Best talk to your husband. I hope he won't be angry with me.'

Anna made no reply. She was chewing at her thumbnail, trying to order her thoughts.

Suicide? Mental illness? She had never imagined anything like that. Her mind called forth the image of a smiling Helen Buckman, cutting roses. It hardly seemed possible. And Guy had not been honest with her. Why? Ashamed? Perhaps he was. There was, after all, some stigma attached. Still, as Mrs Roseveare had said, she was bound to hear sooner or later. Suddenly, Anna wondered, too, if her mother had read the reports of Helen Buckman's suicide.

The housekeeper had left her and gone out into the bedroom, where she was stripping sheets and changing the bed with astonishing speed. After a moment, Anna followed her.

'You believe she was unbalanced, then?'

'She was odd, poor soul. Used to go off by herself for hours and hours at a time in all weathers. And when she came back, you could always see she'd been crying. Desperately despondent, she was. I don't think she had any true friends to talk to. I asked her once or twice if I could be of help, but no, she wouldn't open up. I couldn't think what the matter was, never dreamed she was obsessed with the notion she was ill.'

'What did the rest of the staff think about her?'

'What would they know? It was the same then as it is now, people coming and going all the time. When I started first, there wasn't a soul who had been here as much as three months, except Mr Hoblyn the gardener, and he rarely comes into the hotel. No one really knew her. It was only after she killed herself that it all came out about her mental state. They had to have an inquest, see.'

'Wasn't Mr Buckman any comfort to her?'

'He was very attentive, very concerned, so far as I could tell. Couldn't get through to her, I suppose. Anyway, he wasn't well himself, with that arthritis setting in. That's all I know of it, Mrs Buckman, truly.'

Finishing the bed, Mrs Roseveare smoothed the counterpane, then picked up the morning tea tray to take it outside. She was keen to get off the subject, that was obvious. Anna didn't push her any further. But then, on impulse, she asked the same question she'd put to Sarah.

'Would you say you're happy here, Mrs Roseveare?'

'Mr Buckman pays me well,' came the answer. 'I have room and board as well as my wages. The Buckmans have never been mean with money. Everybody on the staff admits that.'

Admits? The word raised a question in Anna's mind.

'Then do they have complaints of other kinds?'

Mrs Roseveare was cautious. 'Well, employees do grumble. Show me a place of work where they don't. You're all right here if you do your job properly, and I pride myself I do. People who don't measure up don't last long – which is fair enough. After all, we have a demanding type of patron.'

'Yes, of course,' said Anna. 'Thank you, Mrs Rose-veare. I appreciate your candour.'

It was, she reflected, very much the same answer that Sarah had given. The question of being happy was sidestepped, the good wages were quoted instead. Some people would endure a lot for money.

One thing after another. Little slip-ups, lies revealed, illusions destroyed. Anna wondered how much more there was to learn about Guy. Next day she tackled him about his mother.

It was Sunday morning, when they always had their breakfast brought up to the flat on a tray at ten o'clock. Both had just finished their coffee and Guy was writing a letter, while Anna stood arranging roses in the crystal bowl.

The flowers were overblown, drooping with the weight of their heads. One of them had dropped half its petals on to the polished wood of the chess board lying beside it. The opposing armies of black and white chessmen seemed to stare at the fallen petals in disapproval. Anna trimmed the stems and placed the roses as best she could, but they kept flopping sideways, spoiling her display. Her mind was only half on the task, in any case.

'Guy,' she ventured finally, 'there's something I must ask you.'

'Oh?' He went on writing.

'I heard something yesterday which, well, disturbed me.'

The tiny scratching noise of his fountain pen suddenly ceased.

'What was it, Anna?'

'It concerned your mother.'

134

Behind her there was silence. Anna turned around.

He was sitting at an angle, one elbow resting on the back of his chair. In his hand he was turning the fountain pen round and round and round.

'Ah,' he said at last. 'Yes, I can guess what that was.'

He was perfectly calm, not angry or in any other way upset.

'Guy, is it true that she killed herself?'

'Mm.' He tossed the pen onto the blotter, linked his hands. 'Well, yes, it is. I'm, uh, sorry I wasn't entirely straight with you. I thought you might be shocked, distressed. Who told you?'

'Mrs Roseveare. She assumed that I already knew, for which you can hardly blame her.'

'No, of course not.'

'And the reason, Guy? Your mother imagined she was ill?'

A nod.

'She didn't have cancer at all?'

He sighed. 'No, but she wouldn't believe that. She went to see the doctor about a small cyst. That was all it was. He did tests. He assured her it was harmless, but Mother couldn't be convinced. She fretted herself into such a state that she actually did look and feel ill. And in the end, I suppose she decided to cheat her imaginary disease of its victim, go quickly and painlessly.'

'Was it really necessary to lie to me?'

'I didn't want to put you off me, Anna. It was – how shall I say? – a skeleton in the family cupboard.'

'You knew I would find out eventually.'

Guy smiled broadly. 'Better after marriage than before.'

She stared at him. 'Guy, it wasn't anything hereditary, was it? Nothing you could pass on to our children?'

'Good God, no! She wasn't what's called "mad", just morbidly concerned about her health. Mother spent far too much time on her own. She brooded. Worst of all, she read medical books. One should never do that.'

'I still think you should have been honest. I wouldn't have held it against you.'

'Then why does it bother you now?'

A pause, then: 'More evidence, I suppose.'

His brows flicked up. 'Of what?'

'That I never knew you, Guy. Not really.'

Fourteen

Whatever misgivings Anna might have about her husband, the last person to whom she would confide them would be Peggy. One morning in July, they chanced to meet at the local shoe shop.

Peggy had gone there to buy a pair of baby shoes for Joy. She was sitting down, waiting her turn to be served, when the doorbell tinkled and a tall female figure came in. At the sight of Peggy, Anna hesitated briefly, as if debating whether it might be better to come back later. But then she closed the door, took the farthest seat and stared straight ahead of her, just as people did when ignoring each other in railway compartments.

The proprietor was serving an elderly woman who had awkward feet. He kept running in and out of his store-room seeking more choices to offer, while the customer dithered and sighed and fussed. Peggy had already been waiting nearly fifteen minutes and Joy was growing fretful.

Anna's gaze slid curiously towards the infant. Hal's child – but dark like Peggy. Same curly hair, same eyes. A pretty baby, but nearly all Angilley, Anna thought. Briefly, a suspicion crossed her mind. What if the child were not Hal's after all?

Quickly, though, she dismissed the idea. No, Anna remembered the night of the bonfire. The timing was right.

From under lowered lids, Peggy obliquely surveyed her old rival. She hadn't seen Anna in quite a while and was somewhat taken aback by the change in her appearance. She looked like something out of a glossy magazine. Peggy decided she didn't like the hairstyle and make-up. Much too artificial, she told herself and felt a little thrill of superiority. Anna's clothes, though, were another matter. Enviously, Peggy's gaze slithered over the crocodile bag and shoes, the simple green silk dress and neat little brown felt hat tipped stylishly low over one eye. As for the jewellery – Peggy eyed Anna's dainty watch, her gold necklet and earrings and, most of all, the emerald engagement ring. Everything fine quality, tasteful, including the delicate scent which accompanied her into the shop. The sort of perfume which came in tiny quantities in crystal bottles.

As her gaze travelled up again to Anna's face, Peggy found the green eyes watching her from under the shadow of the hat. Peggy's glance flicked quickly away and then dipped to her feet in their scuffed open sandals. Her toenails were dirty, and there was a grease-spot near the hem of her yellow polka-dot skirt. The only jewellery she wore was her wedding ring, and she bought eau-de-cologne by the pint from Lindow's Pharmacy.

The old lady showed not a sign of making up her mind about a pair of shoes. Peggy toyed with the notion of leaving, but Anna might think it was because of her, so she stayed put. Anna, too, was growing restive, but felt just as anxious to hold her ground. Both were uncomfortable; neither wished to be seen to retreat. So they sat and they waited, stared into space or covertly observed each other.

Slattern, Anna was thinking. I'll wager she never

shaves her armpits. I'll bet her underwear's held together with safety pins.

Show-off, reflected Peggy. Like Lady Fan Todd, dressed to death and killed with fashion.

Both girls sniffed to themselves and pulled little faces.

Suddenly, the tension was broken by a small squeal, as Joy wriggled down from her mother's lap and staggered a couple of paces in Anna's direction. She was smiling, holding out a hand to the pretty lady. For a moment, despite herself, Anna smiled too and leaned forward in her chair.

Then the child overbalanced and sat down hard, and Peggy was out of her seat, in haste to bring her back. Lifting Joy to her feet, she held her steady by both hands. Seeing Anna still watching, she said:

'What do you think of her, then? She's called Joy, did you know?'

'It's a nice name,' Anna said coolly.

Peggy sat down again, taking the child on her lap once more.

'She's fifteen months now. Hal adores her.'

See what I've got, said the tone. His child. We're a family.

'Of course,' murmured Anna distantly.

'And I'm expecting another. Found out just last week. It's due next February.' Peggy looked enormously pleased with herself.

The answer was brittle. 'Congratulations.'

'We're hoping to have a boy this time. I want him to look just like Hal. Perhaps he'll be an artist, too. Hal's having another exhibition soon at Mr Jackman's, by the way.'

'How nice.'

'Yes, he's doing very well. He says marriage suits him, says it's improved his work.'

Anna sighed but made no reply. Peggy, however, once on the attack, was always loath to stop.

'It's a wonderful way of life. We're very lucky, don't you think? Hal says that doing what you enjoy is much more important than making money.'

'Oh?' said Anna dryly. 'Well, you can tell him from me that he'll miss a lot in life without it. Did you know that Guy and I went to Switzerland for our honeymoon?'

'Really? Wouldn't give you twopence for all those foreign places. Funny food, and you never know what you'll catch.'

'The scenery was wonderful, glorious mountains and lakes – magnificent landscapes for an artist, if he can afford to travel. We made a few trips over the border and saw a bit of Italy too, beautiful cathedrals and art galleries. I'm sure Hal would love to visit those, so he shouldn't be too quick to sneer at money.'

Peggy's voice dropped low. 'Is that what you married Mr Buckman for, his wealth? He's much older than you, isn't he? And not half so good-looking as Hal.'

She saw Anna swallow, saw her gaze flit nervously towards the shopkeeper, who was finally wrapping up a box for the old lady.

'I happen to think my husband's rather handsome,' she said quietly. 'He's a gentleman. He could have married anyone he wanted, and he chose me.'

Peggy's mouth spread in a grin. 'A gentleman, is he? I'll wager he wouldn't think you such a lady if he knew about my portrait and what you did,' she retorted softly.

It was Anna's turn to blush. Peggy was going to

pursue the subject, but an interruption stopped her. The old lady had paid for her shoes and was leaving the shop. As she went out, the proprietor said:

'My dear Mrs Buckman, I'm sorry you've waited so long. I'll attend to you straight away. Your shoes came in this morning. I think you'll be pleased with them.'

He was beaming, unctuous, rubbing his hands. He turned to a shelf by his counter and took down a box.

'Here! Half a minute!' Peggy stood up. 'I was first, as well you know. What do you mean, *she's* waited so long? What am I, invisible? Twenty-five minutes I've sat here with my kid. Now I expect to be served in my proper turn.'

'Really, Miss Angilley . . .'

'Mrs Pentreath!'

'Mrs Pentreath,' he amended, 'there's no call . . .'

'I'm next,' insisted Peggy, sticking her chin out.

'You don't understand. Mrs Buckman ordered a pair of evening shoes last week.'

'So?'

'I think that gives her priority, don't you?'

'No.' The word dropped like a boulder.

'It will only take a minute, I assure you. Just a fitting.' He took the lid off the box and lifted out a dainty gold sandal.

'That isn't the point.'

Anna remained sitting down, her head cocked to one side, as she listened to this. The shopkeeper held out the sandal towards her.

'If you would care to examine the shoes, Mrs Buckman?'

Anna didn't move, but she opened her mouth to say something. Before she could speak, however, Peggy grabbed the sandal.

'I want a pair of shoes for my little girl,' she repeated. Seizing the other sandal, she flourished it at him. 'I realise that baby shoes cost shillings, not guineas like these silly things, but my money's the same colour as hers, and my family have always been good customers to you. You serve me, right now, or you'll have my husband to contend with.'

Embarrassed, the shopkeeper looked past Peggy at Anna, gave her a watery smile and helplessly spread his hands.

'Please,' said Anna smoothly, 'Peggy was here first. Of course you must attend to her.'

'You're very gracious, Mrs Buckman,' fawned the man, his head seeming to shrink into his shoulders.

Not at all, I'll come back later. I have an errand or two in town.'

Peggy turned around and looked at her. She had won – so why was the feeling so strong that she was being patronised?

Anna smiled at her brightly. 'I'm off to buy some flowers,' she said. 'Guy and I are having special friends to dinner at the hotel this evening. We do a lot of entertaining.'

Peggy's stare was bleak.

''Bye,' said Anna. 'So nice to see you.'

Twenty minutes later, Peggy was walking slowly home, carrying Joy. In the basket slung over her arm was the brown paper bag containing the child's new shoes. Peggy was rattled by what had happened. On the whole, she felt she had come off worst. She had lost her temper, while Anna had kept her composure. Most galling thing of all was the shopkeeper's attitude.

Peggy was a nobody, a nothing, to be shoved aside in favour of a rich man's wife.

Would she have flared up quite so hotly had it been not Anna but some other wealthy woman? Probably not, although she would have had something to say, being Peggy. But it had been Anna, and the gulf between them, the difference in their status, had been painfully underlined.

Anna's talk about Switzerland, Italy, entertaining – it was all a universe away from the life Peggy knew. The smartness of it awed her and made her feel like a peasant. Her only glimpses of glamour and gracious living were gleaned from the cinema screen.

Peggy's reality, Angilley's Bazaar, loomed just ahead. She went in, and there in the shop she found Maisie with a newspaper spread out across the counter. She was studying the racing pages and eating a chunk of toffee, which she bought in slabs and broke up with a little hammer. The pieces were always too large at first, so that a bulge moved around in her mouth, going from side to side, pushing out one cheek, then the other, as she chewed. The chewing made 'clock, clock, clock' noises and forced her to breathe very heavily down her nose.

'You've been a long time,' she said. 'Did you get the shoes?'

Peggy showed her.

'Oh, yes, they're nice. Here, look at this. We had a delivery today while you were out.' Maisie came round the end of her counter, went into the room where the slot machines were. Following her, Peggy noticed that her mother's hem was down at the back and her hair needed combing.

143

'There!' exclaimed Maisie proudly, throwing out a hand. 'Brand new and right up to date.'

It was a gob-stopper machine. Maisie put in a coin to demonstrate. With a clatter, a hideous orange ball arrived in the tray underneath.

Inwardly, Peggy sighed. But she said: 'That'll make us a few bob, Mam. Good idea.'

'And . . .' Maisie went on dramatically '. . . look!'

Across the room by the window was another new attraction, a big glass case containing a model of a medieval castle. In response to payment of a ha'penny, mechanical bats whirred around the turrets and a vampire in evening dress popped up on the roof with dripping fangs. Then there were flashing lights from an upstairs window and Frankenstein's monster appeared on the balcony. Finally, the front door opened and out came a screaming woman in a nightdress, hair standing on end. The sequence was repeated twice, lasting about thirty seconds.

Peggy stared at this automaton in disbelief.

'Oh, just nice for the kids,' she said at last.

'They'll love it, wait and see,' said Maisie. 'It's just like the stuff they go to watch at the pictures.'

Peggy nodded, but within herself she cringed. How easily Anna's smartness could make her feel ashamed of Angilley's Bazaar. A gob-stopper machine, a vampire's castle. Imagine such things at Elestren Manor.

Nevertheless, she said: 'I expect you're right, Mam, you generally are.'

Maisie, pleased, returned to the racing pages. Peggy was just about to take Joy upstairs when Walter came in.

'Here,' he said, 'girl, got something to tell you.'

Peggy looked at him. 'What?'

'Heard it in the pub just now. You aren't going to like it.' Savouring the moment, Walter paused, smirking at his daughter.

Maisie dug him with a finger. 'Well, come on, then.'

'That old chap of yours, he's died.'

'Old chap?' Peggy frowned.

'Your husband's old patron. Had some sort of attack last night and he's gone. No more fancy shows for Pentreath at the gallery.'

'Are you talking about Mr Jackman?'

'Who else?'

'Oh no,' said Peggy. 'Are you sure?'

'It was Pascoe the butcher told me.'

Maisie, chewing in slow motion, cast a doleful look at Peggy.

'Wonder who'll have his shop now, eh?' taunted Walter. 'Somebody, perhaps, who won't care much for the stuff your darling does. Somebody, even, who'll have some other sort of business altogether. How about that?' Leering in Peggy's face, he said: 'Let him try pricing his pictures in guineas in this shop window.'

'You shut up!' Leaning across the counter, Maisie cuffed him. A morsel of toffee shot out of her mouth and stuck to his jacket. 'You nasty article.' To Peggy, she offered frail hope. 'May not be true, maid. You know what a liar he is.'

'Go round there and see, then,' snapped Walter.

'We'll do that, don't you worry,' Peggy said, although she could already guess what they would hear. She recalled all too clearly that day at Jackman's shop when the old boy had seemed unwell.

Trudging forlornly upstairs, she heard her parents bickering on, as Walter turned to cadging. The exchange was so familiar, Peggy knew it off by heart.

With minor variations, she'd been hearing it all her life.

Soon there was uproar, Walter bawling, Maisie chittering and screeching.

'I don't make money for you to drink away.'

'No, you'd rather lose it on the nags.'

'I only ever have a bob each way. You guzzle beer enough each week to float the Padstow ferry.'

And so on and so on. Always the same routine and the same result. In the end she would probably give him half a crown. That and a piece of her mind, so honour was satisfied and each had a good, exhilarating yell at the other.

Groaning, Peggy went into the kitchen and closed the door to deaden the noise. Imagine such behaviour at Elestren Manor. No, they had decorum there, dinner parties and civilised talk around candlelit tables.

In the afternoon, she and Hal went over to Mr Jackman's shop. It was closed, so they called next door at Kellow's the florist's, where the bad news was confirmed. The old man had suffered a fatal stroke.

Crestfallen, Hal and Peggy came away.

'Damn,' he said, 'Jackman was a dear old stick, and he was good to me. I've done fifteen canvases specially for this new exhibition and now it's all off. I suppose I'll manage to sell them sometime, but I feel as if the ground's been pulled from under me.'

Peggy was too glum to answer. It had been a horrible day. First the encounter with Anna, now this. It was, she reflected, their first bit of real bad luck.

Fifteen

Anna's dinner party was an exercise in keeping good customers happy. 'Special friends', she had said to Peggy. The truth was that every so often Guy treated certain regular patrons to a dinner on the house. They were, naturally, people who spent a lot of money at Elestren Manor, people whose continued goodwill he wished to ensure. This was the first such dinner Anna had experienced. The couple to be entertained were a Mr and Mrs Bright.

'Just chat and be your charming self,' Guy told her as they dressed that evening.

'But I don't know them. What can I talk about?'

'Oh, Anna . . .' He was knotting his tie. He glanced at her in the mirror and something flickered in his eyes. It might have been amusement or annoyance, she wasn't sure. 'Oh Anna, you can make small talk as well as anyone.'

She clipped on a pair of pearl earrings and adjusted the straps of her evening gown. It was powder blue with a long, gored skirt. A pattern of ebony beads was sewn on to the bodice. Standing, she picked up her velvet purse.

'All right. Well, I'm ready. Will we have to do this often, Guy?'

'Not really. About once a month, on average. Depends who's staying and when.' Smiling now, he added: 'You may find you enjoy it.'

But she didn't. The dinner was agony. George Bright was middle-aged, with a loud, boastful manner. He manufactured some kind of industrial disinfectant. His wife was called Topsy and had a laugh like a donkey's bray. Mr Bright was a dogmatic talker, going on and on about the Government, taxation and the banks. He emphasised special points by rapping the table with his finger, and plainly considered disinfectant the pivot of the country's economy. He kept asking Anna for opinions on matters of which she knew nothing. Naturally, she could think of very little to say. Whenever she did venture a comment, Mr Bright would explain at length how wrong she was. After a few drinks, he started telling jokes. Anna wasn't stupid and she had a sense of humour, but half the time she couldn't really see the point. Or else she understood but simply failed to find his quips very funny. Still, appreciation was required of her, so she laughed on cue and tried to look lively and attentive. All in all, however, she felt gauche and out of place. Attempts to make conversation with Topsy were fruitless. Mrs Bright was a man's woman and far more interested in flirting with Guy. Anna wished Mr Bright would eat as fast as he talked, for the meal seemed to drag on for ever. After dinner they had more drinks in the lounge, staying up until past midnight, and she thought that hectoring voice would drive her out of her mind.

As the hour grew late, Anna slid pleading glances towards her husband. But Guy kept smiling all the while, maintaining a look of fervent interest in all that Bright was saying. If he perceived his wife's discomfort, he gave no sign of it.

Mercifully, in the end, the drink got the better of Mr Bright and he started feeling drowsy and talking of bed. The Buckmans finally made their escape at twenty-past twelve.

'Oh God, my head is throbbing,' Anna said, as she and Guy walked along the corridor towards the flat. 'I feel as though I've been put through a wringer, I'm exhausted.'

Her husband was silent.

'Please, Guy, tell me it won't always be like that.'

His answer startled her. 'I think it's you, Anna, who should promise better in future.'

The tone was grim. Stopping short, she turned to him – and was frozen by the look on his face. His mouth was downturned, ugly, and his eyes a baleful yellow, the pupils shrunk to mere dots.

'What . . . What do you mean?' She couldn't keep the quaver out of her voice.

'You let your feelings show, that's what,' he growled. 'You sat there wearing a grin like a ventriloquist's dummy, and looking at Bright as if he were a warthog.'

She swallowed. 'Did I? Well, I didn't mean to. I thought I was being pleasant.'

'It wasn't a very good act.'

'Then I'm sorry, but I couldn't help it. Don't tell me you like those two?'

'No, of course I don't like them, but I'm in business, Anna, or had you forgotten? The hospitality business, what's more. That means being nice, come hell or high water. Fail at that and it doesn't matter how good the food and the rooms are.'

'Guy,' she protested, 'I tried my best! I don't know what more you expect of me.'

'I expect you to be witty, amusing. You know, you virtually ignored his wife.'

After the misery of the evening, this was just too much.

'I could hardly get a word in edgewise!' Anna said haplessly. 'And what I did say was never right, so in the end I kept quiet. Mrs Bright didn't want to be bothered with me, Guy, we had nothing in common.'

'Don't make excuses. You were a very poor hostess, Anna. I need you to be an asset, to charm the customers. Bright's a millionaire – did you know that?'

'What if he is?' queried Anna, bewildered. 'He pays the same prices here as everyone else.'

'He has wealthy friends and acquaintances to whom he can recommend Elestren Manor. It's always good business to cultivate people like him.'

Just for a second, her temper flared. 'I'm sorry, I'm not good at being oily.'

At that, he seized her by the upper arms. His lips drew back tightly across his teeth and his words were softly menacing.

'Don't cheek me.'

Anna could only stare up at him, transfixed with fright by his glaring eyes.

'You didn't measure up, do you understand?' He was speaking slowly now, as if she were dull-witted. 'You'll have to do better in future. Is that clear?' His grip on her left arm tightened into a pinch and tears sprang into her eyes.

'You're hurting me!'

He smiled, squeezed harder and repeated: 'Is that clear?'

Cowed, she nodded. His grip relaxed.

Oh, and there's another thing – those flowers you did for the table. Freesias, Anna? Hospital flowers?

Cloying, bloody freesias? Let's have something tasteful next time, shall we?'

'I thought they were lovely . . . Ow!' Another pinch.

'You're arguing,' he warned.

'Yes, all right,' she said hastily. 'I'm sorry, Guy.'

He said no more and they went to bed, but Anna spent a sleepless night. What had she let herself in for? The honeymoon was over, sure enough.

Before the month was out, she found herself in trouble once again.

One evening a couple named Gilchrist checked in. They had asked to be put in a south-facing room with twin beds, but Anna had made a mistake with the reservation.

They didn't take it well. Sarah was on duty when they arrived. She tried to pacify them, but they insisted on seeing the manager. Guy could do nothing except apologise and offer a reduction on their bill. He did it in his usual silky way, but they still went off upstairs grumbling.

As soon as they were out of earshot, he turned on Sarah, who shrank in her seat. His eyes were fierce, his neck and cheeks bloated with temper. In self-defence, she blurted swiftly:

'I didn't take the booking.'

'No? Who did?'

Her eyes darted this way and that.

'Sarah!'

'Mrs Buckman,' she answered, starting as if at the flick of a belt.

His colour was close to maroon. He glared at her a moment. 'Show me the booking chart.'

She held it out. He snatched it from her and slapped

it down on the counter. Tracing his finger down and across the grid, he found the day's date and the name of the couple, 'Mr and Mrs Gilchrist'. The writing was Anna's.

Sarah watched him breathlessly, all eyes. He practically flung the chart back at her, then wheeled away from the desk and tore up the stairs two at a time.

The girl let out a shaky breath, thanking God she was not in Anna's shoes.

Anna was dressing for dinner when her husband stalked in and barked at her so loudly that she jumped and knocked over her box of face powder.

'Anna! The Gilchrists have just checked in. You made a hash of their booking, you silly bitch!'

For a moment she couldn't take it in. She stared at his reflection in her mirror. Gilchrist? Who . . .? Then she remembered.

She swung round on the little dressing table stool with its turquoise plush seat.

'But I'm sure . . .'

'Don't contradict me. I've just had to eat humble pie because of your incompetence.'

'But I was very careful to give them what they wanted. Number twelve, it was ideal.'

'Twelve would have been ideal, I agree, but you put them in fourteen. You know where fourteen is, don't you, Anna? Facing north, and it has a double bed.'

She gazed at him, puzzled, helplessly shaking her head. 'I suppose I must have misread the chart. Can't we move them?'

'Not for three days, the house is full.'

He came forward. Standing right over her, he seemed about eight feet tall, and just for a moment she felt certain he was going to hit her. But he struck with vicious words instead, laying into her with scorn.

'Do you need spectacles, Anna? Are you merely careless, or are you stupid?'

'Anyone can make an error,' she protested. 'I'm sure mine wasn't the first.'

'It had better be the last you make.'

Although she was frightened, Anna stood up. 'Or what?'

His jowls were trembling. 'Or you'll be sorry.'

There was a pause. She was quaking inside, but she said: 'You have some punishment in mind? What shall it be, since I can't be sacked?'

Guy declined to answer that. 'Idiot!' he spat. 'I had to give them the room half price. Brainless bloody woman!'

She summoned her courage. 'Don't speak to me like that!'

He grew calmer, cold. 'I'll speak to you any way I please, I'm your husband.'

With that, he left her. Anna sank down again on the little seat.

I'm your husband, I'm your boss. Was her status really much different to that of anyone on the staff? She returned to making up her face, but her hand was so unsteady now that she made a mess of it and had to start again.

Oh, she was learning all about him now, all right: the quickness of his moods, the minute-to-minute shifts from geniality to biting sarcasm, from easy humour to rage. Guy was demanding and unpredictable. Some days he was graciousness itself and full of affection. Other days he would be cool and silent, almost sulky. Anna was seldom sure what she had done to deserve either.

Most of the staff were afraid him, and no wonder. True, he never roasted anyone without some sort of cause. The trouble was, it took so little; trivial lapses were enough. Everything had to be perfect all the time, and woe betide if it were not.

At least the staff had only to please him in their work. Anna had additional duties, in bed. She cherished a hope that before too long he would want it less often, if only because the novelty wore off. Mother had always said that ardour cooled within a year. Anna fervently hoped it was true. It very quickly became exhausting, always being pulled about and pawed and ridden. Yet, it seemed impossible to refuse him. He would tell her how lovely she looked and how much he wanted her, and be so good-tempered afterwards that she felt she hadn't the heart.

Or was it the guts?

She stared at herself in the mirror. She was wearing an evening dress of jade green crêpe. And so much make-up, such a perfect hairdo. The waves and curls looked almost sculpted round her head.

It was what Guy liked. It wasn't what she liked. Once she had dreamed of being a loose-locked Bohemian – a bit like Isadora Duncan. Instead she was a fashion-plate.

What had he called her? A brainless bloody woman. And what had she been on the tennis court that day some weeks ago? Oh yes – a dumb bitch, that was it. When she was Miss Trevena, he had laughed off her awkwardness, ruffled her hair and called her his 'darling chump'. Now she was Mrs Buckman, and a dumb bitch, a brainless bloody woman.

*

In his changeable way, Guy seemed repentant afterwards. He was almost gentle in bed that night, and the next day he went out and bought her a present. It was a stuffed toy, a black and white cat with a pop-eyed face, a babyish kind of gift designed to melt the heart. Anna accepted the cat and the matter quietly blew over, but she knew there would always be a next time.

Sixteen

The name 'David Jackman' had been removed from the front of the old man's shop. In its place there was a new sign: 'Mitchell's Fine China'. A notice in the window added: *Opening Next Week.*

So that was that, the end of any hope that the place might remain an art gallery. Disconsolately, Peggy turned away and walked on along Temperance Street. She had been to Lindow's Pharmacy to buy some Pritchard's Health Salt and Benger's Food.

It was now September and she was four months pregnant. Soon the holiday people would be gone and with them the best of Hal's income for some time to come. He didn't usually sell much in the winter. They would probably have to use a bit of the money they had in the post office to see them through until next spring. Peggy hated the thought of that, but they had to pay their way.

Coming to the square, she found a small crowd gathered outside the library. They were listening to the local Liberal candidate, who was holding forth on the steps. Labour had resigned in August amid financial crisis, and Ramsay MacDonald had formed a provisional government to manage the country until the voters could have their say. Election posters for all the parties were plastered all over the town, although the result was a foregone conclusion. Maisie Angilley always voted Liberal, no matter what, and in that she was joined by almost the whole population of Trezawne.

Politics meant little or nothing to Peggy, but she stopped to listen, if only because the speaker was so impassioned about something called the Gold Standard. She didn't exactly understand what it was all about, but received a powerful feeling of threat concerning money, a message that everyone's prosperity was in grave danger. Poverty – real poverty – was something Peggy had never known. The Angilleys were scruffy, of course, but they lacked for nothing important. Peggy had always been one to compare upwards, not downwards, envying people like Anna for what they had instead of thanking her lucky stars that she wasn't ragged or hungry. Listening to the Liberal man, however, she felt for the first time ever a sense of being, perhaps, not quite so safe, though she wasn't precisely sure why. Angilley's Bazaar, after all, would always be there doing business – it was that kind of shop, stocking all sorts of things everyone needed. She supposed the disappointment over Hal's lost exhibition had shaken her complacency a bit, and the general talk of depression, debt and unemployment chimed with her expectation of lean months ahead.

Finding the speaker too dispiriting, Peggy continued on her way. Across the square was the *Rex*, Trezawne's little cinema. *The Blue Angel* with Marlene Dietrich was on that week and she paused to look at the billboard outside. Peggy loved the talkies. She was thinking she might ask Hal to take her to see it that evening, when a voice from behind enquired of her:

'Having another one, Peggy? So soon?'

She turned, and there stood Ruby Tabb, clothed in

a limp brown dress and an old cloche hat which flattered her not at all. Peggy frowned at her.

'What?'

'Another baby already?' Ruby nodded at the little bulge that was starting to show under Peggy's frock.

'It's eighteen months since Joy was born.' The reply was somewhat testy. Peggy was vexed to be caught unawares. Had she spotted Ruby first, she would have taken steps to avoid her.

'As I say, not very long.'

Ruby ran critical eyes over her, thinking Peggy's dress too pink, the fabric too thin-looking. Peggy tended to give an impression of wearing no undergarments. No doubt she did wear them, conceded Ruby. All the same, there was often the look of a single flimsy layer over bare flesh.

'Does my condition trouble you for any reason, Ruby?'

Miss Tabb made a careless face. 'I was only thinking how much children cost to raise. Must be frightening, especially in these hard times.'

'People manage – people far worse off than us.'

'Not too well, some of them,' Ruby sniffed. 'Cut your pattern according to your cloth, I always say. Still, if you and Hal feel you can afford it, that's all right.'

'Thank you so much. I'm glad you don't mind.'

The sarcasm bounced off Ruby. 'I suppose your mother's taking care of the little girl this morning?'

'Hal's looking after her.'

'Really?' Ruby's eyebrows lifted. 'Fancy. Not many men will play nanny, but of course, he's different, isn't he, being at home such a lot?'

'I expect that's why she loves him so,' said Peggy

levelly. 'She's more her daddy's girl than mine, you know.'

That was the plain truth. The baby favoured her father and would always go to him when given the choice.

'Some men are great big children themselves,' said Ruby drily. 'That's why they get on well with other kiddies, don't you think?'

'What would you know about men or children?' Peggy asked sweetly, and turned to walk on.

'Enough to avoid them both, dear,' Ruby called.

Peggy responded to that with a short, hollow chuckle. Ruby Tabb had been jilted in youth and everyone knew it. She'd been taking it out on the whole world ever since, making a dead set at anyone who was lucky enough to be happy. Knowing this, Peggy wondered why it should be that Ruby so frequently needled her. Possibly because she did have a way of prodding a person's own little doubts and anxieties. Hal, it was true, was a great big kid in many ways. The needs of children were indeed endless and expensive. And these, as the Liberal said, were uncertain times.

Oddly unsettled, Peggy went home. She was almost there when she heard a ringing of bells, and around the corner beside the bazaar appeared Kelly's ice-cream cart. Cheered to see it, Peggy bought penny cornets for herself and Hal and Joy and Maisie. No ice-cream anywhere compared to Kelly's, she thought, as she went indoors licking her cone. It was rich and yellow, almost, but not quite, like frozen custard.

Hal didn't want his ice-cream, so she polished it off herself and then sat down to a lunch of cold pork, mashed potatoes and spinach, followed by a bowl of figgy pudding. She was eating voraciously now, with a special appetite for sweet stuff. At all hours of the day she would nibble and pick and make little snacks to stand by her. Her favourite was what Maisie called 'thunder and lightning' – bread spread with treacle and clotted cream. Second to that came hard-boiled eggs and mustard, and she always had room to squeeze in a taste of salted whiting, a few cockles, or a chunk of heavy cake.

'It'll be a boy, all right,' said Maisie, as she watched her daughter take a second helping of the plum pudding. 'The way you're eating, I'm starting to wonder if there's more than one in there. You might be having enough to crew a boat.'

Peggy looked up, horrified. 'Lord, Mother, don't say such things!'

'I wouldn't mind,' said Maisie cheerfully. She was sitting opposite, cutting up newspaper into squares to use in the lavatory. A big bundle lay on the table in front of her. The top sheet bore a photograph of Oswald Mosley.

'I don't think I want more than two children,' muttered Peggy. 'Not until we're better off, at any rate. I met Ruby Tabb today. She was saying about the expense . . .'

A snort cut through her words. 'You ought to know better than to take any notice of her.'

'She wasn't wrong, though, and Father's moaning as it is because I'm having a second one.'

'What does that matter? Since when did he have any say in this house?'

'I'm just thinking about the sniping,' sighed Peggy. 'It wears me down sometimes.'

'Mmph.' Her mother paused to save an article about the King, the lavatory pan being no place for royalty. 'Lily Greasypockets said to me I should throw that pair out of here to make more room for you. If it really came down to it, Peggy, if I were forced to a choice, you know, I'd do that.'

Peggy wasn't really listening. 'I wish, too, that we had a steady income,' she mused. 'I wish I could always be sure that a nice sum was coming in on a regular day every week.'

Laying down her scissors, Maisie looked at her uneasily. 'Now, Peggy, what's brought this on? Ruby Tabb?'

'Not altogether. I was listening to the Liberal making a speech in town today. I got . . .' She struggled briefly. 'Well, I can only call it a bad feeling. I felt a bit frightened all of a sudden, about the future.'

'In what way?'

Again, Peggy was hard put to explain her anxiety. It wasn't as if she had any past troubles to haunt her. Her marriage had been untouched by adversity, and she'd always taken security for granted . . .

But that was it, wasn't it?

She said: 'It hit me, I think, that no matter how good they seem, things can all go wrong unexpectedly. Do you know what I mean?'

Reaching across the table, Maisie stroked her face. 'I think I do, and I think it's because you've grown up and you have more than just yourself to worry about, especially now there's another baby coming. But, Peggy, nothing's going to change, love. What could happen, you silly thing?'

'I don't know,' shrugged Peggy. 'Perhaps I'm being

superstitious, thinking Hal and I have been too happy or something like that.'

Her mother took up the scissors again and went on cutting. 'Don't go talking that way, maid,' she said, half-teasing. 'Don't let trouble know you're looking for it.'

Seventeen

That autumn, Anna learned that she too was expecting a child.

'Congratulations, Mrs Buckman,' the doctor said. 'You may expect the birth around the middle of next May. Does your husband know you've come to see me?'

'No.'

'Well, I'm sure he'll be delighted, won't he? Been treating the Buckmans for years, you know. In fact, I delivered Guy.'

This with a complacent smile. Anna didn't care for Doctor Churcher, but Guy had pressed her to register with him because he was a family friend. Churcher was one of those 'top-of-town' people and she sensed he had chosen his career for the money and status it brought, rather than any love for his fellow man. He was good, of course, in terms of efficiency, but not a sympathetic person. Under the polished manner, Anna perceived a hard man, a mechanic, to whom bodies were much like engines, to be serviced and repaired. When, eventually, they had to be scrapped, he was unperturbed. He would doubtless accept his own demise with similar aplomb.

The mention of his long association with the Buckmans prompted her to venture a question.

'You remember Mrs Buckman, then? I've heard all about it, of course.'

'Hmm.' The doctor pursed his mouth. 'Very

unfortunate. I assured her she was perfectly healthy. I thought she believed me. Didn't question what I told her, not outwardly, anyway. There's nothing a doctor can do if a patient's determined to think she's ill.'

He spoke with the air of an oracle who was peeved at being doubted.

'She must have been very depressed,' said Anna.

'Yes, she was. It was all very difficult for Matthew. The arthritis was really beginning to get a grip on him at that time. The last thing he needed was a neurotic wife.'

Anna stared at him, astonished at his callousness. The doctor's gaze flickered a little.

'I realise what a tragedy it was, but . . .' He spread his hands. 'It was all fancy, morbid imaginings. I'm not a psychiatrist, I only deal in genuine bodily ills. She'd be alive today if she'd shown more concern for her husband and been less preoccupied with herself. She knew that Matthew needed her. She knew the disease was going to cripple him. Fine time to leave him, don't you think?'

No compassion for that tormented woman, only for Matthew and his needs. The husband had to be taken care of, but the wife had failed in her duty, wallowed in her own pain instead of attending him. Wicked, wicked woman, to forget the order of things and who should come first.

Anna left the surgery wishing she had stayed with her old physician.

The walk to Elestren Manor was nearly all downhill. Guy had taught her to drive, but she had little confidence at the wheel and rarely used the car for fear of damaging it. In no great hurry to get home, she wandered along the road from the doctor's house. It was now October, and the trees in this affluent part of town were decked in orange and crimson. Leaves fell around her as she walked, showering gold upon her head. The wind made them dance around her feet, and piled them up in corners to look like treasure hoards. Anna cut quite an autumnal figure herself, dressed in a rust-brown coat. Elegant Anna, always impeccably turned out these days.

Nothing less would satisfy Guy.

It was now something over six months since their wedding. Anna was scarcely surprised to find herself pregnant. Indeed, she was almost amazed that it had taken as long as this, in view of her husband's appetite for sex. Anna never called it lovemaking. It was far too earthy for that, too ruttish.

How did she feel about the baby? Anna mused on that as she dawdled along. She was aware of pride, and a feeling of adulthood. Then there were pleasant prospects of someone to love and to love her. Also, she perceived certain side benefits. An excuse to keep Guy at bay for the next few months – at the very least to temper his assaults. She was, after all, in a 'delicate' condition and would have to be treated accordingly. And when the baby arrived, she might escape work in the office, where at any time a blunder could get her into trouble.

Yet, something worried her, prowling her mind unseen like a cat in the undergrowth. At first she couldn't quite draw it out into the light to be examined. It had to do with power, or the lack of it. Yes, being dependent. Children 'set the seal' on a marriage, didn't they? Once a woman had children, she was completely trapped.

Fatherhood, of course, might have a mellowing effect

on Guy. Anna dwelt hopefully on the idea as she made her way back to Elestren Manor.

When she reached the hotel and went in the front door, he was standing in the hall, talking with a smart young woman at the reception desk. Being his most boyish and engaging, for the benefit of a lady guest. Behind the desk, Sarah was working diligently at her ledger.

Buckman saw his wife come in. His glance flitted over her, top-to-toe, and something went from his smile. Following his gaze, the guest looked round at Anna.

'Mrs McSorley,' said Guy, 'this is Anna, my wife.'

The woman acknowledged Anna in friendly fashion.

'Mrs McSorley and her husband will be dining with us this evening, Anna,' he informed her.

'Lovely,' said Anna, on cue. 'I look forward to that.'

'So do I,' said Mrs McSorley pleasantly. 'Well now, if you'll excuse me . . .'

'See you later,' called Guy.

The woman turned and gave a little wave as she skipped off upstairs. The second she was out of sight, Guy's smile was replaced with something near a scowl.

'For God's sake, Anna,' he muttered, 'that lipstick! What's it called? Streetwalker Pink? What must Mrs McSorley have thought of you?'

It was not the first time he had astounded her with something like this, but it still took her breath away.

Behind her counter, Sarah kept her head down and scribbled furiously.

'It doesn't even go with the coat,' he hissed.

'I'm sorry, I thought it did.'

'Colour-blindness coming on?'

She was silent, her face burning red. In front of Sarah. Why did he have to do it in front of Sarah?

'Don't use it again,' he instructed coldly.

'Don't worry, I shan't.' She was furious, hating him. Thoughts of the baby had briefly been driven from her mind. Now she remembered it and said stiffly: 'I've something to tell you. Come upstairs.'

'I'm busy, tell me here.'

'If you insist. I'm pregnant,' she snapped, and turned on her heel.

Sarah's head jerked up and a smile lit her face. She was about to say 'Congratulations', but Anna was already halfway up the stairs.

Stalking along to the flat, she went in and slammed the door. Taking off her coat, she went into the bathroom and patted some cold water over her flaming cheeks. Angrily, she scrubbed off the lipstick, using the back of her hand.

Five minutes later, Guy came up. He was looking sheepish.

'Anna? Is it true? A baby?'

'Why would I lie?' She was sitting, straight-backed, in an armchair, her face rigid.

Suddenly he was all smiles, his nastiness – and any thought of apology for it – forgotten.

'Well, that's grand!'

He came and lifted her to her feet, rewarding her with a smothering kiss that made her fear he might want to take her to bed there and then. Pulling back, she wriggled out of his grasp.

'What's the matter?'

'You know what goes with pregnancy. I feel a bit queasy.'

'Ah.' A nod. 'Yes, you'll have to take it easy, won't you?'

She seized on that. 'I think it would be wise.'

'When's it due?'

'Late spring.'

'Hope it's a boy,' Guy said, grinning. 'I'd love a son.'

'Can't make any promises, I'm afraid. I've no preference myself.'

Or did she? It suddenly occurred to her that she would rather the child was a girl, as if another female, no matter how small, would be an ally. Once more, that part of her mind which was deep and astute was putting two and two together.

'We'll turn the dressing-room into a nursery for him,' Guy said brightly. 'I'm going out this very day to buy him a rocking-horse.'

Anna felt her anger ebb. He was getting carried away now, behaving like a large, over-enthusiastic schoolboy. Guy was always disarming when he started being coltish.

'Don't you think that's a bit premature?'

'I don't care. I'll get him a cricket bat while I'm at it.'

'Guy, it might be a daughter.'

'Nonsense. I must buy some shin-pads too, and a rugby ball . . .'

Despite herself, Anna started to laugh. 'You're ridiculous.'

He seized her, swung her off her feet and whirled her round and round. 'We'll call him Robin,' he persisted.

'And I suppose you'll put his name down for your old school?'

The spinning ceased. 'No, I think not. There are plenty of good schools closer to home. An excellent one at Tavistock, I believe.'

'Well, that's a bridge we won't have to cross for a long time yet,' said Anna, sitting down again.

Guy came and squatted in front of her, his face on a level with hers, his smile so wide and ingenuous now, she could forgive him almost anything. 'I'll have to get you some special clothes,' he said. 'Baggy ones.'

'Oh Lord, not yet!'

Putting out a hand, he pressed it flat against her belly. 'No, you're right. Not yet.' Then his forehead creased, became thoughtful. The hand moved down.

'Guy, don't,' she said quickly.

He blinked. What was in his mind was on his face, as plain as day. Then he voiced it.

'We can still make love?'

'Well – not so much, perhaps, for a while. I think it would be better.'

'Later on. It can't matter now.'

'It might.' She feared to lose her advantage. Closing her hand over his, she tried to force it away.

'What did Doctor Churcher say?'

'I never thought to ask him, but . . .'

'I'm sure it must be safe enough.'

'Yes, but not so much, as I said.'

In a space of seconds, his face showed alarm, then sulkiness, then calculation.

'There are special ways. I've heard about that. I'll find out. I'm sure Doctor Churcher can advise us.'

Anna smiled wanly. Perhaps as time went on, she thought, as her belly swelled, he would want her less. After all, he liked her perfect, didn't he?

'I couldn't do without you, you know. My lovely, lovely wife.'

Now he was at his most appealing. Still, the words

reminded her of what had occurred downstairs at the desk, and she couldn't resist a reproachful dig at him.

'Your colour-blind wife, who wears tarty lipstick.'

Guy made a face of embarrassment and sat back on his heels. 'I'm sorry, I over-reacted.' He spread his arms wide. 'Forgive me! What can I do to make amends?'

'Think up an excuse and let me off having dinner this evening with the – what was the name of those people?'

'Mr and Mrs McSorley' He regarded her with the trace of a frown. 'They're a very nice couple.'

'I'm sure they are, but I'd much rather have something up here on a tray.'

Hesitation. She thought he was going to argue.

'Please, Guy.'

'Very well. We must spoil you, mustn't we? No stress and strain.' He patted her stomach again. 'Above all, we must take good care of my son.'

It was not an easy pregnancy. Anna had heartburn very badly and her back and legs began to ache from the fifth month onwards. Judging by the rate at which she filled out, the baby promised to be large, which confirmed Guy in his belief that they would have a son. Being tall and normally slender, with small hips, Anna viewed the birth with trepidation. Nonsense, Doctor Churcher scoffed. She was a fine, strong woman and should have no trouble at all. Anna certainly looked robust as she put on weight. Combined with her height, the extra girth gave an impression of solidness, but underneath it was a light and narrow frame which found the weight of the child and the extra flesh a tremendous strain.

She hated the visits to Doctor Churcher for check-ups. Guy insisted on going along with her, and she always suffered a terrible sense of helplessness when shut in the doctor's office with the two men – rather like a breeding animal attended by a couple of farmers. Doctor Churcher was very jolly and encouraging, while Guy had the air of a proud proprietor and kept asking earnest questions about Anna's welfare and that of the child. Sometimes she told herself she was being silly and ought to feel grateful to have a husband so involved and so concerned. Yet, she could never quite shake off the feeling of being something similar to a prize cow with a valuable calf inside her. Guy and the doctor did most of the talking, discussing her while she just sat there, or tried in vain to get in a word herself. When she did manage to say or ask something, Churcher usually managed to make her appear a bit foolish, laughing off her anxieties, or explaining things with exaggerated patience. She always emerged from the surgery very subdued.

As Anna grew bigger, Guy bought her a lot of maternity dresses. In truth, she didn't feel very much like bothering with her appearance, but he would tut and chivvy her if she didn't keep her appointments with the hairdresser, or failed to put on her make-up each morning.

'Come on, sweetheart,' he would say, 'the better you look, the better you'll feel. Make the effort. You're always glad afterwards, aren't you?'

She was glad to have him stop nagging her, so she took the line of least resistance. Guy was always amiable, so long as he got his way. He was all affection these days, and called her his 'clever girl'. Indeed, he had been amazingly even-tempered ever since he learned of the baby. Of course, he had not been deprived of very much sex, thanks to helpful Doctor Churcher. Had that been denied him, his mood would have been less sunny.

Eighteen

Winter drew in. Lower Trezawne was a different place entirely during the cold months, eerily quiet and seeming half deserted. There was greyness of sky and sea and stone, a chill and a smell of chimney smoke on the air. Victoria Pier was forsaken and the colourful pleasure ferries were gone, laid up until the spring. Stabled at a nearby farm, Jack Tresize's donkeys were enjoying a few lazy months. The Punch and Judy man's puppets and tent were packed away in a hamper in his cellar, while he returned to cleaning windows until the new season brought his audience back. Stripped of all the gaudy paraphernalia hanging outside, Angilley's Bazaar looked dowdy and much in need of paint.

Up to Christmas, there were fogs and lowering clouds. Then the New Year arrived with shrieking gales, waves smacking over the harbour wall and showering all the houses along the waterfront.

It was on such a day that Peggy had her second child. He took his mother by surprise, not even giving her time to get to the hospital. At seven that February morning, Hal went scurrying up Pawlyn's Hill in the lashing rain to fetch the doctor. Angilley's Bazaar stood stolidly facing a surging high tide. The winds howled around it, rattling the shutters, and soon they were joined by wails from within. From behind a first-floor window came the squalling of a newborn boy. By the time Hal returned with Doctor Wilson, Maisie was already wrapping him up.

'I've seen a cat take longer having kittens,' she told the doctor merrily.

Tired and sweat-soaked, Peggy was dozing. The room looked like a butcher's shop. One glance and Hal retreated, having no stomach for gore. He returned a couple of hours later, after the doctor had left and all trace of the mess had disappeared.

'Well,' said Peggy, 'we've got our son. What do you want to call him?'

Pushing aside the blanket, he peeped at the mewing, red-faced infant and grinned. 'He looks just like my dad. How about Ewan? That's Father's name.'

'It's nice,' agreed Peggy. 'Yes, why not? Ewan Pentreath – sounds good.'

Eyeing her sideways, Hal ventured: 'Perhaps it might be tactful to add "Walter" too? Might make the old devil feel better disposed towards the kid?'

'I doubt it,' grunted Peggy. 'Anyway, it's not a name I like, and the old man isn't stupid. He'd know why we'd done it.'

'To offer an olive branch. What's wrong with that?'

'No, Hal, I don't want any child of mine named after Father. It won't win him over, believe you me.' Pondering briefly, she suggested: 'How about Ewan David, to remember Mr Jackman?'

'Yes, that would be nice.'

'Ewan David it is, then.'

'He's a fine, big baby,' Hal observed.

'Nine pounds three ounces,' supplied Peggy proudly. 'Must have been all that cream and treacle.' Then her smile faded. Absently, she fingered the baby's nose and his tiny right hand. 'I saw Anna in town last week.

174

She's expecting, too. Sometime quite soon, by the look of her.'

Hal's grey eyes regarded her placidly. 'Is she? So?'

'Her child will have all the advantages, won't he? Privileges we'll never be able to afford for ours.'

'Certain things, yes,' he admitted. 'You're not going to fret about that, are you, Peggy? Please, no comparing our children, maid.'

'I'm sorry, but I couldn't help thinking that her offspring are bound to be more – secure.'

'Quite possibly spoilt, and not necessarily happier, Peggy.'

'Mm.' The sound remained sceptical. Sighing, she confessed: 'I've been edgy these past few months, worried a bit about money.'

'Things will pick up, we'll get by.'

Peggy kissed him. 'Yes, of course.'

Secretly, however, she couldn't help feeling that 'getting by' came a poor second when Anna's child was going to be born into plenty.

Thoughtfully, Hal said once more: 'You're sure about the name? We could make it Ewan David Walter. Wouldn't do any harm.'

She made an impatient gesture. 'No, it's pointless, Hal. To tell you the truth, I'd be horrified if Father took a fancy to him and the boy grew up fond of his grandad. I mean, just see what the old man's done to Jasper.'

On that score, there was nothing to fear. Walter didn't conceive the slightest liking for his grandson, especially since Ewan soon made it clear that he wasn't going to be a quiet child.

'Oh, dear God, does it never stop?' Angilley grumbled

one night in bed, as a raucous howling started up for the third time in an hour. 'Nobody's had a good night's sleep since that little bugger arrived.'

It was just past midnight. Maisie was sitting up in bed beside him, placidly sucking some toffee and reading a romance. She was addicted to romances; they were just about all she knew of attractive, courtly men. Walter, lounging alongside, smelt like a drip tray. Coarse, greying chest hair frizzed round the neck and armholes of his vest. Hauling himself half upright, he reached irritably for his tobacco tin.

'All babies cry,' mumbled Maisie through her toffee. 'I expect he's hungry, poor little mite.'

'He must be hungry all the bloody time.' Walter took the lid off his tin, wherein he had hoarded some dogends. He started pulling them apart, extracting the morsels of tobacco and laying them upon a fresh cigarette paper. 'We never had this sort of trouble with Jasper – nor even with her.' He jerked a thumb towards his daughter's room.

'Jasper's created noise enough since to make up for it ten times over.'

'We shouldn't have to be putting up with this sort of thing at our age.'

Maisie calmly turned a page. 'Doesn't bother me.'

'Well, I've got a headache.'

'That's your own fault, that's the beer.'

'And I've got to be up in the morning,' Walter whined.

'Mmph. First job you've had in five weeks.'

He teased the shreds of tobacco into a line, rolled the paper and licked it. Sticking the skinny cigarette in his mouth, he put a match to the end.

'How many more's she going to have, I wonder?' he muttered.

'She can have as many as she wants, and they'll be welcome here,' came the stout reply.

'Not in my book, they won't. Oh God . . .' He clenched a fist and thumped the bed as the screaming went up an octave. 'Why doesn't she get out and tend to him?'

'She's tired. A teasy baby wears a woman out.'

Walter snorted smoke down his nostrils and glowered at a damp stain on the wall. Behind him on the corner of the brass bedstead hung his cap. It was always the first thing he donned in the morning, the last he took off at night.

'It's time they found a place of their own,' he said.

'They will, when they can afford it.'

'They've got money put away, I know they have. Over a hundred pound, they've got.'

Maisie put her book down and stared at him, hard. 'How do you know that?'

'Came across her post office book one day not long ago.'

'She keeps that in her dressing table. You purposely went through her things!'

'Well, he had those exhibitions and I know he sold a lot. I was wondering where the money went.'

'They're saving up to buy a place,' snapped Maisie. 'And until they've got enough, they're staying here!'

'Buy,' snorted Walter. 'What's wrong with renting? They could move out tomorrow and rent a place. Poor Jasper could have his room back then and we'd all have some peace and quiet. He's your own son, your flesh and blood . . .'

'There's more of you than me in him.'

Across the landing, the wailing continued. Then Jasper's door was heard to open and his voice to yell:

'Shut that bloody kid up, will you? Shut the bugger up!'

Immediately, another door swished back. Hal's voice answered, low and threatening.

'One more word and I'll shut both your eyes for you.'

The bang of his door and the click of the catch signalled a hasty retreat on Jasper's part.

Walter glanced at Maisie. She was smiling, still reading her novel. Silence had at least descended. The baby was being fed.

Walter dourly drew on his cigarette. The end of it was growing soggy and starting to come apart. He spat a bit of the paper out and rolled the remaining stub between finger and thumb, contemplating it with narrowed eyes.

Oh, he'd throw them out of here, given half a chance. He'd send them packing, Peggy and Hal and their brats.

'Buy a house,' he sneered again. 'Big ideas, big talk, with nothing much to back it up. He hasn't been doing half so well since old man Jackman died.'

That was the truth and Maisie had no answer for it. Her eyes stayed stubbornly fixed on her book.

'Peggy'll wait a damned long time for that house, I'm telling you. And if she ever gets it, he won't be able to pay the bills. He's just as dependent on you as Jasper or me. I dare say he could get by on his own, but he couldn't support a wife and two kids without your help, and you know it. You just like having them here, that's all it is, keeping Peggy close to you and having the babies around. They can stay for good and always, as far as you're concerned. You don't mind subsidising them. It's me and Jasper get all the abuse.'

Laying her book down, Maisie skewered him with a

piercing glare. 'Peggy cooks and shops and cleans, and she serves downstairs. Hal gives me money each week for their food – which is more than you can say – and I tell him it's ample. They never borrow cash from me, nor shame me in front of other people. Yes, I let them live cheap, so they can save a bit. Yes, I know they'd have a job to manage on their own. But I don't feel like stamping on Hal's pride or Peggy's little dreams. Life does that to most of us soon enough. They may or may not get their house, but I won't kill any chance they have by shoving them out of here while he's still struggling.'

'He'll always be struggling, I reckon,' was Walter's reply.

'He'll always be making an effort, and that's enough to please me.'

Nineteen

All the discomfort of Anna's pregnancy finally seemed worthwhile when she too was rewarded with a son. He was born on 18 May at the local hospital, and they called him Robin, just as his father wanted. A beautiful baby, all the nurses said, eight pounds at birth and crowned with a silky growth of pale blond hair. Anna was enchanted by him, and Guy received him with complacent pride. Of course it was a boy, a handsome boy, another fine male Buckman. Facially, the child resembled Anna, but his father didn't mind. Guy was as breezy as Anna had ever seen him, completely delighted with his son. He kept telling her how clever she was and how proud she'd made him.

'Would you like me to hire a nanny to help you out?' he asked when he came to visit.

'Oh no,' she said quickly. 'Share him with another woman? I wouldn't dream of it. I want to do everything for him myself.'

'I knew you'd be a wonderful mother.'

He squeezed her hand, and then he kissed it. His mouth felt thick and soft and there was the tiniest prickle of stubble. He had brought her two dozen red roses and a solid gold bracelet with broad, flat links. Always a man of extremes, doting when she was in favour, cruel when she was not.

'Of course,' she ventured, 'you won't expect me to do so much now around the hotel?'

'All right. No more shifts in the office, I know how you hate it. Not so many dinner parties, either.'

'Thank you,' she said gratefully.

The baby began to whimper and fret, his face screwing up till he looked like a gnome.

'He wants to be fed,' murmured Anna.

Guy glanced at the clock. 'And it's time I went. In a moment they'll be here to throw me out.'

Sure enough, a nurse came in as he rose to leave. He passed a few engaging words with her as he went through the door, and the girl could be seen to simper. Beaming, she came to the foot of the bed, as Anna unbuttoned her nightdress and began to suckle the baby.

'Your husband's very attractive, isn't he? Aren't you lucky, Mrs Buckman? And now a beautiful son as well. Children are such a blessing, aren't they? Heavens, I do envy you.'

A blessing. Yes, thought Anna hopefully. Life could be better for her from now on. Robin might make a big difference.

And so he did. Three months went by, three very happy months for Anna. She spent most of her time with the baby, and Guy hardly troubled her to do anything else about the place. The life of Elestren Manor went on in the background of her own. In the main she kept to the private rooms and the quieter parts of the garden, and had little to do with the guests.

When Anna wanted an hour or two to herself, Mrs Roseveare minded the baby. Robin Andrew Matthew Buckman, that was what they had christened him. The housekeeper, having no children herself, was besotted by him.

One afternoon in August, Anna left him in her care and went out for a walk in the grounds. In the shade beneath the rhododendrons, she had noticed a narrow path. It went straight along level ground for half a mile, and then downhill to the stream which ran through the grounds of Elestren Manor. There, the track turned to the right and continued some way along the grassy bank between thinly spaced trees. At the water's edge were delicate ferns, and the stream moved sedately over its pebble bed. This was the lower end of a watercourse locally known as the leat. It came down from a source on Bodmin Moor, running past the parish churchyard and onwards down through the town, going underground for part of the way. Then it cut through the woods of Elestren Manor before flowing seawards.

Anna rambled along the bank for about a hundred yards, then saw that the stream passed under a bridge some way ahead. She walked along to it, and found it sound enough except for a single rotten plank. Looking across to the other side, she saw an area which had plainly been cultivated once but had now run wild. There were shaggy stands of azaleas and pale pink rhododendrons, but among them and over them sprang a vigorous growth of weeds. Yarrow was mixed with red campion. Convolvulus and briar rose twined everywhere, and brambles and honeysuckle tumbled over some sort of wooden structure a few yards back from the bank.

Curious, she went across and stopped at the end of the bridge. She could see now what the wooden structure was – a summerhouse. Anna moved forward, pushing the weeds and long grass aside, threading her way towards it. She found the doorway blocked by a tangle of bramble. Peering in through a window filmy with dirt, she could see a wicker table and chairs. On the table was a basket, and beside it lay a pair of pruning shears.

Odd, Anna thought, that this little garden was left untended. It had a soothing, private air, as if it were someone's secret place, a retreat.

Returning across the bridge, she began to make her way homewards, meaning to ask Guy about it. However, before she had gone very far, a figure appeared along the bank of the leat.

It was the gardener, Mr Hoblyn. A sighting of him was a rarity – almost like spotting some wild creature which seldom broke cover or moved about by day. Anna watched him shambling towards her. He was all boots, braces and earthy trousers. His jacket pockets bulged as if he had roots and tubers in them.

'Afternoon, Missis,' he said to her.

'Good afternoon, Mr Hoblyn.' She pointed back down the track. 'I've just discovered the little overgrown garden across the stream.'

'Oh,' he said, 'yes. That was the poor lady's garden.'

'Poor lady?'

'Why, your husband's mother, Mrs Buckman. Used to spend a good many hours there, 'specially towards the end of her life, when she was so very troubled. You know all about her, I expect?'

A memory flashed in Anna's mind, clicked with the basket and pruning shears she had seen in the summerhouse. They were those in the photograph of Helen Buckman.

'Indeed. It was very sad.'

'Her little hideaway, that was,' said Mr Hoblyn. 'I let it run wild when she'd gone. I still think of it as hers, not for other people. Nobody much comes down here, anyway.' he added, pursing his mouth. 'Not even Mr Buckman cares about it.'

Helen Buckman's garden. Now Anna knew what it was she had sensed in the atmosphere of the place. She remembered, too, Mrs Roseveare's words:

'Used to go off by herself for hours and hours at a time in all weathers.'

To the summerhouse, of course.

Mr Hoblyn was hovering, looking at Anna, his cap in his hand. He suddenly interrupted her thoughts with a question.

'Like dogs, do you, Missis?'

'What?' She shook herself. 'Oh – to tell the truth, I've never had much to do with them.'

'Never had a pet, maid?'

'No. Why do you ask?'

His brown face grew eager and hopeful. 'Well, it's like this. My old mongrel's had a litter of puppies. I can keep one, but I can't afford the other two, so I'm looking to place them in good homes. I was wondering if you and Mr Buckman would like one? Be nice company for the little boy as he grows. Handsome pups, they are.'

'Oh,' said Anna, 'I don't know. It's a nice idea, but I'd have to ask my husband.'

'Understood. That's understood, but come and see them, will you? They're all in a box in the potting shed. Won't take more than fifteen minutes. If you can't have one, Missis, perhaps you know someone who will. I think it's likely to be the poor old girl's last litter. I couldn't stand to have any of them destroyed.'

Anna felt she couldn't very well say no, so she went with him. Mr Hoblyn's shed was in a corner of the rose garden at the side of the hotel. He opened the door and motioned her inside.

The place was crammed with rusty tools and flower pots. On a blanket crumpled up in a shallow wooden box lay a sad-eyed mongrel bitch and three squirming balls of fluff.

'Oh . . .' Anna crouched down, stretching out a hand to fondle a fawn-coloured pup. 'Oh yes, they are lovely, I must say.'

The gardener knelt beside the box, picked up a black one and held it for her to see. 'There,' he said, 'he's a beauty. Wouldn't you like him, Missis?'

The bitch whined and whimpered anxiously. Mr Hoblyn put the puppy back and lifted out the third, which was white with brown ears.

Anna sighed. 'I'm tempted, I admit, but it's up to Guy. Which one do you want to keep for yourself?'

'It doesn't matter.'

'Will they grow very large?'

'No bigger than she is.' He jerked his head at the mother.

Anna stood up, eyes fixed on the puppies. She wanted one, all right. Mr Hoblyn had known when he brought her here – one look and she would be lost.

'That little fawn one . . .' she mused.

'That's the female. Other two are male.' He glanced at her from the corner of his eye. 'I call her Tuffet. You might prefer something else.'

Anna debated briefly. Then: 'I'd love to have her, Mr Hoblyn, but I can't give you my answer now.'

'That's all right, that's all right. I'll hold on to her, and you speak to your husband.' Ushering her out, he repeated: 'Lovely company for the little boy.'

Anna supposed that was so, but if the truth were

told she wanted the puppy for herself. Robin might or might not be interested in it as he grew, but she wanted it, all right. Another little creature to be her own.

Guy, in one of his generous moods, hardly questioned the idea at all. The cost was of no consequence, and if she would see to its needs herself, of course she could have the dog.

'It'll be nice for Robin,' she said.

'Hmm. That remains to be seen. I never cared for pets myself, and he may be the same. But I can see you'd like the puppy and I don't mind.'

Anna collected Tuffet as soon as she was weaned and took her back to the hotel. Holding the tiny mite in one hand, Guy turned her this way and that, inspecting her, and then he grinned.

'What did you say she was called?'

'Tuffet.'

He set the dog on the floor and watched her sniffing about the room. 'Better have her neutered,' he said. Then, from his pocket, he pulled a small package and handed it to Anna. 'Here, bought this in town yesterday. You'll have to get the tag engraved.'

It was a dog collar, red leather, with a steel tag large enough for name and address.

'Oh, thank you! Guy, you do like her, don't you?'

'She's very – sweet.' His gaze followed Tuffet about with mild amusement. A toy for his wife. Pretty little dog. Silly little thing, but it pleased Anna.

Then the puppy yipped, a piercing sound of surprising volume from a creature so small. The faintest of frowns appeared on Guy's face.

'Have to keep her quiet, Anna,' he warned. 'Can't have her disturbing the residents.'

186

'Oh, of course.'

Quickly she picked up the dog and shushed her.

'No mess, either. She'll have to be strictly house-trained.'

'I'll see that she is.'

Guy smiled again and tickled the puppy under her chin. 'Quite a family now, aren't we?' he said. 'Mother, father, boy and dog – the perfect picture.'

Twenty

Since Mr Jackman's death, Hal had been granted just one small exhibition at the local library and the sales had not been good. In the summer of 1933, he therefore extended his efforts to include doing charcoal portraits for the visitors. Each afternoon, he would station himself at the end of the quay and set up a sign:

CHARCOAL PORTRAITS IN 20 MINUTES
2/-

He did very well at it, on the whole, with half a dozen customers each day. Bank holidays usually brought a bonanza – he'd find himself with quite a large audience and a queue. The August holiday that year led to something even more lucrative – a commission from an unexpected quarter.

The weather was very hot and the town was crowded. Day trippers had flocked to Trezawne by bus and excursion train. Along with them came hawkers and entertainers, eager to take advantage of the trade. An accordion player wandered up and down the waterfront, passing round a tin for coins whenever he finished a tune. A fortune-teller's booth had been set up on Victoria Pier, and a youth at the turnstile was selling coloured balloons. Stationed outside *The Old Solace*, a man was wearing a sandwich board which promised that the end was nigh and added *Ye know not the hour!* The deckchair man was charging a shilling instead of his usual ninepence, and scarcely a square yard of sand on the beach remained unoccupied. It was packed with snoozing grandmas, dozing dads in rolled-up trousers, cavorting young men and girls in swimming costumes, and busy children.

Hal had been out at the end of the quay since mid-morning. He had brought some paintings with him and lined them up against the harbour wall in the hope of attracting a buyer or two. Visitors came and stood watching him work, making comments, asking questions. Some of them told him they envied him. They said he was a lucky man and they wished they could live as he did.

Near three o'clock that day, he was engaged on a charcoal sketch of a young girl. She sat self-consciously smiling and trying to smooth her hair as it stirred in the wind. Hal worked swiftly at the portrait, shading it, gently smudging lines with the edge of his thumb or sweeping the charcoal across the paper to gain a subtle effect here, a dramatic one there. At length he considered it, then passed it to the girl for her approval.

Another satisfied customer. He always flattered the sitter a little, but more from kindness than any commercial motive. Hal could always see the favourable aspects of any face or any scene, emphasise those and diminish the less becoming ones.

Pocketing the two shillings, he invited his next subject to sit down. As he did so, he chanced to notice among the onlookers a face he knew by sight. There, with his hands in his pockets and head cocked to one side with obvious interest, stood Guy Buckman. He was wearing white casuals, as he so often did, plus a panama hat tipped to shade his eyes.

He remained, still watching, when everyone else had drifted away. As Hal accepted the florin from another delighted sitter, Buckman remarked:

'You're very good. I must say, I like your work.'

'Thank you.' Hal sat back on his folding chair, smiling up at him. So this was Anna's husband – well, he seemed a pleasant sort of man. Hal very nearly asked how she was, but something checked him. He waited to see if Guy would mention her, remark: 'I believe you know my wife,' or some such thing. But nothing came.

She may never have spoken to him of me, reflected Hal. He decided it might be tactful to hold his tongue.

'Your name's Pentreath, isn't it?' Guy enquired. 'I looked at your exhibition at the library back in March. Saw a couple of portraits in oils which I thought were quite impressive. I wonder, would you be interested in a commission?'

Suddenly, Hal had an uneasy feeling. He knew what was coming next.

'What would the subject be?' he asked.

'My wife.'

As he had guessed.

'Yes,' he said slowly, 'I see.'

'I'd be happy to spend, say, thirty guineas,' offered Guy.

Thirty. For one painting. Hal nodded and moistened his lips. He would be very glad of the money, very glad indeed. The charcoal sketches provided a nice little income, of course, but only while the visitors were about.

The fee was tempting, but Hal hesitated, perceiving

potential trouble. Would it be wise to have any contact with Anna? And how would Peggy take it?

Guy went on: 'I own and run Elestren Manor. We have a nice conservatory, and I thought you might paint her there. Good light, plenty of attractive props – greenery, wicker furniture and so on. Like to do it?'

'Umm . . .'

'I'd want my son in the portrait, too. You know the sort of thing, mother and child. He's about fifteen months, so naturally he'd fidget, I'm afraid. Would that be a problem?'

No, that put a somewhat better complexion on things. The very fact that she had a child reminded Hal that a lot of water had gone under the bridge since last he saw Anna. Indeed, it was over three years since that day at Jackman's gallery. Now she had a husband of her own, a son, and a beautiful home. No doubt she had changed a very great deal. They could probably laugh together about what had happened.

Thirty guineas. He wanted so much to accept. But then, there was Peggy to consider. She wouldn't like it . . .

Still, she didn't have to know, did she?

Hal cleared his throat. 'I think I could manage that. Short sittings are the answer with restless children, just an hour at a time to begin with. Once I have his likeness on the canvas and in my mind, I can carry on whether he's there or not.'

'Excellent,' said Guy. 'So you accept?' He held out his hand and Hal shook it. 'When can you begin?'

Hal thought for a moment. He could tell Peggy he was doing some coastal sketches out of town. Thirty guineas – how could he turn it down?

'Next Monday?' he suggested.

'Fine.'

'I'll be along mid-morning.'

'Good. Naturally, we'll give you lunch, and tea in the afternoon.'

'That's very decent of you.'

'Monday, then,' said Buckman, and went on his way.

Very agreeable chap, thought Hal. Anna must surely be happy with him. Yes, it would be all right.

The following Sunday the Buckmans were out in the garden when Guy broke the news to Anna. He was stretched out on a lounger, reading a Sunday paper. Anna was thinning out a flower bed and removing dead heads. It was her own special bed of marigolds. She had planted and brought them on herself, just for the pleasure of it. The whole bed looked like a massive gold and orange pom-pom, spiked with green. Mr Hoblyn declared that he couldn't have done a better job himself, and many of the guests had remarked how beautiful they were.

Sitting back on her haunches, she brushed the hair away from her face, thereby smearing her cheek with dirt. Robin was in his pushchair, watching her with goggle eyes. Smiling, she waved her trowel to him, then blew him a kiss.

The baby's eyes fixed intently on her. Already, a person was there behind them. Infants had often seemed to Anna like empty houses – brand new, everything functioning, but without a tenant. Not so with Robin. Someone was in residence, all right, someone very alert and eager to meet the world. Everybody called him an adorable little boy. Waves of feathery fair hair framed a truly angelic face. Like his father, he had large hazel eyes. Very intelligent eyes, quick-moving and wide with a child's curiosity. His nose was delicately shaped and had come from his mother, while the pouting cherry mouth recalled old portraits of children by Holbein. He was not a child who cried a lot; indeed, he was nearly always smiling.

Robin had much to smile about. He was far too young to know of the money his father spent on him, but his world was full of fascinating things which sparkled or tinkled or delighted his eyes with bright colours, things which felt soft and warm, or smelt nice or tasted good. There was always something new, and life was all pleasant sensations. Robin had never been left to cry at night, never suffered a wet nappy for any length of time. Anna was always there to attend to him the moment he whimpered. He was picked up and carried around a lot, he was sung to and tickled and endlessly admired. Robin was used to cooing voices, beaming faces.

A butterfly wafted past him. Robin reached out a fat little hand, staring after it, amazed, as it flitted away.

'What was that, then?' Anna asked him. 'That was a flutterby, that was. Pretty-pretty.'

Guy turned a page of his paper. 'Don't teach him silly talk like that,' he sighed.

'Daddy's being grumpy,' confided Anna to the tot.

'No, I'm not.' The paper moved aside. 'People speak to children as if they're idiots. It's a wonder that more of them don't grow up soft in the head.' Frowning, he added: 'Good Lord, Anna, you're sweating, and covered in earth. For the life of me, I can't understand why you want to do that when we have a gardener.'

She wiped her forehead with her sleeve. 'I enjoy it. There's a special satisfaction in seeing things grow which you've planted yourself. Haven't you ever tried it?'

'God, no! Couldn't be bothered. Still, if you want to strain your back and your knees and get grubby, that's up to you.'

'It's worth it. It's such a pleasure to watch the shoots grow strong and see the buds unfolding.'

He yawned. 'If you say so.' Glancing towards the pushchair, he grinned at his son. 'What do you think, Robin, eh? Too much like hard work? Yes. Isn't Mummy silly?'

A squealing giggle came from the child.

'Mummy gets funny ideas in her head sometimes,' continued Guy. 'Just like a woman, don't you agree?'

Robin listened attentively, the plump mouth brightly smiling. They were gazing at one another – almost communing. The baby had a tremendous rapport with his father.

Then Guy said: 'By the way, Anna, I hope you've no plans for tomorrow or the rest of next week.'

She looked at him. 'Why?'

'I'm going to have your portrait painted, you and Robin together. The artist will be here in the morning. Local chap, called Pentreath.'

Her stare grew fixed.

'Well, what's the matter? I thought you'd be pleased. He's very good.'

Anna swallowed. 'I, uh . . . When did you arrange this?'

'Saw him last week.'

'Why didn't you tell me before?'

'Forgot about it. I thought the conservatory would be a nice setting. You can wear your white lace frock,

194

you look lovely in that.' He disappeared once more behind his paper.

Anna stood up. 'Was he – keen – to do it?'

'He didn't take much persuading. Shouldn't think he would – I offered him thirty guineas.'

She was silent. Hal, coming here, to paint her? A peculiar blend of alarm and excitement assailed her. Part of her was horrified and fearful of what might result. Still abashed over Peggy's portrait, she wondered how she would face him. What was more, it had taken her long enough to settle into this new life. Since the birth of the baby she'd felt more content, more at ease. The last thing she needed now was anything to disturb her. Yet, she wanted to see him. The thought of it electrified her, just as the sight of a drink might scare and thrill a reformed alcoholic.

'Whatever made you think of doing that?'

Absorbed in the financial pages, Guy did not look up.

'I'm proud of my wife and son,' he murmured absently.

'You could have us photographed. That would be so much cheaper and quicker. Robin will hate sitting still, you know.'

'You'll have to be firm with him. It'll only be an hour at a time.'

She took off her gardening gloves and sat down in a bamboo chair. Tuffet was lying underneath it, resting her chin on her paws. A placid creature, devoted to Anna, she had grown to the size of a cocker spaniel. Sometimes Guy would pet her, but on the whole he didn't take much notice of her. It was Anna who went out walking with Tuffet, played with her and brushed her coat.

She put a hand down to the little dog, felt Tuffet lick her fingers.

Was there any way out of it? Anna wondered. Guy would want an explanation if she refused, and she didn't want him to find out about all that.

To see Hal again – where might it lead?

Perhaps it would cure me, she told herself. I've heard it happens that way sometimes. You see an old flame a few years later and wonder what the attraction was.

Her husband's words came back to her: *I offered him thirty guineas.*

I expect Hal needs the money, Anna thought. I've a feeling he would never have accepted otherwise. I'll just have to be adult about it and see it through.

Twenty-one

Hal arrived at half-past ten on Monday morning. Guy showed him into the conservatory, leaving him to put up his easel where he thought best and arrange an attractive setting for his subject. Hal placed a cane settee and a small table against a background cluster of potted palms and parasol plants, completing the bower with a frangipani and stephanotis. The air was very warm and laden with fragrance. Indeed, this glasshouse would have been unpleasantly hot, were it not for the climbing vines which snaked across part of the roof, casting greenish shadows.

He had just about finished these preparations when Guy returned, bringing Anna and the baby.

'Mr Pentreath, this is Anna, my wife, and Robin, my little boy.'

Hal hesitated. Once again warned by a cautious instinct, he said: 'Good morning, Mrs Buckman.'

Rather stiffly, she nodded. 'Good morning.' She was carrying the child, who for once was looking peevish.

Hal's first thought was that he didn't like her hair. It was far too dressy. She was wearing eyebrow pencil, too, and a dark red lipstick. Peggy had told him of this, after meeting her in the shoe shop. Hal had assumed she was exaggerating, being bitchy, but now that he saw Anna for himself he felt a certain dismay. It spoiled her, all that make-up, and she had such a lovely face. The baby too was beautiful, but . . . For some reason,

Hal felt a curious aversion to him. Probably because the boy was fretful, he decided. A squirming, irritable child would not make his job easy.

'Where would you like me to sit?' asked Anna.

'Just there, please.' He indicated the settee.

Anna seated herself, taking Robin on her lap.

'I think it would be better if the child were to sit beside you. If you put your arm around him. Yes, that's very nice.'

Guy watched for a minute or two, then he said: 'Well, I'll leave you to it,' and disappeared.

Briefly, there was awkward silence. Then Hal asked: 'How are you, Anna?'

'I'm very well.'

'Your husband doesn't seem to know that we're acquainted.'

'No.' She glanced towards the door through which Guy had gone. 'No, Hal, I've never mentioned you. I didn't want him to think he'd caught me on the rebound.'

'Of course not,' he said mildly, taking up his charcoal and starting to sketch. 'Would you mind moving slightly that way, to sit at an angle?'

She did so, crossing her legs. Beside her, encircled by her arm, Robin sat bolt upright, staring levelly at Hal. Anna bent down to him, whispering: 'This nice man's going to paint our picture.'

'Perfect,' Hal said. 'That's just right. Now Anna, turn your head to look at me. Good, like that, keep still.'

His hand moved swiftly, creating her likeness with fluid strokes. Drawing had always been easy for him. There seemed to be some inner control which stopped a line in just the right place, turned the perfect angle, or swept a curve of ideal fulness. Correct proportion and perspective seemed to come of their own accord.

'It must be very pleasant living here,' he remarked, as he worked.

'It's a soft life,' she agreed.

'And your husband – what's he like?'

'He's – extremely generous,' said Anna.

Well, she thought, Guy was certainly open-handed. And he'd been a good deal kinder to her since the child arrived. She could hardly tell Hal that she didn't care for her husband's habits in bed, and whatever she said to him might go back to Peggy, so Anna determined to make the picture a rosy one.

'I've forgotten what it's like to cook a meal or wash a dish,' she said lightly. 'I don't have to do anything, except look after Robin.'

He smiled, switching glances between her face and the image forming on the paper. 'You're very lucky.'

'Yes, I am.'

Covertly, Anna studied him. He was perched on a high stool, one long leg stretched out in front of him. He was wearing the canvas fishing smock she remembered so well. A shaft of sunlight fell upon him like a theatre spotlight.

'And you – are you happy?' she asked.

'Very.' He didn't look up. 'We have a little boy now. Did you know?'

'I saw the announcement in the paper.'

She was disappointed to hear him say that he was happy with Peggy. She had hoped for complaints, for reports that his wife was a shrew, for admissions that he had been wrong and foolish and knew now that he ought to have chosen Anna instead. It offended her vanity to hear he had no regrets. It also made her feel doubly stupid for what she had done to Peggy's portrait.

That was still a matter of acute embarrassment to Anna. She knew he wouldn't bring it up, but while it remained an unspoken issue between them, she couldn't relax. For a while she pondered the question and then elected to try and make a joke of it.

'I, um – I'm terribly sorry about that painting, Hal. Peggy's portrait, I mean.' She forced a laugh. 'I was such a child in those days. I've grown up a lot since then. I had such a pash for you. I hope you can see the flattering side of what I did and forgive me for it.'

'It's all right, Anna. We were all young and thoughtless, weren't we? Not that we're very much older now – but having children makes a difference to us, don't you think?'

'Oh yes,' she said quickly. 'Changes us for the better, no doubt about that.'

He carried on deftly shaping his drawing. 'You certainly don't look very much like the girl I used to know.'

She wasn't sure if that was intended to signify approval.

'You might say Guy took me in hand. He has very good taste.'

'That is a lovely frock,' Hal said tactfully.

He worked on in silence. As she watched him, Anna found herself wondering what he was like in bed. He'd be nothing like Guy, she was certain of that. There were gentlemen and gentlemen – the ones like her husband, who spoke and dressed well, who had money and manners, and the ones created by nature, who might not know which fork to use, but were warm and sensitive. She imagined Hal with Peggy and bitterness rose within her. If Guy had been kind and considerate in that way, it might have killed any lingering feelings for Hal. But he wasn't. She had his money and a smart way of life, but she paid dearly for it almost every night. In that respect, it was Peggy who had triumphed.

Be adult about it, she had warned herself. Easier said than done.

After a while, the child grew restive and started to wriggle. Anna tried to quiet him, but he fought her and struggled to slip off the seat.

'May we stop for a while?' she asked. 'He's girding himself for a tantrum, I'm afraid.'

'Certainly. That's enough for now.' Hal came across to her, knelt down beside the settee and showed her the sketch. 'Like it?'

His face, so close, looking up at her, filled her with longing. A dip of her head and she could be kissing him. Her answer was artificially brisk and blithe.

'Oh yes, and you've done such a lot. I'd forgotten how fast you could work.'

'We'll have another session this afternoon, shall we? I hope to have the whole thing finished in a week.'

A week, she thought wistfully. Just a week. If only it could take a month . . .

But no, this was just what she had feared. No, even a week was too long for comfort. The sooner the painting was finished and Hal was gone, the better.

He was there every morning and afternoon for the next six days, and with every sitting Anna's old feelings revived a little more. After a time he scarcely needed Robin there at all, and so it was just the two of them, alone in the balmy, fragrant conservatory. She would watch his face as he worked, the little frowns, the concentration, the smiles of satisfaction. She had always loved his hands, because they were slim and graceful – especially so when he wielded his brushes. The bony squareness of her husband's hands had come to symbolise brutality to Anna. Those hands were hard on her flesh in bed, they squeezed too tightly, groped too roughly. They looked as if they were meant to hurt, and hurt they often did. Guy would call it passion, he would say he got carried away. Anna couldn't imagine Peggy wincing with pain under Hal's touch. Those fingers manoeuvred the brush and mixed the colours with such delicacy and care.

Over and over, Anna reminded herself that Guy had been good to her in every other way since Robin was born, and comparisons like these were futile anyway. She was firmly married and so was Hal. Both had children and, what was more, Hal was happy with his wife.

Happy with Peggy, content at Angilley's Bazaar. Anna couldn't understand that, yet the fact remained. There was nothing to do but control her feelings and maintain a front of casual friendliness. They chattered of general matters, nothing too personal, and she gave no hint of discontent which might be carried back to her old enemy.

With the licence of superior position, she openly called him Hal in front of Guy. Hal was much more circumspect. When her husband was present, she was always 'Mrs Buckman'. Sometimes Guy would stand at Hal's shoulder, watching him paint. There they were, Anna thought, side by side, what she had wanted and what she had got. The artist and the businessman. Relaxed, untidy Hal, and Guy with his smart suit, gold wristwatch, aftershave.

The fantasy was with her still of a barefoot, shoe-string, unconventional life in a picturesque cottage somewhere. Simple foods and home-made clothes and fires of driftwood. Hal giving free rein to his talent, Anna being his helpmate and inspiration.

This was a bad thing, she knew full well. Better by far if she had never seen him again. Just as she was coming to terms with her life, he had unsettled her once more. When the painting was finished, Anna told herself, she would have to make a determined effort to shut him out of her mind.

A good resolution, but hopelessly broken in no time at all. Guy was delighted with the portrait and had it hung in the front hall. Every time she passed it, Anna was reminded of her old love, and his parting remark on that Sunday when he was packing up his paints.

'I'm glad you're happy, Anna. I'm pleased it's turned out well, and I'm sorry that I upset you so much. I felt very guilty about that, you know. I don't like hurting people.'

Again she had made a joke of it, and sent him on his way with a lighter conscience. After he disappeared down the drive, she had shut herself away and wept for two hours.

Afterwards, Guy's demands for sex became less bear-able than ever. She resented them fiercely, the fre-quency of them, the roughness and the fact that he never asked first. It didn't matter to him if she was feeling like it or not – and indeed she was almost never feeling like it, because he was just like a dog with a table leg, butting away at a thing. Instinct had always advised that it wouldn't be wise to object, and not once in their two and a half years of marriage had

Anna refused him honestly or firmly. On occasion she had made excuses of feeling unwell. Often, he had done it anyway. To tell him point blank that she didn't want it had seemed too much to dare.

But the more she thought about Hal, imagining him a perfect lover, the stronger became the urge to make a stand. Finally, one night when she felt brave, the confrontation came.

'What's the matter?' Guy demanded, when she clamped her legs and turned away, curling up in a self-protective huddle.

'I just don't want it, Guy, that's all. We went to bed this afternoon.'

'So? It's not on ration, is it?'

'I'm tired.'

'Why? You haven't done much all day, except look after Robin.' He leaned over her, putting his weight on her, peering into her face. 'You're not ill?'

She was silent. Why should she have to lie? Why could she not have a choice in the matter, without any need to justify herself? It had always been easier to give in, grin and bear it. A few minutes to satisfy him and keep him sweet, set against hours of ill-temper. Till now she had always weighed the cost and taken the line of least resistance. She could go on doing that for all the years ahead.

Or she could reclaim some dignity and face the music now. The alternative was to accept being made to feel like an animal once or twice a day.

She gritted her teeth. 'No, Guy, I'm not ill. I just want to go to sleep and I don't see why I shouldn't be allowed to do that.'

'Indeed?' His tone became indignant. He was leaning heavily over her and she suddenly felt enraged by the pressure and by the intrusion of his stare. She made a wriggling motion with her shoulder to shake him off.

'Please leave me alone.'

At that, he seized and rolled her over flat upon her back.

'I'm your husband. You're my wife. I want you. Now stop being awkward.'

Awkward. Donkeys were awkward. Cows were awkward. Hold still for the bull and don't be difficult. Anna glared at him.

'Well, I don't want you, not tonight. Dear God, don't you ever get bored with it? Why are you so constantly ready? Is there something wrong with you?'

Briefly, he was taken aback. His mouth dropped open. His forelock, normally combed back, was hanging down at one temple. On either side of her, his sinewy white arms trembled. Then his face hardened and his voice dropped, becoming menacing.

'As long as you cease this nonsense right now, I'll pretend you didn't say that.'

She was quaking inside and her mouth was dry, but she meant to hold out.

'I did say it, Guy, and I meant it. It can't be natural to want it so often. It's not as if we're newlyweds any more.'

He raised an eyebrow and his yellow eyes were baleful, like those of a cat.

'Most women would count themselves lucky to have so much attention from their husbands.'

'Too much of anything, even a good thing, palls.'

'I disagree.'

'And I don't like . . .'

Her mouth worked as she tried to dispel the dryness and take a grip on her nerves.

'Yes?' His eyes never left hers for an instant. He loomed over her, the line of his collarbone clearly visible under the pale skin. She was always aware of the hardness of his bones when he was taking her, conscious of his ribs and knees and elbows. He was terribly strong for someone so lean. 'You don't like what?' he prompted softly.

'Some of the ways you do it, and the things you ask of me. Embarrassing, horrible things.'

There was a pause and then a snort of laughter came down his nose. 'What a little prude it is!'

'No, I'm not! I'm as natural as the next person – but I don't think you are. You can be beastly, really beastly, and I've had enough of it. There are certain things I won't let you do any more. And I'm not spending any more afternoons in bed with you, either. I'm sick of the feel of bedclothes, and you all over me!'

'In other words, you're cold.'

'Oh, think what you like. I don't care.'

He bent his face closer to hers and pinned her by her upper arms. 'Ever heard of marital duty, Anna?'

'Within reason, I don't mind at all. It's the overtime I resent.'

'In my opinion, dearest, you are paid for the overtime. To whom much is given, of her can much be demanded. And I have given you a great deal, haven't I, Anna? A very fine standard of living, you must admit.'

'I'm not a kept woman, I'm Robin's mother.'

Guy smirked. 'All wives are kept women. Father always said that. Still, most of them perform domestic services as well as personal ones. You don't have to do that, Anna. You don't even help in the business any more. This is practically all I ask of you – and you're refusing. Is that reasonable?'

She couldn't think of an argument. She only knew she was not going to cave in now.

'Get off me,' she said flatly. 'Let me be.'

His answer was to pull her nightdress up. His face was set and Anna's reluctance made him doubly eager.

'No!' As he tried to kiss her, she bit him sharply, drawing blood from his lower lip.

With a yelp of shock and pain, he sat back, dabbing gingerly at his mouth. He blinked at the red smear on his fingers, then he stared at her.

He would hit her. Anna was sure he would. For a moment she was terrified. Then, rearing from the pillows, she pushed him backwards, twisted off the bed and scurried into the nursery, locking the door.

She expected to hear him pounding on it any minute, shouting, swearing, threatening her . . .

But from the bedroom no sound came. A silence descended more fearsome than any outburst. Anna waited, listening, then at last sank down in the chair by Robin's cot. The child slept on. After a while, she went to the cupboard, took out a spare blanket and wrapped it around her, then settled herself in the chair again, staring at the door.

Had it been worth it? she asked herself. Tomorrow would tell.

Next morning, well after the sun was up, she ventured to open the door an inch or two and peer through the crack. The bedroom was empty and the clock said ten to eight. Edging out, she crept across to the sitting-room and looked in there. Guy was nowhere about.

Desperate for the lavatory, Anna went into the bathroom.

She came out feeling better for a wash, put on some clothes and went to the telephone to order a breakfast tray. But just as the dining-room answered, she put the receiver down again. She had glimpsed from the window something which at first defied belief.

Opening it for a proper look, Anna pressed a hand to her throat and swallowed hard.

Her bed of marigolds was ruined, flowers trampled or ripped from the ground and strewn in every direction. The fury of the act could be seen in the sprays of earth kicked across the grass and the way the flower heads were torn to pieces. It had not been enough to uproot them, Guy had shredded them as well.

For four days afterwards, he didn't speak to her. If he was forced to communicate, he left her terse little notes. Anna slept in the nursery every night, pushing two armchairs together and stretching out as best she could. Now that she had started this, she didn't know how or when it would end. Part of her was exultant at having resisted him. A more timid and peaceable side of her balked at the consequences, the ugly looks, the terrible, charged silences, the slamming doors. And worst of all, the misery for everyone on the staff. Guy bullied them unmercifully, hurling sarcasm left and right. Three were sacked for virtually nothing, and both the office girls were reduced to tears day after day. What was more, they had some inkling of what it was all about. Mrs Roseveare missed very little. She knew where Anna was sleeping, she saw Guy's caustic messages left around the flat. Everybody knew that 'Mr and Mrs' had fallen out.

In the end, Anna could not endure it any more. So

awful was the atmosphere that she relented. When Guy went up to the flat on the fifth evening, she was waiting for him in bed, resigned.

He made a punishing job of it that night and although he said nothing much thereafter, she knew she was not forgiven. Anna wished she hadn't tried it, and could only be thankful that Guy hadn't connected her little rebellion with Hal Pentreath.

Twenty-two

The portrait of Anna and Robin was much admired by the guests. They remarked upon it to Guy and asked about the artist. Was he local? Where might he be found? The enquiries suggested an idea to him. He thought about it on and off throughout the winter months, and the following spring he decided to offer Hal Pentreath an exhibition.

He turned up one day at Angilley's Bazaar. Peggy had gone out to fetch groceries and Maisie was serving in the shop. She regarded Guy Buckman with plain astonishment.

'Good morning,' he said. 'I'm looking for Mr Pentreath. I believe he lives here?'

'He's my son-in-law,' said Maisie, nodding.

'Indeed?' Guy was genial. 'Talented chap. Is he in? I have a business proposition for him. My name is Buckman, by the way.'

Maisie's eyes flickered over him. 'Classy' was the word which leapt to her mind. A notch or three above Delia Trevena, that was certain.

'He's at work upstairs. I'll show you the way.'

'Thank you.' He glanced about him. 'Business good?'

'Can't complain.'

'Pleased to hear it.'

He beamed at her and Maisie thought him a real gent. She had no sense from him of contempt for herself or her shop. Indeed, it was a peculiarity of Guy's nature

210

that he accepted people like the Angilleys for what they were and didn't mind them. They had nothing to do with him. Their ways and tastes did not reflect upon him. Vulgarity in them was merely amusing, whereas any lapse of refinement in his wife was unforgivable.

Maisie led him upstairs to the loft, where Hal was finishing off a still life in oils.

'Someone to see you,' she said, sounding awed.

Laying down his brush, he stood up. 'Well – Mr Buckman.'

Maisie was hovering at the door. Both men turned and looked at her and she quickly withdrew.

'How are you?' Guy asked cordially, as the door closed behind her.

'Very well, thank you. What brings you here?'

Buckman strolled across the room, hands in his pockets. His steps echoed on the bare boards as he walked around, looking at canvases and sketches.

'That portrait of Anna,' he said. 'We've had a lot of compliments, a lot of people asking about you.'

'Yes, some of them found their way here. I made a few sales.' Hal began rinsing some brushes in a jar of water, drying them with a rag.

'Really?' Guy swung round, his eyebrows raised. 'Good. Excellent. They bought from the shop downstairs?'

'No, they came up here. I sold several large canvases.'

'Indeed? I'm very pleased.' Guy came across to inspect the still life. 'Nice,' he said. 'Anyway, the portrait attracted so much interest, it set me thinking. May I sit down?' Without waiting, he flopped into an old armchair and crossed his legs. 'I was wondering how you would feel about holding an exhibition at my

211

hotel? Naturally, I should want a percentage, but it would be mutually beneficial, don't you think?'

'Oh...' Hal sank down on his stool, trying not to betray too much excitement. 'Uh – yes, I'm sure that would profit us both.'

'Trezawne's a bit short of good outlets, isn't it, since old Jackman died?'

'I admit I've missed him.'

'Hmm. Well...' Guy steepled his fingers. 'I'd be happy to hang a collection of your paintings for, say, a fortnight. A few in the bar, some in the dining-room, some in the residents' lounge. I'd have to insist they were framed, mind you, and I'd want fifty per cent commission on anything sold. But I'd advertise the event for you in the local and regional papers at my own expense. I'd also provide a catalogue to hand out, giving details about each painting, and the price. Professionally printed, not just typed. What do you say?'

Hal considered a moment. 'It sounds pretty fair.'

'It's a way for you to show your work to people with plenty of money. No one who stays at Elestren Manor is ever hard-up. For my part, I'm always looking for new ideas to interest and entertain my guests. People come to see the exhibition, they stay for a drink, some sandwiches, even a meal – it's all good for trade.'

Hal very much wanted to do it. He could see nothing but advantages to the scheme. Except – this would be something he could not conceal from Peggy. It hadn't been too difficult to do a single portrait of Anna on the quiet, but a two-week exhibition at Elestren Manor could hardly escape his wife's notice.

Guy was talking on. 'Do you have much work ready to show? I see a few excellent pictures here I wouldn't hesitate to choose, but I'm thinking in terms of thirty or more.'

Blow Peggy, Hal thought. Why should he be held back by her stupid grudge against Anna? If she wanted her own house, she should welcome any means of obtaining the money.

He still had much of the work he had prepared for Mr Jackman's gallery. Unwilling to sell it cheaply, Hal had held on to it. Nodding towards the shelves and the big cupboard, he said: 'I've a lot of good oils. I'll show you before you go.'

'It's a deal, then?' Guy said. 'Shall we give it a try?'

'Certainly. When would you suggest?'

'Perhaps July? Hotel's always packed in July. Can you be ready?'

'Don't see why not.'

Guy extended a hand and they shook on it.

To begin with, Peggy's reaction was much as Hal expected.

'Something exciting has turned up,' he told her. 'Nothing short of a golden opportunity.'

'Really?'

'I've been offered an exhibition somewhere very smart.'

They were stretched out together on the old couch in the loft. It was twilight and on the window-ledge an oil lamp burned. A lingering chill made it needful to have some heat, so a paraffin stove was also lit. A coronet of pinkish-blue flame surrounded the mantle, and Peggy lay watching it, her back against Hal's chest.

She shifted, looking round at him eagerly. 'Where?'

'Well, it's a hotel.'

Peggy caught the hint of apprehension in his voice and was instantly suspicious.

'Oh, Hal, not . . .?'

'Elestren Manor. That Buckman chap was here today.'

Her face changed, she looked away, slumping back against him.

Hal went on quickly: 'He saw my work on display at the library last year and liked it.'

Silence.

'Very astute businessman, I'd say. Always thinking up new events to draw in trade.'

'I'm sure he's a genius,' grunted Peggy. She stared out of the window. In the dusk the lights strung out along the waterfront looked like a sparkling necklace. 'I don't want you to take it,' she said, after a moment's pause.

'For God's sake, why not?'

'We don't need any help from them.'

'It was his idea, I'm sure, not Anna's. Buckman doesn't strike me as a man who takes advice or lets others persuade him. And it isn't a favour, it's business, pure and simple. He'll take a good commission, don't you worry.'

'Even so, we don't need their patronage.'

'I've just told you . . .'

'Turn it down, Hal, please.'

'I've already agreed to it.'

'Then cancel, tell him you're too busy.'

'That's ridiculous.'

'You can say you've other commitments, enough to tie you up for the next six months!' she said sharply.

'I'll do no such thing! I'm not a good liar. I'd only make myself look foolish, and it's too good a chance to miss. My God, you'd see me decline something I badly need, just because it's offered by Anna's husband.'

'Perhaps you're keen to see her again? Is that it?'

'For the love of God, she's married, and very pleased with her lot in life, according to you. She's content, I'm content. Everything's changed except your attitude.'

'I can't help it. I hate the idea.'

'We need the money.'

'Not that much.'

She pulled away from him and went to the window. Out in the harbour, the boats were black shadows on a glassy sea.

'It's no use arguing,' Hal said. 'I'm not going to pander to you over this.'

'I see,' came the stiff reply. 'And when is this show to be?'

'Most likely July.'

'For how long?'

'Two weeks.'

For a while she said nothing, but stood with her back turned, hugging herself.

'Will you be there all the time?'

'No, just four mornings a week. I might get some commissions out of it, Peggy.'

Grudgingly, she conceded: 'Yes, perhaps.'

'I don't see what your objection is.'

'It's the thought of her, sponsoring the struggling artist.'

'I can't afford to be proud,' Hal said quietly. 'Not that I see any indignity in the arrangement. If the same offer had come from some other quarter, you'd be dancing a jig.'

'She'll be saying next that we're in her debt. I can't be humbly grateful, even if you can.'

'Don't you think my work will be admired?'

'Of course I do! I know it will!'

'Well, if that isn't reason to hold our heads up, I don't know what is. Anyway, Peggy, like it or not, I mean to go ahead.'

Four months passed. All the paintings were finished and framed in time for the show to start on 3 July.

Peggy made Hal wear a collar and tie when he went to Elestren Manor. Good flannel trousers, too. He had refused point-blank to be put in a suit.

'I'm an artist,' he said. 'I don't belong in a jacket.'

'That doesn't mean you have to look like a scarecrow. I don't want you to appear in need of money,' she added grimly.

As a compromise, she bought him a couple of Fair Isle jerseys, which rendered him casually presentable and satisfied them both.

'Sure you won't come along with me?' he said on the day the exhibition opened.

'Me? You must be joking.' Inspecting him yet again, Peggy picked a hair off his shoulder. Then, uneasily, she asked: 'Will you see much of Anna?'

'She's bound to be about. What's the matter, don't you trust me?'

'I don't trust her.'

'Well, don't worry, I don't doubt her husband's around all the time. If she throws herself at me, I expect he'll pull her off.'

Dourly, Peggy sniffed. Reaching up, she brushed back the quiff of his sandy hair with her fingers. 'She's got everything else,' she muttered. 'She needn't think she's having you as well, that's all. I'd mangle her if she tried it. Her and her fancy clothes and face paint.'

'If it's any comfort to you, I prefer my women natural. Like you, a bit dishevelled.' Bending his head, he nuzzled her face, her mouth. 'Sensual, that's the word — as if you've just this minute tumbled out of bed.'

She smiled, then hugged him fiercely, pressing her cheek against his chest. The wool of his jersey still had that new smell, a shop smell. The warmth of him came seeping through it, and her thoughts were full of the dearly loved body just beneath. No matter how much money Guy Buckman had, he wasn't Hal, Peggy thought, and Anna's old desire might merely be dormant rather than dead.

The truth, that it was vitally alive, was something Anna concealed with difficulty. She could only disguise it as enthusiasm for his work. Whenever Hal was at the hotel, she hung about him a lot. She talked at great length about each of his paintings, kept offering coffee and snacks and drinks in the bar. She also rang all the Buckmans' acquaintances and coaxed them to come along and be introduced to this promising local artist.

The exhibition brought Hal Pentreath more money than he had seen since Jackman died. A dozen paintings were sold and three commissions came out of it. A local solicitor wanted a portrait of his red setter. The owner of the Polvarth Hotel asked for three still lifes to go in his dining-room, all depicting elaborate spreads of food. A visiting yachtsman requested a watercolour of his vessel, the *Kittiwake*. Hal was delighted to get so much lucrative work.

A couple of days before the exhibition ended, yet another commission was offered, and at a fee so generous that Hal could scarcely believe his good fortune. He was sitting at the table set up for him in the residents' lounge, when Anna came in with a silver-haired man of some fifty-odd years. He wore a striped tie and a blazer and crisp white trousers. Although he seemed perfectly fit, he carried a walking stick.

'This is Hallam Pentreath, Mr Snow,' announced Anna.

Affably, the gentleman held a hand out.

'Mr Snow arrived yesterday, Hal,' she explained. 'He's staying with us for a month. He likes your paintings very much.'

'Very attractive work,' confirmed Mr Snow, pumping his hand. 'Tremendous atmosphere. Love the fishing scenes. And there's one in the bar I especially admire. Painting of a holy well – wonderful sense of age and cold granite and dripping moss. Excellent, splendid!'

It was what Peggy called a 'haw-haw' accent, clipped and jolly.

'Thank you,' Hal began. 'I'm glad . . .'

'Impressed. Very,' said Mr Snow emphatically. 'Good to meet a solid, traditional artist. Too much pretentious bunk around these days, if you ask me. This modernist tripe – good God!' A snort and a roll of the eyes. 'I've a friend who likes that kind of nonsense. Wouldn't have it in the house myself. Just goes to prove there's a fool born every minute, eh? Oh – dear me. Hope you don't dabble in that stuff yourself?'

'No,' said Hal, who was much of the same opinion concerning modern art.

'Quite right,' trumpeted Mr Snow. 'Damned tomfoolery, most of it. And the way they talk about it! Hah!' He thumped the floor with his stick. 'High-faluting drivel – never heard such rot! Went to an exhibition in London, you know, just a month ago. Lot of ridiculous daubs by some mad woman – well, I think she

218

was mad, that's my opinion. Should have seen her hair!'

Standing slightly behind Mr Snow, Anna winked at Hal and pressed a hand to her mouth to smother laughter.

'Asked her what it was all about,' continued the little man. 'Told me I was supposed to "explore" the colours and "suffer" the shapes, see delirium in a triangle, despair in a square. Went on about the "confusion" in the orange and the "slyness" of the greens, and how the brown was "conscience-stricken". Said I was meant to feel "interrogated" by this canvas, or "chastised" by that one. Ridiculous woman! Mad as a hatter, of course.'

Hal, by now, was grinning broadly. He very much liked Mr Snow.

'It's all supposed to be very clever,' he said. 'Can't see it myself.'

'Nor can I, boy, nor can I.' Mr Snow ambled around the room, inspecting the canvases on the walls.

'Would you like some coffee and something to eat, Mr Snow?' offered Anna. 'I gather you want to talk business with Mr Pentreath?'

'What? Oh, yes, yes. Coffee for two, and some cakes, if you please.'

Anna went to order a tray and the two men sat down together.

'You accept commissions, I'm told?'

'Yes, I do.'

'Well now . . .' Mr Snow folded his hands on the head of his cane. '. . . I have a hobby, you know. Industrial archaeology. Been down here looking around the old tin mines. Fascinating! There's nothing like them anywhere else. So – been thinking. Would like some paintings – oils, about three feet square. A set of four. I've picked out the locations. Abandoned mines, all of them. Be interested, would you?'

'Certainly, although I've a lot of work in hand.'

A waiter arrived with a tray, set it down and poured their coffee.

'As you heard, I'm here for a month,' said Mr Snow. 'Could you manage it in that time?'

'Possibly,' mused Hal.

'Pay you well,' said Mr Snow, taking a bite of Madeira cake. 'A hundred and sixty for the four? Would that be sufficient?'

Hal's chunk of Battenburg almost went the wrong way. He recovered with a gentle cough and tried to sound casual. 'Um, yes, that would be all right.'

'Frames included, of course?' Mr Snow sipped coffee, watching him over the rim of his cup.

'Of course.'

'Done, then?' The gentleman held out his hand again.

'Done,' said Hal.

'Like a deposit, I expect?' suggested Mr Snow. His hand went to his inside breast pocket.

'There isn't any need.'

'Tosh, my boy, of course there is. We must seal our agreement, mark of good faith and all that.' A wallet appeared and Mr Snow extracted four five-pound notes. 'Twenty adequate?'

'Fine.' Hal was quite embarrassed to take a deposit from someone of such obvious quality. Not that he feared Mr Snow would miss it. Anyone who could afford a month at Elestren Manor had to be affluent.

'Married?' enquired Mr Snow, as they finished their coffee.

'Yes. Two children.'

'Indeed? Life's a bit of a struggle at this stage, I dare say? Never mind. You persevere, my boy. It'll be worth it, mark my words. You're gifted. I don't see how you can fail.'

What a nice man, Hal thought. Such a gent.

Twenty-three

There wasn't a single working mine left within fifteen miles of Trezawne, but the cliffs and moors around the town were dotted with abandoned engine-houses. Mr Snow had selected four of the most picturesque.

Hal was lucky, the weather stayed fine and he made rapid progress. On a day in mid-August he was working just a mile inland from Tolgarth beach. The first three paintings were finished. This, the final one, would require a couple more days' work.

Putting down his brush, Hal sat back from his easel for a while to enjoy the sunshine and the hushing wind. The scene before him was faithfully reproduced on his canvas, but as he looked at the old Wheal Resolve, he was seeing this place in his mind's eye, the way it used to be.

Once there was a wasteland here, a tract of muddy pools and churned-up earth, all mixed with rubble and refuse from the mine. Once there were wooden sheds, tram rails, machinery, piles of timber and heaps of mineral dross. And noise and bustle, children labouring in the buddle-pits, bal-girls cracking ore with hammers, gabbling and screaming with laughter. Once there was a great wheel turning and engine beam sedately pumping up and down. And in the dark labyrinth under the earth, where sweating men worked shirtless by the light of tallow candles, there were rumbles and crashes of blasting powder, the constant brittle clinking of picks on granite, and echoes of voices in airy black caverns.

Now there was a rolling swathe of long green grass, clouds of white yarrow, and stately foxgloves, shoulder high. Now the wheel and engine beam and all other things made of metal or wood were gone. All that remained was the engine-house and its stack, granite steadily disappearing under climbing ivy.

This place was full of ghosts. He fancied he could feel them around him, imagined he could hear them faintly. Sturdy girls in aprons and sun bonnets, ragged urchins, cocky young men with loud voices and powerful muscles, broken down old ones with coughs and bent backs. Figures from sixty or a hundred years ago, ambling off to the beer-shop to spend their wages, or going home to some hovel of cob and thatch and a dinner of pilchards.

Once there were tragedies here; a boy of fifteen falling eight hundred feet from the ladder, twenty-nine men crushed to death by a cave-in, another two caught in the blast as their charge went off, one more who just lay down and died for want of air while working in an end.

The adventurers, by contrast, had made substantial fortunes from Wheal Resolve. Hal could picture them as well – stout men in broadcloth who smoked cigars, men with high top hats and gold watch-chains and canny eyes. In 1875, however, with cheap tin coming in from abroad, their instincts had told them to close this mine or face losses, and suddenly everything had stopped, never to move again. Eventually, the same had happened all over Cornwall.

So now the old pits were a curiosity for those of the holiday people who cared for such things. Now they were scenic, romantic. Even slog and disaster became tinted by a kind of grisly glamour with the passing of time. As with ancient wars in history books, the suffering had grown to seem unreal, just a costume play.

These days it was only for artists, like Hal, that the mines could be said to put any bread on the table. People liked to buy paintings and prints of them. What else was so uniquely Cornish, what else was so wistfully lonely and full of the past?

But today was too bright for melancholy. The sky was very blue, completely cloudless, and this was to be the sunniest of the paintings. The other three had turned out moody and he was determined that this one should speak of summer and brilliant colours. Taking up his brush, he went on delicately adding strokes here and there, bringing up sharply the stonework of the engine-house, the carn on the hill in the distance, and the bells of a foxglove in the foreground.

Finally, finished for the day, he stood up to stretch his legs and looked round for Peggy. She had gone to sleep in the grass nearby, her straw hat over her face.

As he came between her and the sun, Peggy felt a chill and stirred.

'Have you finished?' she asked, sitting up.

'For now.'

She looked at the painting on the easel. 'Beautiful. Your Mr Snow should be very pleased with that.'

Hal dropped down beside her, full of confidence. 'I think so. Just imagine, Peggy, forty pounds each. See, we'll be able to buy our own place, and sooner than we thought. Tell me again, was I right to accept Buckman's offer, or not?'

'I'll hit you if you ask me that once more.'

'Where else round here would I have met someone like Snow?'

'All right, all right.' Then, with a sideways glance at him, Peggy asked: 'What about those other commissions, Hal? You've spent all your time working on these mine paintings since the exhibition ended.'

He was lounging back in the grass, propped on one elbow. Plucking a stem, he started chewing the end, not meeting her eyes.

'Well,' he said slowly, 'I've had to postpone one of them, and I did lose a couple of others. The yachtsman, he couldn't wait, and nor could the Polvarth Hotel.'

'I'm not surprised. You promised them before you met Mr Snow.'

'They were only worth about sixty pounds to me altogether. I have to give priority to whatever brings in most money.'

Peggy still looked unhappy. She turned her straw hat round and round in her hands. 'Pity about the Polvarth,' she murmured. Then: 'Did Mr Snow give you anything on account?'

'Yes, twenty pounds.'

She considered a moment. 'That's not very much. Only enough to cover the frames and materials, really.'

'So? The rest will be profit. Still a nice sum, Peggy.'

'Less what you've lost on the other commissions,' she pointed out.

'Why are you pouring cold water?' He grew a bit testy. 'I've only one pair of hands, Peggy. There are only so many hours of light each day. I couldn't help it if the other clients were impatient. I'd have got around to their work if they'd waited.'

She didn't feel like quarrelling. 'Yes, of course. When will Mr Snow collect the paintings?'

'Saturday. That's the day he goes home. A month at Elestren Manor – my God, he must have a mint of money. I only wish I could meet a few more like him.' Taking her hat from her, he tucked a buttercup into the weave and patted it back on her head. 'I'll take you and the kids out somewhere nice for the day just as soon as he's paid me.'

Mr Snow called at Angilley's Bazaar at nine on Saturday morning. Upstairs in the loft, he inspected the results of Pentreath's hard work.

Excellent,' he said, walking slowly along the little row of paintings. 'Excellent, all of them. I'd be hard put to name a favourite.'

Four engine-houses, four situations, four different atmospheres. One was clinging to the cliffs above a turbulent sea. The waves appeared to leap for it in an effort to pull it down. This was a painting full of inky skies and violent elements. Another was melancholy and very still, the building a fuzzy silhouette looming through a moorland mist, and surrounded by gorse and marsh grass. The third was depicted at sunset, its walls bathed in the light of a sky that was pink and gold and mauve, with a few last birds flying off to roost. Finally, there was the mine near Tolgarth beach, besieged by tall grasses and weeds and wild flowers, half engulfed by ivy, a grey derelict upon a brilliant green landscape.

'Yes,' said Mr Snow thoughtfully. 'Lovely. Sunshine and greenery can render anything beautiful, don't you think? That's one of the joys of my hobby, you know, seeing nature take possession again, seeing her – redecorate – so to speak. '

Hal nodded and smiled. All was well, the client was pleased. Hal was looking forward to all that money.

Beaming, Mr Snow reached inside a breast pocket. 'Well now, young man, I believe I owe you another hundred and forty pounds? I'm very satisfied, very pleased indeed.'

From the pocket he drew out a cheque book and pen. For a moment, Hal's gaze wavered uncertainly. He hadn't thought to specify payment in cash. He had taken that for granted because he never dealt in anything else himself. Even Guy Buckman had paid him in cash.

Still, a hundred and forty pounds was perhaps too much to carry around in notes. It was by far the most Hal had ever been paid by any one person and he supposed a cheque was the most suitable way for such a large sum to change hands. Anyway, Mr Snow had practically written it already. He wrote very quickly, with the practised manner of one who paid everything in this way.

'There we are, Mr Pentreath. Splendid work, simply splendid! I shall almost certainly be back next year. Perhaps we can do business again. And I shall definitely recommend you to any of my acquaintances who may be coming this way.'

He held out the cheque. Hal took it, read it. All was correct. Mr Snow's name and address were clearly written on the back. An expensive sounding address – Belgravia.

'Best be off, then. Got the car outside. Any chance you might help me down with these?'

'Of course.'

Ten minutes later, he watched Mr Snow drive off, the paintings safely stowed in the boot. Just before the car turned the corner, a waving hand popped out of the window and a honk of the horn said a final goodbye.

Hal fished the cheque from his trouser pocket, looked at it again and set off straight away to the post office.

It came back a week later. Insufficient funds. Over the breakfast table, Hal and Peggy gazed at the cheque and at each other in dismay.

Then she lost her temper.

'Why didn't you ask him for cash before you let the paintings go?'

'It was a Saturday, remember? And he was just leaving for London.'

'Why didn't you discuss the manner of payment before you accepted the work? How could you be so careless, Hal?'

'I'm sorry, I just didn't think about it. I mean, he gave me a cash deposit, and who'd suspect there was anything dishonest about him? Anyway, perhaps there isn't. He may not have realised that there wasn't money enough in the account.'

'What's the matter?' Maisie said, sitting down to her kippers.

'The cheque Hal took for those paintings. It's no good.'

Walter and Jasper nudged one another and sniggered.

'Shut up,' Maisie told them sharply. 'Oh, Peggy, all that money. My poor love.'

'I'll write to Mr Snow,' said Hal.

'No, you won't,' said Peggy grimly. 'I will. At least, I'll tell you what to say and you can sign it. I know you, Hal, you'd be too nice about it.'

Hal said nothing. He was feeling foolish.

'Some lot of good, he is,' crowed Walter. 'I may not do much, but I always see I get paid. Nobody's ever put one over on me like that. Great dope, to take a worthless bit of paper, instead of proper money.'

'It's nothing to you,' snapped Maisie, 'so hold your tongue.'

'I expect it'll be all right.' Hal tried to sound confident. 'Just a mistake, I daresay.'

'Yes, yours.' Jasper's hollow, idiotic laugh emerged from behind a mouthful of half-chewed sausage. 'Got took in, didn't you, just because he wore smart clothes and talked with a plum in his mouth?'

Hal flushed. It was largely true, he had to admit. Mr Snow was 'better class' and so he had trusted him.

Peggy, who normally sided with her husband, was morosely silent now. Much as it pained her to agree with her father and brother, she felt they were right.

'It's illegal, giving worthless cheques,' said Maisie. 'You can have him up for it.'

'If he can find him,' Walter grunted.

'I have his address,' Hal said. But even as he spoke, he knew the obvious retort – and back it came.

'That could be as useless as his cheque. There may be no such place.' Walter slurped his tea and shook his head, both scornful and amused. 'Gullible, that's what you are, boy.'

'Oh God,' sighed Peggy, resting her head on one hand.

'Well now, don't go crossing too many bridges yet.' Maisie patted her shoulder. 'Drop the man a line today. It may all be cleared up in a week.'

'Cleared up that he's cleared off,' cackled Jasper. 'You daft bugger, you,' he leered at Hal. 'No wonder he offered you such a good fee. He never intended to pay it.'

The truth of that struck home like a sword-thrust. Rage and dismay came together in Hal and exploded. To have that pointed out to him by a numbskull like Jasper when he had not thought of it himself, to be goaded with it and ridiculed, was too much. His arm shot across the table. He grabbed his brother-in-law by his hair and pushed his face down into his food. Jasper squawked and spluttered, lifted his greasy features and started to curse.

Pushing back his chair, Hal slammed out of the room.

The letter was duly sent to Mr Snow. It came back almost by return. There was no such address. Clutching at straws, Hal wondered aloud if the Buckmans might be able to shed some light on the man's whereabouts.

'I doubt it,' Peggy grunted. 'Still, there's nothing else to try. Anyway . . .' An aggressive gleam came into her eyes '. . . I've things to say about this to Madam Buckman.'

'Now, Peggy, it isn't Anna's fault.'

'She introduced him, didn't she?'

'In all good faith, I'm sure.'

'Even so, he was a rogue, and I'm damned well going to make certain she knows it.'

Thus it was that a belligerent little figure stalked up the drive to Elestren Manor later that morning, marched up to the desk and demanded: 'Where's Mrs Buckman? I want to see her, if you please.'

Sarah frowned and hesitated. The woman was windblown, black hair curling wildly about her head. She was wearing a frock striped blue and pink and her manner was pugnacious.

'I'm not sure she's in,' said Sarah cautiously. 'You are . . .?'

'Mrs Pentreath.'

'Oh – the artist's wife?'

'That's right, dear.' Peggy ran a glance over Sarah's neat grey dress with its crisp white collar and cuffs. Office clothes, as Peggy called them. Women who wore such garments always seemed to her like another species.

'Is it important?'

'Yes. I'm not leaving until I've spoken to her.'

'I'll go and ring the flat,' Sarah said uneasily.

'You do that.'

Peggy waited, drumming her fingers on the counter, as Sarah went to the switchboard, put in a jack and pushed the bell switch, keeping her back turned. People passing in the hall looked Peggy curiously up and down, and she responded with defiant stares.

After a moment, a murmur from Sarah told her that someone had answered the telephone in the flat. Things were said which Peggy couldn't catch. Once, the receptionist glanced nervously at her over her shoulder, then turned away, muttering: 'Yes, I'm afraid so.'

Finally, she returned to the desk. 'Mrs Buckman will be right down.'

'Thank you,' said Peggy stiffly.

She paced a little, looking round her, impressed and hostile all at once. Showy old place, she thought. Plush carpets, chandeliers . . .

Suddenly she stood stock-still, spotting Anna's portrait. Peggy knew Hal's work instantly. When did he do that? During the exhibition? No, not then. He hadn't spent time enough here. Slowly, Peggy approached the painting, reached up and touched the rough surface. There was his signature down in the bottom right corner.

She was still staring at it, puzzling, when a voice said: 'Lovely, isn't it?'

Peggy looked up and there was Anna, halfway down the stairs. She was wearing a lemon silk dress and high-heeled shoes of brown patent leather.

'My husband liked it so much, he decided to offer Hal an exhibition.' Anna came to the bottom, a cool smile fixed to her face. 'What can we do for you, Peggy? I must say, this is a surprise.'

Peggy eyed her balefully. 'I never knew Hal did this.' She tapped the painting.

'Didn't he tell you? Must have slipped his mind,' said Anna calmly.

'Like hell,' came the hot retort.

'He did it last year at my husband's request. Is there anything wrong with that? He was very well paid.'

Last year? In secret. He had lied to her, then. Disconcerted, Peggy opened her mouth and then closed it again, glancing back and forth from Anna to the portrait.

Anna folded her hands and her voice dropped low. 'I assure you, there's no cause for suspicion or concern.'

Finding her voice, Peggy snorted. 'Well, you would say that.'

With a heavy sigh and a roll of her eyes, Anna enquired: 'What's brought you here? Please come to the point.'

'All right. It's to do with your Mr Snow.'

A look crossed Anna's face. 'Ah,' she said.

'He's a bloody swindler. He cheated Hal with a worthless cheque.' Peggy's voice was rising, and Sarah looked across, listening. 'If that's the sort of person you have staying here, it doesn't say much for your fancy hotel.'

A couple collecting their key from the desk paused to take this in, all eyes and ears. Anna flashed them an apologetic smile.

'Peggy, please keep your voice down.'

'I shan't! He did my husband out of a hundred and forty pounds. A month's work down the drain. Nothing like it has ever happened to Hal before, not until he came here and met your Mr Snow.'

'Let me begin by saying that he wasn't "my" Mr Snow.'

'He was one of your guests. You go around giving yourself such airs about the nice people you mix with. Well, he, for one, was a bloody robber!'

'I know,' came the flat reply. 'He defrauded us as well.'

Peggy stared at her. 'What?'

'He stayed a month,' Anna explained. 'After the first fortnight, he gave us a cheque to clear his account up to that date. It was duly honoured. When he left, he gave us another for the second two weeks. That one bounced. While he was here, Mr Snow availed himself of the best this house could offer. We've lost rather more than a hundred and forty pounds.' She glanced across to the receptionist. 'Isn't that so, Sarah?'

The fair girl nodded. 'Yes, it is. He gave us an address in Belgravia. It now turns out there's no such road and no such house. If we could find him, we'd prosecute, but there's not much chance of that. It appears there are other traders in town who were cheated as well. Like your husband, Mrs Pentreath, we and they all trusted Mr Snow.'

For a moment, Peggy was deflated. But then: 'Well,

you can afford to lose a bit, you won't miss it,' she told Anna. 'And Hal thought you knew him. He felt he had your recommendation for the old devil.'

'I'm sorry, Peggy, I never dreamed . . .'

'And I think you should be prepared to compensate him.'

'That's unreasonable, and you know it. That's preposterous.'

'Don't you fire long words at me, Anna Trevena.' Peggy was starting to shout, and several people came out of the bar to stand and listen. 'I told my husband not to come here, I told him he should have nothing to do with you.'

One more person emerged from the bar.

'What's going on here?'

Turning, Peggy was confronted by Guy Buckman.

'I've come about your Mr Snow. I'm Hal's wife. Hal Pentreath.'

'Another dud cheque,' Anna explained to her husband. 'Hal did some paintings for Mr Snow.'

'Oh,' Guy said. 'I'm sorry to hear that. It's unfortunate.'

'It's unfortunate,' mimicked Peggy. 'Is that all you can say?'

Buckman surveyed her as if she were a furious terrier. 'What else do you expect me to say? It's no use coming here making a fuss,' he said coldly. 'These things happen. I'm sure my wife has told you that we're out of pocket too? We should have been more careful, and so should Hal. We live and learn, don't we?'

'I've learnt something, all right, Mr Buckman. I'll see to it he never associates with this place again – for more reasons than one,' Peggy added, jerking a thumb at Anna's portrait.

Buckman glanced at it, then back at her. Beside him, Anna was tense and suddenly very pale.

'What does that mean?' he asked quietly.

'It's not a good thing for your wife to spend time alone with my husband, Mr Buckman. It's not that I don't trust him, but she's another matter.'

'I beg your pardon?' His eyes grew very yellow. He glanced around and the little knot of spectators slunk back into the bar. 'Would you care to enlarge on that, bearing in mind that there's such a charge as slander?'

'The truth isn't slander. It's my guess this is news to you, Mr Buckman, so let me enlighten you. Anna's known Hal for many years. He's her old flame. She was crazy for him – and who's to say the fire's gone out? She never tired of him; it was he who dropped her. Anna had hysterics when he chose to marry me. Beside herself, she was. Nearly went mad. Go on,' she demanded of Anna, 'let's hear you deny it.'

At this point, tactful Sarah excused herself and hurried off to the lavatory. Buckman's eyes, reptilian now, moved back and forth between his wife and Peggy.

'That was years ago,' Anna protested.

'Hal did a portrait of me, you know, just after we were married,' continued Peggy. 'Shall I tell you what happened to it?'

Anna cut in swiftly. 'Guy, don't listen to her. She always was a troublemaker.'

Peggy rushed on. 'She walked into Jackman's gallery and put some scissors through it. Must have been just about the time she met you.'

Buckman looked at her long and hard, and then he studied Anna.

'So you're old acquaintances, eh?' he said softly.

'She's dredging up things I'd long forgotten,' quavered Anna.

'Hmm.' Buckman smiled, but his eyes were wintry. 'Well, of course, Mrs Pentreath is upset about the money. But that's no reason to make nasty personal accusations, is it?'

On the face of it, it seemed that telling tales had little effect. Peggy was disappointed. Scowling, she said again: 'You needn't offer my husband any more commissions or exhibitions. He won't take them.'

'Be assured, I shall not.' Guy put an arm around Anna's shoulders. 'Now I think you'd better leave. If you came here to upset my wife, you've succeeded. Let that be enough for you.'

For a moment, Peggy glowered at her old enemy. But then she blinked and her gaze dropped away. Anna was looking dreadful, sick. Briefly, to her own amazement, Peggy felt ashamed. Even more acutely, she felt small. Swallowing hard, she turned on her heel and beat a brisk retreat.

Twenty-four

'Well, well, imagine that,' said Guy. 'Was it a great love affair?' He pushed his hands in his trouser pockets and cocked his eyebrows.

'No, of course not!' Anna moved to turn away and go upstairs.

'Stay!' commanded Guy, as if she were a dog.

'You mustn't take notice of Peggy, she's vindictive.'

'No smoke without fire, though, is there? I doubt it was a total fabrication.' From the corner of his eye, Guy saw Sarah coming down the corridor. As the girl slipped back behind her desk, he said softly: 'Let's go for a drive, Anna, shall we? You can tell me all about it on the way.'

'Now? I don't want to.'

Again she made to turn away, but his left hand shot out of his pocket and gripped her upper arm.

'I insist,' he murmured, with a careful glance at Sarah. 'Something has occurred to me. I have a question or two I would like you to answer.' To Sarah, he said: 'Mrs Buckman and I are going out for a couple of hours. Please ask Mrs Roseveare to look after Robin until we return.'

'Yes, Mr Buckman.'

'Come along, Anna, the day is wasting.' He ushered her outside and round to the place where the Riley was parked.

'There's nothing to tell,' she protested, getting in.

'Then I don't know why you're looking so anxious, dearest.' He slammed his door and started the engine. 'Where shall we go, then? I know – how about the zawn? Tremendous view up there.'

He spoke not another word as the car moved down the drive, past the lawns and iris beds, under the tunnel of beeches and out through the gate. As it started to climb the hill, the sun went in. At the top, the heathery downs were ruffled by a vigorous wind. The sky was clouding over and the huge sweep of ocean was choppy and grey. Now that Trezawne was out of sight, they seemed to be miles from anywhere. The only building to be seen was a derelict cob cottage up on the slope to the left of the road.

At the right, a few yards further on, was a layby. Guy pulled over and parked.

'Now, then,' he said, sitting back expectantly.

Anna looked at him nervously. 'It was nothing, Guy, truly. Just a silly infatuation while I was at school. It was all over years ago.'

'Funny you never mentioned it, though. When I asked him round to paint your portrait, you gave no sign that you knew him.'

Anna swallowed hard and stared out through the windscreen.

'It was all a bit embarrassing. I made rather a fool of myself over Hal Pentreath. I was ashamed of it and I didn't want you to know.'

'I see.' He nodded slowly. 'Yes, I see. Must have been quite an ordeal for you, then, spending all those hours with him while he painted you.'

'I thought at first it might be, but thankfully we'd both become mature enough to laugh about it.'

'You were careful, though, not to let me in on all this hilarity.'

She twisted her fingers together and his sharp glance noted it.

'Well, I'm sorry,' she said with a shaky laugh. 'It wasn't something I wanted raked up, that was all. I wasn't exactly delighted when you told me he was coming to paint my portrait, if you recall.'

He was silent. She could feel him staring at her. At last, unable to bear it, she snapped her head round.

'Well, what is it? Guy, for God's sake, what are you suggesting – that I might have misbehaved with Hal? In front of Robin? In the conservatory, where anyone could walk in?'

'Oh no, hardly that.'

'Then why am I being interrogated?'

The yellow eyes glinted. 'It was after you sat for him that you refused me in bed, now wasn't it, Anna?'

Her gaze flickered, her mouth twitched with fear.

'There was no connection.'

'Sure?'

She stared out at the sea again. 'You've always been too – amorous – for me, Guy. Always. I was just so tired that night, I didn't feel up to it.'

'You make it sound like a ten-mile hike. In fact, you said some very hurtful things at the time.'

'I'm sorry.'

'No, you're not. I'll tell you what my guess is, Anna. You had Pentreath on your mind, you would have preferred him there in my place.'

'That's nonsense, utter tripe!' Panic raised her voice an octave.

'I don't think so.' He was studying her, every tiny change of her face, every bob of her throat. 'That little

239

harridan – what's her name, Peggy? I think she was precisely right, the old fires haven't gone out. Seeing him helped you to screw up your courage, didn't it, my dear?'

'No! I've just explained . . .'

'That you were uncommonly tired that night. Still had the energy to bite me, though. Quite a vicious little nip. Something more than fatigue behind that, wasn't there, Anna?'

'There's nothing I can do if you won't believe the truth,' she said tightly.

He kept on and on looking at her until she thought she would scream. He was plainly mulling the whole thing over. Then, finally, he stirred.

'Let's stretch our legs, shall we?'

Anna didn't like the look on his face and something made her loath to get out of the car.

'I'd rather not. There's a chilly wind and I haven't a jacket.'

'I'd call it bracing,' Guy said. 'Come on, a walk will do you good.'

Seizing her hand, he opened his door, pulled her across the seat and out. She cringed in the blast of wind that hurtled in off the sea.

'We'll go down and look at the zawn, shall we? Breathe some briny air?' He was grinning and hard humour gleamed in his eyes.

He set off briskly, pulling her along behind him. A rough track led down from the layby towards the edge of the zawn a half-mile distant. Anna stumbled along in her high heels, turning her ankle and wincing as little stones found their way into her shoes.

'Guy, please,' she begged, 'I'm going to fall.'

But he wouldn't slow down. Anna tried to twist her hand free, so he squeezed it till the bones crunched.

'I should have smelt a rat when Pentreath had his exhibition,' he called over his shoulder. 'I noticed how bouncy and chirpy you were those two weeks. Couldn't do enough for him, could you? Stupid of me not to guess the reason, I suppose. To think he was there at my invitation. Dear, dear me. What's more, there's another aspect to all this which doesn't exactly flatter me. Lost him to your rival, didn't you? I think I grasp the situation. Did you marry me on the rebound, Anna? Was I second best?'

'I don't know how you can say such a thing, when you're so well off and Hal has next to nothing.'

'I'm not talking in terms of wealth, and you know it – although it may be that my money helped to console you for having to make do with me. Possibly you even thought to flaunt it in front of little Peggy, hmm?'

She had always known he was shrewd, but the depth of his insight now was horrifying. Still, he was seeing only the ugly side.

'Guy,' she pleaded, 'it was that way at first, I must admit. But after I'd seen you a few times, I truly grew to like you. Nothing would have persuaded me to marry you otherwise.'

I did, she thought, I truly liked you – before I found you out.

'Liking doesn't really compare with grand passion, does it? What can I do, I wonder, to make you feel just as ardently about me? I must admit, he's a good-looking chap, Pentreath. Quite a bit younger than I am, too, quite a lot nearer your own age. An artist, thwarted love – yes, all very romantic. While here am I, a boring businessman and all-too-familiar. That's the

241

trouble with marriage, of course. So humdrum, isn't it? No real excitement.'

Close to the brink of the chasm, he stopped. Anna, beside him, was panting. He still kept her hand in a brutal grip.

'Told you the view was magnificent, didn't I? Look, Anna, look down there.' He grasped the back of her dress and urged her forward.

Anna shrieked. He was holding her just a foot from the edge. The walls of the zawn dropped almost vertically to the stone and shingle cove at the bottom. Below her, seabirds cruised back and forth to nests built on narrow shelves in the rock. From up here, even herring gulls seemed sparrow-sized, and strong waves washing the base of the cliffs appeared little more than ripples. Heady scents of salt and seaweed floated up to her, and the cries of the birds echoed shrilly in the abyss.

'Guy, please don't! We're much too close. I'm frightened.'

'Why? I'm here, your husband, looking after you.'

Anna started to cry. Her head was reeling.

'What was I saying just now?' shouted Guy against the wind. 'Oh yes – excitement. Could that be the answer, Anna? What do you think? Has our love-making gone a bit stale, my dearest? Remember that night on the ferry? Would it help if we spiced it up again with some novelty, some thrills? We always do it in bed these days. Same old feather pillows and satin covers. That's very dull, isn't it? Always in private, behind a locked door. Not very imaginative. I'll bet an artist like Pentreath is a lot more creative. I expect he takes Peggy out in the fields in the moonlight and does it under the stars.'

'Shut up! Stop it! Let me go!'

'Yes, artist types always do things like that. Wind-in-the-hair stuff, feet-in-the-dew. Very impulsive and spiritual. Shall we try something similar, Anna? Shall we have a tumble here? Right here and now?'

'You're mad!' she screamed. 'Enough, Guy, let's go back!'

'Lord, no, this is all much too arousing. Mustn't waste a chance like this. By God, I feel I could go for an hour! See?'

He jerked her back against him.

Oh mercy! Anna thought. But of course he was always keenest, hardest, when she least wanted it. Now she was terrified, so his eagerness was all-too-predictable.

In an instant he had her down on the ground and was pulling at her clothes. Her head was no more than a foot from the edge of the cliff and she wondered with sickening fright if the rock was stable, or if there might be a weakness, a section ready to crumble.

But soon another fear took over. With every jerk from Guy, she felt herself shift a little bit towards the drop. Beneath her back she could feel the grass creeping by. Slowly, steadily, with every jolt, he was driving her nearer. He was laughing, looking almost crazy with excitement.

'There now, isn't this novel, isn't this fun?'

Anna wept and tried to push him off. She was giddy with awful sensations of depth and height. In the sky above her, hovering on the updraught from the zawn, was a peregrine falcon. It hung there, watching the struggle with fierce black eyes. She pictured what the bird could see, herself and Guy and the gulf below. Vertigo convulsed her stomach.

Guy was revelling in her fright. 'Enjoying it, Anna?

I am. It's tremendous. Don't know why I didn't think of it before.'

'You'll have us over! You'll kill us both!'

He worked even harder. 'What's the matter, don't you trust my judgement?'

'You want to frighten me,' she sobbed. 'Well, all right, I'm scared to death.'

His grin became ugly, vindictive. 'Good, because that's what you need. Chastisement, Anna. Sins have consequences. I want you to learn your lesson well.'

He carried on and after a minute she felt the supporting ground go from under her head.

'Guy!' she screamed. 'Please! Please! Enough!'

'Not yet. Look, Anna, look down there. Turn your head and see.'

She screwed her eyes shut. 'No!'

'Go on, look!'

Her head and neck were over. She could feel the line of the cliff edge against her shoulderblades.

'Look!' he shouted into her face, and she didn't dare defy him. Opening her eyes, Anna rolled her head, saw the void below and whimpered with terror. Everything was upside down and the walls of rock seemed to fall away for ever and ever.

Above her, Guy was chuckling, peering with fascination down into the zawn.

'What a sensation, Anna, eh? Thrilling enough for you? How many pushes will it take before we overbalance? Think I'll finish in time to save us?'

'Please,' she moaned, 'let me up.'

He was suddenly still, considering her, quite in control of himself. Then he grasped the front lock of her hair and held her face up to his.

'Don't ever deceive me, Anna,' he warned quietly.

'Don't even consider it. Not with Pentreath, not with anyone. You're my wife. You will not hide things from me, or refuse me ever again. Is that clear?'

Gulping, she nodded.

'I want to be sure that you know how strongly I feel about this. I'm proud, you see, Anna. I won't tolerate being made a fool of, so this is in the nature of a cautionary exercise. A stitch in time, if you like. Understand?'

She choked out: 'Yes.'

And suddenly he rolled back, pulling her roughly with him, and dumped her in a patch of heather.

Anna looked up, gasping. He was already walking away up the hill towards the car, fastening his trousers as he went.

Weakly, she pulled her skirts down, closed her eyes and was violently sick.

Late that afternoon, Delia Trevena opened her front door in response to urgent knocking. There on the step stood Anna. She was carrying a suitcase. With her were Robin, very disgruntled, and Tuffet. The taxi which had brought them was just pulling away, and Mrs Trevena saw at once that her daughter had been crying.

'My dear girl . . .'

Anna pushed past her, dragging an unwilling Robin, with Tuffet trotting on her leash. Dropping her suitcase, Anna shut the door and bolted it.

'Anna, what is this? What's going on?'

'I've left him!' came the distracted answer. 'He's a monster and I'm never going back.'

'Do you mean Guy?'

'Of course I do!' Anna's voice cracked. She made for

the stairs, but her mother's stocky figure barred her way.

'Now just a minute, where do you think you're going?'

'To my bedroom.'

'You can't, it's let.'

'What?' White-faced, Anna looked at her blankly. 'You've never done that before!'

'But this year I have. Why should I leave a good room lying empty when I can make extra income?'

'Oh, God!' exclaimed Anna, distraught.

Primly, Mrs Trevena folded her hands. Her expression was stiff and her green eyes frosty. 'I ask you again, what is this all about? Do I take it there's been some sort of quarrel?'

'That hardly serves to describe it,' spluttered Anna.

'Then you had better explain. Go in the parlour, I'll make some tea.' From the corner of her eye, Mrs Trevena spotted Robin pulling the grasses out of the vase on the hall table. 'And you stop that, young man.' She tapped the back of his hand.

Pushing out his lower lip, Robin glared at her. He was two now, and becoming wilful.

Anna took him into the sitting-room. Tuffet ambled after her, tail wagging. Mrs Trevena pursed her mouth and her forehead folded in displeasure. She couldn't abide having dogs in the house, or small children, either. Going into the kitchen, she made up a tray with tea and scones, and chocolate cake for Robin.

'All right, then, let's hear all about it,' she said, settling down in the parlour to pour. 'It can't be so very terrible, surely? All married couples have tiffs, you know.'

Gratefully, Anna sipped the hot tea, putting in extra

sugar. She had no appetite for food, but cut up a small piece of cake into cubes for her son.

'Start from the beginning,' prompted her mother.

Anna blew her nose and debated a moment before doing that.

'I hope it's nothing to do with Hal Pentreath,' said Mrs Trevena sharply. 'I feared there might be mischief afoot when I saw in the paper that he was to have an exhibition at the hotel.'

'There was no mischief, Mother,' snuffled Anna.

'But was it something to do with him?'

Her daughter began to cry.

'It was. Oh, you stupid girl.'

'It isn't what you think!' flared Anna. 'Wait until I tell you what Guy did to me today!'

It all came pouring out about the portrait, Mr Snow, Peggy's angry visit, and finally Guy's exploit at the zawn. Anna's weeping grew uncontrollable as she recounted that, the words broken and swallowed up in sobs. Mrs Trevena's eyes were like marbles and her face turned very red as she pictured her daughter and son-in-law on the cliff edge in broad daylight.

'Thank God it's such a lonely road,' she breathed at last. 'No one saw you, did they?'

'Is that your only concern?' gasped Anna. 'Can't you imagine what it was like for me? I was petrified.'

'Yes, I'm sure it was very unpleasant. Guy shouldn't have done such a thing, I agree. But then, you provoked him.'

'Did I? How?'

'You've just told me you – rejected – his affections that time. This morning he found out why. He put two and two together and he made four.'

'That wasn't because of Hal. I've never liked the way Guy uses me in bed.'

Mrs Trevena made a delicate little grimace. 'Yes, well I do understand your distaste, of course. I never had much trouble at all from your father, but some men have stronger urges. It's unfortunate, I agree, if Guy is one of those. Still, I dare say he'll cool as he grows older. In the meantime it's easiest to be compliant, isn't it? After all,' she sniffed, with a scornful roll of her eyes, 'a minute or two of puffing and blowing, that's all it is.'

Briefly, Anna considered enlightening her, explaining in graphic detail just what it was like with Guy, but she couldn't bring herself to do it, couldn't utter the words.

'Anyway, you may have been unhappy with that side of your marriage, Anna, but don't try and tell me that seeing Hal Pentreath didn't make matters worse.'

'It wasn't my idea for Hal to come and paint my portrait! It wasn't my idea to offer him an exhibition.'

'Even so, you should have been more open about him with Guy. You shouldn't have hidden the fact that you knew him.'

'You told me to do just that when Guy and I were courting!'

'There was no reason to mention him then, and it might have been unwise. But now the ring is safely on your finger, and when Guy asked him along to paint your portrait – well, that was the time to come clean. You could have made light of it. Instead you kept mum and made yourself look guilty, Anna. How else would any husband react?'

'Not like that! No reasonable, normal man would do what he did out there today.' Anna paused to pick up a chunk of cake which Robin had dropped. He promptly dropped another one and stamped it with his little shoe, rubbing chocolate cream into Mrs Trevena's carpet.

'Robin, don't!' his mother whispered fiercely. The child regarded her archly, then he glanced at his grandmother and smirked. Mrs Trevena glowered back.

'You're taking it all the wrong way, in my opinion,' she continued. 'I think it demonstrates how strongly Guy feels about you. If he's madly jealous, it's because he's still madly in love. He wants a lot of sex because he hasn't grown bored with you. It's really rather flattering, Anna. Violent passion. Didn't you see *The Sheik?*'

'Mother, you don't understand. It was all to do with ownership, nothing to do with love, and my husband is not the civilised gent he appears. He's a tyrant. To know a man like Guy, you have to live with him. Or work for him,' added Anna wryly. 'The staff could tell you a thing or two. He's the very devil when things go wrong.'

'Guy is in business, his work brings certain pressures and so, on occasion, he lets off steam. Can't you be a bit more understanding? He may be a little pernickety, but you must adapt to your husband, Anna. That's what marriage is all about, learning to tolerate someone else's habits and whims and foibles.'

'He doesn't make the slightest allowance for mine.'

Mrs Trevena sighed. 'He's the man, that's how it is. He holds the purse-strings – and a nice fat purse it is, too.'

'I don't want his money, or him!'

Mrs Trevena gave her a long, long look. 'My dear, you cannot stay here.'

'I can't go back to him.'

'He's your husband and marriage is for life.'

'Not necessarily.'

'Anna . . .'

'There are good grounds – cruelty, for instance.'

'. . . I will not tolerate talk of divorce. It's immoral and a social disgrace. "Whom God hath joined together",' quoted Mrs Trevena. 'Have you forgotten that already?'

'Please don't make out you're religious. You're not, and neither am I.'

'It's a stigma, Anna, one never lives it down.'

'Seems to me a lesser evil than putting up with Guy. He frightens me. What could be worse, more miserable than that?' Beseeching, she gazed at her mother. 'Let us stay here, please.'

'I've told you, your room has been let. I've a full house right up to the end of the season.'

'Couldn't we share with you?'

'Certainly not. I haven't space for another bed and a cot in my room. Really, Anna, your trouble is you don't know when you're well off, my girl. No marriage is perfect. You just don't appreciate your situation – having money, and staff to do so much for you. Given a chance, I'm sure half the women in Trezawne would trade places with you.'

Would that include Peggy? wondered Anna mournfully. If she were to make the offer, I'd gladly take her up on it.

Robin had wandered from Anna's side and Mrs Trevena suddenly caught sight of him pulling the heads off her favourite potted geranium.

'Robin!' she exclaimed. 'You wicked boy! Come here and say you're sorry.'

The child approached her with dragging feet, looking up at her from under his brows.

'Well?' demanded Mrs Trevena.

Robin threw back his head and spat. As yet, he hadn't mastered the trick of letting much saliva fly, but he liked the noise and the tone of the gesture. Lately, he'd been doing it a lot.

Mrs Trevena was speechless. Angrily, Anna flicked his legs and Robin hung his head.

'I'm sorry,' she said. 'He's upset, he knows things aren't normal. Look, Mother, couldn't we sleep in here? Just for a few days, anyway. A mattress on the floor would do. I need time to think.'

'Anna, you don't imagine Guy is simply going to let you walk off with Robin, do you? Leaving him is quite impractical. You're not using your head.'

'I can manage if you help me,' Anna begged. Then, desperate, she declared: 'I'm not moving from here. I will not go! You must take us in.'

Her mother considered her for a moment, then she muttered: 'Tsk! Fine thing. You made a match any sensible girl would envy. When I think what I spent on clothes for you, not to mention your wedding. Now you want to abandon an elegant home and sleep here on the floor. Well, all right. Temporarily, I'll let you stay. I only pray that you'll come to your senses before too much damage is done between you and your husband.'

'Thank you,' Anna said, relieved. 'Oh, thank you so much.'

'Fine thing,' repeated Mrs Trevena. She stood up. 'Well, I suppose I'd better go and start the dinner. The guests will be coming in soon and now I must cook for two extra.'

'Robin hasn't had his nap,' said Anna. 'May I put him down on the settee for an hour or two?'

'Oh, why not? Make yourselves at home.' Taking the tray, Delia Trevena left the room. Anna removed Robin's shoes and settled him down. When he had fallen asleep, she sank into an armchair, exhausted, to have a snooze herself.

It was an hour later when she drowsily heard the front door bang. There were murmuring voices in the hall. Guests, she thought, coming in for their evening meal.

Then the door to the parlour opened. A familiar voice jerked her wide awake.

'Come on, Anna, we're going home.'

Robin wriggled off the settee and ran to his father, squealing with delight. Scooping him up, Guy smiled at his wife. His long, lean figure towered in the doorway. Behind him hovered Mrs Trevena.

Anna sat up, her heart thudding.

'Your mother telephoned me,' Guy said pleasantly. 'Fancy being so upset by a little tiff. You've blown it up out of all proportion, my sweetheart. Sorry if I scared you, by the way. No more horsing around on cliffs, I promise. Word of honour. It was just a prank, you know.'

Anna stared past him at her mother, appalled by this betrayal. Guilt showed briefly on Mrs Trevena's face. But then she said: 'I knew it was all a storm in a teacup, Anna dear. I knew you were making too much of it. Go on home with Guy and forget all about it.'

Well, now she knew precisely where her mother

stood. No refuge here, not now, not ever. Anna felt hopeless, sick.

Guy held out his hand to her. 'Car's outside. I've left the engine running.' He looked around the room and spotted Tuffet by the hearth. He whistled to her, calling: 'Here, girl,' and the little dog stood up.

Numbly, Anna did the same. Passing the child to his mother-in-law, Guy took his wife by the elbow and picked up her case.

'It'll all look different in the morning,' he said brightly.

On her way out, Anna muttered to her mother: 'I'll never forgive you.'

'On the contrary, dear. You'll soon be thanking me, wait and see.'

'Judas. I'll never trust you again, and I'll never forget this.'

Guy smiled at his mother-in-law. 'She's not herself today,' he soothed.

Mrs Trevena followed them down to the car and put the boy in the back seat. Tuffet hopped in too, and then they were speeding away. Delia Trevena watched it turn the corner and then she went indoors.

Did her conscience trouble her? Was there a twinge? Nothing to bother about. Mrs Trevena had her priorities and Anna's happiness was not at the top of the list.

After all her bragging to the neighbours – indeed, the whole town – about Anna's wonderful marriage, how could she let her throw it away? What would she say to everyone when they asked why Anna was home? The Trevenas would be whispered about and sniggered at and ribbed. Having got her daughter off her hands and into a very smart niche, Mrs Trevena wanted no reversals. Letting Anna's room had increased her income by ten per cent, and anyway, she could never tolerate that dog, or that nasty child.

Twenty-five

Unlike Robin, Joy Pentreath had never been spoilt. Four years old now – or four and a half, as she insisted – she was growing into a little replica of Peggy, in more ways than one. Joy didn't care for her grandad, or her Uncle Jasper. Grandad scowled at her and he didn't smell nice. With Uncle Jasper she simply felt a vague unease. He would grin at her, but she sensed he didn't like her. On occasion she saw him doing things he shouldn't – like taking money out of Grandma's purse. One day she had caught him weeing in the kitchen sink. He had told her to 'bugger off' and carried right on doing it. Another day, he had trodden on her dolly and broken it. He claimed it was an accident, but Joy was not too sure, because his words said one thing and his eyes said another.

On a morning in late October she sat at the kitchen table, emptying out her piggy bank. It was made of white china with big pink spots, and had a round cork stopper in its belly. Every Saturday morning, Grandma gave Joy a threepenny bit to save. It was always a shiny one, specially cleaned with metal polish, so that the coins would look like pirate treasure. Joy loved to look at her threepenny bits, gather them into a heap and see them twinkling. Sometimes she laid them out in rows, or made patterns with them on the oil-cloth.

On this particular day, she was actually going to spend one. Mam and Dad were taking Joy and Ewan on a trip. They were going to the cinema in Wadebridge to see *Tarzan the Ape Man*. Mam was upstairs right now, getting Ewan ready. They were catching the eleven-twenty bus.

Solemnly, Joy considered her coins, trying to decide which one to spend. Although they were all identical, this was something which seemed to matter. The three-penny bits were like old friends. Which one to sacrifice?

As she pondered, the child became aware that she was being watched. Joy looked up and there in the doorway stood her Uncle Jasper. His eyes were fixed upon the coins. Then they shifted slyly to Joy and a lopsided grin split his face.

Soberly, the child stared back. Jasper shambled forward and sat down on the other side of the table. Joy curled a protective hand around her coins and pulled them towards her. Trying to ignore Uncle Jasper, she concentrated once more on her choice. There was one a bit less shiny than the rest which seemed the best candidate. Joy picked it out and put it in the pocket of her tartan dress.

'Got one for me, then?'

Joy glanced up.

'Got a bob or two for your uncle to go and have a drink?'

She shook her head fiercely and began in haste to drop the coins back into her pig.

'Aw, go on,' prodded Jasper. And suddenly his hand was across the table, snatching. His paw engulfed most of the threepenny bits in a single grab. A few spilled out and went tinkling and rolling across the table and onto the floor.

'No!' shrieked Joy. 'Mine, they're mine! Give them back!'

'Shan't,' said Jasper, sneering. 'What do you want money for? Sweeties, is it?' He leaned across the table, pushing his mocking face at her. 'Plenty down in the shop. You can go and help yourself.'

'Mine!' repeated Joy, distraught, and she clawed at Jasper's great clenched hand. 'They're my treasure Grandma gave me!'

'Not any more. Your Uncle Jasper needs them.' He leered at her. 'I'm going to spend them all, right now. They'll be gone in an hour. You'll have to start all over again, collect another lot. And then I'll have them too.'

Climbing down from her chair, she ran around the table and went for him with her tiny fists. Jasper held up the handful of money above her head.

'Here you are. Jump for it, then, little brat. Mummy and Daddy's girl, Grandma's girl, all done up like a dog's dinner.' Scornfully, he tweaked at the white lace collar of her dress. 'Peggy the second, aren't you, eh? Don't like me, do you? Well, I don't like you either, not you nor your brother, so there. Don't want you here, see?'

Joy was hysterical by now, her face red and crumpled with weeping. Jasper, enjoying himself, guffawed.

'Daddy!' Joy screamed.

'Daddy's out, he's gone to buy some paints.'

'I'll tell on you!'

Jasper lightly cuffed her head. 'Tell on you,' he mimicked. 'Whining bloody kid.'

But a second later he dropped the money, yelling and clutching his skull as something hard and knobbly swiped down over it. Joy went scrambling for her coins, and Jasper turned to see his sister standing over him. In her hand was a large string bag full of brussels sprouts.

'Don't you dare torment my child, you toad, or take her money.'

'I was only playing,' protested Jasper. 'Having a bit of fun with her. She's like you, she can't take a joke.'

'You'd have pinched some of her threepenny bits, all right. You wouldn't be above it, I know you. Anything for a pint of beer – anything but work, that is. You're a lazy, mucky article without any scruples whatever. A joke, did you call it? I heard what you said to her. "Don't like you, don't want you here."'

She put an arm around her daughter, as Joy huddled close to her side. The child was glaring now at her Uncle Jasper, a little mirror-image of her mother.

'Well, we don't,' he retorted. 'Father and me, we'd be glad to see the back of you.'

'That isn't news. Father and me, you say. Father and me. It's always you and him – like a double act, with you following his lead. What he thinks, you think. God Almighty!' She was suddenly filled with a surge of exasperation and pity. 'Jasper, don't you ever consider doing something with your life? And can't you see what he's made of you? He likes having someone to booze with him and you serve the purpose. You think so much of Dad, but if he had any care for you, he'd tell you to give up the beer, go out and learn a proper trade, get married and have a family of your own. But no, instead he drags you down the road to ruin with him. Some father! He knows what he's doing, too. The old man's selfish, through and through. You're his only ally, just about the only person in town who doesn't look down on him. So he'll keep a tight hold on you – and you'll never have the things others have, unless you break free. What woman would marry you, Jasper, the way you are now? Look at yourself in the glass, you're twenty-four and a slob with nothing to offer. There's not a girl in town would give you a second glance.'

Jasper had been rolling his eyes and mouthing: 'Yak, yak, yak.' But something about that last remark struck home. Being idle, being a sot, had never seemed especially shameful to him. On the contrary, dodging work was clever and drinking was a man's pursuit. It rankled, however, to think he might be despised by the local girls. Not that he wanted marriage or responsibility – perish the thought – but he had enough male vanity to be stung by their contempt.

His face turned sullen.

'Yes,' nodded Peggy, tossing the bag of sprouts back in the vegetable rack. 'Not one of them would have you as a gift. They all look at Hal, though, yes, they do. And they tell me how lucky I am.' Curling her lip, she said again: 'You'd have taken Joy's coins for beer. Where's your self-respect? And what do you think the future holds for you? All that stands between you and the gutter is Mother. When she and Dad are gone, you'll be completely alone, I promise, because Hal and I won't be bothered with you. If I were in your shoes, I'd be frightened.'

'I'll never need you,' he retorted. 'Nor Rembrandt, neither. He's not so smart, as we've all found out.'

'But still ten times the man you are, and you know it.'

Jasper sat brooding when they had gone. He felt peculiarly disturbed and badly wanted a drink. He didn't like thinking about his life, about making something of it. He just lived from day to day, from pint to pint. Huge anxieties surfaced if he thought about 'plans' or 'becoming something' – frightening, daunting prospects of effort and risk. He wanted to be all right as he was. That would be easy – simply exist and drink. Jasper would just as soon opt out of doing and trying in life. Somehow, it all seemed too much to tackle.

'. . . ten times the man you are.'

How he hated Pentreath. Hal, the good example.

Licking his lips, Jasper swore to himself. He yearned for a beer. He would only have taken a couple of bob from the child – three, perhaps. Enough for the six or seven pints he usually drank midday.

For a while he sat rubbing his head – surprising how much those sprouts had hurt – and feeling very sorry for himself. Then, with relief, he remembered something. Billy Nancarrow still owed him for playing last Saturday night. Billy owed him fifteen bob.

Jasper glanced at the clock. *The Old Solace* was open. Jumping up, he put on his cap and went out. He felt like getting very drunk indeed.

Shortly before three that afternoon, the door of the loft creaked open and a head appeared around it. Bleary eyes surveyed the room.

Canvases standing on easels. A bowl of hazelnuts and apples and oranges set up for a still life. Paints and brushes and piles of drawings. The old chairs and couch draped with colourful fabric remnants. Everything just as Hal had left it.

A malicious gleam appeared in Jasper's eyes. The door opened wider and his skinny figure stepped unsteadily inside. With thirteen pints of ale under his belt, he was in a reckless mood.

He lurched across the room, looking all around him. The loft was filled with autumn sunshine and a sense of peace. Swaying, Jasper glared about him. This workroom made him terribly aware of what he was. Pentreath had a gift. He exercised it and it gave him satisfaction. Jasper recognised that and felt intimidated by it. He was dimly aware of missing something good, and of being a dolt both by decree of nature and by choice. 'Born stupid', his mother often said, 'and happy to drink away what wits he has.' Hal's studio felt like a reproach to him, underlining his deficiency.

He peered at a watercolour pinned to a tilted board. The scene was a courtyard in the back streets of lower Trezawne. White-washed cottages, two old women leaning out of windows to gossip, a cat on a doorstep, polishing her whiskers.

Jasper grunted. 'Huh!' He couldn't focus very well. Sometimes there were four old women, and the cat seemed to float in mid air.

He moved on to a pile of drawings, squinting at them one by one, then tossing them away. They fell to the floor about his feet or fluttered on to the couch. Halfway through them, he scoffed and swore and swept the rest from the table with a violent swing of his arm.

A large oil of a fishing boat caught Jasper's attention and he reeled across to the easel. The paint was thick and rough-looking, almost like putty stuck on in dabs. He put out a hand and rubbed the surface.

It had looked dry, but it wasn't. Jasper stared stupidly at the mess on his palm and then at the picture. A moment ago there had been a lugger and men hauling nets aboard. A moment ago there had been a choppy sea. Now there was a multi-coloured blotch, a bow but no stern, and half a mainsail.

Jasper blinked at it, and then he crowed with mirth. The hand went out again. Paint oozed through his fingers as he clawed them over the board.

Tottering backwards, he viewed his handiwork, chortled and slapped his thighs with glee. The right leg of his trousers now bore heavy smears of oil paint.

'Uh?' he grunted, gazing down at the smudges, head wobbling. 'Oh, bugger,' he slurred. Then he giggled again. His wavering gaze sought other work to spoil and lit upon a stack of canvases propped against the cupboard.

Jasper laid one on a table, considered it, then reached for a tube of red paint. Unscrewing the cap, he squeezed the tube in the middle. A worm of crimson spurted out and plopped upon the painting. Wheezing with hilarity, Jasper took a tube of yellow and did the same again. Then, with the largest brush he could find, he spread the colours.

The painting had taken Hal four days to complete. Jasper destroyed it in as many minutes. Once he had started, he couldn't stop. Just as one beer led to another, so did every ravaged painting make him want the same again. Within an hour he had ruined every picture he could find. The floor was scattered with empty colour-pots and twisted tubes. He had trodden back and forth across the sketches, leaving rainbow imprints of his boots. Screwed-up, torn, soggy with spilt water, charcoal studies were strewn about like litter.

Finally, having exhausted himself and the supply of pictures, Jasper surveyed the room again and shook with merriment. Too sodden even to think about what Hal might do, he clutched his stomach and laughed until his ribs began to ache.

By seven that evening, however, Jasper was feeling anything but jolly. Sitting with Walter in *The Old*

Solace, he took another gulp of his beer. He kept glancing uneasily at the door. The pub was already full, very crowded and noisy. The air was heavy with cigarette smoke and the smell of drink. All around him, men were talking, laughing, arguing. Billy Nancarrow was stationed behind his counter.

Jasper sat in the very corner. Beside him, Walter was droning on about something, but his son paid him no heed. Jasper was not feeling chatty tonight. Jasper was feeling very unhappy indeed on account of his ill-advised prank. He had slept for two hours afterwards and woken up sober. Now he was terrified. Hal and Peggy would be home at any time. Pentreath was sure to guess the culprit.

He shrank into the corner, trying to make himself very small. He had deemed it the wisest course to stay with his father – though what protection Walter could offer, Jasper didn't know.

Walter began to notice that his son was unresponsive to his chatter. He peered at Jasper and nudged him in the ribs.

'Did you hear me? Am I talking to myself?'

'Uh?' said Jasper, startled. 'Yes.'

'What was I saying?'

Jasper didn't answer. A figure passed the window. He followed its movements with saucer eyes.

'What's wrong with you?' demanded Walter.

'Nothing.'

'Yes, there is. You're nervous.'

'Don't feel very well,' came the mumble.

'Finish up your beer and have another. You'll feel better.'

Jasper swallowed another mouthful and pulled a face. He had let it stand so long it was nearly flat.

263

The door opened. Jasper stiffened, went white. A fisherman entered and Jasper breathed again.

Walter's eyes narrowed. 'What's the matter? Who you watching for?'

'Nobody,' said Jasper, but his Adam's apple bobbed. He glanced again through the thick, bottle-bottom windows and a sheen of sweat could be seen beneath the lank strands of hair falling over his brow.

'You're in some sort of trouble,' Walter accused. 'You'd better tell me.'

Jasper opened his mouth and then closed it again. His father would call him all the fools in creation when he knew what he had done. Seizing his beer, Jasper gulped the rest of it down.

'I'll have another,' he said. 'It's your turn.'

Perhaps a couple more would brace him up, he was thinking. It had given him courage enough to do the evil deed. Perhaps it would help him face the consequences too.

Picking up their empty glasses, Walter rose from his seat. With one more suspicious look at his son, he elbowed his way to the bar. Jasper sat with his hands clasped tightly between his knees. So apprehensive was he, that he feared he might wet himself.

Several times more the pub door opened and Jasper's stomach jerked. But, each time, it was someone other than Hal. Jasper began to wish Pentreath would hurry up and come for him, just to have it over with.

Finally, at twenty-past seven, his wish was granted.

Walter had just returned with two frothing glasses of ale. He set one down in front of his son, then saw that Jasper was staring at the door like a frightened rabbit.

'Now, what . . .?' Angilley turned to look, and saw

his son-in-law. Hal had not yet spotted them. He was scanning the room and craning his neck to see over the heads of men who were standing. His eyes were wild and his cheeks were livid. He looked ready to kill.

Walter's gaze snapped back to his son. 'Is it him you're afraid of? Why? You great idiot – what have you done?'

Jasper's mouth worked soundlessly at first. Then he stammered: 'His paintings . . . You know how much I drank this morning . . .'

Walter took a few seconds to comprehend. Then: 'Oh, my God. You did something to his paintings? We'd better go. Out the back door, come on, quick.'

It was too late. Hal had seen them.

Barging his way through the crowd, he lunged across the table, seizing Jasper by his lapels. Walter tried to pull him off and received a clout for his trouble. Staggering backwards, Angilley collapsed in another man's lap and was promptly shoved from there to the floor. There was a crash of breaking glass and beer slopped everywhere as Hal dragged Jasper across the table, overturning it.

'Here!' yelled Billy Nancarrow. 'If you want to brawl, you take it outside.'

A babble of excitement ran around the room. Men grabbed their drinks and cleared out of the way as Hal hauled the struggling Jasper towards the door. He was whining about how sorry he was, swearing it was the beer to blame and he'd only started out to have a bit of a joke, that was all. He squirmed and twisted in Pentreath's grasp, but Hal had a good strong grip on Jasper's collar, and his right arm bent behind him.

Clumsily getting up from the floor, Walter decided to let his fool of a son look out for himself. He wiped his mouth and shook his head, and when Billy wasn't looking, he spat on the floor. The paintings. Walter could make a good guess at what Jasper had done. He wondered how he had managed to father such a blockhead.

With the exception of Billy Nancarrow, everyone followed Pentreath and Jasper outside. Sighing, Billy went on placidly wiping glasses. As soon as it was over, they would all be back and with a bigger thirst.

Outside it was dark and all the lamps along the waterfront were lit. Hal sent his brother-in-law stumbling down the slipway to the beach and charged after him. Jasper made a bid for escape, scurrying this way and that, weaving about on the sand, but to no avail. Pentreath caught him by his jacket and started to use his fists.

There was cheering and whistling and hooting from *The Old Solace* crowd. They ranged themselves along the quay, from whence there was an excellent view, clutching their ale and enjoying this unexpected entertainment. It was not that this was a very good fight, being so one-sided. It was just that the layabout Angilley was getting dusted off.

Soon, people were drawn out of nearby houses by the commotion. Top-floor windows went up and heads poked out, to see a mob grouped on the quayside, and two dark figures down on the beach, flailing at one another.

Jasper was in tears by now. He had taken a dozen punches and could scarcely get his breath. Pentreath was almost sobbing too, with fury and exertion and with grief. Despite his own terror, Jasper grasped the enormity of what he had done to Hal. His precious paintings, all that effort, that work he loved so much.

However, Jasper's first concern was to save his skin, and as the blows went on and on he began to fear that Hal wasn't going to stop until he killed him.

Jasper tasted blood in his mouth and felt the sickening sensation of a tooth hanging by a thread. His left eye was closing, his lip was split, his ribs were aching from body blows. He had managed to land a couple of lucky swipes himself, but he hadn't the fitness or the strength of his brother-in-law. More and more groggy, Jasper staggered this way and that on the sliding sand. His knees were beginning to buckle under him. The street lights appeared to swing around his head, and glowing windows seemed to circle him in the dark. Somewhere up there on the quay was his father, among that shouting mob. The old man wasn't going to help him. Well, what could he do, anyway? Fat, awkward, cowardly Walter.

Jasper began to plead. 'Enough! Please, for pity's sake!'

Hal took no notice, so Jasper folded up, collapsed in the sand and rolled on to his back with arms outstretched.

Hal's response soon brought him back to gibbering life. Taking him by the ankles, Pentreath pulled him down the beach with an alarming speed born of mad strength. Jasper heard the swish of water at the tideline. His eyes flew open, he gobbled with fear and then he shrieked as the cold engulfed him.

Just before his head went under, he thought he heard other screams. Maisie's voice, and Peggy's, urging:

'Stop him, somebody! Stop him! Do something!'

Then he was under and a drumming filled his ears. There came a bubbling whoosh as Pentreath flipped him over. A hand was on the back of Jasper's neck,

267

and Hal's weight straddling his body. Jasper thrashed and kicked and tried to throw him off. It was pitch dark and his face was being pressed against the bottom. In his struggles, he briefly opened his mouth and it filled with sand and water.

Once, he managed to break away, as Pentreath overbalanced and lost his hold. Jasper pulled his head up, snatching air in hysterical gasps. Around him, the water was silky black, with golden reflections upon it from the lights of boats in the harbour. Making a frantic dive towards the beach, Jasper now saw figures running towards him. Peggy, flying down over the sand, with Maisie behind her, and several men who had finally realised that he was in danger of his life.

Then, from behind, he was grabbed again and plunged under the water. Jasper was face-up this time, and above him he could dimly see the dark shape of his brother-in-law. Then there was a flurry all around him, other dark forms moving, another struggle going on. It seemed to take a long, long time before the hands that held him down were wrenched away.

But suddenly they were gone and Jasper surfaced, coughing, sucking frantically for air. Someone jerked him to his feet and muttered:

'He's all right.'

Beside him, standing up to her thighs in the tide, Peggy was hugging her husband, who was kneeling in the water, suddenly spent and still.

'Jasper!' A sharp voice bit through the night. 'Come out here and get on home, you worthless article.'

Through the gloom, he stared at his mother. Maisie was standing at the tideline, hands on hips.

'Well,' she snapped. 'Come on, out! Before the police get wind of this.'

Jasper stammered: 'He tried to drown me.'

'Twenty-four years too late,' said Maisie tartly. 'If I'd known what you were going to be, I'd have done it myself the day you were born.'

'He was going to murder me!' repeated Jasper, outraged.

'He gave you a ducking, that was all,' growled a man nearby.

Jasper flung a look around him, becoming angry now. 'He would have killed me!'

A circle of silent faces regarded him without expression.

'I'll go to the law!'

'You do and you can clear out of my house,' said Maisie. 'Now, go home.'

In the event, however, it was Hal, not Jasper, who left Angilley's Bazaar.

'We can't stay here any longer, not after this,' he said to Peggy later that evening.

'Oh, now don't be silly.' She stroked his face. On his forehead was a cut, and the skin around it bore a sheen of ointment. Bruises were coming out on his knuckles. 'Jasper will never dare do such a thing again, I can promise you that.'

'I don't care, I want to go,' he muttered heavily. 'They've always hated me being here, he and your old man. They can't stand the kids. There's trouble of some sort all the time. Didn't bother me very much at first, but over the years it starts to get you down. There's always an atmosphere at meals – enough to put me off my food sometimes. After this, it can only get worse. Every time I set eyes on that brother of yours, I'll have a job to keep my hands off him. We'll have to move out, we'll have to look for another place.'

They were sitting on the old couch in the loft. All around them lay the wreckage of Hal's precious work.

'Hal, we haven't enough yet to buy a house.'

'I can't help that.'

Alarm stirred in Peggy. 'If we start paying rent, our savings will dribble away.'

'Or that, either.'

'You promised me my own house one day!' She faced him, anxious now.

'And I meant it, then. But things just haven't gone as well as I expected.' His tone grew bitter. He clenched his teeth. 'In fact, it's been one damned thing after another these past three years. Jackman died, Snow cheated me. Now this. I've had a run of bad luck and I feel . . .' He groped for words to explain. 'Almost as if I'm ill-wished and I have to do something to break the spell. Make a change, a big one, turn everything around.'

'Matters can get worse instead of better, you know,' Peggy pointed out. 'That would be a real victory for Dad and Jasper, wouldn't it? They're dying for us to leave. Are you going to give them precisely what they want – and deny me what I want?'

At that, he was incensed. 'For once,' he said hotly, 'I feel inclined to do what *I* want. I married you, Peggy. I lost my freedom before I was really ready. You can't always have everything your own way. What's so terrible about renting a place? Most people do. You only want to own a house because Anna's wealthy and you don't want to feel too far behind.'

'It was you who first suggested buying,' Peggy flared. 'You gave me ideas and hopes, now you're ready to cancel them all because of those two goons downstairs. And don't pretend you haven't had benefits from living here. It hasn't been all sacrifice for you, Hal.'

'Are you saying that I've been a cadger, no better than Walter and Jasper?'

'No . . .'

'You are! So why object when I suggest that we strike out on our own?'

'Oh, God.' Peggy clutched her head, grasping and twisting a handful of hair. 'Hal, we're fighting. Let's stop this, right now.'

He was silent. After a minute or two he stood up and slowly started picking over the débris.

'Can't anything be salvaged?' Peggy asked sadly.

His back was turned. He shook his head. His shoulders were slumped and there was now a broken air about him which tore at Peggy's heart.

Would it indeed be so awful, she wondered, if they were to rent? Nothing they bought could ever compare to Elestren Manor, could it? He'd been right that evening out on the quay. Any sensible person would throw in the towel. And circumstances, it was true, had been somewhat unkind. Every time things were looking hopeful, it seemed as if fate, like a practical joker, stuck out a foot to trip him up. Peggy felt guilty, too, about her behaviour at Elestren Manor. He might have had more exhibitions there, if not for her. In her sorrow for him, she thought perhaps she owed it to Hal to bow to his wishes now.

A short while later, Maisie came up. Mouth tight, she looked around at the mess. 'Doctor's been,' she said. 'I thought I'd let you know the little wretch hasn't suffered any permanent damage. Are you all right?'

Hal nodded. 'I'd have swung for him. Thank God you stopped me.'

'Mmph. I wish I'd never hatched him, that's a fact.' Mournfully, she added: 'All your lovely pictures, son. I can't tell you how sorry I am.'

'It's no fault of yours,' he sighed. Then: 'We'll be leaving, Maisie, just as soon as I can find us somewhere else.'

At once, she was full of concern and objections.

'Aw, now what for? You're as welcome here as ever. I'll see you have no more trouble from those two.' She jerked her head towards the stairs. 'I'd sooner toss them out than see you go.'

'You're kind, but we're moving just the same.'

Unhappily, Maisie rubbed her hands on her apron. 'But what do you mean to do – find somewhere to rent?'

'That's the idea,' said Pentreath.

'But . . .'

'We'll be all right,' insisted Hal. He glanced at Peggy. 'Won't we?'

There was a long hesitation, but finally she said: 'Yes.'

'Winter's coming on, and you have two small children,' Maisie said. 'You could at least wait until spring.'

'I want to go now, that's all there is to it.' His voice acquired an edge.

Maisie appealed to her daughter. 'Peggy, is this what you want? What about your house?'

Committed now, Peggy stood up and clasped her husband's arm. 'I think we'll have to forget about that for the time being. It's no use, Mam, we have to go. Hal would be unhappy if we stayed here now, and if he's miserable, so am I.'

Maisie looked distressed, but she murmured: 'Well, you must do as you see fit, of course.' Then, eagerly: 'I can help you with money.'

'No. We'll manage.' Hal summoned a smile. 'You've been good to us, Maisie. You've given us more than enough already. We can fend for ourselves now, don't you fret.'

Twenty-six

Hal went out early next morning in search of a cottage to rent. By midday he began to realise it wouldn't be easy to find a suitable place. Several landlords refused him because he had children. Furthermore, premises with working space for an artist were not plentiful in Trezawne, and vacancies seldom occurred. Going back to the old lodgings of his single days, he found a sculptor firmly in residence. Hal went home at the end of that first day feeling dispirited.

Next morning, however, he set out again. At the town hall they gave him a list of places to rent and he scoured lower Trezawne from end to end, knocking on doors and looking at rooms, many of which were poky or smelly or dark, unfit for children. By the time he'd exhausted the list, he was footsore and downcast.

Peggy, in truth, was relieved. 'We may have to do as Mother suggests and wait until spring,' she said. 'Don't be too impatient, Hal. We're not in a bad situation here. We couldn't live as cheaply anywhere else.'

If delayed for a few months, she thought hopefully, he might cool down and change his mind, forget the whole idea.

Hal made no answer. He was scanning the accommodation advertisements in the local paper. After a moment or two, he roughly folded the paper and flung it away. Springing to his feet, he paced up and down the loft, hands in his pockets, angry now.

'Damn it, I want to get out. I just want to be away from here. I can't start work, can't settle down to anything until we're living somewhere else.'

'You can padlock the door to the loft if you're afraid Jasper might come up here again.'

'It isn't that. I know he won't. I simply want to go. I just can't think about anything else. There must be somewhere. Must be.' Slumping in the armchair, he snatched up the paper and read the 'To Let' column again.

Late the following afternoon, he came home in a state of excitement.

'I've found a place! It's out of town, but it has everything we need. There's even a garden.'

Peggy was standing at the sink, peeling vegetables. As he seized and lifted her off her feet, whirling her round and round, the potato flew out of her hand and rolled under the table.

'You have?' An uncertain smile lit her face. 'A good place for the children?'

'Perfect.'

'Room for you to work?'

'Of course.'

She linked her arms about his neck. 'Out of town, you say?'

'Up by the zawn.'

A faint frown came to Peggy's face. 'I don't know of any houses up there, Hal.'

'There's one and it's ours. I've taken it. Five shillings a week.'

'Who does it belong to, then?'

'Farmer by the name of Mingo. Know of him?'

She shook her head. A suspicion began to edge its way into her mind.

'It's in good repair?'

'Only needs a bit of doing up.'

He put her down and Peggy took up her knife again, went on peeling potatoes.

'How much doing up?'

'I'll take you out there tomorrow. You'll see for yourself.'

'Is there any furniture, Hal?'

'No, we'll have to buy some.'

'Hmm.' She turned the potato deftly, paring round and round it. 'You've taken it, you say? You've signed something?'

'Yes.'

She kept her eyes on the potato. More and more clean white emerged behind the blade of the knife and the spiral of earthy brown skin grew longer and longer.

'And paid a deposit, I suppose? Some rent in advance?'

'That's usual.'

'How much?'

'A year.'

The potato skin dropped into the sink. 'A year?' she asked, incredulous.

'Why not? It's just the place for us.'

'Couldn't you have asked me first, given me a chance to look at it?'

'You'll love it, Peggy. Just wait, first thing tomorrow morning, we'll go up and see it.'

Early the following day, Peggy stood staring down a rutted track at a wreck of a cottage. Behind her and on either side was open heath, broken only by scatter-

ings of granite boulders and a couple of low field walls
built of rough stone. Beyond the cottage were the Tolgarth road, the cliffs, the zawn, the sea, but Peggy's
gaze was riveted on the single-storey building which
was going to be their home.

The walls were cob and had once been painted white.
Now they were yellowish-brown, like tobacco-stained
teeth. Flaky in places, they looked as if a fist would go
right through them. The galvanised roof was rusty and
the windows filthy. Beside the cottage stood a rickety
shed. The 'garden' was a swathe of nettles and
brambles.

Peggy turned stricken eyes on her husband. 'We
can't . . . Oh, Hal, we can't! Not here!'

'Now don't be so hasty. Come and look inside.'

'I don't want to. You don't expect me to bring the
children here?'

'Why not? They'll have a lovely life. When the place
is shipshape, we'll grow things – flowers and food. It'll
be a lot healthier for them than living in a couple of
rooms above the bazaar.'

'We don't know anything about gardening.'

'Well, of course not, we've never had ground before.
But we'll learn.'

She hung back, reluctant to walk down that path
and look inside the cottage, fearful of what she was
going to see.

'It's nice and dry inside,' he pressed. 'You'll be surprised.'

She ordered her feet to move and they took her to
the door. Sunlight entered as it swung back, revealing
dust and cobwebs such as Peggy had never seen.
Twenty years of dust and cobwebs. For all that time,
the cottage had been empty, through twenty years of

rain and wind and frost and thunderstorms, up here without a hint of shelter.

'When it's swept out and cleaned it'll be all right,' Hal said cheerfully. 'Look, there's a lovely big fireplace in this room, and another with a cloam oven in the kitchen.'

'A cloam oven?' repeated Peggy. 'That's what they used a hundred years ago. I'm accustomed to gas.'

'Yes, I'm sorry about that. We can't have everything, though.'

'That's a prize understatement, isn't it? No running water either, and – oh my God, not even a privy.'

'There's a pump up at the top of the track. It's only a hundred yards. Beautiful water – I sampled it. And Farmer Mingo says he can fix us up with some kind of closet.'

'What kind, precisely?'

'He didn't say, but he promised to provide something.'

'And you trust him?'

'He's not a bad sort.'

'He's very canny, I'm sure. Farmers usually are. I reckon he was one too many for you.' She flashed him a withering glance. 'Like Mr Snow.'

'Peggy, don't. I've done my best. You know I've been looking for days. There was nowhere else.'

'We could have waited until there was. But no, you got the bit between your teeth and now see what you've done.'

'I've found us a home of our own, that's what. If you'd only stop whining and finding fault, you might see the possibilities.'

'Five shillings,' muttered Peggy. 'It's not worth one and six. He saw you coming, that's for sure, and summed you up for the mug you are. A year's rent,' she said wrathfully. 'You're mad.'

Hal fired back, 'I like it here, and I'm the one who earned the money, so I'll say how we spend it. The light is wonderful and there's ample room for me to work. Look, come out here.'

Taking her hand, he pulled her towards the chamber which served as a kitchen. The only facility it had was the open hearth and cloam oven. No sink, nothing else at all. Opening the back door, he led her into a wooden lean-to with large windows and a sloping glass roof. All around it at waist height were shelves with a great many empty flower-pots.

'See? It's not as big as the loft, but it'll do very well.'

Just at that moment, Peggy was not in the least bit interested in Hal's work requirements.

'If you say so. Dare I hope there's a bedroom?'

'Two,' he said triumphantly. 'This way.'

Back through the kitchen and the living-room, he ushered her to a door giving access to a small chamber which could serve for sleeping quarters. Another door connected to an even pokier room beyond.

For lingering moments, Peggy considered, then she went back to the main room and stood at the window facing the sea. Through the dark-smeared glass, the water appeared a grubby blue.

'What if I say no, Hal?' she asked at last. Turning around, she eyed him levelly.

He hesitated briefly. Then: 'I'm coming up here, Peggy. I want you and the children with me.'

'What if I say you can do as you please, but Joy and Ewan and I are staying with Mam?'

'I'll be very disappointed, but I'll still come up here.'

'You'd live apart from us?'

'I'm not remaining at the bazaar and that's final.'

Shaken, she turned to the window again, saying nothing.

'Peggy, please, just try it. If things go badly, then go back to Maisie by all means. I've taken this place for a year. That's not so very long. At the end of that time we can look around again if we're not happy here.'

There was a very long pause, and in the end he left the room and went outside. Kicking his way through the weeds, he perched on a portion of garden wall, looking out to sea. The wind from the Atlantic blew back his hair and chilled his face. In front of him the land sloped away to the road from Trezawne to Tolgarth. Half a mile beyond the road, Zawn Fell cut sharply into the cliffs. The tide was high, with a heavy swell rolling today. Even from here he could faintly hear the hiss and boom of it. Off to the east was a lighthouse, perched at the tip of a rocky headland. In the distance on the western side were two old engine-houses built into the cliffs, with empty windows like square black eyes, and stonework flushed a mellow buff in the winter sunlight.

Another Cornwall here for Hal to paint – forsaken, eerie. A little way inland from here were carns and ancient circles of stones. Fresh scenes for him, a new direction for his work. He wanted to live amid all this and feel the wildness of it around him in every kind of weather, be soaked in it and one with it. Then the atmosphere would come out in his painting, he felt sure.

He prayed that Peggy wouldn't call his bluff. He loved her, he adored his children, couldn't really leave them. They could live an idyllic life up here, he was certain. She simply didn't have his vision of it yet.

After a time, he heard a step behind him.

'Is there a bus?'

He turned and looked at her. In the wind her black hair danced like coiling snakes.

'A bus into town and back again,' she enlarged.

'Mingo says there are two in the morning and two in the afternoon.' He pointed to the road, the layby. 'You can catch it down there.'

'Mm. I'm thinking about the shopping, you see.'

This was hopeful. He smiled. 'Of course.'

She wandered around a bit, kicking at weeds and tufts of couch grass. This would be no place for wearing sandals, that was certain. Heavy lace-ups, even boots, would be more in order.

Still, she owed him a bit of give and take, a little co-operation, she supposed. He had indeed married her when he could just as well have left her in the lurch, saddled himself with a family before he was ready. Now he wanted – what – a sort of artistic adventure? Yes, something like that. Best, perhaps, to let him get it out of his system?

His voice broke in on her thoughts.

'You can buy a lot of stuff up at the farm – butter and eggs and so on. Mingo says his wife makes cheese and jams as well.'

'Got a fine eye to business, hasn't he? He'll sting us for everything, I dare say.'

Hal was silent again.

For better, for worse, thought Peggy. What a rash promise that was, and how lightly made.

She winced to imagine what Anna would say if she saw this place. Which was more important, then? Saving face before that woman she detested, or being a good wife to this man she loved? For Peggy, a thorny choice, but there could really be only one answer.

At last she sat down beside her husband, drew a deep breath and sighed: 'A year, no more, if we're not happy. Is that a promise, Hal?'

'It is.'

He regarded her tensely while she chewed her bottom lip and steeled herself.

'All right.'

'That's my girl!' He hugged her, kissed her. 'It'll be wonderful, Peggy, wait and see. You won't regret it.'

They returned next day with brushes and buckets, soap and mops and cleaning rags. Clearing out the dust and cobwebs was just the start of the job. Nothing much more could be done without water, preferably hot. Hal fetched a pailful down from the pump, but both chimneys responded by belching smoke back into the cottage when he tried to light a fire.

'Blocked with soot, I suppose,' said Peggy. 'Now what are we going to do?'

He thought for a moment, then he said: 'Wait here. I'll be back in an hour or less.'

'Where are you going?'

'Up to the farm. Perhaps old Mingo can help.'

Alone in the cottage, Peggy looked around her miserably. Ye Gods, she thought. I'd accepted that we would never be rich, but I didn't see us living in a place like this. Awful. It's awful, the most desolate dump any nightmare could conjure up. What'll we do for a lavatory? We'll have to use a bucket or something, keep it out in the shed and find somewhere to empty it.

But it was only for a twelvemonth. A year, a year,

no more than a year. She kept repeating that to herself like a magic charm.

After a while she plodded outside to look again at the patch of garden. The wind was soft and balmy today. Around her feet, the grass was dry and yellow. Weeds. The place was overrun with them. Yet – sprawled across the wall there was a rambling rose. Someone, a long, long time ago, had thought it worthwhile to plant a garden flower here.

A faint sound of voices reached her. She went around to the front again and there was Hal coming down the path with the farmer, who carried a shotgun.

'Mr Mingo reckons he can shift it, Peggy. And he has something up at the house we'll be glad of. I'll tell you later.'

The farmer, a skinny little man, was surveying Peggy with bright blue eyes and grinning broadly. He wore a flat cap, a boiler suit and gumboots, all heavily splashed with mud or something worse.

'Morning, dear,' he said. 'Hear the old chimneys are stuffed up?'

Poker-faced, she answered: 'Seem to be. Bird's nests, perhaps.'

'Aw, well, I'll soon blow them out of there.' He slipped two cartridges into his gun. 'Best stay outside.'

Peggy looked at Hal as Mr Mingo strode into the cottage.

'Says it's the way he sweeps his own,' shrugged Pentreath.

Seconds later, there came an almighty bang. A black cloud erupted from the kitchen chimney and another puffed out through the door. There was a pause, and then a second report. The other chimney blew out its plug of soot and a tangle of twigs. Shortly after, Mr

Mingo emerged, shotgun broken over his arm, slapping black powder from his overalls with his cap. His eyes looked even more brilliantly blue peering out of a soot-smeared face.

'Be no more trouble now,' he said. 'Sorry about the mess, maid.' Turning to Hal, he added: 'I'll send my boy down later with the lorry and that little item I promised you.'

'It's good of you, Mr Mingo,' Hal said.

'Aw, don't mention it. Missis hates the thing. Belonged to my old mother, see, and they never did get on.'

Winking at Peggy, he went on his way.

'What was he talking about?' she asked.

'You'll see.'

They went inside the cottage and Peggy groaned. Everywhere lay mounds of brownish-black soot. The walls were coated with it and a fine haze hung in the air, making both of them cough.

'Oh well,' said Hal, 'he didn't charge us for doing it.'

'I should damn' well think not!'

It took the rest of the day to shovel the soot out, sweep again, heat up water and wash down the walls and windows, but at the end there was a marked improvement.

'Doesn't seem quite so bad now, I admit,' said Peggy grudgingly. 'But before you take to your easel again, you're to patch up the walls outside, and the next bit of brushwork you do will be with whitewash.'

It was five o'clock or thereabouts when the farmer's son arrived with the lorry. Cleaning a window, Peggy paused when she saw it stop in the layby. There was something in the back covered over with tarpaulin and tied with rope. Hal went down to help the youth unload it and carry it up to the cottage, where he set it triumphantly down before his wife.

When he whisked away the cover, there stood a commode. A very grand one, too – mahogany, the arms and back extravagantly carved. The pink velvet seat lifted up to reveal an immaculate porcelain fitting with a lid and a rather regal crest in gold.

'We'll keep it out in the shed,' said Hal. 'And God knows, there's plenty of space out here to tip it. I'll dig a soil-pit.'

Peggy stared at it, amazed, and then she burst out laughing, convulsed at the thought of sitting in splendour on such a thing in the tumbledown old shed.

'Nice of him to let us have it, you know,' said Hal, when Mingo's boy had gone. 'After all, it would fetch a good bit if he cared to sell it. I'm sure he must know that.'

'Perhaps he has a conscience, after all,' conceded Peggy.

Twenty-seven

The weather turned cold very early that year. The wind from the sea became a piercing blast which rattled the cottage windows all the time. Hal had whitewashed the place inside and out, but nothing could conceal the roughness of its construction. The walls within were knobbly and the flagstone floors uneven. The window frames were imperfectly shaped – neither quite square nor a snug fit into the walls. A plaster filling had been stuffed in the cracks between the wood and the cob. There wasn't a single door in the house which would open or close with ease. They stuck, they dragged, the latches didn't work or the bolts would jam.

To furnish the place, all the old stuff from the loft above the bazaar was brought up on a cart. Maisie made them a gift of a single and a double bed. The cottage bedrooms offered little space for anything more. Peggy managed to squeeze in a chair and an old tallboy for herself and Hal, but the children's room had nothing except the bed. A pole across a tiny alcove had to serve Peggy for a wardrobe.

For the 'big room', as they called it, they bought some rugs and a dresser from an auction. With an armchair, the couch and a table, their parlour was complete. There was next to no storage space anywhere. Hal bought a corner cupboard for the kitchen, and fixed a lot of hooks into all the ceiling beams, so that cups and utensils, washing and myriad other things could be hung from the rafters.

Peggy wouldn't let Maisie see the place until she had done all she could to make it homely. Her mother was still not impressed. Looking about her, tut-tutting, she shook her head.

'You won't stick it, my dear,' she said. 'I wish you'd come home with me, right now. It's bleak here and the winter's yet to come.'

'I promised Hal I'd try it. I won't go back on that.'

'He shouldn't have asked it of you,' Maisie said. 'I've never criticised him before, but he shouldn't have brought you up here. What about the children, maid? They don't belong in a God-forsaken place like this. It was selfish of him, Peggy, and wrong to take this cottage without consulting you. If a single man wants to rough it, he's welcome, but when there's a wife and family, he has no right to drag them out of a comfortable home and into a hovel. The old bazaar's a scruffy place, but God in heaven, it's a palace compared to this.'

'It's only temporary, Mother.'

'Oh, indeed? From talking to him, I have the feeling it may not be easy to shift him. Peggy, I'm worried about you, love. It's so exposed up here and the isolation could drive you crazy.'

'At the first sign of madness, I'll come straight home.'

'Don't poke fun at me. I tell you straight, I don't think much of Hal for this. It's marred my good opinion of him, that's a fact.'

'He means well, Mother. He's a good man.'

'Means well. Oh yes. We all know about the road to hell and what it's paved with.'

'He thinks he can work well here.'

'He worked well enough at the loft, seems to me. When he married you, he undertook to put you and the offspring first.'

'I can't be too one-sided, Mother.'

Maisie eyed her keenly. 'Peggy, how do you feel about it, truly?'

'I'm hoping it'll grow on me.'

'Answer me straight.'

The girl's gaze flitted here and there, dodging that of her mother, but falling on so many disheartening sights. The cold slate floor, the low ceiling and crooked windows with that patch of nettle and weed beyond, the whole makeshift air of the cottage. Poor people had lived here – miners, perhaps, or farm labourers. This was a dwelling for the deprived, the lowest orders of yesterday.

'Well?' prodded Maisie.

Peggy swallowed hard. 'I hate it,' she said. 'But I promised Hal, and it won't be forever.'

A year is going to seem like forever up here, thought Maisie grimly.

Later that day, they took an old sack and went down to the zawn in search of driftwood. Fifty yards to the east of the chasm, a steep and dangerous rocky path slanted down across the cliff face. At low tide, there was a stony beach at the bottom. Quite close to the foot of the path, a rocky shelf jutted out to sea. It was cloven in two by a fissure, forming a steep-sided gully about twelve feet deep. The crevice was dry now, revealing its shingle floor, for the tide was at its lowest ebb. Far out at the tip of the spur, framed against showers of spray, two men could be seen using fishing rods. Both were in oilskins and one wore a red woollen hat.

'Who are they?' asked Maisie, squinting.

'I don't know. I've seen them out there several times. I think they come here regularly – probably after bass.'

'That's a dangerous spot to go fishing. One big wave could sweep them off those rocks. This is a horrible place altogether, if you ask me.' Maisie shivered, looking round her and up at the sheer, dark cliffs. 'It has a bad feel about it, like a trap.'

She was right about that in one respect; they had to be careful here and watch the tide. When it turned, the water would come right up to the cliff. Anyone cut off from the path would almost certainly drown.

Mother and daughter walked along the beach, picking up bits of rotten timber and anything else which would burn. The currents carried a lot of débris into the zawn, sometimes leaving broken boxes, cork floats, even the occasional oar. The two women threaded their way between the boulders, eyes downward, searching. The sides of the zawn towered above them like great cathedral walls. Sunshine never reached into this dark rift. The sea-smell here was pungent, with tangs of tar and decaying wrack.

As the bag of wood became weighty, Maisie said: 'It's Hal should be down here doing this. It won't be easy to lug this load back up the cliff – no job for a woman, that's certain. Don't you make my mistake, Peggy, I'm warning you. Don't you do all the hard work.'

'He's painting, making money. Anyway, I've just told you, I enjoy this.'

'It may be a novelty now; it won't be so when you've done it a hundred times. It won't be so if you have to do it.' Firmly, Maisie added: 'I'll buy you some coal. I'll have a ton delivered.'

'There isn't any need, we can buy our own.'

'Humour me, let me do it. Keep your money as long as you can. You never know what'll crop up. Expect the unexpected, Peggy.' Maisie paused, put some more fragments of wood in the bag and gazed out at the cold green sea. 'Expect to be disappointed, as well,' she murmured too softly for her to hear. 'That's the wisdom of the ages. Disappointed in people and events. Nothing is ever just what it seems and nothing ever turns out quite the way you think it will.'

When the tide was on the turn, they started to make their way back. Peggy filled her pockets with yellow and orange winkle shells, and bits of glittering quartz for the children. As they neared the outcrop of rock, they saw that the fishermen had gone. The incoming water had already covered the place where they had been.

Maisie and Peggy made a slow ascent of the path to the top of the cliff. It was breathless work, going up, and they took it in turns to carry the sack. Pausing halfway, panting, Maisie pointed down at the gully below, where the sea was now boiling and heaving, filling the crack to the brink.

'Look at that,' she puffed. 'Fall in there and you'd never come out alive. You mustn't ever bring the children down here, Peggy.'

'I know that.'

Shaking her head, Maisie laboured on upwards. 'This is no place for any of you. I always thought Hal had more sense.'

December brought two bad storms, and all the colour of the land and sea faded away. The country around the cottage, wiry and matted, resembled an old pot scourer. The blue Atlantic became a dreary grey under skies perpetually overcast.

Coming down the track from the pump one day, Peggy set her bucket of water down on the path and flexed her freezing fingers. The handle had left a red mark across them and a dented line in the flesh.

She was really discovering now what physical labour meant. At least four trips to the pump every day. Seven, if she wanted to bath the children. She and Hal made do with a strip and wash down. They kept a water butt by the door, but used the contents only for cleaning the house. Twice a week, she faced a walk into town for groceries. Coming back, she rode on the bus as far as the layby below the cottage. Then came the awful climb up a steep earth track with her loaded bags.

Hal hadn't sold a thing for weeks. Maisie kept putting his work in the windows at the bazaar, but it was the wrong time of year. Peggy was glad now that she had let her mother buy her that ton of coal.

Hefting the water bucket, she trudged on her way. They had now been here six weeks. To her, it already felt like six months.

Hal, however, had no complaints. The bleakness all around did not depress him. He said he found it interesting – that even the dullest day could show some beauty, if one had eyes to see it. He was very happy and constantly inspired, disappearing into the lean-to every morning after breakfast and staying there until the light began to fail. He concentrated on painting rocks and skies. Pictures with not much in them, Peggy thought.

Good resolutions forgotten, Hal was scarcely helping at all with the heavy work. He had too many good ideas which couldn't wait. Peggy left him to it. If he didn't paint, he couldn't sell, and in the meantime she was drawing on their savings.

Taking the bucket indoors, she tipped half its contents into a black iron kettle and set it on a trivet over the kitchen fire. For a while she sat beside the hearth, her face illumined by the glow. The children were having an afternoon nap. She would get them up soon and give them their tea. Stew. She made a lot of stew these days, unable as yet to manage the old cloam oven very well.

This is how people lived a hundred years ago, she thought, as she stared at the fire. Up here the twentieth century was nowhere in evidence, with its aeroplanes and electric lights, its telephones and wireless sets. Occasionally, a bus or a car passed below on the lonely road, and she briefly felt that she was still part of the world, still in 1934. But as the vehicle disappeared and the sound of the engine faded, she seemed to be plunged back into a former time.

The children didn't mind it here. They were happy anywhere with Hal. Joy, in particular, spent a lot of time watching him work and dabbling with paints herself. Peggy kept reminding Hal that she would be starting school next year. Reason enough, by itself, she declared, to move back into town. Taking the child back and forth each day was a daunting prospect.

He merely smiled and said they would cross that bridge when they came to it.

Peggy knew now that Maisie was right – it wouldn't be easy to shift Hal from here. He was always saying 'Isn't this lovely?' nowadays. He said it most often in the evenings when they all sat round the fire and he read the children bedtime stories. He was very much in love with the simple life.

Primitive, Peggy called it. Lonely, too. Sometimes, looking down to the cliffs, she could almost believe they were living on the very edge of the world. Like medieval sailors, she imagined a drop into nothingness just beyond the horizon.

January and February were months of drizzle and mist that year. Half the time the cottage was lost in drifting veils of grey, as if it had suddenly been transported to the Celtic underworld. Or else it endured the clammy fret blowing in from the sea, a silent haze of tiny droplets sticking to the windows and soaking everything. In the garden the vegetation had died right back. Hal said this was the best time to clear the ground, but his wife was reluctant to make a start.

That would be something of a commitment, an investment of time and labour for the future, and Peggy didn't mean to spend a future here. When the year was up, they were quitting this place, she was determined.

'Soon be spring,' Hal kept saying heartily. 'Everything will look much different to you then. I'll do the spade work out in the garden and leave the easy part to you. I'll get up the tough weeds and roots and clear the ground.'

But he didn't. Day after day he kept putting it off, always caught up in his painting.

Peggy said nothing. It didn't matter. She didn't intend to stay here.

It had taught her a lot about Hal, this winter. He had no taste for manual work – too much the artist. It was not so much laziness as a matter of priorities.

Always his painting came first. Nothing else was so important that it couldn't be left to slide. It hadn't mattered much at the bazaar, where they had some modern conveniences and the shops were close to hand and there was no ground to till anyway. Out here it was a very different story. Hal had pictured a sort of soulful, rustic existence where he could be creative, communing with the earth and sky and sea.

With me in the background providing the comforts, reflected Peggy wryly.

Oh, he had come here full of good intentions to do his bit. But he never quite got around to it, did he? Too absorbed by an interesting cloud formation or a play of light upon the heath or the shadows cast by a carn in the setting sun.

Sometimes she felt like taking that bucket and tipping it over her husband's head. But – she had agreed to this. Against her better judgement, true, but she had agreed to it. Still, Maisie had been right that he should never have asked it of her. If Peggy owed any debt of gratitude to Hal, she reckoned this twelve-month of graft and discomfort should well and truly discharge it.

Twenty-eight

Not long afterwards, the rainstorm came.

Peggy was woken one night by a deafening din on the galvanised roof. Rising from bed, she went to the window. Huge drops were hammering the glass, driven in from the sea by a strong westerly wind. Lighting the lamp, she lifted it and saw darting silver rivulets flowing down the panes. After a couple of minutes, the gusts grew stronger and the raindrops flew at the windows as if in an angry attack. Peggy heard one of the children crying and padded into their room to reassure them.

'It's only the rain on the old tin roof,' she told her weeping son. 'It'll fill up the water butt for me, so I won't have to go to the pump so many times tomorrow. And perhaps when it's over the sun will come out. We haven't seen the sun for months, have we?' The rain grew heavier still, clattering over their heads as if hordes of imps were out there with tiny hammers. Peggy climbed into bed between the children, taking one under each arm. 'It's all right, truly it is,' she said. 'There's nothing to fear from rain.'

The downpour carried on all night, though by dawn the wind had completely died away. In the town, a film of water covered the streets, running swiftly down the hills and pooling in hollows. The lawns of fine houses in higher Trezawne became saturated, spring flowers were beaten flat and washed from their beds. In the poorer part near the waterfront, people placed buckets and pans to catch the water from leaky roofs. Those who lived in basements, or used them for storage or places of work, sandbagged the doors in case an inch or two of water should seep in.

Still, it was just a cloudburst, people thought. It wouldn't last long.

At mid-morning, however, the rain was still falling just as heavily, and water draining off the land had begun to swell the leat. This stream ran past the churchyard, and the Reverend Smart had been looking at it, feeling troubled. The old retaining walls were less than stout, and he fancied the level had risen about two feet. If the water rose by as much again, it would start to spill over the top.

Not far beyond the churchyard, the leat went underground, emerging again about two hundred yards further down the hill, where lower Trezawne began. From there it flowed between the backs of two long rows of cottages, and thence towards the grounds of Elestren Manor. In days gone by, the leat had been a very useful amenity. Indeed, the original village had grown up on either side of it. Until the late 1800s, it had been Trezawne's fresh water source.

The town had opened up for business as usual that day, but the deluge kept many people indoors and the shops were doing poor trade. At Angilley's Bazaar, Maisie sat behind her counter, knitting. All she had sold by eleven o'clock was a dustpan and brush. Outside, the rain beat down so hard she could scarcely see through it. The long slope of the beach was obscured by a haze of grey. Beyond that was the deeper grey of the sea. Shapes of boats could vaguely be seen riding quietly at anchor in the teeming rain, their bright colours veiled by the downpour.

Peculiar weather, Maisie thought, going to the window. Heavy showers usually came with violence here – screaming winds and churning sea, great waves crashing up against the harbour wall. Not so today. Stillness today, rain coming straight down, and a heaviness in the atmosphere, as if it were so full of water that scant room was left for air.

Every so often, someone ran past the shop, feet splashing, bundled up in a mackintosh and clutching an umbrella. Maisie thought she might close for the afternoon if it didn't stop. What people didn't buy today, they would come and buy tomorrow.

At close to noon, the Reverend Smart looked out of the vicarage window and saw that three of the granite blocks which formed the leat wall had been dislodged and had toppled into the churchyard, as the fast-flowing stream ate away at the mortar and the flood pressure grew. Water was trickling through the gap and a puddle some ten feet across had formed. Two graves were completely swamped, the headstones rising out of a muddy mire.

Fetching his black umbrella, the Reverend ran down the path, his gown flapping. As he reached the wall, another block fell inward and water began to pour around his feet. He saw that the stream had become a torrent now. And worse, the ground on the other side of it was slipping. Soaked with rainfall draining down off Bodmin Moor, the soil of the hill running down to the leat was beginning to slide.

A fear was born in the Reverend Smart, because the land above Trezawne – and indeed, the incline of the town itself – was very steep. The rain showed not the slightest sign of easing and he doubted very much that the local council was alert to any danger.

Hastening back to the vicarage, he picked up the telephone and rang them. The response was sluggish and complacent. He was thanked for his concern and his warning was noted. He was reassured that no disaster was likely to befall Trezawne. He was promised that someone would come and repair the wall when the rain had stopped. The Reverend Smart said a thing or two unbecoming to a clergyman and then slammed the receiver down. Next he dialled the District Council, who were much more attentive, but thirty miles away. They would speak to Trezawne Town Council, they said, and urge them to take some action.

But no one came to look at the situation, and at ten past one a rumble signalled that it was already far too late. For the town, it had been too late by daybreak. For the people, there would have been a chance to clear out of the way, had the alarm been given in time. As it was, they were caught where they stood, in the path of an avalanche of water, mud and stones.

From the vicarage window, the Reverend Smart saw the side of the hill flow forward in a long, smooth motion. It filled and blocked the leat along a stretch of sixty yards. Displaced water erupted on either side. The rushing stream mixed with the soil and turned it into a fluid, then finally chose for itself a new course, straight down Pawlyn's Hill.

Mr Smart could only watch in horror as tons of earth and water swept down on the western end of Trezawne. As it travelled down the hill, gaining momentum, becoming funnelled through narrow streets, the flood reached a ferocious speed and strength.

In the cottages, people looked up from their midday

meals, listening, glancing questions at each other, detecting first a distant roar and then a crashing, hissing sound. An old man crossing Pawlyn's Hill stopped dead in his tracks in the road, looking upwards, stupefied, at what was bearing down on him. There was nowhere to run. The deluge knocked him off his feet and carried him along with it for a hundred yards before his body washed against a wall and stayed there. People were just getting up from the table, going to look outside, when doors and windows suddenly burst inwards and dirty water filled the ground floors of their homes.

As it reached the lowest section of the town, where the streets were most tangled and crooked, the stream broke up, lashing out in different directions, jetting through alleys, cascading down steps and spewing round corners. Basements flooded from floor to ceiling, trapping some unlucky souls inside. The flood kept picking up more and more débris, flushing people's belongings out of their homes and collecting things from their back yards. Old tin baths, firewood, fish barrels, children's toys, even a bicycle, were borne along with it.

Jasper and Walter Angilley were home for their lunch. Jasper, in fact, was caught on the lavatory and saved himself by climbing on to the seat, where he hung on for dear life to the overhead cistern and thus succeeded in keeping his head above water until the big surge had passed. Walter, upstairs in the kitchen, was out of its reach.

For Maisie, there was no such luck. She had only gone down to lock the shop door, intending to take the afternoon off. She was bending to shoot the bottom bolt when she thought she heard screams and shouts. She paused, ears pricked, detecting a hollow booming sound.

Like the sea, Maisie thought, a frown on her face. Just like the sea rolling into a cave . . .

Then water was foaming through the street outside. From the store room came the clatter of breaking glass, as the back window gave way. Seconds later, a wall of water came gushing into the shop. Maisie made for the staircase, but never reached it. As she waded, already waist-deep, towards the counter, a big display stand overturned. The corner of it caught her head a sickening blow and she knew no more.

At dawn the following morning, the downpour stopped at last. Peggy went outside the cottage and looked around. The smell of rain and sopping vegetation was in the air. The ground squelched underfoot. A patch of blue was breaking through the dull clouds out to sea and there was a thick warmth in the atmosphere. Taking the scuttle, she went into the shed for some coal. Both chimneys were wet and the fires had gone out.

The patch of blue sky grew wider and brighter. By the time Peggy succeeded in coaxing the kitchen fire into a blaze, the sun was standing above the horizon, piercing the remaining clouds with spokes of light. She was just about to put some porridge on for breakfast when she glanced through the front window and saw a skinny figure coming down the track. Jasper, of all people. Squinting, Peggy saw that her brother was far more dishevelled than usual. In fact, his clothes were coated with what looked like dried earth. He was glancing about him as he drew near, wary, on the lookout for Hal. She had never expected to see him up here, least of all on his own.

Peggy went to the door and opened it. Jasper was on the step, just poised to knock.

'What do you want?'

He stuffed his fists in his pockets, peering nervously past her into the cottage.

'Got to see you,' he mumbled. 'Something's happened.'

She stared at him. He was very white and looked peculiarly lost.

Foreboding stirred in Peggy, quieting her tone. She stood back. 'Better come in.'

Jasper stalled.

'It's all right, Hal is sleeping. Anyway, he wouldn't touch you.'

Her brother looked doubtful, but stepped inside.

'What's happened, then?'

'There's been a flood.'

She thought she understood. 'You mean the drains have overflowed? The shop – there's damage?'

'No . . . Well, yes. Only, it's more than that.' He gazed at her numbly. 'There's eleven people dead. The town's a mess our end.'

'Dead?' she repeated faintly. 'How? Jasper, who's dead? Tell me.'

He froze suddenly, staring past her. Peggy glanced around and there was Hal in his pyjamas, standing at the bedroom door. Angilley regarded him fearfully and only looked away when his sister took his arm and shook him.

'Jasper!'

He blinked at her, then muttered: 'It was a flash flood, and there's been a landslip up the top of the town by the church. The leat broke. It all came down so fast. There wasn't any warning.'

He backed away as Hal stepped forward, putting his hands on Peggy's shoulders.

'Don't worry,' Pentreath said, 'you're quite safe. Let's have the rest of it, come on.'

Piteously, Jasper looked at his sister. 'Ma's gone.' He sounded unable to believe his own words. 'She was in the shop. Something hit her on the head – a display stand, we think. Place is such a shambles, everything upset and thrown around. We don't know yet if it was the blow that killed her or if she drowned. Father found her face down in the water.'

For a moment, Peggy couldn't grasp it. Maisie? No, impossible, absurd.

But then Jasper said: 'The old man wants you to come and help. The funeral and everything – we don't know what to do.'

It hit her then. There was nothing like talk of 'arrangements' to drive the reality home. Her constant help and champion had suddenly become a thing of which she must dispose. Her mother, whom she had last seen just three days ago, to whom she had bidden such a casual farewell. Maisie had come to the door with her, chewing toffee, and given the kids a couple of bags of sweets. Full of complaints about Walter and Jasper, as usual. Full of concern and advice for Peggy. Dependable Maisie, always the same. Straight from normality to this. It was grotesque.

Peggy's hand flew to her mouth as an anguished cry burst out. Her eyes filled and overflowed, tears coursing swiftly down her cheeks. Turning to Hal, she buried her face against his chest.

Jasper sniffled, ready to cry himself. Holding and

stroking Peggy, Hal asked him: 'When did this happen?'

'Early noon yesterday. You never saw anything like the chaos. They took about sixty off to hospital. *The Old Solace* is wrecked. There were three died in there.' He gazed pathetically at Peggy's trembling back.

'Will you come?'

'God, give her time!'

Jasper quailed and Hal said more calmly, 'I'm sorry. Sit down.'

Jasper squatted on the edge of the couch. Hal sat his wife down there too and went to fetch the emergency brandy from the kitchen cupboard. It was the first time he'd ever seen Peggy in desperate need of a drink.

Two hours later, fortified by several large tots of brandy, Peggy accompanied Jasper down to Trezawne, leaving Hal to mind the children. As soon as they came to the brow of the hill above Elestren Manor, she could see the devastation. A gigantic tongue of mud and rocks sprawled down through the western end of the town. A great section of the land behind Trezawne had fallen away, leaving a semi-circle of raw brown earth exposed, as if an amphitheatre were being excavated. Trees with half their roots exposed were clinging precariously to the slope and likely to fall at any time. A glance was enough to tell her lower Trezawne had suffered most. Peggy mordantly observed that both *Lamorva* and the Buckmans' place were out of harm's way.

Peggy and Jasper scarcely spoke as they continued on their way. She didn't ask how Walter was. She didn't care. Had he suffered any injury, Jasper would have said so.

The area round the waterfront was in turmoil. There were cottages with doors and windows smashed, the ground floors inches deep in sludge. Everywhere, shocked and silent people were sweeping out thick, wet silt. Soft furnishings such as armchairs and rugs were stacked outside to dry, but they were mostly ruined. There were packing cases, too, full of broken, soaked possessions – ornaments, clothing, books. Everyone's house was out through the window, as Maisie used to say. The cobbles were slimy and strewn with rubble. Council men in overalls were shovelling up the mud and larger stones, heaving it all up on to a lorry parked outside *The Old Solace*. Water was still running down Pawlyn's Hill and over the edge of the quay.

Peggy saw the Reverend Smart come out of Jack Tresize's house. She looked at Jasper.

'Poor old Jack was one who got killed in the pub,' he confirmed. 'Don't know who'll see to his donkeys now. Not a bad sort, old Jack.'

No, thought Peggy bitterly. The best always had the bad luck, like Maisie. Strong, reliable Maisie, everyone's prop.

A filthy ooze was all over the floor of Angilley's Bazaar, and coated the walls to a height of several feet. Glass and china crunched under her shoes, display stands and shelving were hurled everywhere. Almost nothing was in one piece, except for steel and iron goods. A jumble of items was washed up in a corner – a doll, a box of fudge, an accordion, heaps of brushes, aprons, loose sweets, a laundry basket and the postcard rack.

Wordlessly, Peggy walked around, with Jasper trailing behind her. She could sense that he was waiting for her to take charge and say: 'Right, I'll do thus and so, I'll deal with all this.' As Maisie would have done, because her men weren't capable. Peggy, however, wasn't feeling exactly resourceful herself just now.

At length, she asked: 'Where's Father?'

'Upstairs in bed. Some shock he had, finding Mother like that.'

Peggy went up to see him. Walter lay against his pillows and eyed her plaintively.

'I can't get over it. My Maisie,' he croaked. 'Will you do all that's necessary,maid? I'm just not up to it. And your brother – well, he don't know how.'

His daughter stood at the foot of the bed, surveying him. Walter didn't look too bad, all things considered. He was wearing his shirt, minus the collar, and his stubble was a trifle longer than usual, but otherwise he seemed very much himself. Three empty beer bottles stood on the bedside table. Indeed, the room smelt heavily of ale. Drinking in bed – Maisie would never have permitted that. He had started as soon as she was gone.

Peggy considered him with weary hatred. Life was hopelessly unfair and that was that. What use to rail? It never made a difference. This waster had escaped unharmed. There he lay in his sweaty shirt, moaning about 'My Maisie' and how he couldn't cope with anything just now. When did he ever? Peggy was feeling like hell herself, sick and shivery inside, now that the brandy's effects were wearing off. Walter and Jasper were going to lean on her, just the same.

Coldly, she said: 'Yes, I'll see to the funeral.' Then a thought occurred to her. 'Is the place insured?'

'Don't know. Maisie always dealt with things like that.'

'We'd best hope it is.' Her forehead creased. 'And did she make a will?'

For a moment her father looked vacant and then he gestured towards the corner cupboard. 'All her papers and stuff were kept in there.'

Peggy opened it, rummaged around and found a writing box. Taking it over to the kitchen, she placed it on the table, sat down and started going through it.

No will. No insurance. Thrifty Maisie had balked at paying out good money for anything as intangible as insurance. As for a will, she had always intended to get around to it sometime. Fit and healthy, she had expected to live for many more years.

Walter was, by turns, elated and disappointed. Not up to making funeral arrangements, he was nevertheless quick enough to consult a solicitor. Since his wife had died intestate, he learned that he could claim the matrimonial home. Scarcely anything worth having was left for Peggy. The property as a whole was greatly devalued by the damage and there would be no compensation because it was not insured. The ground floor needed extensive repairs, and Maisie had left little cash – it had all been tied up in the stock, now destroyed.

Still, the prospect of being the owner brought out the bombast in Walter, and more than a little malice, too. Once the funeral was over, he had no more use for Peggy. Indeed, his horns came forth as they were leaving the churchyard. When she started talking of clearing up the shop, he stopped her short.

'You needn't concern yourself. I don't want you there. The boy and I will see to it all.'

Peggy was scathing. 'Pigs might fly. You'll never get around to it.'

'So be it, then.' He halted, scowling at her.

Hal and the children had walked ahead, while Jasper was ambling round by himself, looking at all the new headstones. There were many fresh graves and the churchyard itself had suffered some invasion by the landslide. A great hump of soil now covered twenty feet of the bottom wall. Up here, so close to the source of the disaster, the gouged out hillside still looked threatening.

'You can't leave the shop as it is!' exclaimed Peggy.

'I will, if I see fit. It's none of your business now. I don't want to see any more of you, madam. For certain, you'll never live in that house again. I won't have you back there, not you, nor your kids, and certainly not him.' Walter jerked his head in Hal's direction. 'Bugger tried to kill my boy. We haven't forgotten. Never will. You'll have to stick with him now, up there where you are or wherever he takes you. There's nowhere to return to, don't you think it. I wouldn't have you under my roof for any money.'

She snorted. 'You surely don't think I'd want to, with Mother gone? You don't imagine Hal would ever agree to move back?'

'I'm just telling you my door is locked. The law's given me the upper hand, see? I'll think about the shop and I'll decide what to do with it, without any help or bossing from you.'

'Which means you'll do damn-all. Couldn't run a business if your life depended on it.'

'And you could?'

'I'd be willing to try.'

'You just forget it, my lady. Jasper and me, we don't want anything more to do with you.' A spiteful smile came to Walter's face. 'Don't know where Pentreath will sell his silly paintings now, I'm sure. They won't be going up in our shop windows any more.'

Dismayed though she was to think that Angilley's Bazaar might cease to be, Peggy managed to summon a cynical smile. 'Think you're going to enjoy yourself, don't you? Think you'll be cock of the walk. Well, I don't believe the future looks very rosy for you, Father dear, now the breadwinner's gone. I don't think you'll get along very well without Mam. Now she's not there to drive you, you won't even do odd jobs. Before long, you'll be selling the furniture to pay for drink, if I know you. Who's going to cook for you, eh, and supply clean clothes?' She thrust her face up to his. Eyeball to eyeball, they glared at each other. 'I know what'll happen to you – and that fool over there.' She tossed a scornful nod towards Jasper. 'You'll stew in your own squalor. You'll live on bread and scrape and shop-bought pasties. You'll get more and more drunk and more and more smelly, and the house will fall to bits around you. Eventually, you'll have the bailiffs coming round. You may think you're having revenge on me, but you're doing yourself no good turn.'

Twenty-nine

Some days later, Peggy stood at the garden wall, gazing out to sea. It was a pallid blue, stippled with white crests of foam. A choppy sea, an aggressive wind. Blustery March, just starting to reveal new green. The gorse buds were splitting open, sulphur-yellow beginning to show through the fuzzy outer pods. Peggy hunched her shoulders, digging her hands in the pockets of her woollen coat. She had put it on to come out to the lavatory. It was mid-morning and she had just put pasties in the oven. She had to learn to use it now, by hook or by crook. Something told her they might well be stuck here after all.

Their savings had dwindled to £40. Frightening that money could go so fast, once they started living on it. Everything cost more than Peggy bargained for, unexpected expenses cropped up all the time. Even though Maisie and the bazaar had cushioned Peggy a lot by giving her household goods out of stock, even so, the cash had run away in no time. Things could only get harder now. No Maisie any more to say: 'Oh, take some from the store, my dear. There's plenty, have whatever you need.'

No more stock, no more bazaar. Even the choice of leaving Hal and going home had been taken from her.

She pushed back her hair as the twisting wind blew it over her eyes. So high up here, so open, above a vast ocean, below a vast sky. So vulnerable, too, as if the wind could pluck the cottage from the earth and carry it off, if it so desired.

But the rent was paid up for another eight months and that was the main consideration for the present. They would get no refund from Mingo if they left, and unless her husband did well in the coming season, she doubted that they could afford to move to a better place.

Turning to go back indoors, Peggy paused to look at the garden. Spring was almost upon her and she hadn't done a thing because she hadn't planned to stay. Now the situation had changed and the plot of ground had suddenly acquired importance. She needed to plant things, food to eat. What would grow in this salt wind? Cabbages, perhaps. Potatoes, carrots. She dug with her shoe at the matted grass and wondered if the soil beneath was good enough, or if the weeds had sapped it of nourishment. Docks, brambles – stubborn villains. And thistles, dandelions, many energetic seeders whose progeny were lurking in the earth, ready to burst forth as soon as the weather grew warmer.

She would have to fight them. Manual labour, that would be her lot, if she wanted to keep body and soul together. No use asking Hal to help, he was embroiled in a painting of the zawn. No use asking Hal. He would say he needed the daylight for his work.

That afternoon, despite the cold, she was sweating as she laboured. Slashing at the brambles and the nettles with a billhook, hauling out the cut stuff with a rake. Chop and drag, chop and drag. Making inroads into the thorny tangle yard by back-breaking yard, building a pile of dead stuff to burn, snagging her clothes and scratching her hands and panting with the exertion. Every so often she had to rest, and sat for a while on the garden wall, sucking at grazes and itching weals, and picking tiny prickles out of her skin. How Anna would laugh to see her, she thought. Peggy, dressed in a pair of old boots, corduroy trousers and a shapeless jersey, her hair tied up in a scarf. Peggy, toiling like a peasant, sweating like a horse.

By the time the light began to fail, she had cleared quite a patch. As she stood surveying her handiwork, Hal came out, looking sheepish.

'I've made the tea,' he said. 'And cut some cake and bread and butter for the children.'

Peggy said nothing.

He looked about him. 'You've made a hole in it, by God you have.'

'Yes.' Putting down the billhook, she pulled off her headscarf and shook her hair free. 'Make a good farm labourer, wouldn't I?'

He blinked uneasily. 'I've got on well today myself. Nearly finished.'

'Bravo,' came the flat reply.

'I can ask a good bit for it. Five pounds, perhaps.'

'Well, don't take any cheques, will you?'

She started towards the door and Hal scurried after her.

'Peggy, you didn't have to do this. If you'd only waited . . .'

'How long? A month of Sundays?'

Going inside, she stepped out of her boots and placed them beside the door, ready for the morning.

'You know I have to paint while I can. The light . . .'

'And I'll have to plant while I can. Vegetables have their seasons, their demands.'

Peggy went into the kitchen, sat down at the table with Joy and Ewan. She poured herself some tea and drank it gratefully. She was aching in every limb and the soreness of her joints made her conscious of each little movement.

'We'll find our feet when the season starts,' Hal promised. 'Lots of visitors about with money – I'll be selling again. I've built up quite a stock of canvases, and I'll be doing portraits on the quay.'

She sighed. 'The bazaar was your shop window, Hal. There won't be another one like it. I really think you ought to consider finding some work.'

He looked astonished.

'Yes, a job.'

'Oh, no, there won't be any need. I've just told you . . .'

'Part-time would do. I'm not suggesting you stop painting, but it isn't enough by itself.'

'It has been up to now.'

'Because we were living at the bazaar, because Mam was helping us out. It's different up here. You said we could manage, but you never did your sums. Have you any idea how little is left in the post office?'

His gaze faltered. 'Well, how much?'

'Forty pounds three and six.'

'We had a hundred and fifty left when I'd paid Mingo!'

'Yes, but we've had to buy a bit of furniture for this place, and you've sold barely a thing since we came up here. Groceries don't come free, Hal. Nor do your paints. Nor do children's shoes and clothes.'

'Don't patronise me. I know that.'

'Nor do bus fares. Do you expect me to carry the shopping all the way up from Trezawne? I think I've done damned well to spend so little, all things considered.'

He was silent. Then: 'Yes, I'm sorry. I'm sure you have.'

'You'll see about finding some work, then?'

A mumble. 'All right, I'll see about it.'

Sometime, he would see about it. Not immediately, though. Next morning he was back at his easel, and Peggy was out in the garden again. And the day after and the day after and the day after that. He daubed and tickled with his brush, while Peggy tore up tufts of coarse grass, forced the spade down into the hard, stony earth and turned it over. He added subtle shadows to his skies and seas, while she lit roaring bonfires and ripped tough roots from the ground. He made first sketches for yet more pictures, while his wife repaired the garden walls, marked out plots for this and that, went out and bought the seeds. He amused the children with painting games, while she knelt down and sowed her little crops.

The plot around the cottage became a neat brown square of soil, divided into a patchwork by lines of little stones. Peggy was proud and resentful all at once, immensely pleased with these results but still irate that her husband had contributed nothing at all.

Hal kept his head down and went on painting. Soon the holiday season would start. Everything always looked better in summer.

Springtime passed, and Peggy's crops grew up. The cabbages did well and the yield of potatoes was greater than she had expected, but the carrots were a failure, so she promised herself to try turnips instead. In flower pots, as a luxury, she cultivated mint and parsley. Not bad results for a first attempt, she thought. But then, one couldn't live on a few vegetables. The children needed meat, and that was dear.

From Whitsun onwards, Hal went back to doing charcoal portraits down in Trezawne on the quay. The town had only partially recovered from the flood, and this year many visitors had gone elsewhere. If he was lucky, he made a couple of pounds a week from the portraits, and then he bought cheap meat and fish, bringing home sausages, pilchards, mince and offal, for the money had to stretch to so much else as well. Gone were the days of roast pork and rump steak, lamb and chicken, and crab fresh off the boat. No cherries or strawberries this year, no clotted cream. Peggy marvelled when she recalled how well they had eaten when they lived at Angilley's Bazaar. A big roast twice a week, always plenty of everything. Even the meals made up of leftovers had been generous. Piles of cold meat and pickles, tomatoes and lettuce. Always fresh fruit in the house. Everything best quality, too. Maisie had never stinted on food. Now Peggy made do with bruised apples, sinewy beef and stale bread. Tail-end stuff, bottom-of-the-box.

It was very clear that Hal had no intention of seeking a job. They were coping, he said cheerfully. *The Buttery* restaurant was going to hang a few of his paintings for him throughout the season. He was bound to make some sales. He had a commission, too, from the Queen's Hotel. They wanted a couple of posters to advertise their Olde Tyme Dancing Night.

Once she had loved him for his optimism. Now it began to get on Peggy's nerves. Good times were always just around the corner. Meanwhile, she was working like a navvy, always digging and hoeing, picking and replanting, always carrying water. And wood – her mother had been right. Foraging for firewood wasn't fun when you had to do it, and now that the coal had been used, there wasn't any choice. Most days, Peggy went down to the zawn and picked up what she could. Often there was little about, so she couldn't cook and they ate cold food.

Well, it didn't matter, said Hal, the weather being so warm.

That was Peggy's only comfort. It was a lovely summer. Hot days and balmy nights and gentle rains. The rambling rose burst out shocking pink, and clumps of white valerian sprouted between the stones of the garden wall. Sometimes Peggy took a kitchen chair outside and sat in the garden peeling vegetables or mending clothes.

One morning she put down her darning and looked out to sea, where a fishing boat was hauling in a long-line. The sky was sapphire blue, with delicate, feathery streaks of cloud like the tails of pure white horses streaming in the wind. The heath was green and purple, the bay so wide and tranquil. For a moment she was almost happy, and the hardship seemed to matter less. This was how Hal felt most of the time, she supposed, because he loved the wild weather as much as the sun. For her, it had to be warm and bright. But then, she was the one who spent hours out in the wind and the pouring rain, doing chores.

She wouldn't have minded so much if he were selling more, but the nature of his work had changed. He kept on doing the charcoal portraits, but his paintings were quite different now. There was less of the chocolate-box prettiness which appealed to the holiday people. He was tired, he said, of doing those potboilers. He wanted to experiment.

As if he could afford an attitude like that, a man with a wife and two young children, Peggy thought resentfully. Instead of putting good meat on the table, Hal was indulging his whims. Well, this was what came of marrying an artist, wasn't it? If Anna knew what Peggy's life was like, she would surely laugh and say she'd had a lucky escape.

Thirty

In truth, Anna had little to laugh about these days. She knew she had never been forgiven. Ever since that evening when Guy brought her home from *Lamorva*, she had been on probation. Under scrutiny. In the doghouse. At His Majesty's pleasure.

She felt terribly alone. She had hardly seen Hal in well over a year. Once or twice she had spotted him doing sketches on the quay, but hadn't dared to go and speak for fear it might somehow get back to Guy. She no longer even knew where Hal was living. He had left the bazaar, that was certain. On reading in the local paper of Maisie Angilley's death, Anna had assumed that Peggy would take over the shop. Obviously not, however. Eight months after the flood, the place was still in a shocking state and showed no signs of resuming trade.

Anna felt she had no one to whom she could turn, and life with Guy was tense these days, to say the least. He was passably civil most of the time, but there were undercurrents. Sometimes she caught him watching her with thoughtful, malevolent eyes, and then she knew he was remembering, mulling over her offences. Now and again he would take a verbal pot shot at her, firing off a mirthless joke.

'Robin must go to the dentist, Anna. Can I trust you not to abscond with him on the way?'

Or, in bed. 'Why are you gritting your teeth, my dear? Aren't you pretending tonight that I'm Mr Pentreath?'

And so on and so on. Anna rarely replied to these barbs. She was afraid to. Better to absorb them than fight back when she couldn't win. She often suspected that Guy would like it if she did, that he would welcome an excuse to . . . Hit her? Yes, or worse. That day on the cliff, she had seen real evil in him. Mother could scoff if she liked, but Anna had been there, Anna knew. Guy could be very inventive in meting out punishment.

To Anna, that is, never to his son. He was very lenient indeed with Robin. Guy had spoilt him shamelessly these past twelve months. It served a dual purpose, cultivating the boy's affection and distressing Anna, for Robin was growing more and more dislikeable. Her beautiful child, becoming a brat, who was loathed by all the staff. She feared for him, and for herself. He didn't care for her these days, he was his father's boy. If she tried to discipline him, Robin would complain to Daddy, and Guy would tell Anna to stop picking on him. Anna couldn't help feeling as if they had formed an alliance against her. She was the outsider, and powerless.

Just how much so, Anna learned one evening in November, one evening when her patience snapped and she dared too much.

It was almost seven o'clock, nearly time to give Robin his bath and put him to bed. In the sitting-room, Anna was looking at the newspaper, which dwelt heavily on the gory details of the Buck Ruxton murder case. By the window, on the carpet, her son was playing with Tuffet.

Suddenly, an indignant squeal made Anna look up.

318

'What are you doing, Robin?' She eyed him from under her brows. 'Why did Tuffet cry out like that?'

The boy turned a smiling face to her. Beautiful cherub, all innocence. The little dog had retreated beneath the writing-table and was watching him warily.

'You're not teasing her, are you? If you are, I shall smack you.'

The smile remained but he looked away, returning to his wooden bricks, building them into a shaky pyramid.

Anna watched him for a minute, then she went on reading.

After a while, the forgiving Tuffet emerged from under the table and stood by the boy, tail wagging. A fat little hand reached out and stroked her. Tuffet sat down at his side, head cocked, watching him at his game.

Five minutes passed and slowly the hand slipped down her back and along her tail. Robin's fingers grasped the tip of it and gave a sharp little twist.

The anguished yelp made Anna jump. Tuffet, bristling now, had skittered back under the table and was growling defensively, eyes fixed on Robin. Laughing, the child picked up a yellow building block and flung it at her, striking her head. Tuffet slunk under the china cabinet, whining.

'Robin!' Anna was on her feet and standing over him. 'What did you do that for? Think it's funny?'

He grinned up at her.

'Oh, you do? Poor Tuffet, you've hurt her. Do you enjoy hurting things?'

The grin persisted, insolent. He wasn't afraid of her, didn't recognise her as authority. Three years old and he knew who was boss. Daddy, only Daddy.

At that moment, Anna felt a tremendous aversion to her son. It appalled and frightened her. Her child, this tiny boy in his blue romper suit and buttoned sandals. She shook herself. Robin was just a toddler, full of unthinking mischief. She tried to touch his conscience.

'I won't let you play with her if you're going to do nasty things like that. You're meant to love her and be kind to her.'

For a second she swore she saw mockery gleam in Robin's eyes. Her words sounded mawkish in her own ears, and she guessed she presented an ineffectual figure to her son. Only if she hit him would he take her seriously. Anna's fingers flexed at her sides. He was smirking at her, daring her. She longed and yet feared to do it.

Robin was studying her with something uncomfortably like amusement. This was fun, this was interesting. Mummy was upset, angry, but she didn't know quite what to do. Experimenting with her, he selected another brick and his gaze swivelled towards the china cabinet.

'Don't you dare.' Anna's voice dropped low.

Robin's pink baby lips closed and curled. His dimples deepened. He passed the block from hand to hand. It was green, with a big letter 'Q' on the side.

'I mean it, Robin. I'll smack you, hard.'

He considered her. He glanced at Tuffet, crouching under the cabinet. He looked down at the cube of wood in his hand.

For a few seconds, Anna thought she had won. 'Put it down,' she ordered.

Robin debated briefly. Only Mummy, was the

decision. No need to listen to her. Defiantly, he hurled the brick at the little dog.

Tuffet saw it coming and a streak of tawny fur shot across the room to dive under the sideboard. Robin's aim was high, in any case. The block went straight through the front of the cabinet. Thin glass tinkled to the floor and a cracking, chiming noise announced the end of a fine porcelain cream jug and sugar basin.

'You . . .!' Anna swooped on her son and Robin's chuckles turned to yells of fright as she started slapping him round the legs and backside.

This was unexpected. Robin screamed for his father with all his might, but Guy was downstairs in the kitchen, talking with Chef amid the clatter as the hotel prepared to serve dinner.

'You're going to bed right now.' Seizing the child by one hand, Anna pulled him roughly into the nursery. 'No bath tonight, no story, no chocolate drink. I won't have you defy me, my lad. I won't have you breaking things and tormenting my dog. You're fast turning into a vicious, spoilt little beast and I won't stand for it.'

Robin shrieked for his daddy, adding that he hated her. His face was crimson with temper and he lashed out with his free hand and his little shoes, pounding her thighs with a pudgy fist and kicking at her ankles. Anna's response was to clip him smartly across the ear, whereupon the screams went up to an unbelievable pitch. Robin's nose was running and his cheeks were wet with tears. As his mother dragged him towards the bed, he resisted by hanging on to anything which came to hand. She had to pry loose his grip on the leg of a table. Enraged, he swept an arm across it, sending toy soldiers flying.

'Yes,' muttered Anna, 'you're your father's son, all right.'

'Tell Daddy! I'll tell Daddy! Hate you, hate you!' Robin bawled.

A chill slid down Anna's spine. She wasn't sure what Guy would do. The china cabinet, a prized possession, had been in his family a long time. He might be sufficiently annoyed about it to take her side for once. He might. If not . . .

If not, she would have to stand up to him, she thought, anger taking over once more and pushing fear aside. This could not be allowed to go on. Robin had to be civilised, lest he grew into a monster.

Beside himself in his tantrum, Robin was squirming in her grasp. She got him on to the bed, wrestled him out of his clothes and into his pyjamas. By the time she tucked him tightly between the covers, he had worn himself out. Dishevelled, Anna stood at the foot of the bed and the child stared sullenly back at her. Both were exhausted. It had been like grappling with a wild animal. Amazing, the strength of a three year old in a frenzy, and Robin was a sturdy boy.

His face was blotchy now and his eyes were puffed. His prettiness had briefly left him, and Anna suddenly noticed something she had never seen before. A downturn to the mouth, a heavy droop which never showed while he was satisfied with life, good-tempered. For the first time, she realised that there was, after all, a resemblance to Guy, and one which might become more pronounced as Robin grew older.

The boy's eyes were cold, unblinking. Even vindictive, Anna thought. Children were supposed to be pure and without malevolence, helpless beings who had to be protected from the world. Not the other way about.

She swallowed hard and then she said: 'Now you go straight to sleep. I don't want to hear any more out of you tonight. In the morning, if you're sorry, I'll forgive you.'

She had meant to sound stern, but somehow it came out weak and tired. Robin scowled and turned his head on the pillow, gazing doggedly at the wall.

Wearily, Anna put off the light, went out and closed the door.

She ordered no dinner that evening; she had no appetite. She cleared up the broken glass and china, then spent an hour consoling Tuffet by combing her coat.

It was past eleven before Guy came up. He had lingered in the bar for over an hour, chatting with some of the residents. Anna had already changed into her nightdress, ready for bed.

As soon as Guy entered the room, he spotted the broken cabinet. He looked at her sharply.

'What's happened here?'

She told him. Expressionless, he listened. Wordless, he went in to see his son.

He was in there a very long time, or so it seemed to Anna. Straining to hear, she caught the murmur of her husband's voice, quite calm, and the fainter, lighter sound of Robin's replies.

Perhaps Guy was telling him off. Or was he? Anna crammed her knuckles into her mouth and sat very upright on the sofa. She was tight with nerves, pressing her knees together and hunching her shoulders to stop herself shaking. She had an impulse to get up and run from the flat, but she fought it. No point putting off the confrontation, if there was to be one. Guy never let anything pass, he never forgot.

At last the nursery door opened. Guy came out, shut it quietly behind him and stood looking at her.

'You hit him,' he said softly.

'I had to, Guy. He really asked for it. We can't let him get away with everything. He'll be a little horror if we do. He won't have any friends . . .'

He cut across her trembling voice, his own becoming curt and harsh.

'On account of that bloody dog, you pasted my son.'

'And the china cabinet . . .'

'Never mind that. It was only a bit of devilment. He's three, he doesn't know any better.'

'He never will if he isn't taught!' She was quaking but she rose to her feet. 'He has nasty inclinations, Guy, he's got a cruel streak.'

'Most children do.'

'Most children are thoughtless, but Robin knows what he's doing. He enjoys causing pain.'

'Oh, rubbish! Stupid, stupid rubbish.'

'It isn't and you know it. You just don't think it matters.'

'I'll tell you what matters to me.' He came towards her and his face was set, as ugly as she had ever seen it. 'You hurt my son, you hard-handed bitch!'

Anna started to back away. 'He provoked me, and he was struggling so. Guy, I love him as much as you do. More. I'm not prepared to see him grow into a bully who's feared and shunned by other children. I'm not prepared to see him become a callous adult. Robin has unpleasant instincts and they have to be curbed. It's for his own good.'

'All this because he teased that dog a little? You're deducing a lot from something so trivial.'

'It's a bad sign when a child likes to hurt animals. Any psychiatrist will tell you that.'

'Ah, I see. Been reading books, have we?'

He kept advancing on her, slowly. Anna edged round behind the settee, as if it offered protection, although she knew he could seize her in an instant if he chose. She was wishing now that she hadn't changed into her nightclothes, feeling utterly vulnerable in the flimsy silk and the swansdown mule slippers. Goose pimples stood up all over her arms, the tiny hairs prickling with fear.

'I really don't think you have the learning or the intelligence to make judgements of that sort on Robin,' Guy said.

Fighting her terror, Anna fired back. 'I haven't been reading books. I've merely observed how much he's taking after you.'

'My, you are brave tonight, aren't you? So I'm – what was it – callous and a bully?'

'Often, yes. Everyone's afraid of you. There's no one on the staff who likes you, Guy.'

'A pitfall of being boss, Anna, not that it troubles me. I don't want their affection, I just want the best out of them. And I get it, don't I? Or else I sack them. Can't exactly sack you, though, can I?'

Her lips felt like crêpe paper, crinkled and dry. Shaking, she passed her tongue across them.

'So I think a spot of retraining is indicated,' he continued. He turned on the radiogram and the sound of a swing band filled the room.

She thought he was going to beat her and blurted out a threat. 'If you assault me, I'll show the whole world what you've done, I swear it. I won't keep quiet like some women do. I'll parade my injuries for every-

325

one to see – staff, guests, all your cronies, every trader in town. I'll shame you, I'll have people whispering and pointing fingers at you.'

He grinned, which scared her more than ever. 'Have to go about it another way, then, won't I?'

Before she knew it, his arm shot out, he grabbed her by the hair and jerked her forward. Tumbling over the back of the settee, Anna found herself sprawled on the cushions. She opened her mouth to scream as Guy loomed over her, saw something large and dark in his hand. Another cushion, coming down on her face.

She managed to utter hardly a sound before the soft mass stifled her voice, shut out the light and cut off all air. Behind it, she felt the full weight of his pressing hand. His forearm was across her stomach, clamping her down. She kicked and thrashed, fists flailing for his head and drumming on his back, but to no avail. Twice, her hands made thudding contact with his skull. The force of the satin pad upon her face grew fiercer still, and she was punished with a jab of his elbow to her stomach.

Time appeared to stretch and there seemed to be two separate people in her head, one distraught, the other one peculiarly calm and just observing. Together they told her she was suffocating, about to die. They told her of the rhythmic thumping her heels made on the arm of the settee, that her slippers had fallen off and her nightdress was bunched up around her thighs, that the radiogram was now playing 'Blue Moon'. She could feel the edges of the appliqué flowers on the cushion, and the squashy texture of the filling inside it. She could feel the shoulder seams of her husband's jacket as she tried in vain to push him off. Then she was seeing red flecks like fireflies behind her eyelids,

326

tiring, despairing, growing dizzy, and at last becoming detached from it all and remembering that day in the chemist's shop when she first met him.

Then she was nowhere in particular, insensible.

The next sensation was of freezing cold. Cold that permeated her flesh and her bones. Then came awareness that she was lying on something hard and smooth. Still in her nightdress, that and nothing else. Anna's eyes flew open.

Solid darkness.

For several minutes, she lay without moving, trying to collect her wits. The last thing she had known, she was being smothered. And now . . .

All around her was a sense of space. Nothing touching her at all, except stone floor and chilly air. Reaching out, groping, she encountered nothing. Anna listened.

Utter silence.

Then her nostrils twitched, picking up familiar odours. Smells of cork and alcohol.

She was in the wine cellar. Had to be. Right in the middle of the floor. Moving a few feet in any direction, she would find racks and bottles, she was sure.

Carefully, Anna got to her feet, not trusting her sense of balance in this total blackness, finding it hard to be certain when she was quite upright. Barefoot, she thought at once about broken glass and moved very gingerly, stretching out her arms in front of her, fluttering her hands in the manner of the blind. She must surely touch something any second . . .

Yes. Wooden shelves, pigeonholes, dusty glass and wrinkled caps of metal foil. Anna had no idea which wall this was. Feeling her way to the corner, she turned the angle and shuffled along again. Racks and bottles, racks and bottles. No break for the door, beside which was a light switch. That was what she wanted first of all, the light. Despite the shuddering cold which shook her, it was light she craved before all else.

Another angle, another wall.

Some of these bottles had lain here for decades, judging by the cobwebs. She had noticed the webs the first time Guy brought her down here and showed her around. Tacky, gauzy strands of spider silk clung to her fingers. Sometimes she felt lumps in the mesh. Remains of dead insects, probably, or even fat little spider bodies. Anna had never been frightened of spiders, but nausea rose in her at the thought of the mess stuck all over her hands.

At last, wooden panels. The door. She fumbled for the light switch, located it, clicked it down.

Nothing happened.

Click, click, up and down.

He had taken the bulb out.

She sought the door handle, turned it. No movement. She felt for a key, but of course, there was none. For the first time, Anna began to cry. On waking, she had been relieved to find herself alive, and then had come the goal of making her way to the door. An objective, a hope of light and even release. Now there was nothing left to do. He had locked her in and here she would stay all night.

In the bitter cold. Her mind now fastened on that with awful intensity. Her toes were aching, stinging with it, her fingers stiff, her upper arms circled by an icy soreness. She suddenly wondered how long she had been here. Only a short time, perhaps – which meant that dawn was a long way off.

Oh, she knew what Guy would do, come down here

and let her out before the hotel stirred, before the breakfast cook came in at seven o'clock. Until then there might be five hours, six.

All that time. She couldn't bear it. Panic gripped her and she started to bang on the door. Perhaps her husband was outside, listening. Perhaps she could appeal, apologise. Anything to get out of here, out of this hole, down so many steps beneath Elestren Manor.

'Guy!' She slammed her palm against the door. 'Guy, are you there? Please let me out!'

No answer came.

Anna hammered with her fists. 'Guy, don't do this. I'm freezing. Please, I'm sorry.'

Silence.

'I won't hit Robin again, no matter what he does.' She leaned her cheek against the wood, tears oozing from her eyes. 'Guy, for God's sake!'

Still no sound from beyond the door. Anger, like magma, welled up in her. She shrieked: 'I'll rouse the whole hotel! I'll yell until somebody hears me! I'll yell until I wake the dead! Damn you, damn you, let me out!' Pounding at the door, she wept and swore and screeched.

In vain.

Calming herself a little, she croaked: 'I'll smash your bloody bottles. Do you hear me? Every one of them. All your precious ports and clarets and Burgundies, all your damned hocks, everything. This'll cost you hundreds! Do you hear me? Do you? You bastard! I'll count to ten and then I'm going to start!'

She began briskly – one, two, three, like a metronome – but at seven her voice died away.

He wasn't out there. She'd known that, really. She was quite alone down here. Her husband was way up above in his warm bed. All those other people, too, peacefully nestled among the feathers, sleeping.

Wretchedly, Anna sank to the floor. She was going to serve the full sentence. Teeth chattering, she huddled up against the door with her knees drawn up, hugging herself in a hopeless quest for warmth. She could scream until her voice gave out, but no one would hear. This cellar was deep below the kitchen and no cries would reach the great granite house above it. As for destroying the wine stocks, she hardly dared think what the consequences would be. In any case, she would surely cut her feet to ribbons in the process.

Quivering, Anna bowed her head over her knees and silently sobbed. Soon she was so cold that she drifted into a semi-stupor. She recalled that people were said to die this way in the snow, becoming drowsy and giving up. Anna wondered if that would happen to her and thought she wouldn't care too much if it did. As she dozed, she dreamed fitfully of fire. The bonfire on the beach, and Hal pouring cider, laughing, joking . . .

When at last she heard a key grate in the lock, it was hours later, half-past six. She was jolted awake by a jerk at her back as the door was pushed inwards. Numb and stiff, she crawled out of the way. The door opened a couple of feet and a dark form was standing there, a silhouette revealed by the light in the stairwell outside. The light was dim, but Anna blinked as if it were radiant. She didn't dare say anything. Guy, without a word, threw something to her, then went away and left the door ajar.

He had brought her woollen dressing gown. Anna clutched it tightly round her, then got to her feet and abjectly followed him up the stairs.

Thirty-one

She had bronchitis afterwards and spent a week in bed. Doctor Churcher came to see her, and stayed to have lunch with Guy. They were such good friends. Anna said nothing about what had happened. She knew she would pay for it, if she did.

Mrs Roseveare fussed around her, bringing hot drinks and brandy, and seeing that Anna's medicines were taken on time. Anna didn't dare to confide in her, either.

Robin looked on with quiet amusement. He didn't know quite how, but Daddy had really frightened Mummy. She wouldn't slap him ever again. Sometimes, Robin stood by Mummy's bed and grinned at her, while he beat his new toy drum. Guy had bought that for him. Consolation for being smacked.

Anna was grieved and frightened to see the way her boy was turning out. A suspicion had formed in her mind that this was something far from new in the Buckman family. Robin, she feared, was going to grow up exactly like his father. His father, with whom he had such rapport, just like the affinity between Guy and Matthew Buckman. A pattern suggested itself and she found herself brooding more and more on the subject of Guy's unfortunate mother. She wished she could talk to someone who had known Helen Buckman well. The obvious person to consult would be Guy's sister, Elaine, but the only communication ever received from her was a card each Christmas. There was never any message, never an address.

And yet – Anna fancied that Guy sent one back. Yes, she was sure he did. One of the hotel's standard cards, as sent to all the suppliers and regular clients. Guy kept a list of names and addresses for that particular purpose. With any luck, Elaine might just be on it.

Anna went through his desk one evening and found it in a pigeonhole. His sister's name was scrawled on the back – clearly an afterthought. The address was care of a hospital. Anna made a note of it, then put all the papers back exactly as she had found them.

Her letter to Elaine was short and cryptic. She wanted to see her, discuss certain matters face-to-face. Could they arrange a meeting? Would it be asking too much for Elaine to come down to Cornwall for a day? Anna couldn't get away without questions being asked.

She posted the letter and waited. Five days, six. No answer came, no telephone call. Anna supposed the letter might take time to find her, having to be forwarded, perhaps. After a while, she recalled Guy saying his sister had wanted to work abroad. If Elaine were out of the country, the letter might take weeks or months to reach her, and one could hardly expect her to travel home from overseas, thought Anna despondently.

Almost a fortnight went by and she had almost given up. But then, one lunchtime, the telephone rang in the flat.

'Mr Buckman's sister is here to see you,' said Sarah's voice. 'Shall I send her up?'

Anna was astonished. 'Yes, of course! Oh – Sarah, does Mr Buckman know?'

'He's gone out for a while with the little boy. Shall I tell him when he comes in?'

'Don't bother. We'll surprise him.'

'Very well.'

A few minutes later, Anna opened the door of the flat to a smart woman of about thirty. The first thing that struck her about Elaine was the family resemblance. Like and yet unlike. Guy's features, but a somewhat finer version. Guy's colouring, too – same brown hair and hazel eyes. Elaine's skin appeared more rosy than his, but that was partly thanks to powder and rouge. Her hair and clothes were well-cut and simple. She looked precisely what she was, an intelligent, self-sufficient woman who dressed to please only herself. At the sight of Anna, something flickered in her eyes; something rather like recognition.

'Elaine? Oh, do come in!' Anna held out her hand and it was taken in a friendly grasp. 'I had no idea you would simply turn up like this.'

'I hope I haven't gone about it in the wrong way?'

'No, not at all. I'm delighted to see you. Come and sit down. Would you like some lunch?'

'It's all right, I ate on the train.'

'You've come down from London this morning?'

'Yes, I received your letter three days ago. It had to be redirected, or it would have reached me sooner.' Elaine took a moment to look round the flat. 'Place has been redecorated, I see. Must say, it's a big improvement. Lighter, more pretty than I remember.'

Taking her hat and gloves off, Elaine sat down, choosing Guy's armchair. For a moment the two women looked at each other. Anna hardly knew now what to say, how to begin.

'I'm sorry I didn't come to your wedding,' Elaine said.

'I wished afterwards that I had, just to see what sort of girl he'd married. I should have guessed, of course. You're precisely the Buckman type.'

'What type is that?'

'Good-looking, quiet.' Her gaze ran over Anna. 'Very fashionable.'

Awkwardly, Anna laughed. 'I haven't always dressed and prinked like this. It's Guy's influence, really.'

'I'll bet.' Elaine eyed her shrewdly. 'Not very old, are you – compared to him, I mean?'

'Twenty-four.'

'That's another thing. The Buckman men choose young, impressionable women. Father was fifteen years older than Mother, you know. Turned her into quite a showpiece after they married. A real credit to him and Elestren Manor.'

As she spoke, she was watching Anna, noting her reactions. Elaine knew what this was all about, why she'd been summoned, Anna could tell. There wouldn't be much explaining to do. Intuition also told Anna this interview wasn't going to bring her any cheer. She felt a sudden need for a drink, and offered one to her sister-in-law.

'Gin and tonic, please.'

Anna poured it, along with brandy for herself.

'Your note . . .' said Elaine, as they both settled down.

'I'm sorry if it was melodramatic.'

'It was careful.'

'I'm very grateful that you've come. It's good of you, I'm sure you must be busy.'

Elaine took a sip of her gin. 'I know a distress call when I hear one.'

'You don't seem surprised.'

'That you need to talk to me? Oh, I'm not.'

334

Nervously clutching her glass with both hands, Anna wet her lips. 'It's about Guy, of course.'

'Of course,' came the dry response. 'How is he? Still as charming as ever?'

Anna stared down into her brandy and smiled bitterly. For a moment there was silence. Then:

'How long did it take you to find him out?' Elaine asked quietly.

Anna didn't look up. 'I knew on the wedding night there was something wrong, but it wasn't until we got back here that I began to see him really clearly. Since then, it's been one thing after another. Little things, bigger things, bad things, worse things.'

'Hmm. Has he been mistreating you – physically, I mean?'

'Recently, yes.'

'So what is it you want to ask me?'

Hesitantly, Anna said: 'I want to know why he's like he is.' Her gaze flicked up to meet Elaine's. 'I want to know how bad it gets, and I want you to tell me about your mother.'

Elaine studied her, blinking slowly. 'What did Guy tell you about her?'

'Before we were married, he led me to think that she died of cancer. Afterwards, when I found out otherwise, he said she was mentally unbalanced.'

A soft, ironic chuckle escaped Elaine. Then she murmured: 'Churcher, the old toad, called her neurotic. Didn't know the half of what went on here, and wouldn't have believed it anyway – not of his friend Matthew Buckman.' Surveying Anna, she said: 'Before I go any further, tell me what Guy's done to you.'

Anna took time to refresh both their glasses and then it all came out. Elaine smiled grimly when she heard what had happened at Zawn Fell and then about the wine cellar.

'Well,' she said, when Anna paused, 'he's more original than the old man ever was. Father was simply a brute. Guy adds a dash of novelty, doesn't he? A new style of persecution.'

'Persecution?' repeated Anna. 'It's not true, then, that your mother killed herself because she thought she had cancer?'

'Good God, no! That was just something handy to tell everyone. Father did an expert job of bending the truth and fogging the issue, and Guy has maintained the fiction for you. It's true that she had been to Churcher, but he told her she was fine and she didn't question that, despite what Guy and Father claimed. After she died, they went around telling people she brooded about it, became obsessed. Even old Churcher swallowed that one.' Elaine's tone became suddenly terse with anger. 'Yes, towards the end she was a bag of nerves, but that was nothing to do with any disease. No disease of the body, no tumour. No silly imaginings, either. Mother had a perfectly firm grip on reality. Reality was the problem – her life was hell. Misery, that was what she died of. Father was a pig to her. The way he treated her – that was the cancer, and it grew from small beginnings in just the same way. It grew beneath the veneer, covered up by their smartness and their money. People didn't recognise it for what it was. When Father humiliated her in public, they said it was just tactlessness, just his thoughtless way. After all, he was such a genial man, always joking and smiling for the world outside.'

Elaine took a long swig of gin, then sombrely went on. 'Up here, in private, the abuse became physical. A

336

pinch, a slap, and then finally full-scale beatings. He usually hit her where it wouldn't show, but if he'd been careless, given her a black eye, for instance, he wouldn't let her leave the flat until it faded.'

The room, with its radiators, was warm, yet Anna felt chilled from head to foot.

'She used to go down to the bottom garden and hide from him,' continued Elaine. 'She would stay down there for hours and hours, just to be out of his way. Then sometimes she would get frightened in case her absence should make him all the more angry, and then she would run back up to the house. Running towards what she feared. They sent me away to school when I was twelve. By that time, she was a nervous wreck; skinny, jumpy and going grey, And of course, the worse she looked, the worse he treated her. Each term when I came home on holiday, she seemed to have aged a year.'

'When his arthritis began to set in, while he could still get around with a stick, he used to rap her ankles with it, or hit her when she was helping him dress. I remember he kicked her once when she was lacing up his shoes. Being incapacitated made him savage. Before the arthritis there were at least lulls when he was good-humoured, even kind to her, but once he was stuck in that chair he was constantly evil-tempered. Father always had a nasty tongue – sarcastic – and he used to sneer at her, mock the things she wore and everything she said.'

'That's familiar,' muttered Anna. Then: 'Why did she stay and put up with it? Why didn't she leave him?'

'Mother was raised in the old-fashioned way. A bad marriage had to be endured, no matter how hellish. If she did have any ideas of walking out, I think she quelled them for my sake. Father would have put on his best act and kept custody of me. Society's hard on women who cut and run. Later, when her parents died, she had nowhere else to go. No money, no training for any career, but most of all, no will or initiative left. I don't think poor Mother had much of that to begin with. She was genteel, very feminine. What spirit she had, Father knocked out of her. I was nineteen when she finally couldn't bear any more and took those tablets.'

'You said she was concerned about you. But not about Guy?'

'Oh!' A snort. 'Guy was happy enough. He grew up worshipping Father. The old man cultivated him, they were thick as thieves. Guy copied him in everything, and that included despising my mother. He was tutored in it, Anna, thought it all an enormous lark when he was small, and then a kind of sinister sport as he grew older. Year by year you could see the little demon developing into a copy of the big one. After poor Mother was gone, I flew the coop at the earliest opportunity and swore I'd never come back. I had a scholarship to go to college. Father would never have financed any more education for me. He expected me to stay here and nurse him. Then he would have started on me. I wasn't going to stand for that; I made my escape and I've never been forgiven for it.'

'Guy told me about his father's will,' nodded Anna.

'Cheap at ten times the price. I wouldn't trade my freedom and dignity for a share in this place,' sniffed Elaine. 'Of course, Guy was full of righteous indignation. I was selfish, a faithless daughter, a regular serpent's tooth. I was the woman who got away, that was what really galled them both.'

For a moment, Anna sat thinking about the things Elaine had told her. Then she said: 'Our son, Robin, is three and a half. I'm worried about him, he's so – difficult.'

'Surprise, surprise.'

'Well, all children get into mischief, of course. They all have their moods and play up a bit, but . . .'

A memory flashed through Anna's mind, the flying wooden brick and Tuffet's squeal of pain.

'. . . he can be cruel, and I think he knows just what he's doing. Robin's precocious. He already understands about power, that some adults are subordinate, that he can goad them and get away with it. I've actually heard him tell Mrs Roseveare: "My daddy will sack you."'

'And he loves his father, of course, prefers him to you?'

'Oh yes, no doubt about that.'

Nodding, Elaine put down her glass and leaned forward. 'You'd better curb him, Anna, if you can. Guy was the same and you don't know where it will lead – possibly into a very great deal of trouble.' Sitting back again, she asked: 'Did you know that Guy was expelled from school?'

Anna looked at her.

'That's right, kicked out,' confirmed Elaine.

'What for?'

'Well, there was a younger boy, one of those unfortunate kids who don't fit in. A butt, picked on by everyone. Apparently he had projecting teeth and carroty hair. The others were always tormenting him, and the worst of them, the ringleader, was my brother. One night he and a couple of cronies thought up a stunt. They tied the poor little devil up in his bedsheet, carried him down to the village pond and dropped him in. After a minute or so, the other two were for pulling him out, but Guy wouldn't have it. He waded in and he held the boy down. He was giggling, they said afterwards, really enjoying it. The others struggled with him. In the end they had to hit him to make him let go. At first, when they got the lad out, they thought he was dead. Luckily, they were able to bring him round and they took him off to the hospital.'

Numbly, Anna stared at her.

'It was just the culmination of a series of nasty tricks. Guy would always go too far, he never knew when enough was enough. To him, someone else's suffering was fun. He'd been warned again and again, but that little incident was the last straw. Now, you know what public schools are like – instil the manly virtues, learn to take it and so on. But Guy was too much even for them. Even his pals refused to lie for him after that. They kept up a front for the school, who naturally didn't want the police involved, but privately they told the Head what happened. It was still touch-and-go that no charges were brought. Father had to buy off the boy's parents. He paid the kid's school fees for the rest of his time there. They were satisfied with that, so long as Guy was thrown out.'

Elaine became thoughtful. 'He was quite indignant, you know. He expected to be forgiven – said it was all a lot of fuss about nothing.' She regarded Anna gravely. 'I'm not out to frighten you unnecessarily, but you asked me here to talk about him and I feel bound to tell you what I think. My brother's a dangerous man. Sometimes he's cunning and covers his tracks, other times he's so worked up, he doesn't consider consequences. And his self-importance makes him feel invulnerable. I can't tell you how surprised and peeved he was that the school punished him. He's a bad type, Anna. I'm sorry to have to say it, but he is. You don't want Robin turning out like that.'

'Oh, my God,' breathed Anna. 'What am I going to do? Robin idolises him. He pays no heed to me. Guy won't let me discipline him. I've told you what happened to me when I tried.'

'Yes,' Elaine said grimly. 'Then perhaps you should simply think about saving yourself. Things won't get any better here, I promise you.'

Anna shook her head. 'I do love my son, even though I detest his behaviour. I couldn't just leave him. Anyway, like your mother, I have no one to whom I can go.'

'I do so wish I could help you, Anna, but I'm going abroad early next year – a sweaty place in Africa, full of tsetse flies.'

'It's all right, it isn't your problem. I didn't contact you for help. I just wanted to know all the facts.'

'And you got rather more than you bargained for. I'm very sorry for you, Anna. I always knew that some poor girl was in for a rough time with Guy. It was my frail hope that he'd marry someone tough enough to deal with him, but of course, that's not the Buckman way.'

'No.' Anna swished the last of the brandy around in her glass, then drank it. She smiled sadly at Elaine. 'I'm glad I've seen you. At least I know now what I'm dealing with.'

Elaine was sympathetically silent. Anna sat back, crossing her legs. 'Anyway, enough of Guy. Tell me about what you do. You must be very bright. I wish I'd used my education, instead of rushing into wedlock.'

For a while they spoke of Elaine's studies, her plans. Marriage, it seemed, wasn't on the agenda. Her parents' example had put her right off the idea. She was just telling Anna about African sleeping sickness when Guy came in with Robin.

At the sight of his sister, he seemed only mildly surprised and drawled: 'My, look what the wind's blown in.'

Elaine smiled coolly. 'Hello, Guy.'

'Why didn't you let us know you were coming?'

'Thought I'd surprise you.'

'Indeed?' He cocked an eyebrow, then bent and told the child: 'This is your Aunt Elaine from London.'

The boy considered her soberly.

'I hear you're called Robin,' Elaine said. 'That's a nice name.'

Still no response. Robin was always wary with unknown quantities, especially ones with steady, searching eyes. This was a woman, and women were usually soft, but Robin's infant shrewdness told him Aunt Elaine wasn't like the others he knew. He quickly decided he didn't like her.

Guy came in and sat down on the settee. The boy climbed up beside him.

'Finally found the time to come and meet your sister-in-law, eh?'

'Yes, we've had a nice long chat, haven't we, Anna?'

'Hmm,' agreed Anna, smiling.

'Splendid. And how's the microbial world? Discovered any new plagues?' Guy grinned from sister to wife. 'She'd love to identify a brand new ailment and have it named after her.'

She's already found one right here in the family, Anna thought. She could call it Buckman's Syndrome.

'That would be Elaine's idea of fulfilment, wouldn't it, Sis?'

Ignoring his gibes, Elaine said: 'I've just been telling Anna, I'm going abroad next year. Central Africa.'

'Ah, yes, the jungle. Mud huts and fever. What a courageous girl you are.'

'Thank you. How's trade? Still charging extortionate prices?'

'Of course.'

'Still the same pampered, idle clientele?'

'Need you ask?'

'Never could stand them, I'm afraid. Selfish types who live for pleasure and never do anything important.'

'You old Pharisee, you. Haven't changed a bit.'

All this with forced smiles. The atmosphere was awful. Anna noticed, too, that Guy was looking at her in a speculative way. Wondering what Elaine had told her, of course.

'How long can you stay?' she asked her. 'We've plenty of room at the moment, haven't we, Guy?'

He made an expansive gesture. 'Acres.'

'I'm afraid this is just a flying visit. I have to go at four.'

'Oh dear,' said Guy. 'A mere two hours.' He clasped his hands across his stomach, beaming. 'Well, what shall we all talk about until then?'

He wasn't going to give Anna another minute alone with Elaine. Still, it was too late anyway, and Anna guessed he knew it. He couldn't wait to get rid of his sister and eagerly drove her to the station to catch her train.

As soon as he returned, he started questioning his wife.

'How did you like her, then?'

'Very well. I admire her.'

'Was she here for long before I came in?'

'About an hour.'

'Wonder what prompted her to come?'

'I think she wanted to meet me just once before going abroad.'

'I see.' Guy pondered a moment, then said: 'Elaine's achieved a lot, of course, but I still think she's wasting her life.' He glanced at Anna from under his brows. 'She's a bit of an agitator, too. Mustn't take too much notice of what she says.'

Anna just gazed at him solemnly, saying nothing. Elaine hadn't uttered a word that wasn't true, she was certain of that. What a predicament she was in. What a man she had married.

Thirty-two

Peggy, albeit for different reasons, was thinking something similar. The first year's rent on the cottage had run out. They should have been moving on to somewhere better, but they hadn't even the means to pay for another month where they were.

Had Maisie been alive, she would have left Hal, taken the children and gone home. That escape route, however, was closed to her now. Walter wouldn't have her back – and life at the bazaar would be intolerable if he did. Instead of doing all the work here, she'd be doing all the work there, while her father and brother boozed. There, on top of everything else, she would have to put up with Walter's abuse. Father, ruling the roost – she could never live with that.

With scarcely any money coming in, Peggy had visions of being evicted and sleeping under a hedge. Fortunately, Mr Mingo was a flexible man. He had a suggestion to make. They could keep the cottage rent-free if Peggy would help out his 'Missis' a couple of days a week up at the farm. 'Missis' needed a hand in the kitchen. How would that be?

She accepted the arrangement, feeling there was little choice. Good of him, wasn't it? Hal said. Sharp of him, corrected Peggy. Who else would want to rent this place? If they left it would just lie empty again. This way, Mingo was at least getting something out of it.

Peggy's labour. Not Hal's. The farmer had summed

345

them up well in that respect. She was the worker and
Hal was the dreamer. He wouldn't be much good to Mr
Mingo.

Joy had started school that autumn. 'You'll have to
take her in and bring her back,' Peggy had told her
husband. 'I've got more than enough to do as it is, and
it's your fault we're living up here.'

He did it without complaint, walking his daughter
down to Trezawne every morning, collecting her every
afternoon. He enjoyed it, in any case, inventing games
along the road and giving the little girl piggy-back
rides for part of the way. If he had twopence to spare,
they rode home on the bus at four o'clock, and Joy
always loved that.

Peggy's work at Mingo's farm consisted mostly of
scouring pans and cooking on Wednesdays and Saturdays. She always took Ewan with her. Eight o'clock
start, four o'clock finish. A long day for the child, but
there was a bonus – breakfast, midday meal and an
ample tea for them both.

Mingo's farm was forty acres, centred round a
granite house and barns. His fields were larger ver-
sions of Peggy's little plot, producing potatoes, cabbages and turnips. He kept a few cows and some
poultry, and a large sty full of pigs. The Mingos also
had a small orchard and kitchen garden. Two acres of
woodland behind the house provided logs to burn in
the kitchen range.

Mrs Mingo was a large, florid and noisy woman, in
charge of a giant kitchen full of Victorian equipment.
She bullied her husband and all the hired men, heaping their plates and chivying them if they didn't eat
enough or ate too slowly. Table talk generally focused
on livestock ailments, with discussions of worms, ticks

and parasites or intestinal disorders. Small wonder that Mrs Mingo drove them out the minute they had finished, just as she drove the dogs and cats and chickens out all day long.

Like Peggy, she was glad of another woman for company, and they swapped complaints, busily tearing their menfolk to pieces as they stood either side of the kitchen table, mixing pastry or cleaning vegetables or preparing meat. Wednesdays and Saturdays were Mrs Mingo's days for making saffron and heavy cake, and for scalding cream. There was always a big earthenware pan of dough rising beside the stove, and another of cream over a steaming pot of water above a peat fire. Peggy would watch the yellow crust forming, knowing there would be a few spoonfuls for her and Ewan later on. Hot fruit pie and clotted cream. Sometimes a basinful to take home with her. Mrs Mingo wasn't mean; there was always some little gift – if not cream, then a few eggs, some cheese, a chunk of brisket or boiled ham.

Her largesse extended to kindling, too.

'Take what you want from the wood,' she said. 'Mingo fells three or four trees every year and saws them up for logs. There's a lot of smaller stuff left lying about. It burns well and you're welcome to it.'

So Peggy got Hal to make her a trolley – a wooden box fixed on to a set of old pram wheels. Thereafter, she always went home with a cart full of wood, and Ewan riding on the top of it.

Thus they continued scraping a living. There had been good crops of blackberries that year, and hazelnuts too. Peggy had walked for miles in search of them, exploring all the country lanes around Trezawne, scouring thickets and hedgerows, filling her basket.

She had made the blackberries into jam and the nuts were stored away for Christmas. Sometimes, on her way up to the farm, Peggy would be lucky and find a few field mushrooms on Mingo's land. She would pick them and hide them along the way, then collect them again as she was going home.

Hal was always delighted by that sort of thing, and would talk about 'living off the land'. He suggested gathering mussels and winkles and catching fish, but he never actually made any effort to do so himself.

If Hal did little, Walter and Jasper were doing even less. Since the flood, they had done precisely nothing. Angilley's Bazaar was still a shambles inside, so it was just as well that the downstairs windows were boarded over. Whilst others had swept the mud from their homes, cleaned up and made repairs, Walter and Jasper had left the place much as it was when the flood had passed. They came and went through the wreckage, stepping over what was in their way or kicking it aside.

Among the items trampled underfoot were envelopes, brown ones, containing bills. Walter knew what they were. He also knew he couldn't pay, so he never troubled to open them.

Upstairs, the house was a scene of indescribable squalor. They seldom tipped a bin or washed a dish. Empty bottles were everywhere, and the bedsheets hadn't been changed since Maisie died. Among the smells pervading the place was a growing stink of rot. Down in what was once the shop, fungus was sprouting from the walls – long dark tendrils, moulds of green and fluffy white, and sinister fleshy brown ruffles. The back yard was piled high with rotting rubbish. Lily

Greasypockets was always shouting over the wall these days about the stench, berating Walter and Jasper whenever she saw one of them on his way out to the lavatory. She had already complained to the council, who in turn had sent Walter a letter, which he ignored.

Outside at the front, children had scrawled rude words all over the boards nailed up at the windows. The local Chamber of Commerce was incensed that the place should be left in such a condition. They had started calling it Angilley's Eyesore.

One day close to Christmas, they sent a deputation round there to complain.

Walter stumbled out of bed at eleven that morning, woken by a loud and continuous hammering at the door. Going downstairs in his vest and longjohns, he found Mr Lindow the chemist on the step, in company with Mrs Kellow from the florist's shop.

The sight and smell of Walter caused Mrs Kellow's nostrils to flare. 'My stars!' she said in disgust, and took a pace backwards.

'What you want?' demanded Walter.

'To speak with you, Mr Angilley, about your shop,' Mr Lindow said.

'It's not for sale.'

'We don't want to buy it. We've come on behalf of the Chamber of Commerce. Everyone's very concerned,' said Mrs Kellow.

'Why?'

'Frankly, because it looks so awful.'

'Huh!' replied Walter. 'No business of yours.'

'We think it is,' said Mr Lindow. 'You're letting down all of Trezawne. Imagine how this looks to the visitors.'

'Couldn't care less.'

'Well, we do!' Mrs Kellow snapped. 'It spoils the

harbourfront and that's what people come here for. Lower Trezawne is supposed to be picturesque, but this place is a slum.'

'Slum?' echoed Walter gutterally.

'There's nothing else to call it. Could you not at least clean it out and give it a coat of paint? Why not let it to someone, Mr Angilley?'

'Don't you tell me what to do with what I own.'

'Would you rather see the place fall down?' asked Mr Lindow.

'That'll take a few years yet. Meantime, I'll do it up and rent it out when I'm good and ready, not before.'

'It's only another four months to the next summer season,' began Mrs Kellow. 'If I may suggest . . .'

'Push off!'

'Now, look . . .'

'Go on, get out of it.'

The door slammed in their faces.

Muttering, Walter went back upstairs. At the top was Jasper, who had been hanging over the banisters, trying to listen.

'Who was that?'

'Busybodies.'

'What did they want?'

'Came here throwing their weight about. I had enough of that from your mother and sister. Nobody's telling me what to do, not now nor ever again.'

Jasper dawdled after him into the kitchen. He was missing Maisie more than Walter was. Pub food and pasties had started to pall, and he longed for proper dinners. Clean laundry, too. These days he itched a lot. Now and again, he actually rinsed a few things out himself, but darning was beyond him. There were holes in the toes and heels of his socks, and missing shirt buttons were never replaced. With Christmas drawing near, he realised there would be no goose and pudding, no mince pies and dark fruit cake this year, unless he cared to attempt the cooking himself. Peggy, he thought wistfully, could turn out a pretty good dinner. He'd be prepared to call a yuletide truce, if Walter was willing.

'Aren't you asking Peggy home for Christmas? Family get-together?'

'No.'

'What about the meal on Christmas Day?'

'We'll go next door.'

Jasper knew the reputation of Billy Nancarrow's Christmas feasts – dried up fowl and soggy sprouts, puddings mostly flour and not much fruit.

'Won't be the same.'

'It'll do for us.'

'We used to have a duck for Boxing Day.'

'Not this year, boy. You just forget it.'

'It was me Hal tried to drown. I'm willing to forgive him.'

'Don't argue with me, Jasper. I can send you packing, too, if I've a mind.'

Disconsolately, Jasper left him and went into the sitting-room. In the corner, in the usual place, he had set up a wan little tree and hung it with baubles in an effort to be festive. A few dejected sprigs of holly were tucked behind pictures around the walls. The fire was laid and he thought he could probably get it going, but there wasn't coal enough to last a day. There by the window was Maisie's gramophone and her carol records, but there was only a single needle left in the little tin box.

Jasper looked around him mournfully. It wasn't

351

going to be much of a Christmas, was it? Being rid of the womenfolk wasn't such fun after all.

Springtime brought work on the land for Peggy. Mingo would pay her a few precious shillings for this. He always took on girls in April, casuals to help pick the early potatoes and weed the fields of young cabbages.

One day in early May, Peggy paused in her work to straighten her aching back. It was nearly noon and her hands had started to swell, with a puffiness and cracking of the skin. She flexed her fingers, examining them in the shade of her wide-brimmed hat.

It was the juice which did the harm, the sap and the tiny hairy filaments on the stems. Most of the other women suffered the same. Peggy looked around her, down the field, which sloped towards the sea. A dozen stooping figures in boots and aprons were working their way along the rows of cabbage plants, pulling up the yellow weed called charlock which grew so profusely among them. The sun was hot and the ground was dry. The world was all blue sky and sea, and brown earth striped with rows of green and brilliant yellow. She had been here four hours and felt as if her spine was ready to snap. Back and forth over the four-acre field, working her way down one row and up the next, leaving behind her a clean line of sprightly green cabbage plants, with the charlock lying in the furrow beside them, going limp and drying up. Before her eyes were soil and stones, soil and stones, endless clumps of the sulphur-coloured weed, endless little cabbages. She could see her own shadow moving over the earth in the glaring sun, and her dusty old shoes ever shuffling forward.

She was being paid sixpence an hour for this, which

was slightly more than she got for picking potatoes. Three days of it would bring her twelve shillings, enough to buy new shoes for Ewan and some underwear for Joy. Her own shoes were stuffed with newspaper because of the holes in the soles.

After a time, she saw two of the women heading towards the hedge where they had left their packages of food. Peggy and several others followed them. It was twenty-past twelve and just as well to sit out this hottest hour of the day. In the shadow of the hedge, they unwrapped sandwiches, pieces of pie, or bread and cheese. As they ate, they compared their aches and pains and their swollen hands, talked about their husbands and their children.

Most of them were older than Peggy, weather-beaten, tough-looking women.

I'll become like that before too long, she thought. I'll have the same coarse skin and features, the same hard hands and loud voice. A yokel in a headscarf, that'll be me, while Anna goes about looking like the front cover of *Vogue*.

The Trevena girl would always be her yardstick, even though reason reminded Peggy that Anna's affluence was exceptional. Try as she might to keep a sense of proportion, she couldn't escape the hideous comparison between the slog and poverty of her own life and the opulence enjoyed by Mrs Guy Buckman. How triumphant Peggy had felt on the day she married Hal. No one could have convinced her then that she would end up like this. Well, she'd been hoist with her own petard. This was what she got for stealing him.

The worst of it was, she didn't think she even loved him any more. Resentment, that was all she felt now, and disillusionment.

She finished her food and sat for a while, then rose and tramped off down the field to carry on weeding. But before she bent her back to it, she stood for a moment, looking out to sea. So blue. That was where Peggy often wished she could go – off into the blue. Summer was coming. She thought about walking off this field and up the lane to the road, just as she was, and disappearing. Walk and keep on walking until she found herself something good. Have a new start, a second chance, be young again. She was twenty-five and felt more like forty. It had taken just eighteen months at the cottage to turn pretty Peggy into a drudge who clumped around in boots and dressed from jumble sales and cut her own hair as best she could. An awful thing was happening to her, and happening very fast. Shouldn't she save herself while she still had a chance?

Preposterous idea. She had two children, so that was that. Her own life had to be written off. Sighing, Peggy bent and went on pulling up the charlock. Later, she was rewarded with four shillings and a turnip. Useful though it might be, Peggy was pretty sick of turnip, especially since she imagined Anna dining on asparagus tips.

Thirty-three

Divorce was always on Anna's mind these days.

'It's immoral and a social disgrace,' Delia Trevena had once declared.

That didn't seem to bother the King and Mrs Simpson. The foreign papers were full of gossip and speculation about them. Anna had read about them in a French magazine, left in the lounge by a guest. It contained a very bold feature on the couple. If Wallis Simpson could discard two husbands and still attract royalty, then times were surely changing, Anna thought.

All that stopped her walking out on Guy was Robin, and with every passing month the child grew further away from her. He was four now and only his father had any real control over him. Occasionally, Guy would put his foot down when Robin did something which annoyed or embarrassed him. The boy adored and respected his father, sensing Guy's power and wanting to be like him. Tall, commanding Daddy, whom lesser people scurried to obey. Of his mother he took little notice, and Anna felt superfluous, to say the least. Yet, if she were to leave, she knew that Guy would tell the world she'd abandoned her child — and indeed she would feel that she had, even though Robin wouldn't miss her.

One morning, she took the boy into town to have his hair cut. They went by way of the harbourfront, because Robin liked to look at the boats. On passing Angilley's Bazaar, Anna noticed that one of the loft windows had been broken, probably by children throwing stones. She paused, wondering again about Hal, where he was. She had only one clue; some months ago she had seen Peggy queueing up for the Polzeath bus, carrying a bag of groceries. That, however, didn't tell her much.

Anna shook her head, taking in the filmy windows, peeling paint and grubby boards. It had been quite a jolly place once, she allowed, even if it was the lair of the awful Peggy. Cheap and cheerful, that was the phrase, and always lively, with children running in and out. Now it was dead and decomposing, a pitiful sight.

Robin, impatient, started tugging at her hand and she walked on. A little farther along the waterfront there was some sort of commotion on the beach, and the boy pulled her towards it.

Down on the sand a gang of urchins were whooping and catcalling, running round and round a rowing boat. Drawing nearer, Anna saw the reason, as a dirty, unkempt figure hauled itself up from the bottom of the boat and snarled around at the jeering boys. It was Walter Angilley. He had plainly slept there all night, blind drunk. As he tried to stand, the children started pelting him with seaweed. One came dashing up the beach with a bucket of water and sluiced it over him. Roaring curses, Walter swung and grabbed at his tormentors, but they simply gambolled around him, far too nimble to be caught. Anna was shocked by the state of him. He had never been any oil painting, but now he looked just like a tramp who'd been on the road for a couple of years.

Robin, excited, was all for joining in the fun and his mother had to drag him away. Looking back over her shoulder, she saw the boys scatter as Walter stumbled out of the boat and staggered towards the slipway, uttering incoherent threats, hurling foul language left and right.

It couldn't have been any joy for Peggy, growing up with a father like that, conceded Anna.

Robin was fractious now, demanding to go on the beach. He had spotted some other small children and wanted to play with them. Anna didn't dare let him. She remembered too many past occasions; Robin stamping on other infants' castles, taking over their little projects, lashing out at any who protested. He didn't know how to get on with his peers, had no social sense at all. It was Anna's hope that school might cure him, or at least temper his behaviour. He was due to start in twelve months' time and a teacher might succeed where his mother could not. A teacher, after all, did not have to live with Guy, could not be attacked, locked in the wine cellar or abused by any other of the myriad means a man might employ to intimidate his wife.

Anna hustled her son along to the barber's shop in Church Street, where he squirmed and fretted in the chair, generally making the man's job hard for him. When Anna wasn't looking, the barber shook his fist at Robin, hissing: 'You keep still, you little brute!' Sullenly, Robin obeyed. By the time he emerged from the shop, all neatly clipped, his face was like a thundercloud and his mood was ugly. He trailed along with his mother, dragging his feet and glaring at passers-by. As soon as he got home he was going to tell Daddy about that man.

Anna made a detour to Temperance Street to buy a copy of *Gone with the Wind* from the bookshop. Going by Drummond's the clothing store, she noticed that they were having a sale but didn't go in. Mrs Guy Buckman never bought goods at sales. Anna had always enjoyed bargain-hunting, but her husband wouldn't want her to be seen doing such a thing – especially at Drummond's, which was a cheap shop anyway. She purchased the novel – currently all the rage – and started back towards home. However, passing Drummond's the second time, she encountered Peggy coming out with a paper carrier. Beside her, holding her hand, was Ewan.

Peggy flushed when she saw Anna. The last thing she wanted was to be caught coming out of a sale. In her carrier bag was a coat she had found for her boy. It was somewhat large and the lining had a tear, but it would serve him for a year or two, she hoped. Her glance flitted down to Robin in his light summer jacket and matching shorts.

Cute, she thought bitterly, eyeing his black patent shoes. What wouldn't she give to be able to dress her son like that? As for Anna's costume, it was just like something Joan Crawford would wear, a wide-shouldered white linen suit with a long, slim skirt. In keeping with fashion, Anna's hair was longer now, loosely wavy beneath a black slouch hat with an eye-veil. Hideously conscious of her own shabbiness, Peggy meant to hurry away without speaking.

Anna, however, couldn't resist the opportunity to try and find out where Hal had gone.

'Morning, Peggy. Been shopping, I see.'

'Yes,' came the muttered response. She moved to

walk on, but Anna continued: 'I was sorry to hear about your mother. What an awful way to lose her.'

The condolence was sincere enough. Peggy eyed her awkwardly, then mumbled: 'Thank you.'

'Where are you living now?'

Instantly on the defensive, Peggy said: 'What's it to you?'

'Just interested.'

'Hal wanted to live in the country. We moved before the flood.'

'Really? Where, exactly?'

'You wouldn't know the place,' said Peggy stoutly. 'Why? Were you thinking of calling on my husband?'

Anna fidgeted. 'Of course not, I was simply curious. I take it you'll never be moving back to the shop?'

A wave of heat rushed up Peggy's face, going right to the tips of her ears.

'How could we? You've seen it, I'm sure. It's not my fault, the mess it's in. You can blame the old man and Jasper for that.'

'Yes, I saw your father earlier,' nodded Anna. 'He looked pretty neglected himself.'

'I hope you're not suggesting I ought to be looking after him?' snorted Peggy.

'Perish the thought, you did well to escape,' said Anna dryly.

Beside their mothers, the two little boys were looking each other up and down. Ewan stared at the pearly buttons on Robin's dark green jacket, then down at his own faded shirt and cotton trousers. He thought he had never seen anything as pretty as those buttons. The sunshine made them glow, and shadows seemed to flow within them each time Robin moved.

Sulkily gazing back at him, Robin pushed out his

lower lip. Ewan tried a smile, but the other boy didn't respond. Fascinated by the buttons, Ewan reached out a hand. He fingered the top one by Robin's lapel, turning it to make the lights dance within it.

Next moment he recoiled with a cry of pain as Robin lashed out with a foot and caught his shin. The kick scraped off a patch of skin and drew small beads of blood. Robin was ready to give him another, but Anna jerked him away.

'My God!' exclaimed Peggy, bending down to look at Ewan's leg. 'What was that for, may I ask?' she demanded of Robin.

Eye to eye with her, he simply curled his lip.

'You nasty little article,' Peggy hissed.

Hastily, Anna pulled her son behind her. It was not for Robin's protection, but more because she feared he might spit at Peggy.

Ewan was tearful. His leg was stinging and Peggy picked him up to comfort him.

Patting his back, she demanded of Anna: 'What's the matter with that little beast? My boy did nothing to hurt him.'

Uncomfortably, Anna said: 'He's a bit out of temper today.'

'Out of temper? He's a savage.'

Anna couldn't argue with that. She glanced down at Robin, cold with fury but terrified to give him the smack he deserved. Now she would have to eat humble pie on his behalf. 'I'm sorry. I apologise for my son.'

'I should think you would, and he needs a bloody good wallop into the bargain.'

'I never hit him.'

'That explains a lot.'

'I've said I'm sorry. Perhaps you'll let me buy some sweets or a plaything for your boy?'

'Thank you, no,' said Peggy, on her dignity. She thrust her head towards Robin, who was peeping up at her from behind his mother's skirts. 'If you were mine,' she told him, 'I'd tan your arse for you. You wouldn't sit down for a week, my lad.'

Robin poked his tongue out at her.

'Hmph.' With acrid humour, Peggy smiled. 'It seems, for all your money, you can't bring a child up decently.'

'He's only four,' said Anna, embarrassed.

'So's Ewan. He'd never behave like that.'

'I'm sure he'll grow out of it,' Anna lied.

'I doubt it. He's spoilt, that's plain to see. Too much of everything and no discipline.'

'That's not true.'

'Prove it, then. Smack him.'

Anna desperately wanted to. He had hurt the other child and he richly deserved it. He had let her down in front of Peggy. Still, she didn't dare.

'I'll do no such thing.'

'There.' A scornful shake of the head. 'He gets away with it.'

'All right, he does,' said Anna stiffly, taking Robin by the hand. 'You're making altogether too much fuss. I'm not going to strike my son to please you, and that's the end of it. Good day to you.'

Peggy watched her hastening off. Robin looked back over his shoulder and thumbed his nose at her.

An angry red mark was showing on Ewan's leg. Peggy bent to kiss it better.

Bitch, she thought angrily. Snooty bitch, with her horrible, pampered child. A well-off brat who could do as he wanted and not be punished for it. What a rumpus Anna would have raised if Ewan had been the one to kick Robin. Because it was the other way about, she made light of it.

Rich child, poor child, different rules. Hadn't it always been the same? Yet again, Peggy felt rage and wretchedness at her lot in life.

Thirty-four

That night when Hal reached for her in bed, she pushed him away.

'What's the matter?' came his whisper in the dark.

'Just leave me alone.' She rolled away from him.

A pause. 'Have I done something to upset you?'

Within herself, Peggy screamed: Where should I begin? Wouldn't it be best to list the things you haven't done – like finding work? But what was the use? It wouldn't change him and she was too tired just now for a row. All she said was: 'I don't want to, Hal.'

'Why?'

'I'm exhausted. Anyway, we can't afford another child.'

Well, that was true, sure enough.

'I'll be careful, Peggy.'

'Don't make me laugh.'

'You're angry with me.'

Silence.

'Tell me what's the matter.'

She debated. Then: 'I saw Anna in town today.'

'Ah,' he said. 'And?'

Peggy told him what had passed between them.

'And because of that, you don't want me tonight?'

'I hate being so poor, Hal. I hate being always at a disadvantage.'

'You married me for better or worse.'

'I didn't know how bad the "worse" could be. And as

I said, we can't afford any more children. Anyway ...'
She hesitated, then struck. 'I don't enjoy it any more.
It's a chore, like all the other chores I have to do each
day. The final one before I'm allowed to sleep.'

When the words were out, she bit her lip, knowing
how much they must have hurt. Once, it had been a
joy between them, and a consolation when other things
in life were going wrong. Now, at last, those other
things were too many, too bad, as far as Peggy was
concerned. Bed was no longer a refuge from them.
Instead, they got in beside her at night, to chill the
very heart of her marriage. She hadn't really wanted
Hal for months. It had simply been, as she said, the
last job of the day.

She waited, wondering what he would say. For long,
dragging minutes he made neither sound nor movement. Then, finally, the bed creaked and just for a
second she felt cool air against her back as he got up.
There followed another silence. Peggy knew he was
still in the room, and after a while she looked over her
shoulder.

Hal was a dark silhouette at the window, staring out
into the night. A thin fog had come down as darkness
fell, and the far-off boom of the horn from the lighthouse sounded intermittently. For a long time he stood
there, watching the dim, distant sweep of the light.
Peggy laid her head down, closed her eyes and pretended to sleep.

When at last he returned to bed, he still said not a
word, but kept to his own side, the very edge of the
mattress, not touching her.

From that night on, his confidence and cheer began to
desert him. Sometimes when he looked at Peggy, Hal

hardly recognised her as the pretty girl he had married, this tired woman in a grubby old apron and boots and headscarf, tight-lipped, with dirty fingernails. He hadn't noticed the change taking place, too caught up in his painting projects. Now, suddenly, he opened his eyes and saw what Peggy had become.

He felt the first stirrings of guilt within him. As a provider, he had failed. And as an artist – well, he wasn't quite so sure any more. The change of style had so far done him no good where sales were concerned. He thought his new paintings showed more merit and skill than the old stuff. But perhaps he was wrong. That was a thought which shook him to the very core. Doubt of his own judgement, his ability. Perhaps, after all, he was mediocre, and should have treated it as just a pastime, fitting it in around a proper job. Bad enough even if one had real talent, to subject one's family to deprivation in the cause of it. Inexcusable if he were simply run-of-the-mill.

He tried to reassure himself. He was going through a sticky patch, that was all. He would cross it, a breakthrough would come and all would be well again – better than ever. He was still young, only twenty-seven, and probably had yet to find his best form.

The straw to which he clung at this time was a forthcoming exhibition. He was going to have a room at the town hall for a week. Some of his new work was going to be shown and he very much hoped it would earn him some admiration. Peggy wasn't interested – indeed, she was pessimistic.

'Who'll want to buy pictures of piles of boulders, Hal? Or just cliffs, or beaches in the rain? It's all so bleak and boring, all greys and browns and dirty whites. If you sell even one, I'll eat my hat.'

'I'll remember that and I'll hold you to it,' he told her the day before the exhibition opened.

By the following afternoon, however, he feared she could well be right.

As it happened, there were two exhibitions on at the same time. Hal had been given a rather small room just inside the main door on the left. Up on the first floor the larger chamber was taken up by the work of a Mrs Fay Tunley. A small notice on the town hall door announced Hal's exhibition. Mrs Tunley had a placard, four by four and beautifully lettered in copperplate. Her show had already been on for a week and had another to go.

People came and went all day. Heads poked briefly round Hal's door, glanced about the room, then disappeared again, after which he would hear brisk footsteps going up the stairs. Occasionally, someone took the trouble to walk around and inspect his work. But they never stayed more than a minute or two, and then he would hear them going upstairs. No one wrote so much as a word in his comments book. All day he sat behind his table in that deathly quiet room.

At four o'clock, dejected, he decided to call it a day. Before leaving, however, he went upstairs to see what the attraction was. He saw Mrs Tunley's work before he saw her, and knew from the moment he entered the room that here was one of Mr Snow's 'mad' women.

Mrs Tunley was versatile. As well as painting, she worked in wood and ceramics. Hal walked around, looking at everything. Here and there, an oddly shaped display stand or block supported an even more peculiarly fashioned bit of pottery or carven wood. A vase, doubled over as if it had been punched in the middle. A lump of ebony, squat and highly polished, with a deep spiral groove worked around it from base to top. Some plates with crows and thunderclouds painted on them. Such were typical exhibits. They all had names: 'Renewal', 'Saqqara', 'Morrigan' and so on. Around the walls, the paintings were luridly abstract.

All of it awful stuff, in Hal's opinion. And the prices were outrageous, yet several items were already marked as sold. He noticed that the visitors book was full of signatures, words of praise. His despondency deepened.

He was just about to leave when Mrs Tunley emerged from an adjoining room. She was carrying another carving. Physically, she was not at all what Hal expected. No wild-haired, mad-eyed eccentric in gypsy skirts, but a dumpy, fiftyish woman wearing a pink suit and pearls.

She halted, looking him over. She didn't smile. Hal glanced down at his shabby old trousers and grey canvas smock.

'I'm Pentreath,' he told her. 'I'm having the exhibition downstairs.'

'Oh,' she said. 'Yes. Oh yes. I had a quick look on my way out to lunch.' The tone was dismissive, bored. 'Quite nice, of course. You have the copier's skill, I grant you.'

'The what?'

'You can copy a scene or object faithfully, represent it as it looks. However, I fear you're a bit out of date.' She set the carving on a pedestal, then, half turning, waved an arm about her. 'As you see, I favour modernism. These paintings around us are not merely to be looked at. They are to be experienced and understood. A certain – interplay – is required, a contribution from the one who observes. Do you comprehend?'

367

Although he stood head and shoulders above her, she spoke as she might to a five year old. Even in his old clothes he looked more graceful than she did. Mrs Tunley was ungainly, her fat feet squashed into high-heeled shoes and the breadth of her backside straining her skirt.

'Certainly,' Hal said drily. 'People can make what they please of what they see. Convenient. And whenever they want a change, they can hang the canvas upside down or sideways, as they fancy.'

She sighed. 'You're poking fun, young man, but I've sold a great many of my works. Can you say the same?'

'Not yet,' admitted Hal.

Mrs Tunley smiled tightly. 'Well, don't be downhearted. I think it's wonderful that you're interested in painting. What do you do for a living?'

So patronising. He knew what she thought, that he was a manual worker of some sort, with aspirations to higher things. Amusing and a bit pathetic.

'I paint, that's what I do. It's not a hobby, it's my occupation.'

'Oh,' said Mrs Tunley. 'Indeed? And have you a family?'

'Yes, two children.'

'Fancy that. Well, shouldn't you think about changing your style? Traditional art is on the way out, I promise you.'

'Rubbish. This is just a fad,' Hal said, glancing round him.

'If so, it's a lucrative fad. I don't wish to hurt your feelings, but one of my paintings would fetch as much as twenty of yours.'

'Hmm. You have the nerve to charge a lot, so people think they're getting something good.'

At that, Mrs Tunley became rather sharp. 'Which college of art did you attend, pray tell?'

'Well, none . . .'

'Did you even receive your basic schooling?'

'Certainly I did. Till I was fourteen.'

'Fourteen.' She rolled her eyes. 'Hardly qualified to judge the efforts of those who've had more training, are you? And if I may give you a word of advice, I suggest you find a job if you have a wife and children to support. To make a respectable income from art is a difficult thing, achieved only by an exceptionally gifted few.'

'Or exceptionally lucky. Exceptionally well-connected. And assuming there are buyers around exceptionally daft,' snorted Hal, jabbing a scornful thumb at a wall full of primary-coloured daubs.

'I've been exhibited in London and Oxford and Bath, I'll have you know,' she informed him. 'Next year I have hopes of showing my work on the continent.'

All those places, big cities. It came home to him forcefully just how insignificant were his own local exhibitions. He had no answer and, routed, he turned to go.

'Perhaps you should try serving drinks,' she called, as he walked towards the door. Hal turned round and she gestured to a tray of empty glasses. 'I offer a glass of wine to everyone who comes in. You could do the same, Mr Pentreath.' She smirked. 'Or you might find mugs of tea to be more suitable.'

At the end of the week he hadn't sold a thing, whereas Fay Tunley's exhibition had been a huge success. There were articles about it in all the local and regional papers. Important people had come from London to see it.

Of Hal's work, there was not a mention.

He was shaken as never before. It wasn't only that he had made no money, that what he considered his very best efforts had been ignored, it was also that prickly encounter with the Tunley woman. She had dismissed his work and rubbed his nose in his lack of schooling, calling up an uncertainty in him which made him furious. Find a job, she had suggested. Don't try to be more than you are, was what she had meant. Remember your place. Stay in it.

Depression began to creep about him like bindweed round a bush, and Peggy's 'I-told-you-so' did nothing to help. Indeed, the failure of the exhibition led to the nastiest quarrel they'd ever had.

'Perhaps now you'll come down to earth and find a job,' she said one lunch-time a few days later.

'My God, a lot of sympathy I get from you.'

'Sympathy? You want that as well? Isn't it enough that I labour to keep us all? Oh yes, and buy your damned paints for you, so that you can keep on turning out stuff you'll never sell.'

The tone was low and sullen. Her elbows stuck out aggressively as she wielded her knife and fork.

'Ready and eager to start a new one, I expect? Another to end up on top of the cupboard along with the rest of your failures.'

'I've had bad luck . . .'

'So have I!' She slammed her cutlery down so hard it could well have broken the plate. 'I had the gross misfortune to marry you!'

That was like a red rag to a bull. In a trice he was on his feet, leaning across the table, snarling:

370

'Sometimes I think you only wanted me in order to spite poor Anna.'

'Poor Anna? Poor Anna!' she almost shrieked.

'Yes, to hurt her. I'm beginning to doubt you ever cared for me at all.'

'You needn't waste any sympathy on her, she's done bloody well out of it!'

'Well, perhaps that's only justice. It's a pity there hasn't been any for me, that's all I can say. I did the decent thing by you. I could have left you to get on with it, but no. Like a fool, I stood by you. And what has it earned me? Nagging and bad temper and ugly looks. You're not even a wife to me any more. Anna wouldn't have treated me the way you do. I'd have had support, encouragement from her.'

'Support?' At once, she too was on her feet. 'What else do I do but support you? Can you imagine her out in the fields with a back bent? Can you see her with hands like these?' Peggy thrust her cracked and calloused palms in his face.

'Why not? She cared about my work. You made your bed, Peggy, but you can't lie in it with good grace. You knew you were marrying an artist.'

'I was very young. I never imagined anyone could turn out to be such a flop!'

'It isn't my fault. I haven't had the recognition I deserve.'

'Oh, that's right, blame everyone else. Wouldn't know a genius if they fell over him, would they?'

'I've never said I was a genius, but I'm better than that Tunley woman, and if her trash is worth praise and money, I'm damned sure my work is. If there was any justice . . .'

'Well, there isn't, you fool, you great child!' She spat

the words at him, hands on hips. 'I learnt that long ago. Why has it taken you so long to find it out? I'll tell you – because you're a dreamer, that's why. Even when all the evidence screams that you ought to give it up, still you keep on daubing, keep on deluding yourself.'

'I'm not deluding myself. It isn't dreaming, it's having faith.'

'Dreaming,' repeated Peggy. 'And because of those dreams, you won't work at anything else. You won't even compromise and find yourself a casual job. No, every waking minute is dedicated to your cursed painting. If you're not actually doing it, you're mooching around thinking about it.' She turned to pleading. 'For God's sake, Hal, let the painting take a back seat. It can still be a pastime, but . . .'

'No! I won't be beaten!'

Her voice became cutting again. 'And meanwhile, good old Peggy goes on bringing home the money, little as it is. You irresponsible, selfish apology for a man! Shall I tell you the truth? Nobody wants this new stuff of yours because it's nothing special. You were all right before you started taking yourself so seriously, before you began "experimenting".'

'Since when were you any critic? Where did you study the subject, may I ask?'

'Where did you?'

'Tuition can stifle and maim what's original in a man.'

'I'm sure it comforts you to believe that,' Peggy said. 'Hal, it's been a mistake. Why can't you admit it? If you must paint, at least turn out things you can sell. Mam understood about that. She sold cheap goods, and we lived well on it.'

'All you ever think about is money,' Hal accused. 'All I ever hear from you is what Anna has and where she's been and how she lives.'

'There's nothing wrong with wanting a nice home and clothes. Any normal man would understand that, but not you.' Her tone became prissy and mockingly mincing. 'No, it's all self-expression and living close to nature. You're a clown, do you know that?'

'Dear God, you're vicious. It's easy to see why Anna hated you.'

'How do you expect me to be, shut away up here in this hovel? I want gas, Hal, I want running water. I want you to bring home some pay.'

Abruptly, he wheeled away, went into the lean-to and slammed the door. Peggy followed him. He turned his back on her and busied himself with rearranging his still life – a pestle and mortar, some candles and bunches of herbs. He moved them this way, that way, tinkering, trying not to listen as Peggy went on scolding.

'I hate every inch of this place. I'm sick of the smell of paint and turps, and seeing you standing there fiddling away with a little brush when other men go out and use their backs – or better still, their brains – to make a decent living. I want . . . Will you leave that alone and hark?'

Stubbornly, Hal carried on, but a wild, explosive misery was building up inside him as Peggy went on and on, repeating the old familiar litany of complaints.

'I want a day of rest every week, and a few little treats now and then. I'm sick of making do, and foraging for firewood. Do you know what I often think about, Hal? Lighting the fire with those precious paintings, that's what. One winter day when we have no fuel, I swear to God I'll do it. They're no good for anything else.'

His control gave way. Spinning round, he bawled: 'Shut up! Shut up, for Christ's sake! Have mercy!'

Peggy stopped short. Her face was set and quivering. Controlling her rage, she said levelly: 'No, you show some to me. Go out to work.'

He turned away and his whole frame seemed to sag, his stance like that of a worn old man.

For a moment, Peggy hovered. She balled her hands into fists, plunged them into the pockets of her apron. Then, ready to cry, she left him.

Hal sat down in the basket chair. For a long time, he stared at the floor. What would he be without his painting? Ordinary. Nothing and nobody, just another man scrabbling for creature comforts. Being an artist had always seemed to him something almost hallowed. Artists were the most admirable people in the world. The great ones were awesome figures, half divine. He had wanted some little portion of that specialness, however modest.

Absently, Hal examined his paint-stained hands, then noted with a stab of shame that they were softer than Peggy's. How long had they been married now? Nearly seven years. And what had he given her? Two children, whom he couldn't keep. Hal felt guilty and defiant all at once. He was what he was, and to some extent she was getting her just desserts.

He looked up, scanning the silent room, the easels patiently waiting. Blank canvas, saying: 'Yes? Let's go. Make something of me. Put something wonderful here, turn me into an object of value, cover me with images and colours that everyone will want and admire. Come on.'

374

Next he surveyed the stacks of work propped up against the old cupboard or tucked in beside it. On top of it were more canvases. And inside, behind those scratched and pitted doors, the shelves were crammed. Countless efforts no one had wanted to buy. He had put them away and told himself their day would come.

Would it?

The latest project, covered by a cloth, stood facing him. Slowly he rose to his feet, peeled back the sheet and examined the picture with newly critical eyes. He could pick out the very last brush-strokes he had made yesterday evening before the light failed. He stared at the painting for minutes on end. It depicted a derelict church, the graveyard overgrown. When first he chose the subject, he'd meant to convey a sense of peace. Instead, it was inexpressibly sad, speaking of loneliness and futility.

It could be changed, Hal thought. He could see how to do it. The mood was entirely created by shadows. He could temper those and add cheerful touches with flowers and wildlife. He ought to be getting to work right now, but all of a sudden there was a frightening reluctance to pick up the brush. He forced himself to carry on, but the painting somehow would not conform to his will, and after half an hour he abandoned it to try something else.

Thirty-five

As the weeks went by, Hal's despondency grew deeper. He was always starting things and not finishing them. Sometimes he stared at his canvases and they seemed to have nothing to do with him at all, as if they had been painted by someone else. At other times he remembered clearly every stage of their construction – the thoughts which had gone through his mind at the time, the foolish optimism and satisfaction. There they now lay, all waste, all disappointment. Hal Pentreath's attempts to be clever, original. Two years of misguided effort. What did he have to show for it? An empty larder, a lowly dwelling, a wife who constantly harangued him, and with good reason. Look at her, look at the children, the way they were dressed. From jumble sales or in home-made garments – and Peggy was no great seamstress. And what did his luckless family eat? The plainest of foods. Wild stuff, for God's sake. Peggy had once boiled stinging nettles for want of any other greens. She was so thin these days, so thin.

She was right, he ought to find some honest work – or at least return to painting the chocolate-box scenes which would bring in an income. Yet now he was reluctant to paint at all, sickened of the whole business. Yes, jaded by what was once the most important thing in life. He rocked to and fro between spells of apathy and periods of desperate endeavour, when he forced himself to work out of sheer outrage at the thought of being beaten, giving up.

But he was disappointed in all he did, becoming afraid to try again each day, fearful that the skill he had was leaving him.

As to his family, his feelings were just as confused. He loved them. He resented them, too, because of their needs. His children still adored their dad, and yet their clothes and their diet were a reproach to him. They didn't blame him, as Peggy did. Hal blamed himself, and yet at the same time, something within him revolted and said:

'Failing wouldn't feel so bad if not for you. I wish I weren't shackled to you and your wants. I was careless one night at Tolgarth beach, and saddled myself for life. It isn't fair. I don't want the responsibility of you. I won't be made to do what you want. I wish I were single again, and free.'

He was furious that Peggy was still refusing him in bed. She hadn't allowed him to touch her for weeks and weeks. She who had used it to trap him now turned it off when he proved a disappointing catch, he thought indignantly.

Yet honesty reminded him that she hadn't really been as cold-blooded as that, and they had loved each other when newly married, they truly had. Part of his mind was a gallery of memory-pictures. Hal and Peggy, Peggy and Hal – brightly coloured, frozen images of happy times. They were once reality, hard as it was to believe, now that everything was going sour between them.

Did Peggy have such a gallery? Hal couldn't tell. He doubted it. If any such recollections survived in her head, they were probably faded, or ravaged by the vitriol of her bitterness.

And how could he blame her? God knew, she had cause for complaint, argued his other self, the guilty one. Sometimes he thought about disappearing from her life, just leaving a swinging door behind him and being gone. Eventually, she could marry again, find a man to give her more of the comforts she craved and deserved.

Leave her? Leave his children? No. No, not Joy and Ewan. Knuckle under, then, admit defeat? Go out and find a job, forget about painting – or demote it to the status of a hobby? Hal was torn and could make no decision.

That autumn, he took to going out walking alone, supposedly seeking inspiration but glad, in truth, to escape those accusing brushes and canvases. Twice a week, three times, then nearly every day as September passed into a fine October. Peggy would ask him at first where he'd been, but after a while she ceased to bother. He took Joy to school in the morning, brought her back in the afternoon. Whatever he did in the hours between, he made no money, that was all Peggy knew. Whether he stayed at home and pottered among his paintings, or went out wandering around and brooding, it was all the same to her. Either way, he earned no income and so she continued supporting them all.

Hal's only aim was to kill some time, stay out of the house and tire himself so that he might sleep at night. Miles and miles across the cliffs and along the beaches he walked. There were beautiful days when the sea was clear turquoise round the rocks, and windy days when it fizzed and frothed about them like creamy soda. Grey days of waves churning up the beach, violent days when he sat for hours watching roaring billows of spray. Beyond Tolgarth, he trudged across wastes of scrappy marram grass and cold, wet sand. So much emptiness, cliffs and ocean going on and on into the distance. He rarely saw another soul. No cottages, either, nothing inhabited, only ruined engine houses or tumbledown abandoned farms. Grass and rock, sky and water. Well, this was what he had wanted, wasn't it, when he took the cottage? Solitude and the elements. And here they were, putting on spectacular shows of colour and energy for him. Yet he never went home and painted anything he saw. Scenes he would once have rushed to capture, Hal now noted impassively. They were too many and he felt he couldn't do them justice.

After a time, he started going inland, trekking through the bracken and gorse of moorland. Once he would have paused to study the lichens on the boulders, or the flecks of quartz and feldspar within the rocks. Now he stepped over them, taking no notice. How much time had he wasted in painting such things? Too much. And what had it earned him? Nothing.

In this way, he dallied through winter and early spring. Then on an afternoon in April of 1937, he found himself heading towards Mengarva Quoit. An ancient tomb, three uprights with a capstone, it stood amid a circle of low hills just a mile north of Trezawne. Coming up over the rise above the hollow, Hal stopped short. Running and snuffling around in the heather below was a little fawn dog. On the grass beside the quoit, resting her back against one of the uprights, sat a woman in a tweed skirt, brown suede jacket and beret.

It was Anna.

379

She was chewing a stem of grass and pensively watching the dog. At first she was unaware of Hal; then Tuffet started barking and bounded up the slope towards him.

A warm smile broke over Anna's face. 'Hal,' she called. 'How good to see you!'

He was equally pleased to see her. Anna, who still thought him wonderful. He trotted down the hill, with Tuffet jumping round him.

'What brings you here?' he said.

'Just walking the dog. And you? Are you looking for subjects, new ideas?'

He flopped down beside her, pulled up his knees and clasped his arms around them. 'No. I just – needed some air.'

She said again: 'Oh, it's splendid to see you! It's been so long. Hal, are you living somewhere near here? Those cottages up by the farm?'

He shook his head. 'We rent from the farmer who owns them, but ours is over near the zawn.'

'The zawn?' She had to think for a moment, then an incredulous look appeared on her face. 'You mean that place with the galvanised roof? I didn't think . . .' She bit off her words.

'. . . that it was fit to live in?' finished Hal. 'Well, you're right, it's not, though it took me a long time to recognise that.'

Anna stared at him. 'How did you end up in such a place?'

'Sheer stupidity,' said Hal.

Her eyes asked questions.

'I was in a tearing hurry to leave the Bazaar,' he explained. 'A few months before the flood, I had one hell of a fight with Peggy's brother. My blood was up and I couldn't wait to move out. I couldn't find a place in town, so I took that one. Poor Peggy, she thought it would be only temporary, but we got stuck there. Not that I minded, first going off. But now . . .'

'You can't afford to move?' She seemed amazed. 'Aren't you selling, Hal? Is your work going badly?'

'To put it mildly. I think I should do as Peggy says and get a proper job.'

'Oh, nonsense! No! Don't listen to that. She ought to be encouraging you. You may be having difficult times, but they won't last for ever. Peggy should have more faith in you.'

Ah, music to his ears after so much self-doubt. Dearest Anna, loyal Anna. Still, he said: 'You don't know what it's meant for her.' Then he smiled. 'Anyway, never mind us. How are things with you?'

She debated her answer. As the silence grew longer, his smile disappeared.

'Anna?' He turned her face to him.

'All right.'

'Just all right? I thought you were happy?'

Hesitantly, she admitted: 'There's been some trouble since last I saw you. Guy's not the easiest person to live with, to tell you the truth.'

His eyes narrowed. 'Oh?'

'He isn't always reasonable. He's very – critical.'

'Of you?'

'Of everyone.'

He spent a moment digesting this. Then: 'There's nothing more, is there, Anna? Nothing worse?'

She wanted to confide in him, but it might go back to Peggy, and anyway, how could he help?

'No,' she said quickly, then added: 'We argue a lot. It

largely concerns our son. We don't agree about the way he should be brought up.'

'Oh.' His brow furrowed. 'I see.' Then he remembered Peggy's fury because Anna had refused to slap her boy for kicking Ewan. Supposing Anna to be a soft and doting mother, he asked: 'Is your husband more strict than you would like?'

A wry little smile crossed her face. How easily people misconstrued what they saw and heard. Too strict with Robin? Ye Gods! The boy had recently started at the nursery school. Already there had been indignant notes from the teacher.

'Yes, that's right, he's strict,' she said, inwardly adding: *But not with Robin, with me. I'm the one who doesn't dare step out of line.*

Hal stretched out his legs, leaning back beside her against the stone.

'When Peggy and I fight over the kids, it's because of what they're lacking, all the nice things they don't have, all the treats I can't buy them.'

'Are they happy, though?'

'Yes, on the whole, they are,' he mused fondly. 'It's Peggy who feels short-changed – herself and on their behalf.'

Anna turned to look at him. 'You're not getting on so well any more, you two?'

'It's because of the way we have to live.'

'Are things very bad between you?'

He stalled a few seconds before admitting: 'Pretty grim.'

She touched his hand with a rueful smile. 'Seems we have similar problems.'

'I wouldn't say that. Be glad you have some money,

Anna. Be glad your husband is successful, even if he's difficult.'

'Money?' She gave a tiny snort. 'I'd just as soon do without it.'

'You don't mean that.'

'Yes, I do. Between you and me, Hal, I made a mistake. I haven't been happy, except for those few months when Guy and I were courting, and the first year after Robin was born. The truth is, I bit off more than I could chew. I've never quite lived up to my husband's expectations. He should have married some stylish, seasoned woman ten years older than me.'

'Was it he who tried to make you look like one?'

'He felt it needful to improve me,' nodded Anna.

'Well, he was wrong, it's gilding the lily.'

Pleased, Anna smiled. Tuffet came running up to her and licked her face. 'I have to go back soon,' she sighed, ruffling the little dog's coat.

'Shall I walk some of the way with you?'

'Yes, I'd like that.'

A short time later they set off southwards and soon reached the brow of the hill above Elestren Manor. This was where the Tolgarth road made a broad arc, almost clipping the cliff edge. Anna paused, looking across the heath. About a mile distant squatted the cottage.

'That's your place, over there?'

'Yes.'

No wonder Peggy didn't want to tell me about it, she reflected.

It certainly wasn't the quaint, charming nest of Anna's imaginings. Just for a moment she felt almost sorry for her old enemy. To say that Peggy's fortunes had declined was putting it mildly.

Still, she had a gentle husband, and that was more than Anna could say. Reluctant to part with Hal, she said: 'I take a shortcut through the woods from here. It saves me walking down the hill and then all the way up the drive. Will you come a little further with me?'

Hal looked down at her hopeful face. He was in no hurry to leave her.

'Why not?'

They started down the hill. About fifty feet below the crest grew a sycamore tree, where a footpath struck off to the right. Hal had always known the track was there, but had never explored it. The woods here bordering the road were all part of the hotel grounds. A wooden sign was nailed to the tree trunk: 'Private Property. Keep Out'.

Anna started along the track, with the little dog running in front.

'I always come this way when I take Tuffet up to the quoit,' she said. 'It leads down to the leat. I think I must know every yard of the grounds by now; I go walking a lot.'

'I suppose you have to, when you've got a dog.'

'It isn't only that. I'm glad to slip away on my own for a couple of hours every day.'

They were making their way down a shadowy path now, steep and slightly treacherous. Pine trees grew on either side, their roots snaking right across the track. A slippery carpet of fallen needles covered the earth.

'I thought you were so content with Guy.'

'Everyone does. Everyone outside the hotel, that is. The staff see and hear a lot'

'He seemed such a pleasant, easy-going sort.'

'So much for appearances.' Halting a moment, she

turned to face him. 'You know, he was not best pleased when he found out how well I knew you. There was . . .' Irony coloured her tone. '. . . quite an incident.'

He frowned. 'How . . .?'

'Peggy told him, that day she came round about Mr Snow's cheque.'

'Oh damn!' He was briefly angry. 'Peggy and her mouth!'

'Guy hasn't trusted me since. I'm not supposed even to speak with you.'

'He's jealous as well?'

'He guards what he thinks he owns,' said Anna, walking on.

They came down to the level ground on the bank of the watercourse. He walked with her to the end of the bridge and there they stopped.

'You'd better not come any further,' she said. 'But Hal, may I see you again?'

He fidgeted, half shook his head. 'Oh Anna, I don't know . . .'

Imploring now, she gazed at him. 'Please? Look, I'm always out with Tuffet – virtually every day. Why don't we meet?'

'But your husband?'

'To hell with him.' She felt reckless now, seeing Hal after all this time, not knowing when she might see him again if she didn't seize the moment. 'What harm can it do?'

He was tempted. If Peggy no longer wanted him, why should she mind?

Yet, he still loved her, even if she had turned against him, and nothing in the world was more precious to Hal than his children. Things could get worse. Oh yes, they could, if she ever learned that she was seeing Anna.

There was a silence. Then she pressed: 'You can tell me all about your work. Perhaps it'll help somehow. I promise I won't ask too much of you, Hal. We both need somebody to talk to, don't we?'

It was enough to sway him. He longed for a sympathetic ear where his painting was concerned. He remembered the old days, talking with Anna for hour after hour. Anna, with her total faith in all he did. Peggy would get up and leave the room if he started explaining his troubles to her. She was sick of his work and his woes.

He moistened his lips and then said: 'Could you come here on Sunday, around two o'clock?'

'I think I can.'

He glanced across the bridge. 'Over there, perhaps?'

The bottom garden. Where better? thought Anna. Her smile was radiant. 'Yes, of course.'

He left her, returning the way they had come. Anna watched him until he disappeared up the path through the pines.

Sunday, just four days and she would see him again. They would have so much longer to talk . . .

Talk? Why not be honest? she chided herself. She wanted more than that, wanted him, craved to know what Peggy knew. Physical comfort, a taste of real love from the man she had longed for all these years. No other could have spurred her to take the risk.

Guy's warning that day at the zawn sounded once more in her head.

Don't ever deceive me, Anna. Don't even consider it.

If she were caught, what would he do – beat her? Probably. Well, if she stayed with him long enough, he would start that anyway, just as Matthew Buckman had with Helen. Might he even kill her? Did she care? What kind of life was it, in any case? Loveless and full of fear. Anna was willing to venture it for a chance to steal some happiness with Hal Pentreath.

She turned thoughtful eyes on the bottom garden and Helen Buckman's summerhouse. What a very appropriate place it would be. In a way she could almost feel she was taking a little revenge for them both.

Thirty-six

Next morning, Anna sought out Mr Hoblyn. She wanted a word with him about the summerhouse.

'Open it up?' he said. "Course I can, Mrs Buckman, if you want.'

'It's so girt about with brambles and ivy, I just can't move the door. Do you think you might clean it out a bit, too?'

'Certainly, no trouble.' Cocking his head, he asked: 'Want the old garden put straight, do you, Missis? Used to be nice one time. Mind, it would take a week or two.'

'No,' said Anna quickly. 'I rather like it as it is. As you said yourself, it was the late Mrs Buckman's retreat, so we won't disturb it. I'm just afraid the summerhouse will rot under all that growth, and that would be a shame. What I can see of it looks very pretty. When can you make a start?'

'This afternoon, if you like.'

'That would be grand.'

He regarded her curiously. 'Sure you don't want me to cut the weeds and tidy the garden?'

'Oh no, there are so many wild things down there – foxes, squirrels, nesting birds. Let's leave them in peace.'

Mr Hoblyn shrugged. 'As you please, my dear.'

Early on Sunday afternoon, Anna stepped inside the summerhouse and looked around. Mr Hoblyn had swept it out and cleared all the corners of cobwebs. All he had left inside was the old cane settee. The place was full of green and gold light and the scent of flowers.

Perfect, Anna thought. Secluded, peaceful – lovely.

At her feet sat Tuffet, swishing her feathery tail on the floorboards.

'I'm taking the dog for a nice long walk,' Anna had told her husband.

He had barely been listening, and just muttered vaguely: 'Oh yes, all right.'

She knew she was taking a terrible chance, but daring had kindled within her, and also defiance. He thought he had cowed her, brought her to heel, but she wasn't going to be like poor Helen – innocent, faithful, and still mistreated in spite of it.

Standing by the side window, Anna watched the bridge and the track beyond. Hal would be here soon. They would have two hours together, two priceless hours. How wonderful, after all these years, to have him to herself again, if only for a short time.

He was late and for a while she fretted, fearing he had changed his mind, but at last a fair-haired figure appeared along the path. Anna stepped outside, waving and beckoning to him. He hurried across the bridge. Taking his hand, she led him into the summer-house and closed the door.

'I was starting to think you wouldn't turn up,' she said.

'I wouldn't leave you waiting here, you ought to know that.' He glanced around him. 'I didn't notice this place before.'

'It was covered in bramble, that's why. I had the gardener clean it out for me. Guy never comes down here, hardly anyone does, so this can be our hideaway.'

Our hideaway. Her face was eager, her eyes were shining.

Hal had a momentary impulse to go, leave before he waded deep, deep into trouble. But loneliness stopped him, bade him stay.

Smiling, Anna went on:'I've brought a bottle of wine and a couple of glasses, smuggled them out for us under my jacket.' She poured and handed him a glass as they both sat down on the cane settee. 'Have you been working this morning?'

Throwing back a gulp of wine, he shook his head. 'I can't do a damned thing. I haven't finished a painting in seven months.'

Sipping, she lowered her glass and stared at him. 'Why?'

'It all seems pointless. I never like what I've done any more. In fact, when I look at a canvas, I barely know what to do, just can't seem to remember how. It's like losing a special sense, something's gone and I can't seem to call it back.'

'Gone? I doubt it very much. Withdrawn, perhaps, which is not the same. The tide goes out, but it always comes back in, you know.'

'But seven months, Anna . . .'

'And I'll bet you've worried every day of it, that's half the trouble. You can't just lose your talent, Hal.' She laughed. 'But it may be a bit like a donkey – sits down sometimes and refuses to budge. The harder you push it and pull the reins, the more stubborn it gets.'

He grinned. 'It's a pleasure to talk with you, Anna. You're always so full of good sense.'

'Mm,' she said wryly, topping up his glass, 'here I am handing it out to you, after making a mess of everything myself.'

390

As they shared the bottle, he told her of all that had happened to him in the past three years; what Jasper had done in the loft, the flood, and how Walter Angilley had got his hands on the property. He talked at length and with bitterness of his failed exhibition, and Mrs Tunley, all the disparaged work on which he had pinned so much hope.

Listening to him, saying little, Anna drank more and faster than he did. The wine quickly went to her head. As Hal drained the bottle into her glass, she let something personal slip.

'I haven't had this much to drink since my honeymoon. On the second night, I drank myself silly on schnapps so that I wouldn't know much about it when we went to bed.'

'Oh?' Alerted, he eyed her sharply. 'Don't tell me there's trouble of that sort, too?'

She hedged a moment, but finally muttered: 'Guy makes it degrading, he likes it that way.' Then, perceiving a danger, she blurted, pleading: 'You won't tell Peggy?'

Reaching out, he stroked her cheek. 'No, of course not. May God strike me dead if I do. Poor Anna, I'm so sorry if it's been that way for you.' After a brief hesitation, he confessed: 'Peggy and I don't do it at all.'

Her stare was disbelieving.

'She won't have me,' shrugged Hal. 'It's partly punishment. That and a lack of feeling which I don't think she can help. She's always tired.'

Anna was astounded and, to her shame, secretly thrilled.

Tentatively, she said: 'It seems we're both in need of comfort, doesn't it?'

He was silent, looking at her.

'Whenever I'm with Guy, I wish it could be you. He doesn't make love, it's just sex. He's the only man I've ever had, but I know it shouldn't be like that. I often think about you and Peggy together, I can't help it, and I wish I were in her place.' She stopped, then looked up and fixed him with intent green eyes. 'I still love you, Hal. When you came to paint my portrait, I put on such an act, but I still wanted you.'

He had known it would come to this. He had his needs and she was still in love with him. All the same, he was cautious.

'Anna,' he said gently, 'I don't want to hurt you again. All that anguish of yours because I married Peggy, it was so . . .' he groped for a word '. . . mistaken. Anna, Peggy's my kind. I couldn't leave her for you, even now, and I love my children. I'm very fond of you, but . . .'

'I don't care. That's enough for me. It's far, far more than I have as it is. Believe me, nothing you've ever done or ever will do could upset me as much as Guy has over the years. He never loved me at all.' She swallowed, then said, 'After six years with him I've no room for pride. I'll settle for consolation.'

He gazed at her. She was so lovely, and it had been so long. She was unhappy, so was he . . . If he had any lingering doubts, they fled.

All thoughts of right, wrong and consequences were discarded along with their clothes. From beneath the cane settee, the little dog watched, bright-eyed, as the two bodies twined on the summerhouse floor. She sensed delight, pure happiness, a wild and fresh excitement.

Afterwards, Anna thought: I knew he'd be like this.

She lay looking up at the summerhouse roof, with Hal's sleeping form stretched half across her. The bare

392

boards beneath her were hard, but better by far than any soft bed shared with Guy. She knew now what she'd been denied and tears glistened in her eyes.

Oh, the comparison – wonderful, dreadful. What it could and should be, set against what it had been for the past six years. How she envied Peggy for having all that time with a lover who knew the meaning of the word. How could she be tired of him, not want him any more? Anna would take all she could of Hal, no matter what the dangers.

All through the summer which followed they met there two or three times a week. After a month or two, being caught began to seem less and less likely. The garden was a safe haven, their own private world, and Anna became more and more relaxed. Rarely did anyone come near, not even Mr Hoblyn. Once, an old couple ambled past on the other side of the leat. They were guests from the hotel, exploring the grounds, but the bottom garden was too overgrown to tempt them.

She had given Guy no reason to suspect her, performing her marital duty as always. There was no getting out of that, but she took it like a dose of nasty medicine, and was even a little bit bucked to think that Guy didn't know he was sharing her.

'I'm going out with Tuffet,' she'd say, when half the time she planned to go no further than the summerhouse, where Hal would be waiting.

Anna didn't know how long it could continue, never wanted to look beyond the next meeting. It didn't do to think around the situation or focus on its limits. Whenever she did, the summerhouse seemed like a single, tiny sunlit spot with a dark world all around it, and she knew that all the joy she had was borrowed and might be abruptly taken from her. She savoured her time with Hal, lived it intensely, as if she could somehow store it against the day when it would end.

'How I love it here,' she said to him one afternoon. 'I live for these hours with you. The rest of life is just marking time.'

June sunshine fell on a makeshift bed of cushions and quilts, dusty rays sloping in through the windows straight at the corner where they lay. A bottle of wine, half empty, stood on the floor beside Hal.

Anna was lying on her back, her arm across her eyes. Against the scarlet of the quilt, her skin was very white. 'Oh, I wish we could go off together,' she murmured. 'Just you and me – disappear and never come back.'

It made him uneasy when she said things like that. It pricked his conscience. He loved to come here to see her. It was wonderful to forget everything for a while and make love. But now and again, when she started to talk in this way, he grew edgy.

'I could never leave my children,' he said, 'and I couldn't offer you a halfway decent life.'

'I know. I know there's no future in it. I'm only building castles in the air.'

'And you have your son to think about.' He rolled over, looking down at her, concern in his face.

'It's all right, Hal. I was well aware of the complications when I started this. And I did start it, didn't I, this time? You needn't feel bad.' Anna smiled up at him, tracing a finger down over his nose and mouth. 'Perhaps it's best of all this way. We both know what happens to people in marriage. We can be purely friends and lovers, can't we, without any of that?' The smile faded away, a faint frown took its place. 'What would Peggy do if she found out?'

'God only knows.'

'Come after me with a rolling pin, I expect,' chuckled Anna.

'I don't think it would be any laughing matter if either of them tumbled to it,' Hal said soberly. 'What if Guy divorced you and kept your son?'

That, reflected Anna, would be the least she had to fear. She debated a moment and then admitted: 'It wouldn't break my heart. Where Robin's concerned, I'm already licked, I'm afraid. You misunderstand about him, Hal. He's his father's son, he doesn't care for me. If I were to vanish tomorrow, he wouldn't miss me a bit.'

He stared at her. 'I thought . . .'

'I know what you thought – that I dote upon him, and Guy is hard on him. You couldn't be more wrong. They're as close as can be, and Robin despises me, just as much as his father does.'

'Despises?' repeated Hal, peering closely into her face. 'Did you say despises?'

'That's how it is.'

'Why?'

'It's the way the Buckmans are. Things were just the same between Guy's father and mother.'

He studied her for a moment. Then: 'Anna, Guy doesn't hit you, does he?'

'No. He's never hit me.' came the level reply.

'What *has* he done? I want to know.'

'I've told you, he's very critical, and as I've mentioned, he's rough in bed.'

He was poised above her, very still, and watching her carefully.

'You're afraid of him, Anna.'

'He has a nasty tongue when he's displeased.'

'It isn't physical?'

'No.'

'You'd tell me, wouldn't you?'

'You'd see for yourself.'

'If he knocked you about, I'd kill him.'

That's what I'm afraid of, Anna thought. You'd go up there and confront him, possibly beat him black and blue. Then he'd have you charged with assault and I dread to think what would happen to me.

'He doesn't knock me about, and you mustn't interfere. You could only make things worse for me.'

Turning, he sat up, took the wine bottle and emptied it into their glasses.

'If it's that bad, Anna, you ought to divorce him.'

Accepting the glass from him, she sat up and put a cushion at her back.

'I wouldn't have grounds, nothing I could prove, nothing acceptable to a court. And Guy wouldn't divorce me, even if he knew about this. I know his ways. He'd simply put a stop to it and make me pay for ever more.' Wryly, she added: 'I suppose I'm reaping what I've sown. Nobody made me marry him. I was silly enough to let him bedazzle me, and weak enough to let myself be hurried into it, but I wasn't exactly forced.'

'You didn't deserve a miserable marriage, Anna.'

Taking a gulp of her wine, she sighed. 'No, and sooner or later I'll leave him – though God knows where I'll go or what I'll do. Get a job and a room somewhere, I suppose. The prospects aren't exactly golden. Without a divorce, I couldn't remarry. Life's unforgiving, isn't it, if you make a hash of things? Genuine fresh starts are very rare. There are always scars and stains and echoes from the past.' Fretfully, she waved her glass, as if to dismiss these thoughts. 'Oh, why are we talking about all this? The very things I come here to forget.' She wound her fingers in his hair and pulled his head down to her, kissing his eyelids. 'Tell me how your work is going. Are things any better yet?'

'I did a couple of watercolours last week, but they weren't up to scratch. If not for the charcoal portraits, I wouldn't be making a penny. I keep waiting for it all to come back – the zeal, the old flair – but nothing happens.'

'It will. Be patient, it will.'

Good old soothing Anna. He kissed her gratefully.

'What a mess we've all got into, haven't we?' he murmured. 'What a bloody awful tangle altogether.'

She took his glass away, set it beside her own, then slid down into the quilt again, stretching up her arms for him.

'Yes, but let's at least forget it for these few good hours we have.'

Thirty-seven

September came. In the rose garden, Mr Hoblyn was dead-heading the floribundas. In earthy clothes, with earthy hands, he moved among them, snipping, singing to himself a favourite hymn. Another beautiful day. There was going to be an Indian summer, he felt sure.

Suddenly his peaceful work was interrupted. A clipped voice said: 'Good morning, Mr Hoblyn.'

He looked up and there on the path stood Guy, hands in his pockets. The old man nodded.

"Morning, sir.'

'The roses have made a lovely show this year. Well done.'

'Thank you.' The gardener allowed himself a smile of pride. 'They haven't finished yet, not by a long way.'

'Excellent.' Guy began to walk on. Then, as something occurred to him, he came back. 'Tennis court needs a bit of attention,' he said. 'I'd be glad if you'd sweep up. And the rhododendrons are starting to get out of hand again. They're growing through the fence and throwing too much shadow. Calls for a bit of lopping, Mr Hoblyn.'

'All right, yes, I'll see to it.'

'Good.'

Cutting a specially lovely bloom, the gardener handed it to Guy and said: 'For your wife, sir.'

He smiled indulgently. 'I'll see she gets it.' But then the smile disappeared as he noticed the shears Mr

Hoblyn was using. A frown replaced it. 'Where did you get those?'

The old man glanced at them. 'Oh,' he said, 'from the summerhouse, sir.'

'They were my mother's, I do believe.'

'Yes, I think they were.'

Guy reached out for them. 'Haven't seen them in years. You found them where, did you say?'

'The old summerhouse, Mr Buckman, down in the bottom garden.'

'Thought the place was completely overgrown? Restoring it, are you?'

'No, your wife just asked me to open the summer-house up, clean it out a bit. Inside, I found your mother's basket and her shears.'

Passing them back, Guy observed: 'That's odd. Anna never mentioned anything to me about the summer-house. She didn't ask you to put the garden straight?'

'I offered, but she wouldn't have it. Prefers it as it is. Mind you, there is a kind of charm in a garden gone wild.'

Briefly, Guy looked puzzled, abstracted. Then: 'Indeed,' he said, with a quick, mechanical smile. 'Well, Anna's quite a romantic, you know. Imaginative.'

The smile hadn't reached his eyes. They were hard and full of speculation. Mr Hoblyn blinked uneasily. He didn't like young Buckman, any more than he had liked his father.

'I must ask her about it,' Guy said lightly. 'Anyway, do carry on.'

Mr Hoblyn returned to his trimming, but as Guy walked off, the gardener paused again to watch the lanky figure striding up the path. Grey suit and after-shave, shiny shoes. Elestren Manor's despot. Mr

399

Hoblyn remembered him as a young boy, ignoring his mother's pleas to behave. He remembered Guy and Matthew Buckman, riding roughshod over everyone. Something troubled Mr Hoblyn. He had given a secret away. He went on cutting, the sun still shone, but he had lost the inclination to sing.

At lunch-time, Guy sat alone in the bar, pensively drinking Scotch. Behind the counter, the barman self-consciously busied himself with polishing glasses and cleaning around. The presence of the boss made him edgy.

Guy, however, was taking no notice of him. He sipped his whisky and thought about Anna and her order to Mr Hoblyn. Clear out the summerhouse, but let the garden be. Was she spending time down there, the way his mother had? Elaine had probably told her all about that. But his mother had been in a dismal state of mind, while Anna . . .

He swilled the Scotch around his teeth, seeming almost to be chewing it.

. . . while Anna had been rather cheerful these past few months. She was anything but depressed. He had noticed how rosy she often appeared when she came in from walking the dog.

Fresh air and exercise always enlivened her, she said.

Where did she go, then, with Tuffet? Guy put his empty glass on the counter and signalled for a refill. The barman poured him another and went away. Absently picking at peanuts, Guy drank some more. He could hardly recall the last time he had seen Anna going off down the drive with Tuffet, so she clearly didn't take her into town. Of course, the grounds were

400

seven acres, no need to leave them at all. There were lots of little woodland tracks.

But the summerhouse – it seemed pointless to Guy to bother with it unless the garden, too, was put in order. His thoughts circled round again to his mother. For her, it had been a retreat. What was it to Anna?

Another thing – she never took Robin with her, did she? Never. If he wasn't in school, then she would ask Mrs Roseveare to babysit. It wasn't that Robin minded-being left. He didn't care for Anna or the dog. Still, it began to trouble Guy that his wife had habits and private doings of her own, hours of the day when she separated herself from being his wife and Robin's mother. Hours when she was someone in her own right.

Doing what? Why the summerhouse? A sort of den?

The barman asked if he wished to order lunch. Guy shook his head.

He didn't like mysteries. He didn't like anything to be concealed from him. How could one keep control without knowing all that went on? Without his knowledge, without his agreement, Anna had given the gardener an instruction, and a baffling one at that. Guy was piqued – and he was suspicious.

What was Anna doing today? Oh yes, she was having her hair done this afternoon. Well, perhaps while she was in town, he would be the one to take the dog out, for a change. Or let Tuffet take him.

'Where do you want to go, then, girl? You show me the way.'

It was ten to three. Out on the lawn behind the hotel, Guy stood waiting while Tuffet gazed up at him. At first the dog seemed confused, uncertain. It was strange for the man to do this. She kept looking around for Anna.

'Go on, wherever you like,' said Guy. 'I'll follow.'

He had changed into boots and corduroy trousers and a jersey. Tuffet sniffed at his feet and looked at him, tongue lolling.

'Ready when you are,' he said, controlling his impatience.

Tuffet hesitated, then set off at a trot towards the path through the rhododendrons. Guy trailed along in her wake. The track, he noted, was very well-worn, wider than he remembered. In front of him sauntered Tuffet, her coat shining amber where shafts of sunlight reached it through the shrubbery. She loitered here and there, distracted by interesting scents, but she certainly seemed to be setting course for the bottom garden. Guy stayed several yards behind her, letting her lead.

Soon they came to the stream. Without hesitation, the dog went right, and after a while they reached the bridge. Tuffet bounded over it, as if eager to meet someone.

Stepping into the overgrown space of the garden, Buckman looked about him. Everything was still. Bushes and tall grasses stood motionless, briar roses and honeysuckle locked together, hugging each other, not a petal stirring. There was, he fancied, an air of secrecy about this place, as if everything had frozen, tensely guilty, at his approach. He had an irrational feeling that if he walked back over the bridge and went away, it would all come alive, start to sway and dance.

Beyond the leggy, tangled azaleas, stood the summerhouse. Tuffet had gone straight to the door and was trying to paw it open.

Moments later, Buckman was inside and looking round him. What he saw brought a twist to his mouth. A rumpled nest of blankets in the corner. Half a dozen cushions, and a scarlet quilt. An empty wine bottle. He picked it up. On the cane settee lay a couple of others.

What did she do, come here and drink?

Yes, but perhaps not alone. Buckman's sharp gaze fixed on the ledge of a small side window, where two glasses stood.

What did this place suggest to him? Secret love on sunny afternoons. Quiet laughter and heart-to-heart talk. Clinging bodies and wistful partings. Deceit.

Was she seeing someone? Who? He wondered about Hal Pentreath. Guy had hardly seen the man these past three years. He had spotted him once or twice on the quay, doing portraits, that was all. Guy didn't even know where Pentreath lived these days.

But perhaps Anna did.

Would she dare? Did she still possess enough spirit and nerve? And here, of all places, on his own land? Could he have underestimated her?

He looked about him again. The very meeting place suggested Hal Pentreath, a man with no money to take her anywhere better. Of course, this bower would appeal to Anna and that silly romanticism of hers – the wild garden, the weathered old summerhouse and her penniless artist. It would all add up.

A calm, cold anger filled him. He suddenly became aware of Tuffet looking at him. She was sitting several feet away and watching him uneasily. Animals were said to sense emotion, he recalled. As if she could feel his mood, the little dog had grown subdued and nervous.

Guy took one more look about him, then he turned and left. Tuffet dawdled in his wake, reluctant now to get too close.

During the next few days, Guy slyly kept Anna under surveillance. He noted what time she went out with the dog, what time she returned and how she seemed. A fairly consistent pattern emerged. She was generally out for a couple of hours, but two or three times a week she took somewhat longer. The evenings were now drawing in. If she chose the latter part of the day, she always returned just as dusk was falling.

Buckman also made a careful check of the wine-chits and stock book, observing that Anna quite often had a bottle sent up to the flat. That little habit had suddenly started back in April. The first entry was dated the nineteenth.

'Mrs B. 1× Saint-Emilion.'

April. Five months ago. He'd never seen an empty bottle about the flat in all that time, never smelt alcohol, never caught Anna up there taking a drink by herself, never found her tipsy. No, those bottles had all gone down to the summerhouse, hadn't they?

To be shared with someone?

There was only one way to be sure of her guilt, and that was to follow her. He chose an afternoon later that same week. It was half-past four when he saw her set out with Tuffet across the lawn. The mongrel skipped along beside her. Anna was almost skipping too, her footsteps light and quick and bouncy.

Elestren Manor stood bathed in mellow sunshine. The light winked brightly on the windows, turning them into squares of silver. From behind those shining panes of glass, Buckman's eyes, like frosty agates, watched his wife as she slapped her thighs and whistled to Tuffet. Anna's laughter echoed back across the grass as the dog frolicked round her. She did look happy, didn't she? Much too joyous for someone merely taking her dog for a walk.

After she disappeared down the path, he slipped out through the French windows of the lounge and crossed the lawn, following his wife at a careful distance. He padded down the shady path which led towards the leat. The rhododendrons swayed and whispered around him, already armed with fat, scaly buds for the following year. Somewhere ahead, he could still hear Anna whistling and calling to Tuffet.

He spotted her again as she emerged on to the bank of the stream. Sunlight filtering through the trees made stripes on the ground and glittered on the water.

Guy trailed her to the bottom of the path, then stood in the shadows, watching, as Anna went on towards the bridge. He was a dark, unmoving figure in the gloom beneath the shrubbery. Even if Anna had turned around, she wouldn't have noticed him there.

But she had no suspicions. She hurried on and the dog set up an eager barking as she neared the bridge. It sounded like a welcome, and it was.

Along the path from the other direction came Hal Pentreath.

As Anna ran to him and was swept up, swung round, kissed, the only change in Guy's face was a tightening of his mouth. The dim light among the leaves picked out the glitter of his eyes. He had confirmation now.

So Anna hadn't truly come to heel after all. Well, he had ample time to deal with her. As for Pentreath . . .

Guy became very angry indeed as he thought about Hal Pentreath. Forgetting his place and reaching for the wife of important Mr Guy Buckman. An unschooled Cornishman, drinking Mr Buckman's wine and trespassing on his property. Hal, who was nobody and had nothing – except youth, of course, and greater physical attraction. Guy, not far off forty now, was at a disadvantage there.

Did they laugh at him when they were together? Quite possibly. Certainly, many others would laugh if ever it became known that Guy's wife was deceiving him, and with such a person as Hal Pentreath.

How long had she thought she could get away with it? Anna wasn't really very clever at subterfuge. Perhaps she had planned to run off with Hal? That would be more humiliation than Guy could stand.

What, then, was to be done about it?

Later that evening, as Hal walked home, a figure shadowed him, moving stealthily through the trees on the right hand side of the path. It followed him along by the leat and then up the wooded hill towards the road. Once, only once, at the crack of a twig, did Pentreath pause uneasily and look behind him down the winding track. The figure hung back in the trees and waited.

Shrugging, Hal went on.

At the end of the footpath, he stepped out on to the tarmac road and walked the last few yards to the brow of the hill. In the failing light, the figure followed him as far as the top. Baleful eyes saw him leave the road and set off across the heath. They watched him all the way to the cottage.

Guy was enraged. His wife, who had such a luxurious home, was carrying on with a man who lived in a shack. It could hardly be worse.

When Hal disappeared, Guy looked back down the road. At the foot of the hill, where it curved, was Elestren Manor's gate. Thoughtfully, he strolled down, pausing a moment to note where the footpath emerged from the trees. There was, he observed, a sycamore just at that point, and a big bay laurel. At the bottom he halted again, looking back up the road. From the gate, one could clearly see the sycamore and the laurel – and anyone stepping out from the track between them.

He would have to give it some thought, but he already had an idea of what he might do.

Thirty-eight

Some days later on another fine evening, Hal said goodbye to Anna and set off homewards. Twilight was closing round him as he made his way up the woodland track, all the world becoming blue and grey. Everything was quiet when he came out on to the road, and his quick glance down the hill failed to note the big dark car parked under the trees at the side of the road near the hotel gate.

Hal walked up to the top of the hill, where he paused for a minute, gazing out over the bay. On either side sprawled jagged headlands, black silhouettes in the dusk. Below and away to his right, Trezawne was a crescent spray of yellow lights. Westward across the heath, another solitary point of light marked the cottage.

He had a sudden exciting desire to paint this scene, a flash of that old enthusiasm he had feared was forever lost. Perhaps Anna was right. He had passed through a tunnel, a crisis of faith, and was nearing its end. Hal was enormously cheered by the thought.

Moving on over the crest of the hill, he didn't see the sudden start of light under the trees near the bottom. Nor, at first, did he notice the low growl of an engine coming up behind him. By the time he became aware of that purr, it was gaining on him fast. Turning, he flinched from the brilliance of headlamps shining full in his eyes. Hal stepped back a couple of feet off the road – as far as he dared to go, for he was on the seaward side and this was the place where it ran quite close to the edge. Behind him was a sloping drop, and beyond that the cliffs fell straight down to the sea.

Shielding his eyes from the glare, Hal waited for the car to pass. He couldn't see a thing except those blazing lights, but the driver could surely see him, so he felt no anxiety.

Although – he realised all of a sudden that the car was on the wrong side of the road. Then, instead of veering away, the lights pulled towards him. The purr became a snarl, and next thing, the car was off the road and mounting the verge. Yelling and waving his arms, Hal stumbled backwards. The car followed him, surging forward, making him retreat. And then there was nothing beneath his feet but empty space. He screamed out, then he hit grass and started rolling, tumbling.

First the slope and then the precipice. He knew what was waiting down there: an eighty-foot drop. He was bowling towards it with awful speed, scrabbling for handholds and finding only grass which tore away, or rubble that promptly came loose from the ground and bounced along with him towards the edge. Flailing about him, he caught at the stem of a gorse bush and tried to hold on. But it bent with the force of his falling weight, and then the spines were ripping through his hands and he was on his way again.

He didn't think about the car, about who or why, only that any second now would come the final plunge and the end of him. Abruptly, there came a crack, and a hot lance of pain shot along his right leg. He howled as it grew worse, excruciating. Then it stopped. Everything stopped, because he had hit something, first with his body and then with his head. A jolt and a sickening bang to his skull took him into oblivion.

Perfect silence descended. The car had gone.

It had been pitch dark for an hour. For the third time, Peggy looked out of the cottage window. Hal was usually home before this. Within her, there stirred a faint unease. But then she sniffed and told herself he was big enough to take care of himself, and if his dinner was spoiled by the time he came in, it would serve him right. She had just put the children to bed and they had been asking for him. Some father – not able to feed and clothe them, and now too late even to kiss them goodnight.

The clock ticked on and she kept consulting it. Where could he be? In town, in the pub? Hal was never much of a drinking man. Anyway, he had no money, so far as she knew. The oven was going cold and so was his food, cottage pie congealing on the plate. Let him make do with bread and cheese, then, Peggy thought angrily.

But her temper was covering something, a growing anxiety.

Ten o'clock, half-past ten, twenty to eleven . . . This was worse than strange, this was bad, there was something very wrong. Going into the big room, she sat and tried to get on with some mending, but couldn't concentrate. The stillness and silence in the cottage seemed ominous tonight. His missing presence disturbed her terribly, everything felt abnormal.

After a time she abandoned her sewing and went outside. There was no moon, but the sky was peppered with stars. A shaft of lamplight from the doorway cut across the garden. Beyond the gate, the line of the track faded off into darkness. A cold breeze touched

Peggy's face. She listened but there was no sound of approaching footsteps.

Oh Lord, she thought. Hal . . .

Then she grew angry again and stormed indoors. She would play hell with him when he returned. In fact – yes, in fact, she would lock him out. Let him sleep in the shed, that would teach him. Let him spend the night on the commode! With a bang, she shot the bolt.

And then she pulled it back again, sank down in her chair and stared at the door with worried eyes.

Perhaps he had left her. Perhaps she had driven him off, finally said something so wounding that . . . What had she said today? Her mind roamed back. Nothing more than usual. She might, of course, have repeated herself once too often.

Would it matter, then, if he had gone?

No, snapped Peggy the long-suffering drudge. Good riddance.

Yes, whispered the girl who had married him and now remembered the happy days. It matters. Where is he? Where is he? Have I done this, with my temper and my tongue? I've said cruel, wicked things that no one should say to another.

With provocation, retorted her harsher self. He'd try the patience of a saint.

But so many things could have happened to him. There might have been an accident – or had he been feeling wretched and reckless enough to do himself harm? That was a thought to freeze her with horror. How did one go through the rest of life bearing guilt for something like that? Fraught with awful imaginings, Peggy went to the kitchen cupboard and finished off what remained of the brandy.

411

She couldn't go to bed. At eleven-thirty, she settled down in the old armchair by the fire. The hands of the clock crept up to midnight, passed it and went on to mark the small hours. Eventually, she fell asleep, her head laid back on a cushion, a hand on each arm of the chair. The candle burned down to a stub, the wick fell over into the melted wax and went out.

Towards dawn, Peggy woke to see shreds of pink and gold in the sky above the horizon out over the sea. Airy puffs of colour delicately melting into one another, or boldly splashed across the sky in ragged stripes.

Joy and Ewan were still asleep and Hal had not come home. The fire was out and Peggy was chilled to the bone. Stiffly, she rose and went to look in on the children. At least now that daylight was here, she could go out and look for Hal – better by far than that helpless waiting. Her best course, she supposed, was to give the kids their breakfast and take them to school, then make some enquiries in Trezawne.

As it turned out, however, no search was required. At just after seven, news came to her door. A hammering shook the wood and she ran to open it, finding Mr Mingo on the step.

'Been an accident, dear,' he said. 'Your husband. Can I come in?'

A few feet more and he would have gone right over. A few feet less and the farmer might not have seen him from the road. Hal had been extremely lucky.

'Your husband is fortunate, Mrs Pentreath,' the doctor said. 'He has a badly fractured leg and some concussion, but he's probably going to be all right. The boulder struck his head a nasty blow, but it also stopped his fall. By all accounts, he came within two yards of being a dead man. How it happened we can't say, although we found some alcohol in his blood. He may have lost his bearings and strayed off the road in the dark.'

Standing beside him, a nurse chipped in: 'Mind you, there was something else. When they brought him in, he was mumbling about a car and lights.'

Peggy glanced down at her husband, motionless in the hospital bed. His head was bandaged, his leg in splints and plaster.

'A car?' From under her brows, she looked at the doctor.

'Nurse is right. I believe he did make mention of a car.'

'He was hit?'

'I think not. No sign of that. It's hard to be absolutely certain, but I'd say his only injuries were those which occurred as he fell.'

Puzzled, she shook her head. 'Thank you.'

'It's Mr Mingo you must thank. He and his farm hand made a risky descent to rescue your husband.'

'Yes. Yes, of course. I'll be seeing him later.'

She sat down by the bed and gazed at Hal. The nurses had put screens around, so that Peggy was scarcely aware of the nine other patients on this ward. His face was striped with scratches and there were dressings on his hands. Peeling the lint back, Peggy found gashes on his palms.

A car, she pondered. But there was plenty of room for pedestrians on that road. Room for large vehicles – buses, drays, farm lorries like that of Mr Mingo. Had the driver been drunk? It was a possibility. Or perhaps there had been no car at all and Hal's words were simply ramblings, meaning nothing.

For an hour she remained by the bed, but he made no move, no sound. Peggy was shocked, bewildered, but most of all grateful to have him alive – and after all the times she'd said she'd be better off without him.

Somebody had put a posy of cornflowers by his bed. Fingering the petals, Peggy suddenly recalled the bunch of pinks he had picked for her at so much risk long years ago. Just after his first exhibition, when the future had looked as rosy and golden as the dawn this morning. Newquay, halcyon days, when she still thought the world of him. He had risked his neck to fetch her those few silly flowers.

Lord, they were so happy then. When they were naked, she used to think how beautiful he was. What had happened to them? Only life and its letdowns. Which of them had changed the most? She had, she supposed. Until only a year ago, he'd been the same optimistic, laughing man who had bought her the yellow dress and drawn those caricatures in the sand. The man who gave piggy-back rides to the kids and read them bedtime stories. But then the spirit had gone out of him, because in his work he had made some mistakes and turned up a blind alley. What had Peggy done but make it worse for him? Hadn't she been the very devil, a cold and carping bitch?

Peggy closed her eyes and tears welled out under her lashes. They were guilty tears, and tears of relief, and tears for the loss of that old happiness. Oh yes, there was fault on both sides. She had worked as no woman should have to work when there was a man around, but a thing like this had a way of putting everything back in perspective. Six feet more and he would have gone over, he would have died. Until last night she had thought that she no longer loved him at all. Yet, under all the exasperation, it had still been there.

Later that day, as Peggy went home, she stopped for a while to look at the spot where Hal had fallen. Halfway down the slope was a broken gorse bush, and there near the cliff edge a big granite boulder, just as Mr Mingo had described. She thought again about the car and her eyes ranged over the ground beside the road. The weather was dry and the verge was wiry, yet she fancied there was a flattened area, long and thin and curving. It could have been a single wheeltrack, but she wasn't sure. A more definite imprint was left in a bare patch of soil, where a pattern of ridges was stamped in the earth, resembling the tread of a tyre.

But then, who knew how long those marks had been there? Several days, perhaps even longer? It hadn't rained for a week, and indeed, they could have been made by Mr Mingo's lorry when he stopped there to climb down after Hal.

Peggy gave it no more thought. There was probably nothing to it.

Thirty-nine

Squatting beside the car that same morning, Guy dug a couple of stones from the tread of his offside front tyre and threw them away. Straightening up, he walked around the Riley, inspecting it. Not a mark. It had gone very well; he hadn't even had to touch Pentreath. He had thought he would have to hit him and then push him over the edge, but in the event it had all been extremely easy. There would probably be something about his death in this evening's papers, if the body had been found. It would be entertaining to watch Anna reading that.

Would it be sufficient punishment for her? Hardly. She was truly going to suffer now. He could think of a hundred ways.

Beginning with her dog.

Opening the door, Guy slid into the driver's seat. In the back was Tuffet, whining and pawing unhappily at the windows. Guy had taken her from the flat while Anna was in the bath. Tuffet rarely went out in the car, and instinct now seemed to warn her that something bad was afoot. She barked at Guy as he got in.

The door slammed, cutting off the sound, the engine started and the Riley cruised away down the drive. From the back window peered an anxious tawny face, watching the hotel swiftly recede from sight.

An hour later, Guy returned. He went up to the flat, carrying a bundle wrapped in a blanket. The moment he entered the sitting-room, he was confronted by a worried Anna.

'Guy, I can't find Tuffet, she's disappeared.'

Her husband merely raised his brows.

'I've been all over the hotel looking, and outside calling. She doesn't . . .'

Her words tailed off. Dropping her gaze to the bundle, Anna eyed it for several seconds, then breathed: 'What have you got there?'

Guy held it out to her.

From the moment she took it and felt the floppy weight, she knew. The little body was still warm. Anna stared at her husband, then down at the tartan blanket.

'Well, go on, open it.'

As she put the bundle down on the settee, a flap of the blanket fell back, revealing two front paws and a sharp little snout. Anna's hand flew to her mouth. Kneeling, she pushed off the rest of the wrapping, and dissolved with an awful cry. Shoulders shaking, she wept, and stroked the light brown fur. For several minutes she could neither think nor say a thing.

Standing behind her, his hands in his pockets, Guy was faintly smiling. If she felt this strongly about the dog, how much more would she grieve for Pentreath? That was going to be exquisite, he was looking forward to it.

After a time, Anna croaked: 'What happened?'

'I had her put down.'

'Why?' She shot to her feet, her face anguished.

'She snapped at me.'

'What?' Anna was incredulous. 'She wouldn't, she never snapped at anyone.'

'Calling me a liar?'

417

'Yes!' Her voice cracked and she swiped at her running nose with the back of her hand. 'Where did she bite you? Come on, show me!'

'I was too quick for her, but she tried. Can't keep a dog like that around where there's a child.'

'She never once tried to bite Robin, even when he was tormenting her! It was always Tuffet who needed protection from him.' Anna's voice went up high and thin. 'You had her destroyed just for spite, simply because you were feeling like it!'

'Don't get hysterical. I assure you she didn't suffer. Gone – poof – just like that.'

She choked: 'Oh God!' and dropped to her knees again by the settee, crying incoherently into Tuffet's coat.

'It was I who let you have her,' Guy said softly. 'I was entitled to take her away. Who's borne the expense of feeding Tuffet these past five years? I have. Who's settled the vet's accounts? I have. Now I've decided not to do so any more, and that's my right.'

'There was no need to have her put down!' moaned Anna. 'We could have found her another home.'

'Never occurred to me,' shrugged Guy. 'Anyway, it would have been a lot of effort. Animals always make work, Anna. I don't know why you wanted to be bothered. All that bathing and combing, all those tiring walks. You won't have to do any more of that now, will you? Such a chore, all that traipsing about.'

Anna's face turned white. Yes, gone was her excuse for disappearing into the grounds for hours. It would be more difficult now to go on seeing Hal . . .

Then came an inward question to make her heart lurch. Did Guy know? Was that why he had destroyed her poor dog? She turned her head slowly, eyeing him fearfully through the tangle of her hair.

But Guy returned her gaze quite blandly. No, he would surely be insanely angry if he knew of her affair. This was just another of those mean, spur-of-the-moment acts of his, like the summary sackings of staff which went on all the time. In this case his whim had been to take the life of her pet.

Fury seethed and rose in Anna like milk boiling up in a pan. There he stood, mocking her, confident that she could never harm him. He was the one with the sinew and all the practice in dealing out hurt. How she longed for once to turn the tables and wipe that smirk off his face.

And God in his wisdom had provided a means, hadn't he? No matter how big or strong the bully, there was always one sure way to fell him.

She didn't dare think about what would come after, only that she had to do it before the courage of wrath deserted her. Glaring now, she rose to her feet, took three paces towards him and pushed her face right up to his.

'Bastard!' she spat, and in that instant her knee made jarring contact with his groin.

His eyes bulged and his mouth flew open. Out of it came a single, strangled cough. Anna watched him double up, clutching at his fly. What pleasure, what delight, to see him sinking to his knees, tears streaming down his face. Speechless with pain, he glared up at her.

'How do you like it?' Anna hissed. 'Being on the receiving end? Not half as much fun as dishing it out, is it, Guy?'

Recovering his breath a little, he gasped: 'You're going to be so sorry you did that.'

'I'm leaving you,' she fired back. 'I'm clearing out this very day. I know what's in store for me if I stay here. I don't plan on going through what your poor mother endured.'

A wheezing chuckle escaped him.

'Leave me? Where could you go? Your mother won't have you back.'

'I don't care. I'd rather sleep on a park bench than spend another night with you.'

Panting, he said: 'Forgetting Robin, aren't you? You needn't think I'll let you take him away. Or do you mean to abandon him? Dear me, what will everyone say?'

'They can say what they like. I can't do him any good by remaining here and being shoved around. He's learning by bad example, just as you did. I know how little he thinks of me. I know you're his favourite.'

Swaying to his feet, Guy put his weight on the back of a chair. 'Perhaps I underestimated you,' he allowed. 'You show more guts than I expected of you.' Gradually, he was straightening up, though his face remained the colour of lard. 'What's made you so bold, Anna, hmm?'

Again she wondered briefly if he knew about Hal, and again she dismissed the idea. He would have confronted her with it, wouldn't he?

Crossing to the settee, she gathered up Tuffet's body. 'I'm going out to bury my dog,' she said. 'Then I'm going to pack my things and shake the dust of this place off my feet.'

Stalking out into the little hall, she tried the door. It wouldn't open. Anna rattled the handle. The door was locked.

'I thought there might be a bit of a scene,' said a dry voice behind her. 'Didn't want Mrs Roseveare walking in on a private quarrel.'

Anna spun around. He was leaning in the sitting-room doorway, still stooping and holding his crotch, but grinning now. He held up a key, then dropped it into his pocket.

'Come inside now, there's a good girl.'

'No! No, you let me out!' She backed against the door.

'I said you were going to be sorry, Anna, and by God, you are.'

She thought about trying to kick him again, but as if he guessed what was in her mind, he wagged a warning finger.

'Oh no, you won't catch me that way a second time. Reckless of you, Anna, when you know I always take reprisals, one way or another. I'll give you credit for that bit of spirit, but I can't allow you to get away with it.'

He advanced within arm's length, and suddenly his fist was coming at her face. Screaming, she turned her head aside and the blow caught her cheekbone. A scything pain and the wet warmth of blood told her the flesh had split. A second later, the bundle was wrenched from her arms. She heard a thump and then her husband seized her by the hair, dragging her back into the flat.

What followed was a tumult – being thrown this way and that, pummelled and slapped and kicked, crashing into furniture, finding herself face down on the floor, then hoisted up and slammed against the wall. At one point her head was being banged against God-knew-what, and then her arm was twisted behind her until she shrieked with agony. There were glimpses of Guy's

421

face, grinning, ugly, and always his swinging arms and flashing hands. At least once, she passed out, only to find herself revived by a deluge of water as he held her head under the cold tap in the bathroom. Then she was being beaten again, flung about like a soft toy in the hands of a destructive child. She thought that someone must surely hear and intervene, but no one did.

Hitting the floor one last time, Anna lay on her back, too weak to stir. The ceiling seemed a great height above her, the carpet a dark plain stretching away all around. She felt it prickle against her cheek as she lost consciousness again.

Night had fallen by the time she woke. She was lying on top of the bed and a single table lamp was on. Bright splinters of light came at her, darting between swollen eyelids she could open only halfway. Her eyes felt full of fluid, the flesh around them stiff and hot and sore. One of her cheeks was stinging, and her bottom lip felt inflated, grotesque. She tried to raise her head, but flopped back again, moaning.

Pain everywhere. Arms, legs, back, ribs – she ached from head to foot. Anna could almost swear she felt the bruises surfacing on her skin, blossoming black and purple, spreading out all over her. There were sharp pains that told of pulled muscles, and a dull throb where one of her fingernails had been ripped below the quick. How had that happened? She couldn't recall.

For minutes she lay too weak to move. Remembering. Tuffet was gone. It returned to her like another awful blow, and she let out a cry. What had he done with her body? It would be just like Guy to drop her in a dustbin.

Tears oozed out of Anna's eyes, spotting the turquoise quilt with moisture, mingling with bloodstains.

Then what? Oh, there had been a row and she had kicked him. Anna groaned, turning her head from side to side. She must have been mad. Even so, the punishment had been more than she'd bargained for. Beyond the imagination of one who had never been beaten before. Nothing Elaine had described had prepared her for this.

Where was Guy now? She froze, listening.

No sound but the ticking clock on the bedside table.

What time was it? Again she struggled to lift her head, blinked to clear her sticky eyes and peered at the dial. Five to eight.

He was downstairs, then, overseeing dinner. Being the polished proprietor, exuding wit and bonhomie among the guests.

She had to escape. But where to go? Perhaps, if her mother saw her like this . . .

No, that would be the first place Guy would look, and Mrs Trevena could not be counted on. He would come after Anna, that was certain. He would bring her back. She was one of his belongings. As for the world at large, it preferred to turn a blind eye. Whatever went on between husband and wife, outsiders shrank from becoming involved. It was too intrusive, it wasn't done, and the Buckmans' 'friends' would not want to look squarely at anything so embarrassing. The owner of Elestren Manor using his wife as a punch bag. They liked to pretend that only the lower orders did things like that.

There was just one person who cared enough to protect her, and that was Hal. Regardless of Peggy, that was where Anna would have to go. First thing in the morning . . .

But what about tonight? What was going to happen later when Guy came up to bed? Would he leave her alone or set about her again? Might he even be planning another night for her in the wine cellar?

The thought of that gave Anna the strength of desperation. Now. She had to go now, before he came back, before he could start on her a second time. Pushing herself off the bed, she stumbled to the wardrobe and surveyed herself in the mirror. She was mottled with plum-coloured bruises. Her lower lip was puffed like a doughnut, her left eye was black and her right cheek cut open. That was where the blood on the quilt had come from. Rusty-brown smudges and streaks of it covered that side of her face.

Flinging open the wardrobe, Anna changed into a pair of slacks, a checked jacket and walking shoes. Around her neck, she tied a green silk scarf. Next, she went to her jewellery box and threw back the lid.

Anna never had much cash and possessed no chequebook of her own – indeed, there hadn't been any need up to now. Whenever she wanted something in town, she could simply have it charged to Elestren Manor. Ready money had now become vital, however, and the only way to get some would be to sell her trinkets. The box was full of pearls and rings, gold bracelets and dainty watches. Anna snatched them up and hurriedly stuffed them in glittering tangles into her jacket pockets.

Ready, she paused a moment, looking at the nursery door.

Robin. She was leaving Robin.

Anna went to the door, quietly opened it and looked

inside. The slice of light from the bedroom fell full upon her boy's sleeping face. He looked saintly in sleep, yet already he was becoming another devil like his father. She swallowed the lump in her throat and shook her head. Now that the beatings had started, Guy would employ them again and again, and it wouldn't edify Robin to witness that.

Anna softly closed the door, and the boy didn't stir.

Going to the bedroom door, she found it locked. Well, of course. Just like Matthew, Guy wanted the evidence kept out of sight. The telephone was in the sitting-room, so she couldn't reach it to ring for help. But there was something Guy hadn't considered – the balcony and the parapet connecting it to the next one along.

Unlatching the window, Anna slipped out on the little balcony. Strains of music reached her from the dining-room below. Nervously grasping the railing, she looked along the ledge. The nearest guestroom window was number four, about twelve feet away, and it was in darkness. The occupants would be downstairs, having dinner. Their door to the corridor was probably locked, but at least she could use their telephone, ring the office and ask the girl to slip up with the master key.

Yet, was it worth the risk? For a moment, Anna's courage failed her. She couldn't, she dared not, she was bound to slip and fall. There was nothing to hold but the side of the building, and she could be killed or crippled. Better to bide her time and await another opportunity, no matter what tonight might bring.

But then she collected herself. Elestren Manor was built of granite. Its walls were knobbly and there would be little handholds, enough to steady her.

Anna went to the dressing-table and picked up a

marble figurine – Ceres with a sheaf of corn. She put it in the pocket of her trousers, then returned to the balcony, summoned her nerve and climbed out over the rail. Which way to face? Outwards, she decided, preferring the feel of the wall against her back. Flattening her palms against it, she started shuffling, inch by inch, towards the neighbouring balcony of room four.

Of all the horrible sensations she had known in her life, this was surely the worst. Worse than childbirth, worse even than being hit. After a couple of feet she paused, desperately wanting to go back. The ledge on which she stood was only twelve inches wide. She could hear and feel the fabric of her jacket dragging against the rough stone when she moved, and there was an eerie sensation that the wall was about to heave and thrust her outwards, off her perch. Thankful for the darkness, Anna kept her eyes closed, lest the lights from the downstairs windows should remind her how high she was, make her giddy and cause her to overbalance.

Go back? Go on? She stood rooted, debating, but finally bravery won. She shuffled another foot, then another, another . . . Once she was halfway there, the dilemma would end.

It took ten minutes, although it seemed three times as long to her. At last her fingers encountered cold metal, the railing of the other balcony. Gripping it for dear life, she cautiously lifted one leg over, then swung the other after it.

Safe.

Turning, she tried the window. It wouldn't budge. Anna delved into her pocket and pulled out the marble figurine. Holding Ceres by her head, she smashed the heavy base through the pane beside the catch. The noise was no more than a tinkle, but to her it seemed enough to wake the dead. Hastily reaching through the hole, she unlatched the window.

A second later, Anna was inside. Without much hope, she went to the door and turned the handle.

To her joy, luck was with her; they had left it unlocked. She opened it slightly, peeped out, listened. Still faint strains of music from downstairs, a distant burst of laughter from the bar. Within sight, just yards away, was the door to the service staircase. Cautiously poking her head out, Anna looked down the corridor.

No one. Quick! At any second that dreaded, dark-suited figure could appear. She ran for the stairs and scurried down them.

She had nearly reached the bottom when she was suddenly confronted by Sarah and Mrs Roseveare. Off-duty now, they had just emerged from the kitchen, carrying their supper trays, en route for their rooms upstairs.

At the sight of Anna, the housekeeper nearly dropped her dinner, while Sarah simply froze and stared at her with open mouth.

'My dear life!' Mrs Roseveare breathed. 'What's happened? Mrs Buckman . . .?'

'Let me pass! Oh, for God's sake, get out of the way!'

'You look as if you've been hit by a train,' the receptionist whispered.

'No, just my loving husband. Please, move!' Anna started to cry. 'I must go, I have to get out of here.'

'You need a doctor, let me help you.' Mrs Roseveare bent to put down her tray.

'No! I'm not staying here another second,' blurted Anna. 'I can't let him get hold of me again.'

With that, she barged between them and Sarah's tray went flying.

A moment later, Anna was in the draughty passage between the bar and kitchen, where every morning the hotel's suppliers brought in fresh food, and the brewery men rolled in great kegs of ale. The tradesmen's entrance. Thanking God, she flung open the door and vanished out into the night.

Forty

Putting another piece of driftwood on the fire, Peggy settled back in the old armchair. There was no other light in the cottage but that of the flames caressing the cracked stump of wood. Their brightness reflected in Peggy's eyes and her curly hair threw shadows like Celtic spirals on her skin. She had been back to the hospital that afternoon, but there had been no change. Hal had shown no signs of coming round. They said it could be days before he did.

Alcohol in his blood, the doctor had told her. Had her husband taken to drinking, then? Was that where he went when he disappeared for so many hours, *The Old Solace* or some other pub? If so, then where did he get the money? Peggy had thought she knew all about Hal. She had also believed that she no longer cared what he did. Resentment of her poverty had been her chief obsession for so long. Focusing on that, she had forgotten that Hal was once her most prized possession.

Now, though, her mind was engaged in speculation. What had he been doing while out by himself? For over a year now, she hadn't let him touch her. He hadn't made a fuss about it, accepting the deprivation with sorrowful silence. Or seeming to. But a man was a man and could she blame him if he went elsewhere? And weren't there plenty of women in Trezawne who would find him attractive?

For a long time, Peggy's face was still, like a sculpture in the firelight. But at last she sighed and shook her head. Probably there was an innocent explanation. Perhaps he had met the Penpraze brothers in town and they had bought him a few pints. And he wasn't such a satyr that he couldn't endure a year of celibacy. Really, it said a lot for him that he hadn't turned nasty about it, as many men would.

Closing her eyes, she felt soothed by the warmth of the fire on her cheeks. She had so nearly lost him, might have been burying him in a couple of days from now, if not for kindly providence. Peggy took it as a lesson and a warning. She had been in the lean-to earlier on, looking at all his abandoned work, all the palettes and brushes encrusted with dried paint. He used to take such care of his materials. Neglect of them suggested despair and the thought had been troubling her that he might not have have fallen, but jumped.

When he came home, she resolved, it would all be different. She was going to be a loving wife to him again.

For a while she sat without thinking, just listening to the sputter of the fire. But then she became aware of a sound disturbing the quiet of the night outside. Very faint at first but growing more distinct, there came the rhythmic thump of hurrying footsteps. She heard a rattle of stones from the track, the squeak of the rusty latch on the garden gate . . .

Peggy's eyes fluttered open.

More footsteps, loud and heavy now.

Turning her head, she stared at the door, and at once a frantic thudding broke upon it.

Peggy's first dreadful thought was that her husband had taken a turn for the worse, that he was dying, and this was someone sent to summon her. Her heart turned over. For lingering seconds she couldn't move.

The hammering increased. It would frighten the children. Peggy pushed herself up out of the chair.

Then the banging stopped, replaced by a sobbing voice.

'Hal? Hal! You have to help me. Let me in.'

It was strained, a breathless whine which Peggy didn't recognise. Lighting the oil lamp, she went to the door.

The figure outside stepped back, retreating a little into the dark when Peggy opened it. Briefly there was silence. Then: 'I must see Hal. I must. Peggy, please.'

The voice, now under control, was sounding more familiar. Even so, Peggy doubted her ears. No, surely not?

'Anna? Is that you?'

'Yes,' came the cracked reply.

'What do you want?' Stepping forward, Peggy held the lamp up. Anna backed off further into the shadows.

'Let me speak to him.'

'Why?' demanded Peggy suspiciously.

'Please, don't send me away. Where is he? I have to see him.'

Impatiently, Peggy said: 'He isn't here,' adding unhappily, 'Hal's in the hospital. There was an accident yesterday night.'

'What?' came the dazed response.

'He had a fall. He nearly went over the cliff over there where the road runs close to the edge, about half a mile above your place.'

She could feel Anna's shock, like a thrill in the night air between them.

'Is he all right?'

'It's on the cards he will be. Now, I'm asking you again, what do you want with him?'

After a pause came the whisper: 'Never mind. It's no use now. I'll go.'

She sounded broken, hopeless. Abruptly moving forward, Peggy thrust out the lamp and peered at her old enemy.

The sight made her catch her breath. Her lips formed the words 'My God!' but no sound came out. For a moment she simply stared, astonished.

'What in heaven's name happened to you?' she breathed at last.

Shrinking from the light, Anna muttered wretchedly: 'My husband did it. I came to see Hal because I was frightened and there was nowhere else to go. I'm sorry. I shouldn't have.' She turned away.

It seemed fishy to Peggy that Anna should come here to seek Hal in her trouble. What had she just been asking herself – if he might have a woman somewhere? Halfway to making the logical guess, Peggy was surprised to feel so little anger.

'Wait.' She caught Anna's arm. Anna hesitated, looking at her with a hint of hope.

There was a pause, then Peggy waved a hand towards the door. 'Come in, if you want,' she said awkwardly. 'It's all right.'

She stood aside. With a whispered 'Thank you', Anna limped into the cottage.

Peggy followed, looked at her once again, longer, and gave a soft whistle. Anna's face was a travesty of itself, bloated almost out of recognition, smeared with the remains of its heavy make-up.

Barring the door, Peggy indicated the armchair. 'Sit down there, go on.'

Numbly, Anna did so. Not noticing the cottage at all, Peggy realised. This had been one of her nightmares, that Anna should see this place. Now here she was, and too distraught to give a fig.

With a panicky jerk of her head, Anna looked up at her. 'Hal . . .?'

'He was very lucky. Concussion and a fractured leg. He's been out cold since he was found.' Dryly, Peggy added: 'I have to say, he doesn't look half as bad as you do.'

Anna's gaze moved this way, that way, as if she were recalling something and hadn't heard that last remark. 'Yesterday evening,' she murmured distractedly.

Surveying her, Peggy slowly shook her head. Anna Trevena, the girl she had envied all her life – this battered creature, suddenly stripped of all pretence and pride. Shouldn't Peggy be feeling triumphant? Shouldn't she be taking her chance now to jeer?'

Instead there was merely pity and bewilderment. Her husband had done it, Anna claimed. Guy Buckman? Elegant, polished Mr Buckman?

From the bedroom, the children peeped out, woken by the knocking and the sound of a strange voice. Peggy shooed them back to bed.

'Better take your coat and scarf off,' she told Anna brusquely. 'I'll boil some water and we'll clean you up. Think you've any broken bones?'

'No. Just let me rest.'

Peggy brought the trivet in from the kitchen and set the kettle on it, then sat down on top of the wood box by the grate. For a space, she eyed Anna silently. Then she asked: 'Why seek out my husband, Anna? Why didn't you just go home to your mother?'

The questions were quietly charged with accusation. Her eyes were searching Anna's face.

Anna stared down at her lap. 'That's the first place Guy will look for me. Anyway, I can't trust her. She won't stand up for me.'

'Oh? How do you know?'

'Experience.'

'I see. But surely you have other friends to help you?'

'Most people don't like interfering between a husband and wife.'

'That's very true. So why should Hal be different?'

Anna's gaze shifted guiltily towards her, then darted away. Peggy knew now. Yes, he had been seeing her. Well, of course. Peggy answered the question herself.

'Because he's more than a friend, isn't he?'

Wetting her lips, Anna nodded. 'Sure you don't want me to go?' she added wryly.

There came a short, soft chuckle. 'Not so very long ago, I'd have torn your hair out,' Peggy said wearily, leaning her head back.

Something like a smile moved Anna's face.

'But since he's had this accident, I've done a lot of thinking and – well, I'm not so angry or surprised as you might imagine.' Stiffly, Peggy conceded: 'I understand why he came to you. I don't like it, but I understand. He must have told you how things have been between us.'

'Yes.'

'I've had plenty of cause for complaint, mind you,' Peggy snorted. Then her voice dropped, subdued. 'But it really shook me to see him in that hospital bed, and realise how close he came to being killed. I looked at him lying there and thought that if I hadn't been such a tartar, he would have been home with me. I drove him, that's why he was always out – and why he turned to you,' she ended, sighing.

The kettle began to sing. She rose and fetched an enamel pan, filled it with hot water and poured in a drop of disinfectant.

'Here, see to yourself.' She handed Anna a piece of lint. Soaking it, Anna started gingerly wiping her face.

Watching her, Peggy said: 'It's hard to believe that husband of yours could dole out a beating. He doesn't seem the type.'

Anna's laugh was bitter. 'What is the type? A man in a cap and hob-nailed boots? A guttersnipe? A drunk? Guy was stone-cold sober when he did this to me. His speech, his clothes, his manners, his money, they just hide what he is.'

'Has he hit you before?' frowned Peggy.

'No, but there have been other things, just as bad in their way.' Anna moistened her puffed lower lip. 'I've been frightened of Guy almost since the day I married him.'

Peggy stared at her.

'Oh yes.' Sour humour coloured Anna's tone. 'That's something for you to think about, isn't it? All this time. You thought he cherished me, because he bought me lovely clothes and jewellery, didn't you? I wanted you to think that, I confess.'

'What else would I assume?'

'Quite. Actually, though, I have to be like everything else he owns. A credit to him, smart, impressive. There's trouble if I'm not.' She pressed the lint against her forehead, letting the liquid trickle gently down her face.

For several minutes, Peggy said nothing, digesting this. Everything she had envied so much – just a front.

435

To think of all the time she had spent in gnawing herself with jealousy, and beating Hal about the head with 'Anna's wonderful life'. She'd torn herself and him to pieces over an illusion.

'It's really been that awful?'

'On the whole. I won't say there haven't been good days, but on balance it was the biggest mistake I ever made to marry Guy.'

'And now he's found out about Hal? Is that why he beat you?'

'No. We had a fight because he had my dog destroyed, and I . . .' Breaking off, Anna stared at the fire. 'Guy never mentioned Hal,' she said slowly, 'not once. But . . .'

They looked at each other. Things were coming together in Peggy's mind, pieces slotting into place.

'What if he does know, Anna? Just how vengeful is he?'

'What are you getting at?'

'Well,' said Peggy thoughtfully, 'when Hal arrived at the hospital, it seems he mumbled something about a car that night on the road.'

The lint dropped from Anna's fingers into the pan.

'You mean he didn't just fall?'

'I'm not sure. Of course, it may have meant nothing, just an injured man's ramblings, and apparently he'd had a drink or two.'

'Yes, he . . .' Even under the bruises, Anna's guilty flush could be seen. 'He'd just left me. We'd had a bottle of wine between us.'

'Had you, indeed? I see.' Just for a moment, Peggy felt the old hatred gather again, but quickly she shook herself free of it, striving to be dispassionate. They had always vied for Hal. Now Anna had stolen a share of him. Back and forth, the old tug-of-war, nothing really new.

A question broke in on her thoughts. 'Do you mean to say he was struck by a car?'

Peggy lifted her brows. 'There aren't any injuries to suggest that. But as I was coming home, I looked at the spot where he fell. I thought I could make out tyre-marks on the verge.' She made a descriptive motion with her hand. 'A long swerve, like this. Of course, there's no telling when that happened, and it might just have been some driver who'd had too much to drink.'

'Or it might have been my husband? That's what you're thinking?'

Peggy spread her hands. 'You know him better than I do.'

Yes, indeed she did. Nervously, Anna recalled her talk with Elaine.

'My brother's a dangerous man,' she had said.

'He told me Tuffet snapped at him,' she murmured. 'That was a lie, I'm certain. He said he was saving me the chore of walking her so much. I wondered at the time, but then I thought he couldn't possibly know, or he would have confronted me with it.'

'Not if he'd just bumped your lover over a cliff,' said Peggy astutely. 'He wouldn't admit he knew a thing about any affair. But is he capable of going that far?'

The question needed little debate. 'I'm afraid he might be.'

Peggy's mouth twisted. 'My, you were taking a hell of a risk, weren't you?'

'Yes.'

'And endangering my husband.'

'It never occurred to me that he might go after Hal.'

'Did you tell him what Guy was like?'

'I didn't tell him much. I thought it best. It could only have spoiled things.'

Fixing her now with a cold stare, Peggy warned: 'He's still mine, Anna. You needn't think I'll let you take Hal, just because he's had a fling with you. Just because we're sitting here beneath a flag of truce and because I've taken it calmly, don't imagine I'll graciously stand aside for you. I'll give you such a fight . . .'

Anna cut in. 'Oh, you don't have to tell me that. Anyway,' she muttered, 'you've won before you start. I knew what the limits were all along. Hal made them clear enough.' Resignedly, she looked at Peggy. 'You always had the edge with him and you still do. You can reclaim him whenever you want, you and your children. I know where I stand. I've just been a port in a storm these past few months. I knew I was only borrowing him and I wasn't too proud to do it. Now the rightful owner wants him back and I'll have to bow out. He always loved you best. I should have accepted that long, long ago, and I shouldn't have taken up with Guy just to prove something to you. There – I'm giving it to you on a plate – I've been a total fool and I'm paying for it. If it makes you feel triumphant, fine, enjoy it. I'm past caring.'

For a space, there was just the crackle of the fire. The last of the antagonism seemed to run out like sand from an hour-glass. Anna was too tired to keep the grudge alive, and so was Peggy. Finally, sadly, she said: 'I'm not gloating, Anna. Perhaps I'm growing up a bit.' Rising, she patted her shoulder: 'I'll fetch you something to eat and drink. You must sorely need it.'

Alone in the sitting-room, Anna looked around her. The place was rough, depressing. Peggy, she acknowledged, wasn't the only one deluded. Would Anna have liked this? Not for long. She suspected that after a while she would have reacted just as Peggy did. Indeed, she would not have endured it so long or so well.

They had fought all these years and both been so wrong. And what was it all about, anyway? How did trivialities become so huge in people's minds as to change and shape their lives?

Peggy brought her soup and heavy cake and a mug of tea.

'Is it all right?' she asked, as Anna ate.

'It's fine, Peggy, thank you.'

'Plain old stuff, I'm afraid.'

'It's very tasty.'

Heaping driftwood on the fire, Peggy settled down again. 'Dreadful old place, this, isn't it?' she said uneasily. 'Must look like nothing on earth to you.'

'It looks like hard work.'

'I should say.' Wistfully, Peggy added: 'I always wanted a nice house. One like your mother's, perhaps. Some hopes.' Hesitantly, she confided: 'I envied you so much when we were kids.'

Slowly, Anna said: 'I'm sorry if I seemed snobby. It may interest you to know that I was jealous too. You were far more popular than I was.'

'And I used to keep you out of the games,' nodded Peggy, her forehead creasing at the distant memory. 'My little bit of power, that was. Spiteful of me, wasn't it? But then, of course, you were always making cracks about Dad and Jasper.'

'You once called my mother a sow.'

'Did I?'

'Hmm.' A faint smile lifted Anna's battered features.

'It was just about the time I first met Hal. Before you knew him.'

For a while they sat quietly watching the fire. Eight years on from that bonfire at Tolgarth beach. Twenty years from their first little scuffles in school. They had never actually talked before, not once in all that time. Each had been an unknown country to the other, and all they had ever exchanged was sniper fire across the border. It felt peculiar, and intriguing, to sit here swapping confidences with the foe, the demon herself.

In the grate, the flames flowed round the driftwood, and shades of orange, black and yellow rippled across the embers with the draught. Another fire, another turning point.

'Whipped up quite a little war, 'didn't we?' Peggy said. 'Hal used to tell me how stupid it was. It got on his nerves more and more as time went on. That, and trouble over cash. I always set more stock by money than he did. But it is important, say what you like,' she added stoutly. 'There's no charm whatever in being hard up. It means cold and worry and sweat and exhaustion. It's not romantic, it's bloody awful. One day when we were fighting, he said you wouldn't have minded it. Hah! What do you say, Anna? Care to try it?'

'I think not. I couldn't cope with this place the way you do.' Anna put her cup and dishes aside, then smiled. 'I don't know how you manage it, but you make very good heavy cake. I'd almost forgotten how much I enjoyed good old Cornish food.'

'I suppose you eat a lot of foreign stuff at that hotel?'

'I did.'

'Does that mean you're not going back there?'

'I'd sooner die.'

'So what will you do?'

'I'm not sure. I'll have to think about it, but not tonight. I can't tonight, my head aches so.' She looked uncertainly at Peggy. 'May I stay?'

'You're welcome to use the couch. I'll get you a blanket and pillow.'

'You're being very kind.'

Peggy threw the last of the wood on the fire. 'Well, can't turn you out into the night, can I?' came the brisk reply.

Forty-one

The next morning at just after nine Guy was sitting in his car outside Mrs Trevena's house. Anna wasn't there, her mother hadn't seen her. Damn, damn, damn! In a sudden access of temper, he slammed his palm against the steering wheel.

He hadn't dreamed that she could get out of the flat, that she would have thought of taking such a route, or had the courage to attempt it. For sure, his mother never had. What a huge embarrassment this was, what a lot of bother Anna had caused him. It had taken Guy until nearly midnight to pacify the old couple from number four and move them to another room. Worse, there were whispers going around among the staff. Sarah and Mrs Roseveare had seen Anna on her way out, seen the state she was in, and word had spread like wildfire. They all knew, and the bolder ones looked at him with open disgust.

Where was she? Where the hell was she? Oh, she would suffer for this, by God she would. At first light he'd been down to the bottom garden in search of her. Next, he had called at Churcher's house and that of her old physician, Doctor Wilson. He had even tried the hospital, but to no avail. Scowling, Guy sucked his teeth. Had she gone seeking sanctuary with any of their acquaintances? Probably not. Anna had never been close to Guy's friends. In any case, there were dozens of them; he could trawl around from house to house all day and not find her. Indeed, it would be the last place he wanted to find her – displaying her bruises among his respectable cronies.

He could kill her for leading him such a dance. Snarling, he started the engine. Perhaps she had left town altogether. He had seen that her jewellery was gone. Pulling out into the road, he roared along to the junction and turned right, down Pawlyn's Hill.

The question was, had she simply run off in a blind panic and was she now wandering aimlessly about, or had she planned on going somewhere in particular? There was no Pentreath to whom she could run . . .

His feet went down hard on the brake and clutch and the Riley stopped with a jerk in the middle of the road.

But of course, she didn't know that, did she? Why had he been so slow?

Would she dare, though? What about that wife of his, that Peggy? Thoughtfully, Guy pursed his mouth. In desperation, Anna might have had the nerve to go there. He smiled. If she had, she was in for a shock. There wouldn't be any Hal to protect her, just his grieving and probably very hostile little widow.

Guy decided it might be worth a visit to the cottage to make enquiries. If nothing else, he would enjoy hearing all about Hal Pentreath's 'accident'.

From behind him came the impatient toot of another car. Buckman drove on down the hill, turned left at the bottom and set a course towards Zawn Fell.

In her kitchen, Peggy was frying eggs. She was just about to dish them up when she chanced to look out of the window.

Her mouth went dry. Down in the layby, a big black

car had just come to a halt. Licking her lips, she watched, and a few seconds later the driver got out.

Dropping the pan of eggs on the trivet, Peggy ran into the big room. Anna was sitting with the children, drinking a mug of sweet tea. Tight-lipped, Peggy took it from her hand and grabbed her by the arm. Anna looked up, startled.

Peggy said: 'He's here. Come on, you'll have to hide.'

'What? Guy?' Terror whitened Anna's face.

'He's just pulled into the layby. Hurry, a couple of minutes and he'll be up the hill.'

But Anna was rigid with panic and fright.

'Where can I hide? There's nowhere. Oh my God! Oh, Peggy . . .'

'Move! Stand up!' Peggy shook her. 'Now! You'll have to go in the outhouse and keep quiet. I'll try to fob him off.'

Anna started weeping, shaking. 'He won't believe you. He'll find me . . .'

'Do as I tell you!' Peggy snapped. 'Stop wasting time.'

Over the top of Anna's head, she glanced through the window again. Guy had started up the track and his long legs carried him fast.

'I won't let him take you, I promise. Anna, move!'

'He'll beat me to a pulp!'

'He will not! If I must, I'll take the garden shovel to him.'

'He's as strong as a bull. You can't fight a man.'

'Get up!' Peggy hissed through gritted teeth.

On legs which seemed to be dissolving, Anna rose to her feet. Grabbing the checked jacket, Peggy thrust it into her arms and bundled her out of the door and round to the lavatory, where she sat her down firmly on the pink plush seat of the commode. Anna's fingers gripped the arms and her eyes were huge with fear.

'Peggy,' she begged, 'don't accuse him, whatever you do – about Hal, I mean. Don't threaten him with the police, don't provoke him. For your own sake.'

'I'm not that stupid. Now, be still, be silent,' Peggy ordered tersely.

Trembling, Anna nodded, and Peggy closed the door.

Racing into the cottage, she shepherded the children into her bedroom. 'Now listen,' she said, 'there's a nasty man coming here. He's looking for the lady and he mustn't find her. Understand? Not a word. You haven't seen her. It's all right to tell a lie this once.'

Ewan asked: 'Did he hurt her face?'

'That's right and he wants to do it again, so . . .' She pressed a finger to her lips.

Gravely, the boy clamped his mouth shut and sat down on the bed beside his sister.

Seconds later, there came a sharp tap at the cottage door. Shutting the children in, Peggy went to face Guy Buckman.

He was wearing his best hotel-manager smile.

'Good morning, Mrs Pentreath.'

She just looked at him.

'Is your husband about?'

She still made no reply. Her eyes flickered over him coldly. Guy looked her up and down. One corner of his smile dropped just a little. There were things about Peggy that bothered him. She wasn't dressed in mourning black and showed no signs of weeping.

She drew herself up. 'My Hal isn't here, Mr Buckman.'

'Oh? Out somewhere painting, I take it?'

'I'm afraid not. He had an accident, night before last.'

'Oh dear,' said Buckman.

'He's in hospital.'

'Hospital,' he repeated gravely. His mind could be seen working overtime. 'Indeed? What sort of accident was it?'

'A fall. He went halfway down the cliff over there near the top of the hill.'

'Good Lord! Well, I'm extremely sorry to hear that. Will he be all right?'

'Eventually. Anyway, what did you want with him? I thought I made it clear we would do no more business with you, Mr Buckman.'

'I'm sorry you still feel aggrieved. However, it's nothing like that,' said Guy, remaining pleasant. 'It's to do with my wife, as a matter of fact.'

'Anna? How does she concern us?'

'May I come in?'

'I'm rather busy.'

'Shan't take more than a minute or two of your time.'

Shrugging, Peggy waved him inside. The top of his head brushed the ceiling beams. Straight-faced, he glanced about him.

'So, what about Anna?' prompted Peggy.

His hands went into his trouser pockets and he shuffled his feet with an awkward laugh.

'I was wondering if you'd seen her, if she might have called here?'

'No. Why would she do that? You're aware there's no love lost between us?'

'Quite, quite.' He spread his hands. 'I'm clutching at straws, I know. Fact is, we've had a silly quarrel, Anna and I. She ran off last night and I don't know where. I've looked all over town for her and I'm starting to feel worried. Since they were close at one time, it did occur to me that she might have come to see your husband. Bit of a long-shot, last resort, but worth investigating, I thought.'

'Even if Hal had been here, I wouldn't have made her welcome, would I?'

'No, of course.' He was looking round him. 'You haven't seen her, then?'

'Isn't that what I've just said? Now, if you'll excuse me . . .'

'Mm.' He wandered into the kitchen and Peggy followed him. Opening the back door, he glanced at the lean-to. 'That's where your husband works now, is it? Trust he's not severely injured? How did it happen?'

Peggy's gaze was on his back, her eyes glistening. As if you didn't know, she thought. If I had any doubts, they've gone. After the beating you gave Anna, I don't think you would have dared come here if you'd thought you might have to face Hal, if you hadn't felt certain that he was out of the way.

'No one is sure. He has head injuries and he hasn't woken yet.'

Guy turned. 'Think he'll be kept in hospital long?'

'I couldn't say.'

'We must hope there aren't any permanent effects.' He smiled.

Peggy, expressionless, was thinking: You feel safe and powerful, don't you? It's your sort who get away with murder and you know it, you and your razorblade accent and your tasteful ties.

Quietly, levelly, she asked him: 'How did you know where we lived?'

Something went through the air. She felt it come from him like a shiver. He was briefly disconcerted. Then: 'Anna mentioned it, I think.'

'And how did she know?'

A shrug. 'I've no idea.' He sauntered back to the big room. 'Anyway, sorry to have troubled you at such a distressing time, Mrs Pentreath. Please convey to your husband my wishes for a speedy recovery.'

'Thank you, I will.'

'Jolly good. Well, I'll be on my way. Perhaps, if you should see Anna . . .'

His voice stopped short. Peggy's gaze followed his and fell upon the flash of iridescent green between the cushions of the couch.

Anna's scarf.

Buckman slowly turned on Peggy that yellow-eyed stare which always cowed his wife. Then he silently bent and pulled out the square of silk, dangling it in front of Peggy's eyes.

She declared: 'That's mine.'

'I hardly think so.' His voice had changed.

'It is!'

'I bought this for Anna last year.'

'One similar, I expect. No doubt they're mass-produced.'

A quiet, threatening, 'No.' Stepping closer, he stood over her. 'Where is she, Mrs Pentreath?'

'She isn't here. She came and then she left again. It was Hal she wanted to see, not me.'

'Why didn't you say so in the first place? Why deny she had been here at all?'

'Because I saw what you'd done to her,' flared Peggy. 'We may have been old enemies, but I felt sorry for the poor bitch. Anyone would. I gave her some tea and off she went.'

'Pull the other one, Mrs Pentreath.' Gesturing towards the bedroom, he demanded: 'What's in there?'

'My children.' She backed towards the door. 'You can't go in.'

'Where's the harm in letting me look?'

'This my home! I'll say where you can go and where you can't. You'll frighten them.'

'Nonsense. I'm a father myself, you know.'

Flattening her back against the door, she barred his way.

'Move aside, Mrs Pentreath, there's a good girl. I don't want any unpleasantness with you.'

'I will not! Go away! You wouldn't dare do this if Hal were here.'

Bending his head, he pushed his face down to her. 'I have come for my wife and it's not your business to interfere.' The words came out low, slow and deliberate. 'Couples have their skirmishes, as you must surely know. Such matters are strictly private.'

'Not when the wife is beaten senseless.'

'I think if you knew what lay behind it, you'd cease to sympathise with Anna, Mrs Pentreath.'

'Tell me, then.'

She waited, meeting stare with stare, challenging him. But he was too careful to mention Anna's affair with Hal.

'We had an argument about her dog. Sweet, defenceless Anna kicked me in the groin,' confided Guy.

'And you repaid her a hundredfold.'

'I'm afraid I forgot myself, and forgot my own strength. Now I'm here to take her home and look after her. It won't happen again.'

'I've told you, she's gone.'

'Oh, I've had enough of this.'

So saying, he flung her out of the way and Peggy stumbled sideways, crashing into a table. The lamp on the top of it fell over, hit the floor and smashed, and she found herself sprawling amid broken glass in a pool of paraffin.

'Get out of my house!' she screamed. 'Get out, get out, get out! I'll go to the law, I'll report you for this!'

Ignoring her, Guy went into the bedroom.

Wincing, Peggy picked herself up. Something was wrong with her ankle; she'd heard a crunch, felt a tearing sensation, and now it screamed under her weight. It was probably sprained.

'Satisfied?' she spat, when Buckman came out again.

Disappointed, he scowled at her. 'Would have been easier simply to co-operate, wouldn't it, Mrs Pentreath?'

She growled: 'Well, now you've seen for yourself. Anna isn't here, and I'm going to bring a charge of assault against you for this. I'll have you prosecuted, you . . .'

A little clatter interrupted, the sound of something falling over in the outhouse. Buckman's head went up, he listened, and then a movement caught his eye. His head snapped round. Through the window, he saw a woman in a checked jacket running down the track. Anna, making a beeline for the car.

Buckman laughed aloud. The Riley was locked and the keys were safely in his pocket. Diving for the door, he rushed outside.

Anna pounded down over the path. The steepness of it threatened at any second to pitch her forward and send her sprawling on her face. The thud of her footsteps filled her ears, and her eyes were fixed on the bumpy brown earth over which she ran.

She had sat there in the outhouse, paralysed with

fear, staring at the flaking door, expecting all the time to see it wrenched open and her husband standing there. And then the sound of Peggy screaming, of breaking glass, had panicked her. She thought as she bolted that if she could reach the car she would simply drive and drive and drive until the fuel ran out. And after that she would sell the Riley and disappear. It was nearly new and worth a lot of money. Whatever she did now could hardly make things very much worse for her. Guy knew of her affair, he had probably tried to murder Hal, so what were the prospects for Anna? For the present, all she could think about was putting a few hundred miles between herself and her husband.

She was halfway down the path when a bark from behind her made her whirl around.

'Anna!'

She saw him starting towards her, coming down the track half sideways, crab fashion. The sun was behind him and he was a dark, leggy outline against it.

Anna galloped on down to the road. Loping across it, she yanked at the driver's door, but it wouldn't budge. Sobbing, Anna scurried around to try the passenger door, with the same result.

'Anna!' The voice rang out again. 'Enough of this! Come on, I'm taking you home.'

Frantically, she cast about for an avenue of escape. She had to get off the road, or he would follow in the car. Despairing, Anna stared about her. If only there were other people. Curse this lonely place! To her left, half a mile down over the heath, lay the zawn, and in the other direction nothing but the cliff path to the beach.

There was no more time for debate. Guy had almost

reached the road. Spinning away, Anna took off and headed for the cliff path.

'It's all right,' she heard him calling. 'I promise I won't hurt you.'

Her only answer was to quicken her pace.

'Don't be so bloody stupid,' he roared. 'Where do you think you're going, anyway?'

Soon, the brink of the drop was in sight. Behind her, Guy was gaining. Anna veered towards the rocky path descending the cliff and started down. Jumping from step to rough-hewn step, she paused to look upward and saw that Guy was no more than forty feet behind.

Where, indeed, could she go? The tide had only just turned. It was dropping, but so far there was nothing at the bottom but a narrow strip of wet shingle, leading nowhere. He was going to catch her, wasn't he? Why not simply stop and take it? He was angry enough to kill her. Well – she might as well be dead. It was all over now with Hal. Guy knew, so did Peggy, and the worst had come to the worst.

Yet she struggled on and reached the foot of the cliff, making a dash for the rocky spur, stones and shingle sliding away beneath her feet. Hard going, and if she tripped now Guy would have her in a matter of seconds. The sound of his crunching tread, so near, suggested he could almost reach out and seize her.

'Anna . . .' His panting said he was winded. 'You bitch! Come here. Come here!'

She got as far as the gully and there her way was barred. It was eight or nine feet wide, too far to jump and there was no way around it. Water rose and fell within the rift like the breathing of a monstrous creature. It slapped against the rocky sides, and on its surface the foam was whipped up thick and scummy.

452

Flounces of weed along the slippery walls heaved up and down. Every few seconds, a gush of swirling white water fumed in over the deeper green beneath.

Then Anna shrieked. Guy's hands were on her, jerking her round to face him, grasping her by the collar of her jacket. Without a word, he started to slap her, once, twice, then a third time.

'Glutton for punishment, aren't you?' he said. 'Well, I'll see you get all you can take.' Bunching up handfuls of her coat, he raised her on to the tips of her toes, and pushed his face so close to hers that all she could focus upon were those glaring eyes.

'Strictly entre nous,' he hissed, 'I know all about you and Pentreath, though I'd never admit it to anyone else. Wouldn't want the world to know my wife had such bad taste. But I'll know, I'll never forget and you won't be forgiven, Anna. I'm not a forgiving man.'

She sobbed. 'All right, you know. Was that why you had poor Tuffet destroyed?'

'Indeed so, dearest. No more walkies, no more passion at the summerhouse. My, what an ingrate you are, after all I've given you. Now, if you remember, I did warn you, Anna. Up there, above the zawn – do you recall? Of course you do. In spite of that, you've been rash enough to defy me, and you're not going to wriggle out of the consequences. You already have a fearsome list of offences for which to atone, so come on home with me quietly now and don't make matters worse.'

For a moment, defeated, Anna went limp. But then she saw something to kindle a hope of escape. Coming down the cliff path were two men with fishing rods.

Both wore oilskins and one had a red woollen hat on his head.

Anna screamed out to them: 'Help me! Please!' and started to fight.

Guy glanced up at the path. The men had stopped halfway down. They were staring, pointing.

'Help me!' Anna shrieked again.

He shook her, growling: 'Shut up! Shut up, will you? Shut your mouth!'

'I won't!' She howled with all her might. 'You're hurting me! Let me go!'

The men came hurrying down the cliff. Guy, enraged, started swiping her head from side to side with long swings of his arm. Back and forth, back and forth. All the world would know what he'd done to his wife. So be it, then. The cat was already out of the bag, in any case. Peggy had seen her, and the hotel staff would soon be gabbling it all over town.

Anna tried to keep her head down, squirming to escape his grip. The fishermen were hastening across the shingle now.

Thrashing wildly at her husband, Anna heard a voice shout: 'Hoi! You! You pack that in! Let her go! Hear me? That's enough!'

In a minute they would stop him. In a minute it would cease . . .

Suddenly, lashing blindly, she struck him with her forearm across the throat. Guy was caught off balance, and as he stepped back his left ankle turned in a crevice of the rock. Briefly, he was poised on the edge of the gully, flapping his arms like some distracted bird in an effort to stay upright. Then his other foot came down on a patch of wet green weed and shot out from under him. One second he was teetering on the brink, wearing a look of pure astonishment, the next he was falling backwards, arms outstretched.

There was a splash and he sank. Then a surge of water buoyed him up and hurled him at the apex of the gully. Shocked and gasping, Anna saw the current suck him back, floundering, and smash him in again. Next moment, arms clasped her from behind and pulled her back from the edge. The man in the red woolly hat rushed past her, dropped on to his knees and reached out for Guy, trying to catch his hand.

But the tide kept snatching him away as if it were playing a game. Guy went under, surfaced, went under once more, bobbed back up, choking, stretching up his arms, was seized by another wave and thrown against the slippery walls, where his fingers clawed for a hold but found only rotting weed. His shouts were half-drowned by the boom of the sea and the cries of gulls.

Anna stood unmoving, coldly watching. The sea was hurling him around just as he had thrown her about the flat.

Before very long, his struggles began to grow weaker. At last, the fisherman stood up, knowing the man was past help. Very soon, Guy was floating face-down, going in and out with the swell, along with a few bits of driftwood and other flotsam.

Both men looked at Anna. Blood was seeping from a fresh cut at the corner of her mouth. The other marks of violence stood out starkly on the whiteness of her skin.

'Who was he?' one of them asked. 'What was it all about?'

'My husband,' came the dull reply. 'A domestic upset.'

'Your husband?' repeated the second man. 'Your husband treated you like that? But you're a lady. And him – he's dressed like a gent.'

An attempt at a smile stretched Anna's mouth. 'Camouflage,' she said.

Forty-two

The following Saturday, Peggy was visiting Hal at the hospital. In the grounds stood a chestnut tree with a wooden seat built all around the trunk. Peggy pushed him down there in a Bath chair and they sat together in the broken sunlight under the leaves. Four days had passed since he awoke. There was much she had to tell him, much to discuss, but she had put it off until today.

For a long time he just sat listening while Peggy talked. The bandage had been removed from his head and a line of stitches could be glimpsed beneath his hair. He was white-faced and very subdued, his gaze resting intently on his wife, wavering only now and then to reveal a stab of guilt or a momentary agitation. When at last she had finished, he stared down at the white wool blanket over his legs.

'Anna never told me how bad it was,' he said quietly. 'I knew she was unhappy, but she always insisted he wasn't violent.' Tensely, he regarded Peggy. 'I suppose you're very angry?'

'What's the good of that?'

'I've been unfaithful. I don't know why you're being so reasonable.'

'You mean it isn't like me to be civilised?'

'Especially since it was Anna. You always hated her so much.'

'Yes, well . . .' Peggy pulled a guilty face. 'She was such a mess that night, so pathetic. The things she told me about her life with him – I couldn't see her in the same light after that. And you wouldn't have gone to her, would you, if I hadn't been such a shrew?'

He was smiling now.

'Would you?' prodded Peggy.

'No,' confirmed Hal solemnly.

She looked sheepish.

'So,' he said, 'the war's over, is it? Between you and Anna, I mean?'

'I think so, yes.'

'Going to be friends?'

'That may be asking a bit too much, but at least we won't be enemies any more. There's going to be an inquest into Buckman's death. I've told her I'll speak up on her behalf, if necessary.' Peggy eyed him sideways. 'I've also told her to stay away from you, not just for my own reasons, either. Wouldn't look good, would it, for her to come here visiting when her husband's just drowned? She'd soon lose public sympathy if people suspected she'd been having an affair.'

'I hadn't thought of that,' he mused. 'Stands to inherit a lot of money, doesn't she?'

'All being well. It's fair compensation, I suppose, and you've had justice too. Buckman's dead and gone, so we can't complain.'

A rush of wind set the branches tossing overhead and sent flurries of fallen leaves bowling across the lawn. Leaning forward, Peggy tucked the blanket more snugly about his legs. Then, from her coat pocket, she pulled a piece of folded paper.

'I forgot. The kids made this for you.'

It was a home-made card, with a bunch of flowers clumsily drawn and coloured, and the words 'Get better, Dad' inscribed in large, round letters.

He looked at it for a long time, smiling. 'I see they've been at my watercolours.'

'It took them all of last evening,' nodded Peggy. 'They've missed you so much, Hal. We all have.'

Both hopeful and doubtful, he gazed at her. 'Is it truly this easy, Peggy? To patch things up, I mean?'

'It can be, if we make our minds up to it. I'll forgive you if you'll forgive me. I feel I can afford to jettison some pride. Anna did, that night she came to the cottage. She dropped the whole act, so I'm not going to stand on my dignity, Hal. I want my husband back.'

'And the chancy life that goes with him?'

'I believe I promised something like that at the altar. You know, the other day I remembered something Mr Jackman once said to me – that you might have your ups and downs, but I should always encourage you, even if the road was rocky, because one day you'd be a real success. I forgot that too easily, Hal, and I'm sorry. As you always said, I knew I was marrying an artist.'

He shook his head. 'It's been too hard for you, maid. I'll find a job as soon as I'm well. I can still paint in my spare time.'

'No. I don't want to feel in years to come that I might have thwarted you, stifled your gift. I don't want to end up feeling guilty. Anyway, you'll be miserable if you can't have time enough for your work, and what's the point of staying together if one of us feels like that? I've managed up to now and I can carry on. I only ask one thing – just do a few potboilers, Hal, to help me out. Apart from that, try something new and keep on trying until you hit the mark, as I know you will. Who can tell?' she said, broadly smiling, 'Good times might be just around the corner. We've had our spate of disasters, seems to me, and it's time for the wheel to spin the other way.'

The verdict on Guy Buckman's death was one of misadventure. Trezawne was shocked and enthralled by reports from the inquest. Doctor Churcher maintained that Guy was a delightful chap, who must have been provoked beyond endurance by a neurotic wife. Violence, he said, was quite uncharacteristic of the man he knew. Guy was as pleasant a person as one could wish to meet. Buckman's employees painted a picture entirely different, and damning statements came from Mrs Roseveare, Sarah, Peggy, and lastly the two fishermen. The woman, they said, had just been defending herself as best she could. The doctor who examined Anna said she had been the victim of an extremely vicious assault.

As the general perception of Guy began to change, Delia Trevena loudly proclaimed him a monster. She was outraged, she said, and appalled to think she had been so completely deceived by his charm. She was filled with anguish on behalf of her poor, dear child. Tongue-in-cheek, the neighbours listened while she huffed and puffed her indignation. In future, she declared, she would view any manfriend of Anna's with a much more critical eye.

However, under all the bluster, and side by side with all the embarrassment, there swelled a little bud of hope and excitement. An idea suggested itself to Mrs Trevena, replete with pleasing prospects of lifelong comfort. She cherished it in secret until all the business pertaining to Guy's will was settled, whereupon she paid her daughter a visit to offer help and advice.

Anna had been waiting for it.

Mrs Trevena was chatty as they sat together over afternoon tea. She devoured scones with jam and cream, glancing about her with calculating eyes. Anna ate nothing and said very little at first, but slowly sipped her tea and listened, expressionless.

Her injuries had healed, and a simpler hairstyle and lack of make-up made her look younger, yet a lingering air of strain lent a new maturity. Beside her on the settee, Robin was dourly quiet. His daddy had gone and much had changed. He was bewildered, unhappy – and wary of Mummy, who was no longer to be trifled with. He was having to treat with a new and different power. He didn't like it much, but was starting to learn discretion. Every so often, he still tried to flex the old muscles, but it was always a mistake.

After a while, Mrs Trevena ceased prattling about peripheral matters and came to the point.

'Anna, dear,' she said, putting her cup and saucer back on the tray, 'have you given any thought to the future?'

'In what respect?'

'Concerning the business, and how you're going to manage. You'll need assistance, won't you?'

'Will I, Mother?'

'Well!' Mrs Trevena laughed and made a wide-embracing gesture with her hands. 'It takes some doing, you know, to run a place like this, and you've precious little experience, Anna. Guy did all that, didn't he? He never taught you the ins and outs.'

'I've coped well enough since he died. I have good staff.'

'Oh, Anna, you haven't been trusting everything to them? That's madness, they'll rob you blind. There's such a lot to know about this trade, dear; the accounting and finance side of it, the laws which affect it and so on. It's very demanding. You have to be able to judge a prospective employee, you have to be tough enough to fire people and haggle with suppliers. You're such a gentle person, Anna. I'm not at all sure you're up to it.'

'You think I should hire a manager, then?'

'Oh no,' said Mrs Trevena quickly. 'I mean to say, that would cost a lot of money, wouldn't it?'

'I have a lot of money, Mother.'

'Yes, yes, I know, but it seems a waste to bring in an outsider and pay a large salary.'

'What shall I do, then?' Anna's eyes were wide with innocence.

Her mother wriggled her buttocks forward until she was on the edge of her chair.

'Why, let me take charge, of course. Anna, I have a wonderful idea. I can sell *Lamorva* and move in with you. We'll pool our resources.'

A light of baleful humour danced in Anna's eyes, but Mrs Trevena failed to see it and blundered on: 'You wouldn't have to pay me a penny, dear. All I'd require would be room and board. I'd have my own capital in the bank, earning interest.'

'Hmm,' pondered Anna, smiling. 'And you wouldn't have any more cooking or cleaning to do, would you? You'd only have to supervise my staff.'

'Quite. After all, I am getting on in years, Anna. I'm fifty-three, you know. It's a slog, running *Lamorva* all by myself.'

There was a pause, a lengthy one. Then: 'I would have helped you at home,' said Anna softly. 'If you'd taken me in when I asked you to, I would have been

462

there to share the work, but you preferred to let my room.'

Uneasily, her mother fidgeted. 'I thought I was doing the best thing for you, Anna. I thought you were in danger of throwing away an ideal marriage. I didn't dream that Guy was such a brute.'

'But I told you, in no uncertain terms, what he was like.'

'Yes, but it seemed so incredible. Like most people, I was fooled by him.'

'I'm your daughter, yet you didn't believe me. You thought I was exaggerating, being hysterical.'

Flustered, Mrs Trevena poured herself more tea, just for something to do with her hands.

'As I've told you, I didn't realise how cruel he was.'

'I don't think it would have made much difference if you had.'

'Anna!'

Her daughter's voice dropped low. 'You really do have the devil's own nerve, to come here and ask me if you can move in. Mother, nothing would induce me to have you here, even if you could run this place – which I doubt. You tell me it's beyond my capabilities – but you always said I was such a bright girl, didn't you? Well, I'm going to be as bright as I can be and do the job myself.'

Mrs Trevena's jaw dropped down as far as it would go, squeezing a little roll of fat out under her chin.

'Anna . . .' A tremor entered her voice. 'You're my only child. I don't want to live alone in my old age. The house is terribly empty in the winter.'

'Take in a lodger or two,' suggested Anna.

'Strangers? I'll want my family.' She forced a smile in Robin's direction. He scowled at her.

'I shall need all my rooms for letting,' Anna said implacably.

'You're an unforgiving, unchristian girl!'

'And my, it does feel good.'

A muscle twitched under Mrs Trevena's right eye. 'So, you're not going to be gracious, now that you have the whip hand?'

'I was at everyone's mercy all the years I was married – yours, Guy's, even his,' Anna said, nodding at Robin. 'Now, yes, the tables are turned and I'm in charge. I'm sorry.' Her voice was gentle but firm. 'But it wouldn't do for us to live together and that's all there is to it.'

'You'll become bossy and wilful, Anna. There'll be trouble when you remarry.'

'I'm not at all sure I shall, but if I do I'll be extremely careful in my choice, and I certainly shan't be taking any advice in the matter from you.'

Filled with umbrage, Mrs Trevena stood up, put on her hat and coat. As she buttoned it, she said: 'However unpleasant your marriage, you've ended up well off. Don't you think you owe me some gratitude for that?'

'No. I earned it, by God I did.' Anna's gaze flickered regretfully. 'I wish we got on better, Mother, but I don't believe we ever will. Would you like me to drive you home?'

'No, thank you,' said Mrs Trevena flatly.

'Anyway, I'll see you out.' Anna stood up and held out a hand to her son. Squirming off the settee, Robin grasped it and all three went downstairs.

Watching her mother's stocky figure tramping off down the drive, Anna felt a sense of final release. She was the boss – albeit unsure as yet in that capacity. She would learn, she would cope, she felt strong enough, even exhilarated. Free, still young, a survivor of seven dreadful years with Guy. She would be all right.

Robin looked up at her. 'Nana's angry. She wanted to live with us.'

'Ah, well, we can't have everything we want in life.' Anna raised her eyebrows. 'Can we?'

'No,' sighed Robin heavily.

Going inside again, Anna spoke to Sarah. 'Anything interesting tonight?'

'A table for six – a golden wedding anniversary party. Lionel's making something special.'

'Really? Well, tell the dining-room to put a complimentary bottle of champagne on the table.'

'Yes, Mrs Buckman.' Sarah wrote the order down. 'How are you today, Robin?' she asked the child.

'All right,' came the dull reply.

'All right, thank you, Sarah,' corrected Anna pleasantly.

Resigned, the boy repeated the words. He had to be polite to everyone now, and aggravating the staff brought sure-fire punishment.

'Very good,' said Anna. 'We'll make a true gentleman out of you yet.'

Forty-three

At the cottage, Hal returned to his easel and life went on much as before. The fracture had left his leg with a certain stiffness and a tendency to ache in cold, damp weather, but apart from that he was as good as new and very grateful to be alive. He was building up a stock of views to sell in the coming season. They would move, he promised Peggy, just as soon as he could afford it and find a place in town. This time, he meant it.

Taking nothing for granted, however, she planted new crops in her garden and made her twice-weekly treks to the farm. It wasn't so bad, she told herself now. There were worse things in life than hard graft.

Walter Angilley would never have come around to such a view. His son, however, was beginning to find the price of idleness unbearable.

Stumbling into the kitchen one morning, Jasper tried to light the cooker and nothing happened. He struck two matches and jabbed at the hob with them, but no little circle of flame appeared. Jasper turned all the knobs, he sniffed and then he groaned. First the water, now the gas – both disconnected. The bailiffs had been around twice and failed to find anything much worth seizing.

Walter simply didn't care. There was something wrong with him, Jasper thought. He had started to notice it some months past. The old man's faculties seemed to be deteriorating. He couldn't remember things from one minute to the next, couldn't take in what was said to him, and kept falling over. Walter Angilley was fifty-six, and had drunk a dozen pints a day since he was twenty. It was a miracle, acknowledged Jasper, that Father was still functioning at all. He might not be so tough himself, he might not last so long.

Staring stupidly down at the cooker, Jasper wondered what to do now. He was filthy, unshaven, his vest full of holes, his blue and white pyjama bottoms grey with dirt. Opening a cupboard, he found a packet of stale biscuits and a hard saffron bun. He sat down at the table and made a breakfast of them, washed down by what remained of yesterday's milk.

The house was cold and dark and filled with the wet-earth smell of rot. The fungus, a creeping, devouring presence, was in the walls and underneath the floorboards beneath his feet. One morning he feared he might wake up and find it growing over him. Everything had stopped in this house, nothing worked; even the clocks had all run down and their keys were missing. No colour any more; it was all obscured by layers of dust and grime. No chatty voices, no good scents of food, no busy comings and goings, just this lonely, dreary squalor.

How long had his mother been gone? Slightly over three years.

'We'll please ourselves now, boy,' the old man had said. 'We'll live as we like, with no one to nag us.'

Jasper had been convinced they were going to have a high old time.

Draining the last drops of milk, he set the bottle down. In an hour or so, *The Old Solace* would open and they'd be among the first in. Same routine almost every day. In the pub till half-past two, sleep the afternoon away, back at the bar in the evening, reel home and collapse at about eleven. Round and round, day in, day out, in endless – tedium. Yes, tedium. Jasper realised all of a sudden just how bored he was. Drinking had always been something easy to do with himself. It would fill a few hours, knock him out for a while, then occupy the evening too. He enjoyed his beer, no doubt about that, but shouldn't there be something more to life?

Was he what they called an alcoholic? Jasper rubbed a hand over his stubbly chin, looking lost and anxious. Walter was, for certain. He couldn't live without his booze. But Jasper wasn't sure about himself. Was there a difference between mere bad habit and actual need for the stuff? Did one eventually lead into the other? Either way, if he carried on, he was going to end up like Walter, only it wouldn't take so long for Jasper to fall to bits. Walter had at least been fed and looked after for most of his life. Jasper, already neglected and malnourished at twenty-eight, would probably be very lucky to see his fortieth birthday.

Screwing up the empty biscuit packet, he stared down at the sticky oil-cloth. It was criss-crossed with cracks, and bits were crumbling off it.

Saving himself would mean staying sober, getting a job and going to it every day – a tremendous demand. He could scarcely imagine how such self-discipline would feel – just as he could barely imagine how it would be to have a girl, as other young men did. A girl of his own, a normal life, sex ... Nervously, Jasper licked his lips.

'Aw, you don't want to be bothered with women, boy,'

the old man had said. 'It's overrated, I tell you straight, and you pay dearly for it. Tie yourself to a woman and she's on your back till the day you peg out, carping and criticising, expecting this and expecting that. She won't let a man be his natural self and enjoy his life. Come and have a pint, boy. Come on, it's my round.'

Peggy had been right. The old man had simply needed a drinking companion, somebody to share his weakness with him. After all, he was never liked and had no other friends. Yes, he had always discouraged Jasper from seeking a girlfriend, and Jasper had hardly minded, being full of ale most of the time. Yet – Walter had been no celibate in his younger days, fathering two children by the time he was Jasper's age. And who was on whose back, anyway? Poor Mother, what had Walter and Jasper ever given her? They were just a couple of cadgers, though Jasper had never been very conscious of that when she was alive, regarding home and its comforts as a right. He was Maisie's kin and therefore entitled to live and eat in her house, he was male and therefore entitled to service. He had actually thought more of Walter than of her. Yet, what had Walter done for his only son, except point him towards destruction?

A sense of being deliberately cheated and ruined arose in Jasper. One of Walter's favourite phrases echoed in his head.

'That'll do for us.'

Nothing on God's earth was important to him except his beer. Everything else could be sacrificed. That would do for Walter, and he didn't give a damn whether it was good enough for his son.

Jasper sat for a long time, brooding on his

predicament – so immersed in it that he didn't notice the passing hours. It was not until after midday that he asked himself why his father was so late in getting up. Walter would normally have been dressed and in the pub an hour before this.

Rising from the table, Jasper padded across the kitchen, cursing and hopping as he put a bare foot on a fragment of broken china.

'Father?' he shouted across the landing.

There was no reply.

Walter's door was closed. Jasper thumped on it and then walked in.

Angilley was lying on his back with his mouth wide open. There was vomit on the bedclothes round his chin. Pulling the curtains to let in the light, Jasper peered at him. No rise and fall of the chest. He prodded him with a finger. Walter's head flopped sideways. He was stone cold.

Jasper was, by turns, astonished and indignant. Frightened, too. Gone. The old man had gone, and left him alone in this mess. Just like that, as if he had said: 'Well, thanks for keeping me company. I'm off now, I've had my life. Don't know what you're going to do with yours – you, who've missed all the boats. Still, it's not my worry.'

For fully five minutes, Jasper stood staring at the corpse. Then, exploding, he kicked the bed three times and began to cry.

Later, Doctor Wilson came and wrote the death certificate.

'Can you cope with the arrangements?' he asked, surveying Jasper with candid disgust.

Jasper looked blank.

'Better go and see your sister straightaway, then.'

The physician snapped shut his bag, then jerked his head in Walter's direction. 'Want to end up that way, son? Not a pretty sight, is he? Think about it.'

The day after the funeral, Peggy was walking around the house with Jasper trailing in her wake. She kept tutting, and saying 'Dear God', and glaring at him over her shoulder. The gangling Jasper followed his dark little sister, wringing his hands. Finally, Peggy turned and looked up at him.

'I don't know what you think I can do,' she said brusquely. 'You surely can't expect us to move back into a hole like this? Even the cottage is a king to it. I swear I can see the walls decaying as I speak. It'll cost a small fortune to put this place right. We haven't got it and nor have you.'

'I'm handy,' said Jasper. 'I can do plastering, wood-work, all sorts of things.'

'Pity you didn't do it before, then. It would have been just a modest job after the flood. Now you might as well knock it down and rebuild from scratch. Not that you're capable of doing that. I've no faith whatever in your handiwork.'

He hung his head like a scolded child.

'We'd have to employ professional craftsmen and they cost money. So do materials, if you recall.'

'I'll get a job,' offered Jasper.

Peggy was caustic. 'I'm hearing things.'

'I mean it.'

'Oh yes? And what can you do?'

'Something on the boats? Share fishing, perhaps?'

'You're no seaman, Jasper. I don't think there's a skipper in town who'd risk having you on board.'

471

'I could do as your husband used to do – work as a cellarman.'

'And take your pay in kind?'

'No, Peggy. No, I swear.' He gazed at her pathetically. 'Please come home. Look, the loft isn't too bad. You and your family can live up there until the house is fixed. Peggy, let's get the shop going again. You could run it, just as Mother did.'

She shook her head. 'It's a tall order, Jasper. I don't see how we can do any of it without capital.'

'Borrow some. Ask a bank.'

Her laughter was sharp and scornful. 'Oh yes, they'll be really eager to lend to us, won't they? Hal and I are penniless and you're a known drunkard.'

'Don't keep saying that! I haven't touched a drop since Father died.'

'Coming on for a week. Bravo.' Cynically, she asked: 'What are you hoping, Jasper – that I'll be your meal ticket, just as Mother was? Are you on your best behaviour to entice me back here? How long will it last?'

His Adam's apple bobbed, and with something close to dignity, he drew himself up straight.

'You can own the place,' he said. 'You can have it entirely in your name and throw me out if I let you down. I'm giving you my word that I want to improve myself. If I break it, you can send me packing. Will that satisfy you?'

More than a little surprised, she surveyed him thoughtfully. At length she conceded: 'Well, you may have it in you to change, I suppose, especially now that Father's gone. But we're daydreaming, aren't we? I'd like it, I'd love to restore the bazaar and have it as it used to be, but it will depend on finding the money,

472

and I don't know if we can. We could offer the deeds as security, of course, but this isn't exactly a desirable property any more. They might not lend very much on it, and if we fail we'll all be out on the street.'

'Still, surely it's worth a try? What have any of us got to lose?'

'Not very much, I agree. All right, I'll see what can be done.'

'Will Hal mind about me being here?' ventured Jasper.

'He never bears grudges for long.' Severely, she added: 'I'm warning you, though, I'll take you at your word. Slip back to your old ways and out you'll go.'

A smile lit Jasper's face. Peggy smiled back and took his arm. 'You're looking gaunt,' she said quite gently. 'Come home with me. I'll give you some supper and we'll talk it over with Hal.'

Hal was enthusiastic about the idea. The banks were not. Renovating and re-stocking, they said, would cost far more than the place was now worth. They were unconvinced that Peggy could make a go of it, and deterred by her husband's occupation.

'Banks don't care a lot for artists, actors and the like, or so I've heard,' said Hal as they started home to the cottage. 'We're supposed to be fickle, unstable, just general bad bets.'

'I don't think it helped that we look so shabby, even in our best.'

'But, damn it, the shop's in a prime position,' he grumbled. ''It used to be a little gold mine. They must know that.'

'They do, but it was Mother who made it so, and she's gone. Now it's just "Angilley's Eyesore" and they

473

haven't any faith in the rest of us. Father died owing money everywhere, and everyone knows that Jasper hasn't got much of a head on his shoulders. As for you and me, we live in a shack and we've never had such a thing as a steady income. Can't blame them, I suppose, for being wary.'

She paused, for Hal had stopped in his tracks and was looking thoughtful.

'What is it?'

'Faith,' he repeated. He glanced down the road. They had come to the outskirts of town. Round the next bend was the gate to Elestren Manor, and beyond that the steep rise of the cliff road. 'Who'd have faith in us?'

'Precisely. The old bazaar's been a laughing-stock for years.'

'Anna,' Hal said.

'What?'

'Anna.'

Peggy looked horrified. She opened her mouth, closed it again, then vigorously shook her head. 'Oh – no. No, Hal.'

'Why not?'

'Because ...' She waved her hands, not knowing where to start.

'Yes?'

'We can't! I won't!'

'Still too proud?'

'No! Well – yes.'

'I thought you'd grown out of that? I thought the feud was over?'

'It is, but that doesn't mean I'm ready to go begging to her. Anyway, it's a cheek.'

'No, it's a business proposition. We're not asking for

a hand-out. We'll repay her, with interest, just as we would a bank.'

'Out of the question.' She was pacing, muttering. 'It feels – I don't know – it's just not right. We've buried the hatchet, it's true, but we're not exactly bosom friends, she and I.'

'I don't think she'd refuse me if I asked her.'

Peggy looked at him sharply. 'No, I'm sure of it. Still loves you, doesn't she? You mustn't play on that, it isn't fair.' Jabbing a finger at him, she added: 'You've toyed with her enough, been unfaithful to me, nearly got yourself killed. You stay away from Anna from now on.'

'I don't think she'd refuse you, either,' Hal said quietly.

Mutely, Peggy shook her head.

'You and your dignity,' he sighed. 'Don't you want the bazaar back, Peggy?'

'Yes, but some other way.'

'We tried every bank in town. We don't know anyone else with as much cash as Anna has. I doubt she'd even miss it.'

'I will not eat that much humble pie!'

'For God's sake, she knows how poor we are.'

'Poor, yes, but not beholden.'

Wheedling, he said: 'Imagine it – the house and the shop done out, all freshly painted. All the shelves full of goods again, lots of my paintings in the side window. Brand new shiny slot machines, that sweet old smell of fudge, and the sweet old sound of coins in the till.'

Her eyes acquired a wistful glaze and he pressed harder.

'Maisie would have liked it, wouldn't she, Peggy? Think of it – a grand re-opening, a smack in the teeth for all those who've been jeering and sneering these past three years. Show them, Peggy. You're your mother's daughter.'

She struggled with herself. He was right, she knew he was. Her resistance began to flag. They walked on until they came to the hotel gate and stopped again.

Briefly, Peggy stalled, then she said: 'Perhaps we should go in together?'

'No, you were right. It isn't fair for me to approach her. You say you've made your peace, you two. Now prove it.'

Resigned, she turned and started up the drive. She looked about as eager as someone walking to the scaffold. Peggy Angilley, asking Anna Trevena for a loan. Peggy, about to do the unthinkable.

Forty-four

On the terrace outside the residents' lounge were white
cane tables and chairs. There, in a quiet corner, Anna
was sitting, reading Warwick Deeping. She was clothed
in a simple tweed skirt and a white silk blouse with a
big floppy collar. Only a good string of pearls at her
throat and a fine gold wristwatch gave any hint that
she was an affluent woman. Her hands were bare; she
would never again wear the wedding or engagement
rings Guy had given her.

Spring sunshine lay on Elestren Manor and the
shrubbery was coming into flower. Around the lawns
the irises stood to attention, their long buds like spear-
heads between the tall, pointed leaves. Little had
changed since Guy's death, except the atmosphere.
Everyone was so much happier these days.

Laying down her book, Anna reached for her orange
juice and that was when she spotted Peggy coming up
the drive, wearing the same blue skirt, striped jumper
and knitted beret in which she had appeared at the
inquest.

Raising a hand, Anna called out to her. Peggy cut
across the grass and came up the three steps to the
terrace.

'Hello,' said Anna, cautiously friendly.

Peggy nodded awkwardly. 'Hello.'

'Please, sit down.'

Peggy took the other chair and almost at once a waiter appeared.

'Will you have some tea?' asked Anna.

Clearing her throat, Peggy murmured: 'No, thank you.'

'Orange juice?'

'Um – all right.'

Anna sent the waiter off to fetch a fresh jug and another glass.

'I'm pleased to see you,' she said. 'I still haven't thanked you properly.'

The other looked surprised. 'For what?'

'For trying to help me and hide me from Guy. For your evidence at the inquest.'

'Oh well, I only told them what happened,' said Peggy dismissively. 'It was the simple truth.'

'But not quite all of it. If you'd told them about Hal and me, I doubt they would have been so sympathetic.'

'Why should I bring that up? I have my pride. I didn't want the whole world knowing. Least said, soonest mended. I've taken him back and it's all over now.' Peggy's eyebrows lifted. 'Isn't it?'

'You have my solemn word,' said Anna patiently. 'I told you that night at the cottage I knew where I stood.'

'That's all right, then. Anyway,' continued Peggy, 'your husband deserved what he got. I didn't want people going around making excuses for him, saying he was a wronged man. What reason was that to try and kill my Hal?'

The waiter arrived with a tray and she accepted a glass of iced orange juice.

'How is Hal?' Anna asked.

'Working again, thank God. In fact, I've never seen him turn out so much so fast. Either he's making up for lost time, or else his brush with death has taught him not to waste it.'

Anna smiled into her glass. 'Troublesome creatures, men,' she said, taking a sip. Over the rim, her green eyes surveyed Peggy humorously. 'How silly we women are to fight about them.'

'Mm. I can't disagree with that – not any more.' Then, recalling her errand, Peggy eyed Anna uncomfortably and asked: 'Did you know my father died two weeks ago?'

'I did hear.'

'That's what I've come about, in a way. I mean – something connected.'

'I was wondering,' nodded Anna.

Putting her glass down, Peggy pushed her hands into her lap, picking nervously at her fingernails.

'He, um . . . Well, you know what the place is like?'

'Yes,' came the grave reply. 'What's to become of it now? Did he leave it to you?'

'Oh, he didn't make any arrangements. He wouldn't, not him. But my brother has asked me to take it over, try to restore it and run it again.'

'No easy task,' observed Anna.

'No.' Peggy chewed her lip, tried to meet her eyes, then quickly looked away again. 'I could do it, mind you, I'm sure I could. Only . . .' She wrung her hands and prepared to abandon her pride.

'. . . only it needs expensive repairs, not to mention new stock,' ended Anna, quite matter-of-fact. 'How much will it take?'

'More than we have. I mean – oh, let's face it, we don't have anything and the banks don't want to know us.' Squirming with embarrassment, Peggy gazed at her across the table. 'Hal thought, suggested . . .' Again she ground to a halt, loath to plunge in and ask.

'That I might come up with a loan? Yes, of course.'

Peggy stared at her. 'Just like that?'

'Why not?' Sitting back in her chair, Anna crossed her legs and smiled. 'I have all sorts of reasons for wanting to help. I want good will between us, Peggy, from now on, and I'd like to make amends of some sort to Hal for what Guy did to him. I'm sure he'd be glad to have his old studio back and to know that you were leading an easier life.' She thought for a moment and then confided: 'There's something else, as well, which follows from what you said – or rather, didn't say – at the inquest. You see, Guy didn't really provide very well for me in his will. He left most of what he owned in trust for Robin. I had to contest it. Luckily, the courts were very generous, which is why I'm comfortable now. I suspect they would have been far less open-handed had they known I'd been an unfaithful wife, however brief the affair, however miserable my marriage. A man is forgiven these things, a woman is not. So you see, it's partly thanks to you that I'm in a position to offer a loan. It's therefore the least I can do. Anyway,' she chuckled, 'Guy would be enraged and that's reason enough by itself.'

A slow grin spread across Peggy's face and within her there rose a surge of fellow-feeling. Not-so-starchy old Anna was capable of devilment. Peggy appreciated that.

'You're not bad at all, really, are you?' she said.

This was high praise after a lifelong feud, and Anna knew it.

'You're truly willing to trust us – me – with your money?' continued Peggy.

'I'm sure you're very capable, well able to make a go of it. Hal isn't practical,' sighed Anna with fond amusement, 'but you are. Anyway, if I can manage this place – and I haven't done too badly so far – the bazaar should be a piece of cake for you.'

'You won't be sorry,' Peggy promised, eager now. 'I'll repay you with the proper interest just as soon as I can.'

'I shan't want any interest.'

'Oh no, you must have it,' said Peggy firmly. 'I wouldn't want to feel I was taking advantage.'

'All right,' agreed Anna reluctantly, 'but I won't accept more than a third of the normal bank rate. Now that's a condition, Peggy. I'm not out to profit.'

Peggy was about to argue, but she checked herself. What else was this but a gesture of friendship? To reject it would be churlish.

'Thank you, Anna,' she said warmly. Then, looking around her, she murmured: 'It must feel good to own all this.'

'It certainly feels better than being owned.'

'You'd best be careful next time you marry.'

'If I do.'

Glancing at her, Peggy laughed that off. 'You're too young and too good-looking to remain alone for long.'

'I don't feel quite so young inside myself,' came the rueful reply.

'Nor do I. Still that's no cause for sorrow; we were such a silly pair when we were girls.'

Both of them laughed and Anna asked hopefully: 'Are we friends now?'

'Friends,' confirmed Peggy. 'Yes, we are. I think it's high time.'

Together, they sat in the sun and drank their orange

juice, as if there had never been a day's ill will between them.

Four months later, on a dazzling summer day, Peggy was standing out on the quay, looking proudly up at her new signboard.

Angilley's Bazaar, it said in dark red letters. The shop had never had a sign before. Now it had a new roof, new windows, new stock and slot machines, even new furniture upstairs. Smells of paint and sawn timber still lingered about the place, which had only been open a week. In the side window, a score of paintings awaited buyers, and round the door hung a choice of straw sun hats, tin buckets and spades, and kites and raffia baskets. Inside, it was crammed with goods; Angilley's Bazaar, back from the dead, as gaudy and busy as ever.

Glancing down to the end of the jetty, Peggy saw her husband engaged on a charcoal sketch of an elderly couple. As for Jasper, well, he had been sacked from a job or two, but he was trying. She had never expected miracles of him.

A pair of small girls in striped bathing suits came running up the slipway from the beach and dashed into the shop, clutching handfuls of pennies. Peggy followed them inside, feeling buoyant again in her bright cotton dress and sandals.